D1602291

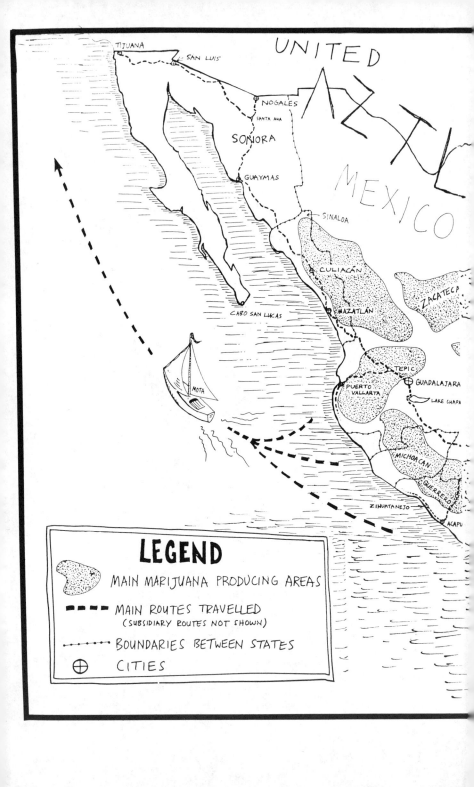

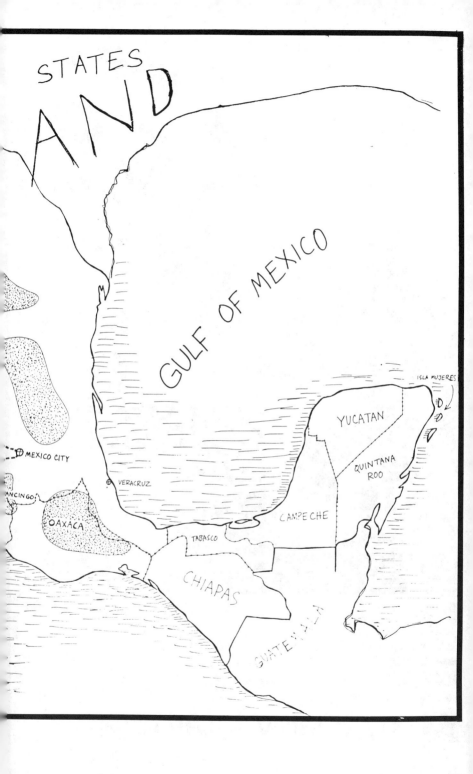

WEED

by Jerry Kamstra

Adventures In Mexico

photos by Roberto Ayala

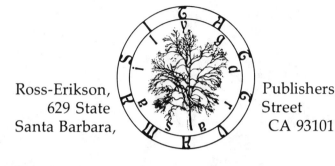

Ross-Erikson,   Publishers
629 State   Street
Santa Barbara,   CA 93101

The Ross-Erikson logo is derived from elements of the eastern and western mystical traditions. Inside the ouroboros encirclement is the Ash Tree, from which, according to Celtic mythology, all things in the world derive. Surrounding the tree is its Celtic name, *yg drasail*.

Within the rim of the ouroboros are the words TAT TWAM ASI (Thou Art That), from the Chandogya Upanisad, vol. IX, ¼, which is the reply by the philosopher Aruni to the question of his student Shvetaketu, who asked him, "What is the Absolute?"

Designed by

JERRY KAMSTRA

Acknowledgements

I want to give special thanks to Maitland Zane and Jon Pelzel for loans that paid the rent during the writing of this book. I also want to thank Roberto Ayala (Angel del Valle), without whom this book could not have been written. Roberto took over half the photographs in this book, and all the rest are from his personal collection.

I also want to give special thanks to my family and friends, my children & my ex-lives for their continual support and understanding for one whom "the dust of Mexico has settled in his blood."

Cover photograph by Roberto Ayala

Design by Jerry Kamstra

Text by Fred Usher

Airbrush work by Dennis Hoey

Jerry Kamstra is the author of *The Frisco Kid* and the forthcoming *Stand Naked and Cool Them — North Beach and the Bohemian Dream — 1950-1983*. He spends his time in various ports of California and Mexico.

Roberto Ayala is the author of the forthcoming: *Los Sembradoves — The Marijuana Growers*. He has been a student of Mexico and Marijuana for over 30 years. Over 50 photographs from his personal collection appear in Weed: Adventures in Mexico.

He has attended the San Francisco Art Institute where he studied humanities under Richard Miller, and photography under Jerry Burchard. He also majored in art and La Raza studies at San Francisco State University.

ROBERTO AYALA

Monday is fine for any old kind.
Tuesday give me the Purple.
Wednesday is comin' so it's Indian Black Gungeon,
Guaranteed to please the people;
Thursday night Michoacan is right.
Friday will be very heavy.
Bring in the Gold for when I'm old
Saturday all will be ready;
Sunday it's said is the Day of the Dead
And if you have it you smoke Panama Red.

Marijuana smuggler's song

This book is dedicated to the campesinos of Mexico, and to my father, and to the memory of my mother. It is also dedicated to William Fortner, who died in Mexico while on a run.

Copyright © 1974, 1983
by Jerry Kamstra

Photographs © by Roberto Ayala

Published by Ross-Erikson, Inc., Publishers with PEERAMID PRESS, 629 State Street, Santa Barbara, CA 93101

First published by Harper & Row, Inc., and Bantam Books, Inc. under the title: Weed: Adventures of a Dope Smuggler.

Library of Congress Cataloging in Publication Data

Kamstra, Jerry.
    Weed: adventures of a dope smuggler.

    Autobiographical.
    1. Narcotics, Control of—United States. 2. Kamstra, Jerry. 3. Marihuana.
    4. Smuggling—United States. I. Title.
HV5805.K35A3   364.1'57   73–18665

ISBN #0-915520-62-1

CONTENTS

PREFACE

It is difficult to be objective when writing about Mexico. I love Mexico. I love the land and the people, especially the poor people, the campesinos, the people of the fields. I also hate Mexico. I hate the injustice and poverty and inhumanity and greed of much that goes on there. Mexico is a land divided between beauty and ugliness, between poverty and wealth, between all the dualities that make everything exciting and meaningful. By circumstances beyond my control I got into the heart of Mexico through marijuana. I became a smuggler and because of that I entered the Sierras where few gringos go. This is not to imply that I entered some Shangri-La of the imagination forbidden to other people, but only that there are areas in Mexico where few gringos are allowed—or even consider visiting. This has not always been so. At the turn of the century the mountains I visited were home for many gringos, silver miners and their families who lived and died there. One night after scoring a ton of marijuana and preparing it for shipment to the United States, I slept on one of their graves. It was the grave of the young wife of an American mining engineer; she had died of fever in the high mountains.

In this book I use the terms *gringo, American, campesino,* and *Mexican* with some forethought. *Mexicans* are Americans because they live in North America, but the term *American* has come to denote citizens of the United States, and that is what my term is meant to mean. *Gringo* is not a pejorative when I use it. The word is used by all Mexicans and sometimes it is used pejoratively, but wide usage has calmed the term. Here it simply refers to a non-Mexican, whether from the United States, Canada, or Europe. *Gringo* is also used by some Mexicans to describe Black Americans and *Chicanos,* that is, people of Mexican descent born within the boundaries of the United States. *Campesinos* means people of the fields. For me the campesinos are Mexico. They have little to do with the social and political life of urban Mexico, but they are the country's lifeblood, its heart and gristle. They are the people who rose up out of the fields with Zapata to defend their lands and homes and won—somewhat.

This book is about the Mexican marijuana industry. It is also about Mexico, or my own particular view of it. During the last decade and a half Mexico has changed greatly, and is still changing. Many of the changes have been brought about by two causes: an incredible influx of tourists who have inundated the country—and marijuana. To those who may be skeptical that marijuana has wrought many changes in Mexico, I say this: Thousands of the young kids who have gone to Mexico in the last few years have gone there for one reason, to score weed. In visiting Mexico the young kids trail after them a fantastic youth culture, peculiarly American, particularly potent to other youths everywhere. The cross-pollination that is occurring right now between Mexican and American youths is a more potent force than any cultural exchange programs between the two countries. The young gringos are like bees swarming over the flowering marijuana plants that grow in Mexico, sucking sustenance from them and depositing in turn new mores and attitudes, new styles and manners. No place on earth is immune from the American presence, and part of the purpose of this book is to show how that presence is affecting Mexico and the marijuana industry. For me the two things are linked together, each separate, but involving one another like the spokes on a catherine wheel that spins and spins until they become indistinguishable.

Part of the reason for writing this book is to counter some of the misconceptions about marijuana and the marijuana smugglers; I want people to know exactly how they and the marijuana industry operate. Marijuana itself is no longer important to me, but it is the thread that holds this book together. Without it, it would never have been written. It is also what is going to sell the book, so light up!

Finally, I wish to state that this is one man's odyssey. The observations I make in the book are mine, based on living and traveling in Mexico for over fourteen years. I have read other books about Mexico and have picked up some confirmation of my ideas from them, also some refutations, but on the whole this book has been lived and written by a self-educated traveler-smuggler-writer-adventurer who has no one but himself to blame if anything said here is false. The conclusions I have reached about marijuana and its effects are based solely on my observations of the industry and of my own friends for many years. They have nothing to do with official government reports and scientific experimentation, the last place I would expect to learn anything about marijuana.

JERRY KAMSTRA

Chilpancingo, Guerrero, Mexico
San Francisco, California
1970–72

1.

THE BORDER

I'm on federal probation for the "illegal importation of marijuana." That's smuggling in The Man's language. The Man is the law, the heat, the police, the fuzz, the pig. He comes in all forms, as regular cop, as Customs agent, as the FBI, as Treasury agent, IRS official, undercover narc, Immigration official. Sometimes The Man is also your connection, that is, the man you score, or buy, dope from.

I fell at San Luis, Arizona, at a full-moon midnight, August 30, 1966, with two hundred kilos of Michoacan *mota* in my car. *Mota's* a Mexican slang term for marijuana, specifically the flowering tops, the *colas de zorras* or foxtails, as they are called in Mexico.

Falling at the border with a load of weed is what every marijuana smuggler dreads. The whole smuggling trip is designed to avoid just those hassles and the hip smuggler is attuned to every sign along the way, ready to alter even the most carefully planned run if the vibes aren't right. Each of us carries our own vibes around with us though, and my partner Jesse and I had been missing some pretty big signposts along the road of late. We were six weeks into a run that was supposed to last two weeks and had taken delivery of our load outside Santo Tomas two nights before. In a small resort town along the west coast

of Mexico we transferred the load into another car that we had stashed there and headed up Highway 15 toward the border. On the morning of the thirtieth we turned off of Highway 15 onto Highway 2, the cutoff road that leads from Santa Ana to Tijuana. Three hours out of Santa Ana I spotted a cluster of people on the road ahead. I was drowsy from the heat but my head jerked up when I saw them. Jesse slowed down and I stuck my head out the window. The warm air blasted my face like a furnace. "Maybe we better stop," I said.

Jesse continued down the road, only slower. Both of us were wary. I scanned the highway ahead. Eight or ten people were standing beside a truck. I looked at Jesse. "I don't see any soldiers. Maybe it's farmers." Jesse didn't say anything.

A hundred yards further along we slowed almost to a stop. An old Mexican stepped out on the road and waved his sombrero. As we drew near I could see it was a family of Mexicans, old folks and young, standing beside a broken-down truck. Jesse stopped the station wagon and we got out.

"*Ah, gracias, gracias, mil gracias,*" the old man said. He held his
sombrero in front of his breast in a supplicatory manner. His family
stood beside the truck, scanning our faces with what appeared to be,
if not hostile, at least indifferent eyes. They didn't look like ordinary
Mexicans. There was something gaudy, almost outrageous about their
appearance. Except for the old man, they all hung back in the shadow
of the truck, a ragged, noncommittal group.

While the old man explained his problems to Jesse, I looked them
over. There were three young girls, from fourteen to eighteen, I'd say,
a middle-aged couple, an old crone fanning a baby, obviously the wife
of the man talking to Jesse, and a couple of tough-looking young
dudes in their late twenties or early thirties. They all had a carnival
look about them. The three girls were barefooted and wore long skirts
that touched the ground. The hems of the skirts were frazzled, and
although the material was filthy, underneath the dirt I could see that
the colors had once been bright. One of the girls stared at me in a
quizzical, straightforward manner. I felt slightly embarrassed and
turned away.

I could see what was wrong with the truck. It had tandem wheels in the back, and one set of wheels was off, lying in the dust. The young men had been wrestling with one of the tires, attempting to repair it. All the tires were bald, with the cord showing through in a hundred places. It looked like an impossible task. As I watched, one of the young men grabbed a tire iron and started beating the tires forcefully. The whole scene was one of bedraggled poverty, heightened by the heat and desolation of the desert road.

"We are having much trouble with our troque, *señor, muchos problemas, las llantas están muy viejas,* the tires are very bad, *malas,* as you can see. . . ." The old man gestured to the dilapidated tires with a resigned wave of his hand.

"Where are you going?" Jesse asked.

"Ah, *señor,* we are going south, Mazatlan . . . if we can have our tire repaired, it is very difficult. . . ."

The middle-aged woman broke in. "Do you have water, *señor?*" Jesse nodded and reached for the water bag hanging on our bumper. The young girls crowded around as the woman drank. After everyone had drunk his fill, the woman, who was a large-boned creature with flowing skirts, approached Jesse. "You are kind, sir. Perhaps you would like to have your fortune read. . . ."

As she spoke the three girls surrounded me. One of them reached out and took my hands in hers. I was startled, but the girls appeared unconcerned, smiling and gazing at my hands. I felt uncomfortably boyish in front of them, yet I enjoyed it. "They're gitanas," Jesse said, "gypsies. They want to tell our fortunes."

The idea that Jesse and I should be stopped in the middle of the desert by a band of gypsies was incredible. I sensed the old hustle and rapidly calculated in my mind how much money I could afford to squander. Immediately my mercenary attitude repelled me. How often was I stopped in the desert by gypsies?—never. While the two young men working on the tire watched, the three girls led me into the shade of the truck. Jesse was squatting in front of the older woman. "Give me one hundred pesos," she said abruptly, and just as abruptly Jesse complied. "Money is nothing," the woman said. She quickly ripped the hundred-peso note in half and tossed the pieces to the wind. A bemused smile covered Jesse's face. The young girls meanwhile were examining my palms. One of them, the prettiest one, stroked my hand with her fingers. She said nothing as her fingers moved over my palm, just smiled softly. I glanced nervously at the two tire changers but they too were smiling. Nobody seemed the least disturbed by the ritual. I was beginning to relax. While the cute girl was stroking my palm, the other girls edged in closer. The oldest looked at my right hand intently and then took my left hand in hers. All three girls murmured. The youngest girl's smile disappeared as she traced the lines of my palms. She held both my hands together and spoke. *"Veo mucha tristeza, mucha tristeza,"* she said. "See much sadness, much sadness." I smiled uncomfortably. The girls shook their heads slowly, sadly.

At that moment Jesse stood up and dusted off his pants. The woman walked to the back of the truck and sat down on the tailboard with the old crone. She said nothing. I fumbled in my pocket for some money to give the girls. I had a Buck knife on my belt which one of the young men was eyeing. I took it off and gave it to him. As Jesse and I walked back to the car the old man followed us, smiling. Jesse reached inside the car and grabbed a flashlight and handed it to him. *"Gracias, señor, gracias,"* he said.

Neither Jesse nor I spoke after leaving the gypsies. I could not get the image of the young girls out of my mind. The one especially who had looked at my palms and then into my eyes, saying "Very sad, very sad." A melancholy feeling swept over me. I suddenly felt very alone. I looked out over the desert. The heat waves shimmered in the distance. The mountains looked like scar tissue formed by prehistoric wounds.

That evening as we approached San Luis, I said to Jesse, "I don't understand why she tore the hundred-peso bill in half. It was such a waste of money."

Jesse laughed. "She didn't tear a hundred-peso bill in half; it was phony." I looked at him. "I gave her a hundred-peso note and she had a phony one tucked in her sash. She switched them around when she

squatted down. She tore the phony one in half. It was a good trick."

"What did she say about your palms?"

"The same old shit, a long life, meet a pretty girl, come into money, you know."

I said nothing. Time had already mellowed the experience of the afternoon and I had other things to look forward to. I was going to drive the load across the border that night and I wanted to be sure everything was right. Jesse and I had over $40,000 riding on the trip.

It was eleven P.M. when we arrived in San Luis. The station wagon had been acting badly, with weird clunks grinding out of the transmission. We stopped at a Pemex station outside of town and tried to find the trouble. We could discover nothing. We drove into town and discussed our last-minute tactics over coffee. The plan was for Jesse to get out of the car and walk across the border while I drove the load across. Once safely through, I'd pick up Jesse and we'd drive on into Yuma. We had done it a dozen times and each time had been successful. This was one of our nicest loads yet, however, 200 kilos of Michoacan. We had paid $5,000 for it. In San Francisco we would be able to wholesale it for about forty thousand. Not a bad profit for six weeks' work.

After coffee I drove through town to the border checkpoint. Jesse got out of the car two blocks from the border and I went on alone. The night was beautiful. It was midnight and a full moon shone overhead.

As I aimed the '59 Ford station wagon into the inspection stall I felt good, a little nervous, but that natural nervousness that keeps you on your toes. The transmission was still making weird noises, so after parking my rig in the stall I stepped out of the car and walked around to the front and raised the hood to inspect the engine. I was kind of glad about the mechanical problem. I figured it might take The Man's mind off his business.

The first inspector to check out my car was a patsy, an easygoing dude, middle-aged, who peered perfunctorily under the front seat and opened the glove compartment and then came around and stood beside me and stared into the engine just like I hoped he would. I was

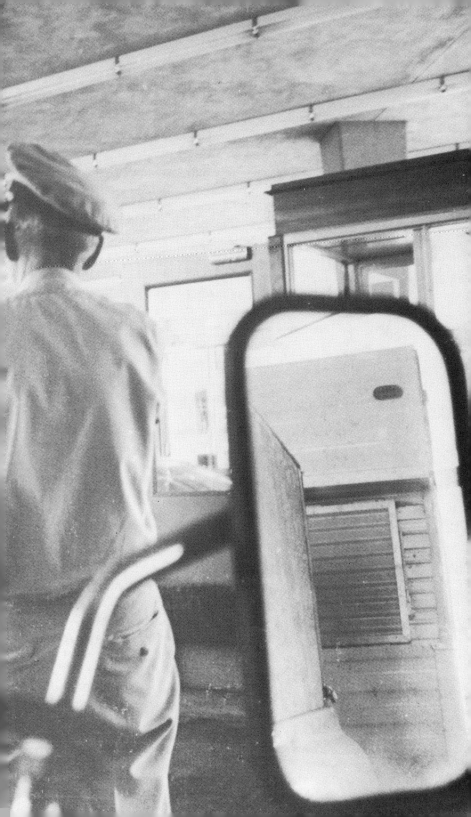

feeling pretty breezy when the second dude opened his office door and started walking toward me. Dude number two was one of those lean-necked types, a son of one of those mid-America dirt farmers who fled west after the nineteen-thirties' dust clouds blew away his farm. I knew I was in trouble the minute I saw him because he had that lean, thin-lipped Okie look that characterizes a certain type of man prevalent in the Southwest and in many small towns throughout California; he's the guy who watched his daddy plow hard dirt all his life and decided there must be something easier to do in this world for a dime so he became a deputy sheriff or border patrol cop, joining the very same breed that used to beat his old man on the back with a stick when the large ranches and railroads wanted him to move on. Now the son wielded the stick, and because his early life had been so hard he figured he might as well make it hard on others. I felt my stomach sink as he walked slowly toward my station wagon. With a calmness belied by the hollow feeling in my gut, I casually closed the hood, then went around to the side door.

There's a pattern customs inspectors look for when rigs drive into the inspection stalls. A good inspector can sniff out a smuggling operation, picking up the little telltale signs some smugglers inevitably give off. It might be a look in the eye, it might be a too cool indifference on the part of the driver, it might be a jittery dance the smuggler goes through to keep his butterflies down. Experienced inspectors look for any action that is abnormal. In my case it was getting out of my car and raising the hood.

The irony was that I had a legitimate mechanical problem, and in the helter-skelter last-minute adjustments one makes when approaching a customs checkpoint with $40,0000 worth of weed, my two-bit brain figured that the inspectors would be just as interested in the problem as I was. I was right with inspector numero uno, but numero dos had too many years on the job; he looked out of his window and smelled something fishy. When he started walking across the tarmac toward my rig I was already figuring distance and windage to the Mexican border. The approaching moment was one every smuggler imagines but there is really no adequate way to describe the feeling that goes through your body. Every nerve is exposed and tense, like a wire, and at the same time a weird floating unreality seems to seep under your skin; you see it happening but reality refuses to register. You don't believe it.

As inspector number two approached I opened the driver's door and sat down in the front seat. I suddenly remembered all the incriminating evidence I had in the car: photographs and notebooks, paraphernalia and accouterments you never think about until The Man's about to come down on your ass. What I especially wanted to get was a photograph of Jesse and me that we'd had taken a couple of weeks before in a Mexico City nightclub. The photograph was stashed behind the sun visor. If the heat got the photograph and checked it out I was finished, because Jesse was one big hombre as far as they were concerned, wanted on both sides of the border.

While the inspector opened the rear door of my wagon and started prodding the upholstery, I quietly slipped the photo out from behind the visor and put it under my shirt. Number two was a dogged son of a bitch, and after rifling my furniture he pulled out a little light on the end of a long flexible cable and tried to stick it down inside the doors. Fortunately all the kilos were wrapped in black plastic and he couldn't see anything, but for good measure he tapped the side of the Ford, running his knuckles along the rear quarter-panel like a piano tuner tuning a piano. His thin, smirky lips got thinner as he worked his way along the side of the car, then he turned to me and said, "I think I'll go get a screwdriver and take off this panel." I stood beside the car while he walked over to the office and returned with the screwdriver. He reached inside and started taking out the screws on a small rear panel and I gingerly patted my pockets to make sure I was ready. The photograph was safe, so was a bag of amphetamine pills I'd snatched, and as the panel came off revealing a dozen beautifully wrapped kilos, I took off too, making like Speedy Gonzalez for the Mexican side of the border.

Strange feeling, fleeing. Everybody was surprised by my exit, including me, and I remember thinking at the time that this sure is like a grade B movie. I had on a pair of huaraches I'd purchased in

Mazatlan a couple of years before and as I hightailed it toward the Mexican side one of the son of a bitches broke. The run from my car to the border was about 50 yards and as I rounded the chain-link fence into Mexico, I did it in sort of a hop, step, and jump, dangling my broken sandal off my left foot. When I took off, the customs agents started running after me shouting, "Stop! Halt!" and the Mexican border guards jerked up out of their sleep. I caught a glimpse of two or three of them lumbering up out of their chairs as I sped into their territory, not flying, but going a little faster than running. I suddenly thought as I sped over the ground that I had no place to go, just into Mexico, away from U.S. Customs, away from my car with $40,000 worth of weed in it, with one huarache, a photograph, 200 amphetamine pills in my hip pocket, $50 cash, no papers, nothing.

You may wonder why I ran toward Mexico, and I'll tell you. The minute I realized that the second inspector was going to spoil my fun, I saw penitentiaryville dance before my eyes. Smuggling's a heavy rap on any man's border, but if I had to fall I wanted to fall in Mexico, not the U.S. My reasons for this were twofold: First, when you're busted in Mexico, they only want your body, they don't imprison your mind. Institutions in the United States want both your body and your mind. American prisons don't feel they're doing their job unless they've twisted your head around until it fits into one of their square slots. The psychological damage done to most cons by the U.S. penal system is much more damaging than any time they have to do. Time passes, but the head changes the U.S. prison system puts a con through are almost impossible to overcome.

In Mexico it's different. Mexican prisons are physically rougher, granted: the food's terrible, facilities nil, care inadequate, concern nonexistent—but at least your head is free.

Second, a prisoner in a Mexican penitentiary is also left free to operate; that is, if he has the chutzpah and brains, the know-how and access to some money, he can set himself up in business, rent a small apartment in the prison, and invite his family in. He can, in other words, live a reasonably normal life, even if it is in a confined space. A prisoner in Mexico can also, if he has any real money, buy his way

Gordon Ball, 1968, young film-maker, in the carcel in Puerto Vallarta.

ROBERTO AYALA

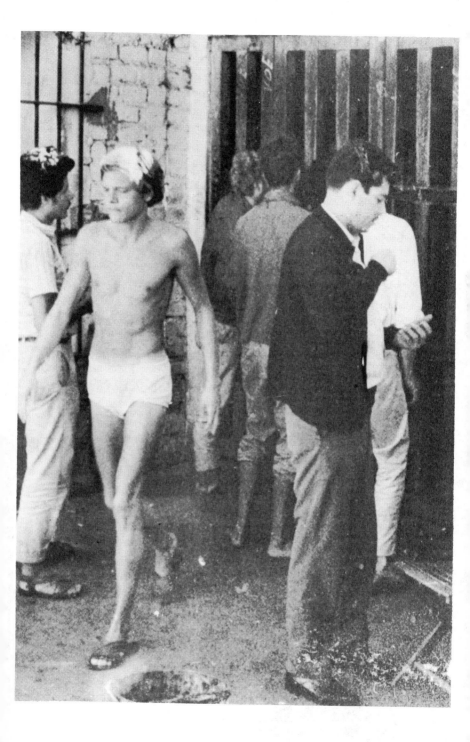

out. In fact, one of the laws in Mexico is that if a prisoner's sentence is under five years, he can post a bond and go free. Also, while violence is against the law in Mexico, jail breaks are not, so if a prisoner decides to make a run for it, he can do it as long as he does it nonviolently. If I could get across the border into Mexico I could hide out, and eventually make my way home. If I couldn't make my way home, I could survive in Mexico. I had lots of friends in the country and considered Mexico my second home. And even if I eventually got busted in Mexico, it was still better than being busted in the United States.

All these thoughts were racing through my head as I ran. About twenty yards inside Mexican territory I took a quick look back over my shoulder and saw the Mexican guards running after me with their cannons out. The gringo border guards were yelling, and then somebody shot at me. It sounded like a very large bee sailing past my right ear. Right in the middle of my run I said to myself, well, now you know what it feels like to be shot at. It's weird when you consider what a .45 caliber bullet can do to you. I imagined my spine severed and walking around with wheels for feet for the rest of my life. The thought didn't last long though, because I hauled ass and made it around the side of an adobe hut. I was full of pills and panic, so I loped fast, noting as I ran all the possible spots to fall, crawl under, up, on, or over. I ran into a *cul-de-sac*, however, an area of adobe huts and ten-foot-high walls with no exit. The moon was like a searchlight shining down just on me so I dove under a woodpile that happened to be leaning against one of the buildings. Fifteen Mexican Federales tromped into the area and began shining flashlights and kicking everything they could see—then the gringos, fat-faced customs agents panting like blowflies as they huffed and moaned and shouted orders to one another. They looked for me for twenty minutes, sometimes standing not one foot from where I lay, then they left, climbing over the walls as they presumed I must have done.

One Mexican guard, who weighed about three hundred pounds without his cannon, stayed. I could have reached out my hand and touched his boot. My legs were sticking out of the woodpile and I

knew if he turned around I was had. I tried to make my legs look like wood, blending them into the shadow next to the wall, but it was hard. I'm six foot four and there just wasn't much room under that woodpile. When the Mexican turned around with his flashlight my blood literally ran cold. I know Mexicans too well; he had me, baby, all he had to do was pull back that hammer and let go. It must have amazed him that I was lying right behind him, because when he saw me he yelled.

To this day I know that yell was involuntary. If he hadn't yelled I would have been dead, because nothing raises a Mexican border guard's status more than to have a gringo to his credit. He yelled though, and the gringo customs agents came running. The Mexican shouted, "*Arriba, cabrón!*" and man, you've never seen anybody *arriba* himself out of a pile of old boards as fast as I did. Even so, as I wriggled out of the wood the Mexican pointed his gun between my legs and pulled the trigger. Ka-plow! The sand splatted up under me. Mexicans have something about the balls. If you could understand the Mexican's relationship with his manhood, you could understand Mexico. In the most sophisticated regions of Mexico I've seen a man's balls—or lack of them, rather—kill him. More than anything else, the Mexican wears his balls on his shoulder; touch them, refer to them, ignore them, be near them even—you've got yourself gonad trouble! There have been a hundred explanations for this phenomenon, but as the gringo border guards ran up and pinned my arms behind me I wasn't thinking of any of them. I was just thankful that I still had a pair.

Running away from guns is one thing; having one shoved halfway up your ass is another. I could feel the gringo border guard getting his rocks off as he dug the barrel of his .45 into the small of my back. "Gwan, whyncha make a run for it, you son of a bitch," he said to me as he punched and pushed me toward the U.S. side. "I won't miss like the greasers. . . ."

I was hustled back across the border. I thought when I made it into Mexico I'd at least have a chance. I didn't think the Mexicans would return me to the U.S. side. What I hadn't figured on was the unwritten

rule that prevails on the border. Legally the gringo heat had no hold
on me once I was behind that chain-link fence, but if they could rush
over and grab me out of the Mexicans' hands, then nobody but me
was going to complain. Too, the Mexicans knew that if they squawked
they'd get all kinds of shit the next day from their *honcho* boss, who
got half his bread from the U.S. Customs. In effect, I was worth more
money on the U.S. side than on the Mexican side, and as far as my
being legally busted on the Mexican side, who knew that but me?

I was handcuffed to a door while the immigration people phoned
Calexico for Speedy Blue. Speedy Blue (I learned later) was chief
honcho for the customs district that included the border from Calexico, California, to Nogales, Arizona. The Man must have thought he
had a big one in me because he phoned Speedy at 1:30 A.M. and three
or four hours later Speedy appeared, trailing a Chicano agent named
Gomez, who was his running mate. I was locked down below in the
immigration holding cell by this time, still buzzing on my Percodan
and thinking about all the books I'd write during my five to ten years
in the joint. Even in those circumstances the Percodan made me feel
good. I wasn't used to the drug, didn't even know what it was derived
from, but my running partner stayed high on it all the time, and he
advised me to use it too, which I occasionally did. I was told later it
has a synthetic heroin base. I say this though, if I hadn't been stoned
on Percodan, I wouldn't have run the San Luis border at that time.
My natural vibes were fucked up. This was the first time I ever crossed
with a head on; usually I went clean so I could read the vibes. The
whole trip had been a bummer though, and Percodan was just another
sign. I wasn't reading the signs so I ran into a wall. That's all there
was to it.

When Speedy Blue and Gomez came downstairs to the holding cell
where I was pinned, the first thing they did was read off all the rights
I was entitled to: a lawyer, silence, phone call, help, all the rights you
never knew you owned. "Hell," I said, "that sounds great. I'm not
going to say anything until I have an attorney present."

Speedy Blue looked at me and smiled. To appreciate Speedy you've
got to see him. He's a short, squat dude with a roll of fat around the

middle, dressed in Levis and sweat shirt, cowboy boots and a .45—not in the holster, but tucked inside his belt like the Mexicans. And Speedy has an accent, a twang like a cold wind off a flat plain. Being a Southern California boy by birth, I've always been a little mistrustful of accents, unless, of course, girls wore them. Speedy wasn't a girl though; he was a chubby trooper who had found his cause in the U.S. Customs Bureau and was working his way up with a .45 tucked in his belt and an impounded Chevy Impala for catching baddies. He was stocky and sly, and I knew when I saw him that he dug his image, sort of a legal gangster who dressed like one of the boys. When I said I'd wait for my lawyer, Speedy smiled and said, "Well, lissen, Bigtime, yore gonna be waitin' in Yuma County one helluva long time."

I didn't need a fortuneteller to tell me what Speedy meant. Talk or rot. Right then I started talking. I talked for two hours and to this day I'm right proud of the extemporaneous spiel I let Speedy have, complete with blueprints, maps, reasons, names, dates, everything! I mean, I created! There I was, sitting in a cell with a carload of marijuana outside and no place to go. Speedy and Gomez thought they had a big one, and I saw no reason to make them feel any different; so while Speedy chewed, I rapped out a whole scheme that was not only plausible—after talking it for an hour, it became real. My story was true, brother! Later, when I was repeating the rap to my wife I looked up and she said, "You really believe that, don't you?" I realized then that I did. Nobody can tell a lie like a man who believes it.

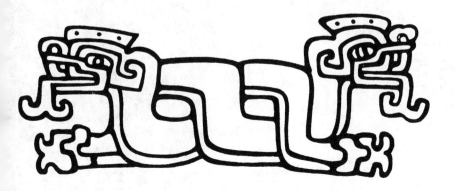

2.

THE ROAD

I started smuggling in 1962. At the time I didn't smuggle marijuana out of Mexico, I smuggled guns, Levis, cameras, cars, and TV's *into* Mexico. It never occurred to me to smuggle marijuana because in 1962 I wasn't interested in the weed. I was into a writing bag and my trip was smuggling small items into Mexico and enjoying the financial benefits and way of life down there, living and grooving in a country where life was relaxed, the beer cheaper, and people less uptight. Jesse was into the weed-smuggling game in a sort of half-assed way, and he wanted me to join him, pointing out the bread that could be made, the ease with which it could be done, etc. He was all the time walking around with a head full of dreams and no money though, so I never got too interested.

I had my own little scene worked out, which involved buying Levis wholesale and smuggling them into Mexico to sell. Early in the sixties anyone with a little cash and a car could pick up a load of Levis from one of the wholesalers for a couple of bucks a pair, take them south, and sell them for ten bucks a pair. I had successfully smuggled quite a few loads down. My scam was having my wife sew the Levis into a mattress and then having her and the kid sleep on it for the first few hundred miles into Mexico. Whenever we drove through an *aduana* checkpoint and the guards poked their noses in the window, my wife would moan and I'd yell, "*Enferma! Enferma!*" The Mexicans would shake their heads in sympathy and pass us on. Never a lick of trouble and we'd always end up with enough bread to last us for six months.

In 1963 I was living in Big Sur when a friend named Larry came down for a visit. Larry had a '59 Chevy and a little cash and he wanted to pick up on my Levi scam. I told him all I knew and gave him the name of a good wholesaler. He decided right then and there to outfit his rig so he could haul 500 pair of pants down south. He removed the partition between the back seat and the trunk of his Chevy, and cut out all the excess metal with an acetylene torch. He decided to imitate my mattress idea for stashing the Levis, so he had his chick cover the nicely wrapped pants with new mattress ticking and then sew a professional looking binding around the edges.

When Larry was ready to go I gave him the name of a connection in Culiacan, a young dude named Daniel who would act as broker and sell all the Levis for ten percent of the action. To those who might wonder about Levis as a smuggling commodity, the fact is they are a popular item all over the world. There's something about a pair of American Levis. In Mexico the local product was made out of an inferior grade of denim, and to wear a pair of *norteamericano* Levis was a badge of status to most Mexican kids. The San Francisco-based Levi Company has since opened a factory in Mexico and now manufactures Levis in the country. An agreement to supply Russia with blue denim was recently reached. In Russia, in 1973, Levi pants sold for as much as $100 a pair.

Photo overleaf by Roberto Ayala

When Larry finished his preparations, he and his chick took off for Culiacan. He linked up with Daniel, and in less than a week's time the two had struck up a partnership. Daniel guided Larry around the country and peddled Levis to individuals and retail outlets. It took two weeks for Daniel to sell the Levis, then he suggested to Larry that it might be a good idea if he invested some of his profits in *mota*. As with me, it had never occurred to Larry to get involved in the weed-smuggling business. Daniel's brother-in-law was a big supplier though, so with that opportunity available to him Larry decided to try it.

On his first trip Larry bought twenty kilos with part of his money and stashed it in the door panels of his Chevy. He had no trouble getting it across the border, and once he reached San Francisco he sold it easily within a week. After that he started smuggling twenty or thirty kilos back across the border every time he took a load of Levis down, and in no time at all he was able to buy a house in the city and hire a mule to do the running for him. A mule is someone who is paid to drive loads across the border, usually for a flat fee. Larry and Daniel's partnership grew, and inside of six months the two of them were responsible for bringing 300 kilos a month into the bay area.

In the meantime Jesse heard about Larry's success and came down to my place in Big Sur and started talking up dope smuggling, using Larry's success as a lure. I didn't need much of a lure. I knew a good deal when I saw one. I was broke at the time, trying to support a wife and two kids and a writing habit, so I went over to see Larry and hit him up for $2,000, payable in three weeks with another thou interest. Larry loaned me the bread and three days later Jesse and I were on the road to Mexico.

On our first trip we stopped in Culiacan and I called an old friend of mine named Chuy. I didn't want to use Daniel because he and Larry had a partnership going and I didn't want to break in on it. Chuy was a good man though, and the minute I called him he came over. I told him I wanted all the weed that $1,700 would buy, and if possible I wanted it that evening. Chuy took the money and our station wagon and told us to meet him in Virginia Café at 10 P.M. Jesse and I sat out the day in a hotel and at 10 P.M. we went to the café. The Virginia is a corner café with two sides open to the street, situated directly across from the Culiacan post office. Ten minutes after we sat down Chuy drove up in our station wagon. He sat down at our table and said, "Eighty kilos, that's all I could get on such short notice." "Did you cover yourself in the cop?" I asked. Chuy nodded.

We finished our coffee and Jesse and I split for Mazatlan, 150 miles to the south. We could have gone north, but the grass wasn't stashed in the wagon. It was sitting in back in a sleeping bag and we had to find a place to stash it. We knew Mazatlan so we went there. It was the off season and Jesse had a friend who owned a trailer court where we could stay while we stashed the weed.

Around midnight we drove into the trailer court and hipped the owner, who gave us a spot in the back. We rested that night and the next day took off all the side and door panels on the wagon, wrapped the kilos in plastic bags, and stashed them inside the panels. It took all day to stash the weed, and later that evening we took off for the border.

Approaching any border is ominous, even when you're clean, but our first trip was a breeze. I was driving and when we reached the customs checkpoint there were only a couple of cars ahead of us. When our turn came I drove up and yanked the emergency brake on and jumped out. The inspector came out of his office and looked in our wagon. I had copped a crazy mélange of toys, paper animals, and baskets and goodies for the old lady and kids. Jesse sat in the passenger seat and play-acted like he was asleep. One thing I hadn't counted on was that each traveler was only allowed so much duty-free booze. We had too much. The inspector looked at our six bottles of El Castillo rum and his eyes gleamed. He pulled the jugs out of the car and called me inside his office. "You'll have to fill out these forms, sir." He shoved a fistful of paper at me. "What's this?" I said. "Can't a man take his own booze across the border?" "It's only orders. I'm supposed to stop all but two quarts per man, any more and you have to pay duty." "It's a ripoff," I said. "How much is the duty?" He looked it up in a book and it came to $15. "You guys are being paid by us and you're working for the liquor lobbies," I said. He looked at me like I read *The New Republic.* I signed the papers and gave him a twenty. He went next door for change and when he returned he handed me an elaborate receipt. "I'm gonna write my congressman," I said, slamming the car door. "Sorry, sir, only doing my duty." He tipped his cap and I drove off with $15,000 worth of weed.

It took Jesse three weeks to sell the grass once we got it to San Francisco. I took the two thou plus the thou interest back to Larry and said thanks. Jesse and I had our stake now, so we took off again and in a couple of weeks were back in the city with 125 kilos. Not top shit, but good enough to sell. With the second load we took a little more time, renting a house and garage so we could peddle in leisure. At this time weed was going for about $170 a kilo, not bad for a brick that cost $15. My part in the operation was copping and driving, and Jesse took care of the selling. When the 125 kilos were sold, Jesse and I were ready to set out big.

To deal dope big you have to have good connections in both Mexico and the U.S. Quality wasn't important in the early sixties, people would buy anything that got across, but anyone who wanted to make big bread had to be able to cop weight. That's where Jesse and I had it made. The Hernandez brothers, Roberto and Juan, were big-time dope dealers in Mexico, some say the biggest. They weren't, but they were big enough. Both of them were fugitives from the United States, ex-U.S. citizens who had fallen and were taking advantage of the one free fall allowed nationals by the Mexican government. A free fall means that if a person of Mexican descent is arrested in the U.S. over some beef—narcotics, theft, etc.—and can make it across the border to Mexico, he can remain there in relative safety as long as he stays clean—which means as long as he pays his *mordida.* A *mordida,* or "bite," is a bribe. All of Mexico operates on the *mordida* system. You buy your way in, you buy your way up, and you buy your way out if you get caught. The Hernandez brothers operated out of Tijuana, the asshole of Mexico, that particular border town being the small end of the funnel for a dope-smuggling operation that encompasses much of Mexico and involves high-up officials on both sides of the border. Jesse had spent some time in a Mexican joint with Roberto Hernandez and knew him well. With that connection—with that knowledge really, for we never had to use the Hernandez brothers as connections, it was enough simply to know them—Jesse and I were able to ascend into the highest ranks of marijuana smuggling.

As partners Jesse and I worked well together, his Mexican temperament balancing perfectly my gringo sensibility. We worked together from 1964 on through the middle of 1966 and got a lot of loads across the border with few hassles, and I had a nice scene together in Big Sur with some land and a book on the way. My bust at San Luis brought all of this to an abrupt halt. I was sentenced to two years in the federal penitentiary, sentence suspended, and placed on five years' probation. Under the terms of my probation I was not allowed to leave the Northern California Federal District without the permission of my probation officer. For all intents and purposes my smuggling career was over.

Less than a year later I was back in Mexico. I wasn't there to smuggle weed, however, but to write about it, and Jesse and I had $5,000 in our pockets to do the job. The bread had been provided by *Life* magazine and we were going up into the mountains to search out the marijuana fields and do the greatest dope story of all. After we'd found the fields, a photographer would fly down and take pictures of the whole process—cultivation, harvesting, bricking, transportation.

The *Life* marijuana caper started one night when Jesse showed up at my house in Capitola. I was making a clean scene with my wife Judy and my two children by a previous marriage, writing a novel, and working occasionally to bring in a little money. Jesse told me he had met a photographer at a Haight-Ashbury party who'd heard him rapping about Mexico and marijuana and thought it would make an interesting picture story. Eugene Anthony, the photographer, thought he could interest *Life* in doing it. Jesse and Gene flew to Los Angeles and talked to the West Coast editor of *Life*. As a result of that meeting an informal agreement was entered into: *Life* would provide $5,000 expense money for the expedition into Mexico, but would assume absolutely no responsibility for the participants in the venture. At first

Gene Anthony wanted an established writer to accompany them but Jesse wanted me to go for a number of reasons: first, I was an ex-running mate of his; second, I had smuggled marijuana and I knew Mexico; third, I was currently writing about Mexico and marijuana; and fourth, he was afraid to take anyone else.

I thought through the hassles I'd have to overcome before I could go. In the first place I was supposed to fill out and mail in a probation form on the first of each month outlining where I was living, where I was working, how much money I was making. The monthly reports didn't cover my whole probation scene however. I was also subject to unannounced visits by my probation officer, Mr. Chandler. Usually when he dropped by I was busy working on my novel or on some children's books, which seemed to impress him. After I'd been on probation for eight months, Chandler had lightened up considerably, he'd even grown a beard, and we got on reasonably well. But if I split for Mexico, I'd have to set things up so he wouldn't suspect that I was violating my probation.

Despite the risk, I decided I couldn't turn the assignment down and signed six monthly probation report forms, dating them for the up-coming months, signed and sealed them in separate envelopes, and left them with a friend for mailing on the first of each month. As far as Chandler's personal visits were concerned, I could legitimately miss one or two simply by not being at home when he arrived, and if he called or wrote to make an appointment, my friend could cover for a while. If things got real hairy and Chandler demanded that I report to his office, I could take a plane home—that is, if I was in close enough touch with my friend to know about it.

So Jesse and I were in business again. He sent off letters to connections in Mexico, while I got hold of some phony ID papers from a connection in Oakland. I needed a driver's license, a birth certificate, and a few credit cards. For 200 bucks I got the lot, complete with pictures. Within a week Jesse had a favorable reply from one of his most reliable connections. We serviced his station wagon, putting on some new tires and other gear courtesy of the credit cards, and we were ready. Jesse also brought along his Pentax and I took a Polaroid camera and some writing equipment. On a Sunday afternoon, two weeks after Jesse came to my house in Capitola, we were off on the first leg of our journey south.

When I made my decision to accompany Jesse I didn't realize that it would eventually lead me into the farthest reaches of Mexico, one of the strangest and most perplexing countries in the world. Nor did I know that later Jesse and I would not only do the story for *Life*, but we would use the money they gave us to buy a marijuana field, and that we would eventually smuggle the resultant ton of weed out of Mexico into the United States. But strange things happen when the dust of Mexico enters your blood, and my veins have long been full of the Mexican earth. What follows then is the story of our adventure.

During my early days of dope smuggling the run between San Francisco and Guadalajara had become like a commute to me, so it was easy to fall into the old road rhythm. I feel exhilarated every time I leave one place and head for another, and leaving San Francisco and heading for Mexico brought out that on-the-road excitement.

Our first night out Jesse and I outlined an itinerary that we hoped would get us into the mountains within two or three weeks. That it was to take longer was inevitable, for nothing happens on schedule in Mexico. We stopped in Los Angeles at an all-night surplus store, where I bought some gifts for Mexican friends, and after sending a wire to our connection telling him we were on the way, we sped over the desert, through Indio, El Centro, Yuma, heading south.

On the morning of September 17, we crossed the border at Sonoita and stopped at a café for breakfast. It was dawn and the early morning air was invigorating. Jesse got out of the wagon to stretch, then walked around behind the adobe hut to take a leak. Inside the café we ordered coffee. I was tired from having driven all night. The whole journey down the west coast of Mexico lay before us, and I looked forward to it. Jesse and I had made the trip many times, but this time it was going to be different. We would actually be going into the mountains. On previous runs we had always delivered our car to a connection and then split for a short vacation at the seashore while our grass was bricked and stashed in our car. Many times we'd rendezvous at a friend's ranch in Mochis where a stockpile of grass was kept by a few entrepreneurs for an assorted clientele of West Coast smugglers. It had always been a fairly relaxed operation, organized in a casual way. We made the arrangements, delivered our car, paid our bread, spent a day or two or a week at the most on the beach, then returned and picked up our loaded car and split. One, two, three, four, right down the line.

Jesse and I had done it many times, each time learning a little more, getting a little bit more professional, watching while others fell, learning from their mistakes, mostly the junior high school types and hippies from the Haight, ivy-league college kids and self-styled busi-

Photo overleaf by Roberto Ayala

ness types who smuggled kilos over in their underwear. We saw surfers and straights fall; we saw sons of doctors, lawyers, state legislators go down. Everyone came to score and each had his style. Jesse and I came and we had our style too. We'd made the run together from the start, and it worked right up until that full-moon midnight in San Luis, Arizona. That night was behind us though, and everything was perfect for this trip, money in our pocket, letters out to connections and answers back, and everything moving along in the slow rhythm that I liked, the rhythm that was enunciated by the mountains themselves, slow and timeless. Everything was perfectly coordinated so that it wouldn't fail—but the one thing that's constant about marijuana smuggling is the possibility of a failure. It's built in, just as the generator on your automobile is built to go only so far before it fails. Everyone who makes the drive down Highway 15 into Mexico looking to score knows that there are only two types of dope smugglers, those who've fallen and those who are going to fall.

The old woman brought our coffee and shuffled back into the kitchen to make *huevos rancheros.* The coffee was good, strong and black and hot. Mexico has the best coffee in the world. I listened to the kitchen sounds and cupped my hand around the tin mug. It felt good to rest.

"We'll make Guaymas by one and be in Los Mochis tonight," Jesse said. He stirred milk into his coffee.

"You're going to have to drive," I said. "I'm going to sack out in the back."

"I'm glad we're across. I always feel better when I get into this country." Jesse added sugar to his coffee as he spoke, stirring it slowly.

As a Chicano, that is, an American of Mexican descent, Jesse benefits and suffers from both cultures. From three cultures really, because behind his Mexican and gringo blood lurks the blood of the Tarascan Indian. He speaks fluent Spanish and wears a droopy Zapata mustache. His own view of Mexico is unique because of his position, and I derived a lot of my opinions and attitudes about the country from him, always refining them, however, with my own sensibility, because I feel that Jesse has a somewhat distorted view of Mexico by

the very nature of his background. Our relationship is one of mutual respect and of heightened tensions and stubbornness when we work together. His reserve and conservatism, a cohesive tendency to pause and think everything out fully before moving an inch, is constantly accented by my prodding impulsiveness, a need to go forward continually, always moving in the direction I feel necessary. As a consequence our two temperaments tend to balance one another and we get along reasonably well, though at times we have terrific fights that leave us both either laughing hysterically or detached from one another for days. As a working team, we somehow make it. Partly it is because one of us always seems to have that element the other lacks.

Jesse is a fastidious dresser in a casual, Bohemian way, tending to boots and costume clothing long before the fad caught on with the hippies and the younger set. He had spent five years in a penitentiary for the possession of one marijuana cigarette back in the early fifties, when dope wasn't the big thing it is now. After his release from prison he landed in North Beach and took up photography, and now he was smuggling weed across the border to help supply the fantastic quantity being blasted all over the country by everybody. After I'd been busted, Jesse had continued to make runs every three months or so, and at the time had a reasonable business going. By reasonable I mean that perhaps $100,000 had passed through his hands in the last year or so. Money is slippery though, especially money derived from marijuana. One of Jesse's credos is "Never get greedy." Consequently he is always generous with the farmers and subsidiary people involved in the trade. We both have seen too many older and more experienced smugglers succumb because of greed. The greedy ones always fall, if not at the border, then somewhere further on down the line.

We finished our coffee and ordered second cups when the old woman brought our *huevos rancheros*. The hot, spicy smell of the eggs enticed me. I was verging on that delicious edge of fatigue you get after having been up for a long time. The past few days had been hectic, and the actual driving on the road was a release. I always go through a complete physical rejuvenation during a run, eating little and purging my body of all the poisons of city living. When I enter the desert I consider it as a ritual, a cleansing and fasting time that clears my head and makes me more aware of the nuances and vibrations floating around the people and places I will be visiting.

My one weakness is *huevos rancheros*—eggs fried very lightly, laid on a tortilla, and smothered with hot chili. Jesse and I had devised a route down the west coast of Mexico that included all the restaurants that served good *huevos rancheros*. Like the American hamburger that changes so much from district to district, *huevos rancheros* are subject to local interpretation. We had suffered through many incredibly inept variations before establishing the chain of small adobe huts, fancy hotel restaurants, and wayside stands that served what I considered to be the best *huevos rancheros* in Mexico. We had stopped at the restaurant we were now in a number of times. The old woman is one of the world's great undiscovered cooks, bringing forth from her extremely modest kitchen the most savory coffee and the tastiest *huevos rancheros* in Sonora. I gobbled mine down joyfully as Jesse spoke.

"This country's like another world, even the terrain is different. Every time I cross that border I feel a thousand pounds of bullshit and bad living lift off my shoulders. I'm going to quit all this crap and move back down here one of these days."

"I wonder what it is about this country that makes it so much different from the States," I said. I, too, felt the release of an invisible pressure from my shoulders, or, to be more exact, off my head, when I crossed the border.

"People are less uptight down here," Jesse said. "They aren't caught up in that bullshit control and conform crap that everyone is into back in the U.S. And they're people from the land, campesinos, poor people, most of them anyway. The rich ones down here are just as bad as the rich ones back home. The Mexican upper class is more middle class than the American middle class. Plastic? Man, they eat that shit up. They consider it the height of refinement if they can serve their coffee in plastic cups. Very few of the rich Mexicans are hip to their own culture, they never go down to the market place and spend twenty centavos for a pottery cup to drink their coffee out of; no, they'll get plastic melmac cups for a dollar apiece and think they're living. It's a strange country, but to really understand it you have to get close to the people, the campesinos. . . ."

At one time, Jesse had lived in the mountains of Michoacan for several years, living the simple, hardworking life of the Indian. Living with the Indians had affected him, creating in him, for one thing, an infinite capacity for passing time. No journey with Jesse is ever direct. By definition it is circuitous, rambling, open for chance and the vagaries of the road. Nothing can keep him from waylaying a journey, interrupting himself and whoever is with him to explore another village, inspect a new crossroad, visit a ruin so he can capture it with his camera.

Jesse had also mastered the art of dissimulation. With him nothing is ever as it appears. This was partly a throwback to his Tarascan blood, but it was also necessitated by the realities of his life. Jesse operated with supercaution because of his prison experiences, and also because he was a fugitive, actively sought by the FBI. His dissimulation, therefore, is designed partly to leave a cloud of ambiguity and doubt along his trail. Nobody knows his real name, no one knows where he is from, no one knows anything concrete about him at all. Jesse seemed to have taken to heart Don Juan's dictum of "erasing all personal history," though not quite for the reasons Don Juan had in mind.

One of the hangups about Jesse's dissimulation is that it had become a way of life, creating bizarre situations when his need to cover up his trail involved his friends. My relationship with him was often tense because of the fantasies he engaged in; he seldom told the truth about anything. Often I had to deal spontaneously with his fabrications as they surfaced. One time in a restaurant in Taos, New Mexico, Jesse told the waitress that we were Indians from Alaska. Nothing serious, even worth a laugh or two later, but it was I who had to follow through with Jesse's lie. These incidents occurred often on our journeys together and after awhile they began to bother me. More often though, Jesse's tales were simply humorous, designed to relieve the tension and make the time go by easier.

Jesse also had one of the most incredible memories I have encountered and his tales contained minute details and embellishments. During his youth he had studied law for a semester or two at a junior college and his capacity for logic and structured detail amazed me. He was contemptuous of people who didn't think things through logically and arrive at the same decisions he himself arrived at, and during his stay in prison his ability to organize rational approaches to everything served him well; he was personally responsible for the release of twelve prisoners who had been imprisoned illegally. He was an expert on writs and justly proud of his legal ability. As we drove down the Mexican highways he would regale me with prison stories and Mexican stories and life stories, tales that were indexed and repeated, and uncovered, wrapped up in his own particular lexicon of words that presented, finally, a whole picture of the world in which he lived.

It was through Jesse's friends that we were going to be able to get into the mountains. After my arrest and retirement from the business in 1966, he had set up a whole smuggling chain, one that started in the mountains, linked into the towns and hamlets, and crossed over to the city where he took over. After a load was delivered to San Francisco, it was spread up and down the West Coast, to Chicago, and sometimes to New York. It was an established route, the connections were reliable, and it was fluid enough to be able to suit the climate, heat, temperature, temper, and times.

Our chain was unique in the sense that Jesse and I now had access to the mountains, to the fields where the grass was grown, and at the same time we had buyers in the States who would take the stuff—a hundred kilos or more at a time—and start it through the filtering-down process to the streets. We never dealt on the street level, leaving that to others in the chain, for it is on the street where you are most apt to fall.

The mystique of grass is strange, and it has become a sort of status symbol in the States to fall behind it. It is also a status symbol to be a big dealer, the bigger the dealer the higher the status. Of course, the biggest dealers are completely unknown to the lower levels, those dealing on a super-professional level, those who would kill (and have

killed) a border guard if their security is threatened. Jesse's and my dealing was on a more or less amateur-professional level—professional in the sense that we hauled large quantities of marijuana, but amateur in the sense that it wasn't important enough to kill for it. We always figured that if we fell we would handle it innocently, working out a nonviolent plan to deal with the situation as it occurred.

We finished our breakfast and walked back to the car. It was still early. I could hear cocks crowing in the distance. A few early-morning workers walked by, heading out into the campos to gather firewood or down to the river to fish. Many of the Mexicans had green cards that allowed them to cross over the border into the U.S. to work in the fields. They were beginning to line up at the immigration checkpoint.

Jesse drove as we headed out of town. I sat in the passenger seat and watched the early-morning scene. Sonoita is a typical border town, less outrageous than most, being a little off the beaten track for most tourists. The downtown section resembles a lot of small southwestern Texas and Arizona towns, somewhat less prosperous looking, less neon, a little more dust and more heat. On the outskirts the adobe shacks tumble into each other, hovels and shanties, knocked together with mud, tin, tarpaper, and whatever. Poverty in Mexico, unlike poverty in the United States, is less well hidden. You may have to drive into the back streets to see the squalor, but when you see it, it is really wretched. Most North Americans are not aware of the poverty of the majority of Mexicans, but they are not aware of the poverty of a lot of their fellow Americans either, so I guess it doesn't make that much difference. It's said that the majority of the Mexican people are suffering from some form of malnutrition; my own experience, in more than fourteen years of traveling and living in the country, tends to confirm this.

As we left Sonoita and headed into the desert, crossing over Highway 2 to link up with Highway 15 and then down to Guaymas, I looked out over the desert and saw the sun peek up over the mountains. The soft blues and purples of the desert lightened and I felt genuinely at peace with myself. Tired and content, I climbed into the back of the wagon and went to sleep.

From the collection of Roberto Aya

At noon Jesse stopped for lunch in Caborca. After eating I climbed into the front seat again and we drove on to Santa Ana, the town where Highway 2 cuts into Highway 15. From Santa Ana on, the road is long and straight, through Hermosillo and then Guaymas. Sometimes the road skirts a river, but mostly it runs through the flat Sonoran desert of northern Mexico, which is broken abruptly by high jutting peaks and distant mountain ranges. In the distance the mountains seem to take on human form, sleeping women, old men, craggy profiles peering up at the sky. It is said that when the King of Spain asked Cortez what Mexico looked like, Cortez crumbled a piece of paper in his hand and tossed it on the floor. "Like that, your majesty," he said. It is an apt description of Mexico. Long distances and vistas that are breathtakingly beautiful combine with sheer mountains and plunging *barrancas* that gash through the country like prehistoric wounds.

I have never lived on the desert, always seeming to need the sea, but the Sonoran desert enthralls me. I expect that there will sometime be a "desert period" in my life. There are great similarities between the desert and the sea; each has its own grandeur and demands its own sacrifice.

We pulled into Guaymas about six in the evening, made it over to one of the beaches, stripped to our shorts, and ran into the water. The water was warm and it felt good. After bathing we went into town and stopped at our special restaurant. I ordered a bottle of Bohemia and an omelette with green chili. Jesse had *carne asada,* a large steak cut thin and cooked well done. After eating we walked around Guaymas, down to the docks to watch the fishermen, into town to stretch our legs and let the food settle before continuing on to Mazatlan.

We wanted to be in Mazatlan before noon the following day, in time to make our connection and arrange for rooms. The distance was about 800 kilometers, ten hours of normal driving. I wanted to stop and see some friends too, renew some acquaintances, and drop off a few items I'd brought down with me. Whenever I went to Mexico I brought Levis and shirts, a few tools and some handguns to lay on Mexican friends—braceros I'd met in the States, people beside the road I'd made acquaintance with, families and individuals that somehow had entered my life and remained close.

I felt a perennial debt to Mexico that began on one of my first trips there, one of those magical tours that some divine travel agent had arranged. Just out of the army, I had packed my ditty bag and gathered papers, intending to make a journey to Tierra del Fuego, the trip you will never make if you are chosen town clerk, as Thoreau said. I hadn't been chosen town clerk, so I wanted to make the trip, hitchhiking through Mexico and Central America, bumming my way through South America to the tip, back up to Montevideo, and then catching a boat to South Africa, and up through Africa to the Mediterranean. A noble plan that didn't work out quite that way.

At the Nicaraguan embassy in Los Angeles, I met Raul and his Aunt Nano and their dog Allie. Raul was driving a bus to Managua, Nicaragua—a bus he had purchased and filled with every necessity for the trip and his subsequent settling down in his home town. We agreed that I would drive the bus as far as Managua, at which point I would strike out on my own. It was a good arrangement, and lasted all the way to the Mexican border. At the border the Mexican spirit of casualness and abandon and red tape and *mordida* and *mañana* and

impossible juxtapositions spoiled Raul's plans. We were shuttled from one border town to the next until finally, he, the bus, me, the dog Allie, and Aunt Nano ended up in El Paso, Texas, astraddle the Rio Grande River, wondering what to do. It seemed Raul hadn't the proper papers. The Mexicans didn't think he was actually going to take his two refrigerators, stove, and three television sets all the way to Nicaragua. Raul ran out of money before he ran out of patience. After four days waiting I left Raul still astride the Rio Grande, Aunt Nano still riding shotgun, and faithful Allie still at her side. Raul had given me $20 for the chauffeur job, a twenty I returned with sad apologies and the guilt of Judas. I felt I was abandoning a faithful friend. I had spent ten days yo-yoing back and forth along the border with Raul and his bus, and I still wanted to see the Land of Fire.

I hitchhiked on down to Chihuahua, got a ride in a station wagon full of Mormons returning from a basketball tournament in Cedar City, Utah, a tournament, I eagerly pointed out, I myself had played in four years previously. The Mormons weren't impressed, but reluctantly drove me to a small, lonely outpost fifty miles north of Chihuahua, where they turned off the road into the desert to their own lives. I spent the night huddled in the chilly air beside a gas station. In the morning I got my first real ride with a real Mexican—a ride that took me over a thousand miles into Mexico and opened up the country to me.

Carlos, the salesman who picked me up, sold salt and was determined to hit every small store in northern Mexico. From Carlos I learned about Mexican generosity. During four days of peddling, eating, sleeping, talking, laughing, lying, and listening, he never let me take a peso from my pocket. This Mexican characteristic has been reaffirmed a hundred times since, by all types and classes. When a Mexican befriends you, you are a guest, and a guest does not pay. I have been a guest in the most humble homes and it is the same—the best bed, the most generous portion always belongs to the stranger.

Carlos took me from the outskirts of Chihuahua, through the back-country roads of Mexico, visiting towns and villages all along the line, Ciudad Delicias, Sancillo, San Francisco de Conchos, Jimenez, and Hidalgo del Parral, the town where Pancho Villa was assassinated.

In Hidalgo del Parral, Carlos put me up at a fine hotel and the next morning treated me to delicious *huevos rancheros* in the dining room. On the street I read a plaque put up on the spot where Villa died. All along the way, through miles and miles of Chihuahua and Durango and Zacatecas, I sat beside Carlos. We screamed words at one another over the howl of the wind outside his panel truck; *los aires, pais, ventana, calle, carretera;* I repeated the words in English as we taught one another our respective languages.

So I had remained faithful to many of the friends I had met in Mexico and I enjoyed stopping along the way, to say hello, to drop off a few items that ordinarily my friends would be unable to obtain. One of the joys of making money from marijuana is the ability to spread some of it around, repay the people, as it were, with some of the things they need. A gun, which in the United States is the product of one; or perhaps two days' wages, is for most rural Mexicans the product of four or five years of work and sweat. When one sees the incredible ancient firearms used by many of the campesinos, guns wrapped with wire to keep the barrel from falling off, pistols that came in with the conquest, one appreciates the value they put on their weapons. Too, a weapon for a Mexican who lives in the campos is more of a necessity than a plaything, as it usually is in the U.S. A gun is part of a campesino's everyday life; it is as important as his machete, as necessary as the shirt on his back.

Mexico is still an agrarian society, and most Mexicans still root their living out of the soil. The majority of the people, both Indian and mestizo, are campesinos who bear the weight of the affluent class upon their backs. The middle class has not yet developed to the extent of wielding any real power. The rapid industrialization that is taking place is bringing with it an increase in the middle class, however, workers and technicians who will eventually bring many changes to Mexican society.

At present, the campesino who travels a day's journey into the mountains to cut firewood to sell the next day for five pesos (40 cents) is a common sight along most of the roads traversing Mexico. A burro, a machete, a gun, are all necessary tools for him, and all save the machete are hard to come by. Subsistence living does not allow a Saturday afternoon visit to the gun shop to buy a firearm. When the average campesino has enough to eat, that is a day for rejoicing. It is hard to convince most gringos—and many Mexicans too, for that matter—of this fact.

Jesse and I left Guaymas as the sun went down, the liquid red ball settling on the sea like a slowly deflating balloon. I drove as we crossed the bridge south of Guaymas and headed into the town of Empalme. Empalme used to be one of the northern dispatching stations for braceros, the Mexican laborers who make their living by working six or nine months at a time on farms in the United States. The braceros were processed in Empalme, then placed on trains for the journey to Benjamin Hill and Calexico, the northern terminals for the Mexican railroad. One late afternoon I drove past Empalme and saw a sea of sombreros spread out before me, rippling and moving in waves; over 10,000 patient campesinos were crouched on the ground waiting to go north.

South of Empalme the country started getting greener. We were entering the great, lush, Sonoran agricultural belt. Thousands of bugs smashed themselves on the windshield and we had to stop our car a number of times to scrape the goo off. Alongside the road, huge trucks loaded with cotton were lined up waiting their turn at the gin, many of them so overloaded their springs sagged under the weight. Once while hitchhiking north from Guadalajara I was picked up by two Mexicans delivering a load of pottery to the market in Tepic. Their

From the collection of Roberto Ayala

truck was so burdened down with clay pots from Tlaquepaque that
it rolled and swayed from side to side as it lumbered down the highway. I must have been the straw that broke the camel's back, for just
south of Tepic on a flat stretch of road, the right rear spring sang out
like a band of steel reaching its breaking point—which it had. The
truck heaved over to the side of the road when the spring snapped,
determined not to go an inch further.

It's a rule in Mexico that if you have a car or truck, you load it twice
as full as is humanly possible, then you drive it twice as fast as it is
capable of going. I have never experienced worse drivers than those
who rampage over the highways of Mexico. When a Mexican gets in
an automobile he becomes another person. Perhaps it's the nature of
machinery, perhaps the nature of the Mexican himself, but I know few
Mexicans who do not, upon climbing into a car, become demons in
human form.

The Mexican driver is the rudest, loudest, craziest on the face of
the earth. He has absolutely no sense of machinery. He treats his car
as if it were an omnipotent chariot capable of carrying him over
cobblestones, bricks, dirt, and mud with the mere turning of a key and
the plunging of accelerator to the floor. He scatters pedestrians,
refuses to recognize obstacles, and plays chicken with every approaching vehicle. In Mexico City cabs shoot at you, buses run you down
at the curb, drivers curse and race one another on crumbling and
nonexistent highways, vehicles careen in and out of traffic like bumper
cars in a carnival, all with serene equanimity. When I first walked the
streets of Mexico City I ran for my life, and I was no green country
boy; I was brought up in Southern California, where the automobile
is a deity of its own.

The Mexican mechanic is noted for his ability to keep anything
going. He can patch the most dilapidated piece of junk together to give
that last few miles, while the Mexican driver is renowned for his
ability to make junk out of the newest piece of equipment in an
incredibly short period of time. A famous anecdote concerning the
Mexican driver's stubbornness involved the Count del Valle de
Orizaba, whose coach met another coach on a narrow street. Neither
coach would back up for the other, so for three days and nights the

two coaches faced one another while spectators cheered them on and servants ran back and forth to both coaches with food and instructions. Finally a bystander devised a contest for the two embattled noblemen: whoever could throw a sword farthest and have it land upright in the ground would be allowed the right of way on the narrow road.

I have long puzzled over what insane hand created Mexicans and then invented automobiles to put them in. Could it be God's own method of population control?

When a Mexican acquires a car his whole psyche changes. Owning a car raises him up a notch or two above the common peons and he isn't going to let anyone forget it. According to Jesse, this habit comes from the old days when only the wealthy could afford to own carriages and the common practice was to run down any peons who happened to get in the way. The emerging middle class of Mexico now beginning to drive automobiles continue this practice. Anyone outside an automobile is fair game. And courtesy is unheard of. In fact, courtesy is discourteous. I am tempted to exclude Mexican truck drivers from my criticism, being an American romantic who likes to believe in those vagabonds of the road, but in all honesty I cannot. The times I have been seated in twenty-ton rigs roaring down the narrow, rutted Mexican highways and cringed as the drivers swerved maniacally

around gigantic buses on blind curves are too numerous to mention. All one can do in such a case is lower one's head and pray. The burned-out carcasses of smashed buses along the roads and arroyos are mute testimony to those prayers that weren't answered.

A few miles north of Esperanza, we turned off the highway and headed east on a dirt road. Manuel Zubiaga, a friend I'd met some time before, lived twenty kilometers down the road. I had a gun and some clothes and a few other things for Manuel and his family.

Four years earlier when I had been driving down this same highway, I had just left Empalme when I saw Manuel standing alongside the road. He had his hand raised in the typical Mexican fashion, index finger upright, asking for a ride. I gave him a lift, depositing him finally on this same dirt road to his home. Manuel had been waiting for two weeks at the embarkation center in Empalme, trying to get a job as a bracero. He had failed and he was on his way home when I picked him up. As we drove down the road we talked about braceros and Mexico and the United States.

As far as the Mexicans are concerned, the bracero program is a great opportunity to go north and work for a few months and get some money together so they can ease the grind of poverty at home. I've always been in favor of the program as far as the individual Mexicans are concerned. At the same time the callousness with which many of them are exploited by unscrupulous farmers in the United States bothered me. Also, the falsehood that home-grown workers didn't exist, that there were no North Americans who could or would do stoop labor—a lie propagated by the large owners—rankled me. It especially bothered me when a single trip into Stockton or El Centro or Indio would dispel that figment of agribusiness's imagination in one afternoon. What the growers meant was that North American harvest workers, the so-called fruit tramps, would not do stoop labor for the wages the Mexican bracero would accept. Seventy-five cents an hour is a fortune for most Mexicans. When the minimum wage was raised to $1.40 an hour, it was paradise. The average American working for $1.40 an hour is rooted in the deepest poverty. But the average laboring Mexican, that is, someone who works at a municipal job like a traffic cop, is paid the equivalent of about $1.80 a day.

Another reason why Mexican braceros were so popular with the North American grower was the ease with which they were controlled, transported, and then expelled after the completion of a particular harvest. North Americans, even poor North Americans, are less easily hustled, less easily satisfied, less easily dispersed, simply because they are in their own country. It's a moot question who is worse off, the Mexican campesino or the North American fruit tramp. The only thing that seems to be constant about both groups, now that the bracero program has been curbed, is that, aside from Cesar Chavez, nobody seems to be doing much of anything to help either group, despite all the government reports.

Manuel and I became good friends after I picked him up, and I stopped at his house a number of times on subsequent trips to Mexico. The road to his village was narrow and rutted, and we inched along, a large cloud of dust billowing up behind us in the darkness. We passed groups of white-clothed campesinos trudging along, their dark faces illuminated as they turned to stare at our passing lights. They walked in pairs and singly, a column of farmers heading home after the day's work. At a familiar spot I turned off the road into a clearing beside a group of huts. Manuel lived with his wife, Guadalupe, and three children, Marta, Antonio, and Francisco. The huts were arranged in a casual circle around the clearing, adobe and sticks pressed together, the familiar wattle and daub construction of many of the outlying settlements in Mexico.

As a community, Manuel's settlement wasn't much, a place where a dozen or so families lived together, sharing the day-to-day problems of survival. Some of the men worked in the cotton fields belonging to the large landowners in the area, others scratched a living gathering firewood or doing subsistence farming. Many, like Manuel, made their own way to Empalme each season and tried to get on the bracero train; if, like Manuel, they failed, they returned to their villages or moved further south to Obregon or Los Mochis to get work on the large ranches there.

I could see the oil lamp burning through the cracks in Manuel's hut as Jesse and I approached. Inside, Guadalupe was preparing the meal —chili, tortillas, and some beans. Manuel was at the door at the approach of our lights, his familiar face smiling as we got out of the car. I had purchased a bottle of tequila in Guaymas and reached into the back of the wagon for it. We would have a few drinks, talk, I would leave the things I'd brought, then Jesse and I would be on our way.

When we parked, Manuel ran up to our car.

"*¿Qué pasa, hombre?*" he shouted as we slapped each other on the back. "Lupe, put some more food on, Jeronimo *y* Jesse are here!"

In the corner of the hut Lupe smiled shyly and busied herself over her stove. The children stayed in the corner of the room, smiling at us. Jesse and I ended our greetings and then sat down on boxes placed on the dirt floor. I held up my jug of tequila and Manuel whooped for joy. He ran to the alcove beside Lupe's stove and produced a clay bowl and two small fruit glasses.

"It's been a long time, hombre," Manuel said, after we'd filled the cups and sipped some tequila.

"Too long, *mano,*" I said, rolling the fiery liquid around on my tongue. "I can see you're still alive though. Have the gods been good to you?"

Manuel shrugged and laughed. His lean face was etched with fine lines that stretched and retreated around his eyes as he smiled. Manuel was part Yaqui Indian and the wiriness of that race traced itself in his bones. His eyes sparkled with a toughness that belied the soft, almost whispering voice he used when he spoke.

"Aye, *mano*. Things are this way and that, you know. One is never through with the struggle."

"*¡Verdad!*" I said. We lifted our glasses.

"And you, my friend, have the angels been keeping you covered with their wings?"

"More than enough, Manuel." We all laughed.

A peculiarity of Mexicans—and most Latin Americans for that matter—and something many gringos have a hard time getting used to, is the florid speech of many of the people. Mexicans are a nation of poets, their everyday speech embellished with aphorisms, epigrams, and sheer verbal fantasy. This is as true of the uneducated campesinos as it is of the aristocracy, the language of poetry seeming to fall effortlessly from their lips. In the mouths of politicians the art of language is extended to incomprehensible length, according to a rule that if a thousand words will do, ten thousand will do better.

While we exchanged pleasantries and sipped our tequila, Lupe placed clay bowls of chili, hot and steaming, with tortillas and beans before us. Although we were probably using up a whole week's fare, both Jesse and I knew the uselessness of resisting—and the loss to Manuel and Lupe could be made up when we left. I had grown tactful in my benevolence and had developed a reverse sense of being insulted unless my gifts were taken as readily as their gifts were offered. The whole pantomime of offerings and refusals was done with much back-slapping and laughter. There is an art to receiving as well as to giving, and if one travels much in Mexico, one has to learn the rules. The difficulty is, of course, until you learn the rules you're bound to make a lot of mistakes. Once in Mexico City I made the mistake of admiring a painting I saw on a friend's wall. Zap! The painting was off the wall and in my hands before I could say another word. I stuttered help-lessly, wondering what I was supposed to do with the painting. I looked at it closely, pretending to be inspecting it as a connoisseur, and handed it back. "Very nice," I said. "No, no, it's yours," my friend said. Try as I might I couldn't make him take his painting back. I learned later that in Mexico anything you admire is yours, so I made my way through the country admiring other people's belongings si-lently.

It was getting late and Jesse and I had to leave. I had given Fran-cisco, Manuel's oldest son, a rigging knife that I carried on my belt and he was huddled in the corner eagerly examining it with his brother and sister. I went out to the car and got the Levis and gun for Manuel and placed them on the table. I was a little embarrassed because beside what I had brought I could see the immensity of things that were needed. I gave Lupe a squeeze when she emerged from her corner and wished I'd thought to bring some utensils for her. It had

never entered my mind. While no one was looking I slipped a hundred-peso note on the table to restore the supply of food Jesse and I had eaten and to tide them over for a while. It would last them for weeks. Manuel was examining the gun and I could see incredible disbelief and new-found possibilities of ownership on his face. With some haste and without formalities, just the traditional *abrazo*, the arms around each other, Jesse and I bid goodbye to Manuel and went outside to our car. Manuel spoke softly.

"*Bien viaje, mano*," he said. "Watch for God along the road."

We laughed as Jesse turned the wagon around in the clearing. Manuel's parting statement had more than one meaning. The first time I had picked him up after leaving Empalme, I had cursed the horses and cows on the road as intractable instruments of destruction. "In Mexico," Manuel said, "we call the cows God, they move for no man and sometimes they send him to hell if he drives too fast."

Being sent to hell by a Mexican cow is no idle possibility. During the late fifties it was not uncommon to see dozens of dead animals—burros, horses, cows, dogs, etc.—along the narrow, unfenced highways. During one stretch of about seventy-five miles between Obregon and Los Mochis, I once counted seventeen dead animals. The slaughter got so bad and the resulting automobile accidents so numerous that the Mexican authorities finally passed a law holding the owner of the animal struck down on the road responsible. Before that law many indigent campesinos would lead their already half-dead animals out on the road at night hoping that someone—preferably an ignorant gringo—would hit them. Then they could collect money for an animal they were glad to be rid of. Any animal hit on the highway is left for the vultures to clean up.

On the other hand, many Mexican drivers seem to get a secret joy out of killing animals along the road. Innumerable times I have seen truck drivers swing their rigs into animals grazing peacefully along the shoulder. In fact, the lack of regard most Mexicans hold for animals is one of the most striking characteristics North American tourists notice. Perhaps because life is hard for most Mexicans, not much sympathy is left for the mongrels roaming the streets. The

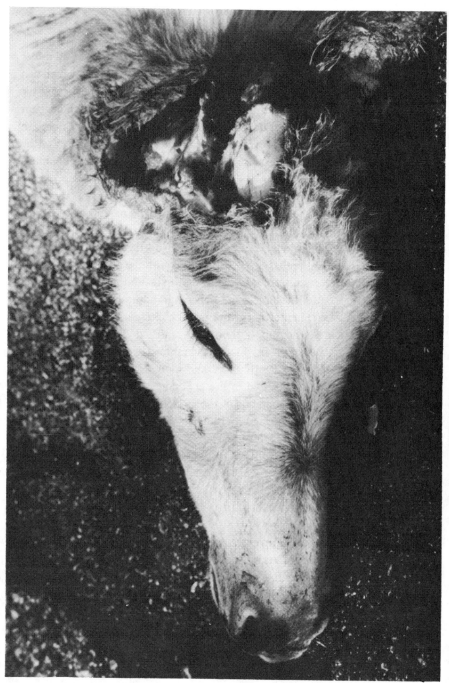

Mexican treats his working animals, the burros and horses and mules that are his livelihood, with a callous brutality, treatment which can be equated, I guess, with the way the modern Mexican treats his machines. The rule of thumb seems to be to work any machine, be it truck or mule, until it drops. That's just the way things are done. In the last few years, however, fences have been built along most of the main highways, and because of the new law the death rate for animals and automobile drivers has gone way down.

Jesse drove the station wagon back along the narrow dirt road to Highway 15, then turned south toward Mazatlan. Since the early sixties the area along Highway 15 from north of Ciudad Obregon south to Mazatlan has been cleared, and with the advent of extensive agricultural expansion, new dams, and irrigation facilities is rapidly becoming one of the largest and richest agricultural belts in the world. Many Mexican landowners work under contracts with North American combines who supply the money and tell the farmers what to plant. Purchase of the products is guaranteed by the North American backers, and consequently more and more of the winter fruits and vegetables now being sold in the U.S. come from northern Mexico.

The agricultural methods of the large farmers have been imitated somewhat by some gringo marijuana smugglers, many of the bigger operators contracting for their weed just as the North American agricultural interests contract for tomatoes. If marijuana is ever legalized, I picture vast ranchos of marijuana growing in Sonora and Sinaloa, all of it controlled by American tobacco companies.

When Jesse and I first started smuggling marijuana, Los Mochis and Culiacan were two of the stop-off places where supplies of weed were stored by Mexican entrepreneurs. Since Operation Intercept, the marijuana industry has moved further south, the states of Sonora and Sinaloa having become much too hot for safe dealing. Many of the big dealers in the area still act as brokers, however, traveling south to the east and west coast states to purchase ton lots of weed for delivery and sale in their own states. In most areas of Mexico the marijuana industry is controlled by a few large entrepreneurs, although the nature of the industry is such that many small farmers and dealers can make out if they have the right connections. In practice most big deals, involving ton lots of grass, are handled by a few large entrepreneurs. The small individual farmers often cannot supply the amount of marijuana a particular entrepreneur needs, so they will band together —either in a prior contractual agreement with the entrepreneur, or else in a cooperative among themselves—to make up the amount needed in a particular area. This partly explains why the quality varies so much even in the same shipment of marijuana, and why it is often so difficult to cop really large amounts of super grass.

Jesse drove all night down Highway 15, through Guasave and Guamuchil and Culiacan. Culiacan is the Salinas of Mexico; one of the richest communities in northern Mexico, it is similar to the California town in the sense that it is the center for much of the agricultural industry going on in Sonora and Sinaloa. For years Culiacan had also been the center of the Mexican marijuana industry, the central location where most of the weed bound for the California border was warehoused, bricked, etc.

Because Culiacan became known as one of the centers of the weed industry in Mexico, it also has become one of the centers of the anti-weed forces in the country. The town now crawls with American undercover narcotics agents who work with Mexican officials, and it is full of finks and fingerers. Culiacan is also one of the roughest places outside of the state of Guerrero as far as weed-related shootouts and killings are concerned. Marijuanos from Sinaloa don't hesitate to use their weapons to protect their sources and supplies. The district attorney for the state of Sinaloa is a cripple because of a shootout involving marijuanos. Before being appointed District Attorney, Señor Coppola was a federal narcotics agent. He was leaning too heavily on the local contrabandistas in Culiacan, however, so one night he was ambushed and machine-gunned. Fortunately, for him, and, unfortunately, for everyone else who thereafter fell behind dope in the state of Sinaloa, Señor Coppola wasn't killed. The machine gun attack crippled his arm and left him with an intense hatred of anyone caught with dope. Now Federal District Attorney in Mazatlan, Señor Coppola prosecutes all would-be weed smugglers and dealers arrested under his jurisdiction.

When Jesse and I first started smuggling, Culiacan was the center of our operations. Although successful smugglers no longer use the town for active dealings, or even for storage purposes, Culiacan is still the communication center for the Mexican weed industry. Most of the big dealers maintain links with the place, and many of them still live there. Nothing happens in the weed industry in all of Mexico that the dealers in Culiacan don't control, or at least know about.

Nowadays Jesse and I consider Culiacan a town to be passed through as quickly as possible, no stops, no sightseeing, no visits of any kind. At the Rio Culiacan bridge, Jesse paid the five-peso toll. Across the bridge we turned left and picked our way through the streets. Culiacan has a university, and the city throbs with new construction and industry. Diesel buses blasted fumes into our faces as we waited at traffic lights, and light Moto Guzzi motorcycles rattled by with their ear-splitting mufflers, two and sometimes three students astraddle each cycle.

When Jesse and I first started smuggling our connections were in Culiacan where many of our friends lived. Carlos, son of one of the wealthiest families in Culiacan, was a Mexican rebel when he was young. He was never involved in dope, but he did tear a mean swatch throughout much of Mexico and parts of California with his insane Mexican energy. Once, Carlos's parents left for a six months' vacation in Paris. His father, who ruled the family with an iron hand, left him in charge of the ranches. Carlos took it upon himself to plant sugar cane on one of the largest spreads, instead of the tomatoes his father had stipulated. Carlos's decision to plant sugar cane coincided with Castro's embargo on sugar shipments to the U.S. from Cuba. Carlos reaped a fortune for his father by selling the sugar to the United States, but when his father returned and found out that his orders had not been carried out to the letter, his sense of macho overcame his common sense and he stripped from Carlos all authority on the ranches. In anger Carlos got drunk one night and took off in one of his father's airplanes and buzzed downtown Culiacan. Swooping in

over the large cathedral in the center of town he succeeded in knocking off the neon-lit cross on top, plummeting it into the main square.
The next day Carlos absconded with 70,000 pesos from his father's
bank account—the money was owed him for the season's business—
and fled to California. He was twenty-three years old at the time. I
met him soon afterward while he was running a crew of braceros in
Salinas. After spending a year in California Carlos returned to Mexico
and tried to reach an accommodation with his father. When it proved
futile he settled in Mazatlan and started his own construction business.

Halfway through Culiacan Jesse cut off the main road and headed
for the south end of town, away from the noise and traffic. It felt good
to be out on the highway again.

Mexican towns begin and end so abruptly that the transition seems
like no transition at all; you're out in the middle of nowhere and bang!
suddenly you're in the middle of bustling streets with thousands of
cars and motorcycles and kids and people and burros trudging and
bumping and falling over one another, gasoline fumes, and squalls of
babies, honking horns and carnivals on every street corner. Whenever
I enter a town in Mexico I imagine what it must have been like
entering a medieval town in Europe. In Mexico there are no stone
gates guarding the entrance, only Pemex stations planted beside the
road, dusty, fumey, but welcome because you need to buy what they
have to offer. Culiacan, although already beginning to suffer from
progress's middle-aged spread, is the classic example of a city planted
in the middle of nowhere; after passing the last big Pemex gas station
on the town's south end, Highway 15 is absolutely barren on both
sides, no houses, no buildings, only the rolling expanse of brush-
covered desert, much of it in the process of being cleared for agricultural expansion. Thirty miles south of Culiacan we stopped at a small
roadside restaurant that perches on a flat bluff overlooking a river.
The early-morning sun was glinting off the water, softly, looking like
molten silver. As I watched, two *vaqueros* drove a small herd of *vacas*
down the steep embankment to drink. On the far side of the river half
a dozen women were at the morning's wash, beating white shirts and
trousers on the rocks, then hanging them over outspread branches to
dry.

About noon, twelve hours after leaving Manuel's house outside of Guaymas, Jesse turned the wagon down a side road a few miles north of Mazatlan and headed toward the beach. We were on a cutoff road that ran across a marsh and linked up with the motels and trailer courts lining the beach north of Mazatlan. We had originally started using the bypass road to avoid crossing the *aduana* checkpoint just outside Mazatlan, but in the last few years the authorities had moved the checkpoint forty miles north, near the Tropic of Cancer, so no one could slip by undetected. It was still relatively easy getting through the checkpoint, however, since the Mexican *aduana*'s main concern was inspecting cars with Mexican license plates. If you did happen to have something in your car like, say, a diesel engine you were smuggling into Mexico to install in a boat (which I did), a hundred pesos would see to it that you got through safely.

As we drove down the palm-lined road, swerving from side to side

to avoid the potholes, I could see the tops of the larger hotels in downtown Mazatlan.

Mazatlan's main beach is beautiful, stretching in a graceful arc in front of the shops, motels, and private homes that have sprung up on the northern edge of town in the last ten years. In 1957 this stretch of beach was relatively deserted; today the roads are being paved all the way out past hundreds of homes and projects being built to accommodate the increasing tourism. When I first visited Mazatlan there were only three trailer courts in the area, a few camping sites where travelers could park for the night. One of the trailer courts was where Jesse and I wrapped and stashed our first load of marijuana. Nobody stashes weed in cars in the trailer courts nowadays. Today they are full of campers and kids, the beaches are crowded, and the Federales drive by almost hourly on their longhair patrols.

Mazatlan's a crazy town, Mecca for a lot of American tourists

making it south along the road, preamble to the Mexico they've come to expect from all the books and travel posters they have read. Every time I enter the town I am reminded of my first entrance in 1957, off a bus from Guaymas after an all-night ride, the bus doors whooshing open to the blare of mariaches, music, and people. In 1957 the bus station was located beside the Hotel Belmar, which at that time was *the* big hotel in Mazatlan, and the esplanade which ran in front of the hotel was packed with Mexican and gringo swingers, gaudy and colorful and full of fiesta. I thought I had discovered paradise because the music and dancing continued all night and into the next day, and continued for four more nights and days, ending one night with me standing beside an old Mexican with hoary feet and beat huaraches in front of the Church of the Immaculate Conception with 5,000 other people watching the last of the pre-Lent carnival fireworks disappear in smoke and glitter and noise. "Sputneek!" the old man yelled, turning to me with his no-front-teeth smile as an exploding shower of flame rocketed off in the evening sky. I laughed and yelled back and savored the word that belonged to neither of our languages until that year and suddenly was common to both.

I stayed in Mazatlan for two weeks. As the peons cleaned up the carnival debris with their long stick brooms and pushcarts, I walked around the esplanade until it ended and I found myself on the south side of town, where the roads gave way to dirt and dust and the La Paz ferry. I got my first vision of Mexico and the United States as related entities on the back side of town, the side away from the glitter of tourists and hotels and fireworks. I was standing at the harbor, beside the detritus and gloom that accompanies every bayside drift; I looked up and saw one of those tarpaper and tin shacks that so many Mexicans live in, saw a little naked girl with a pot belly and sores standing among six or seven black *zopilotes* (vultures) who were pecking at the bloated body of a dead dog; beyond, mirrored in the bay, was a gleaming white-hulled American yacht. That image has remained with me to this day, and every time I enter Mazatlan I think of carnival and fireworks and that little girl, who must now be twenty.

Mazatlan has changed since 1957. The changes in the town reflect the changes throughout Mexico, and they are not only physical, but cultural and psychological as well. Many of the cultural changes

Photo overleaf by Roberto Ayala

occurred indirectly because of weed; marijuana has played an important role in formulating the social and moral attitudes that prevail
today, a bigger role than most people realize.

When the first beat travelers hit Mexico during the fifties, the
possibilities of easy access to marijuana, while not their primary goal,
were never far from their minds. During the fifties, marijuana was
used casually in rural Mexico by thousands of campesinos, and in the
cities by artists and Bohemians. It never presented a problem and was
seldom publicized, having been part of Mexican pharmacology for
centuries. When the beats arrived, weed was not popular among the
young university crowds, who would eventually make up the intellectual élite of the country. Marijuana has always had a stigma attached
to it in Mexico, and its use among the upper and educated classes was
frowned upon because it was considered an Indian thing, a palliative
of low-class country people and artists and Bohemians.

The beats had no trouble finding marijuana when they arrived.
Having rejected the success-oriented life of the U.S., and being psychologically and emotionally aligned with the campesinos, they gravi-
tated naturally toward those parts of rural Mexico where the use of
marijuana was relatively open and free. In *On the Road* Jack Kerouac
described the scene as it was in 1950:

. . . As we waited in the car Victor got out and loped over to the house and
said a few words to an old lady, who promptly turned and went to the garden
in back and began gathering dry fronds of marijuana that had been pulled off
the plants and left to dry in the desert sun. . . . Presently Victor's tall brother
came ambling along with some weed piled on a page of newspaper. He
dumped it on Victor's lap and leaned casually on the door of the car to nod
and smile at us and say, "Hallo." Dean nodded and smiled pleasantly at him.
Nobody talked; it was fine. Victor proceeded to roll the biggest bomber
anybody ever saw. He rolled (using brown bag paper) what amounted to a
tremendous Corona cigar of tea. It was huge. Dean stared at it, popeyed.
Victor casually lit it and passed it around. To drag on this thing was like
leaning over a chimney and inhaling. It blew into your throat in one great
blast of heat. We held our breaths and all let out just about simultaneously.
Instantly we were all high. The sweat froze on our foreheads and it was
suddenly like the beach at Acapulco. . . .

It was the beats who first adapted themselves in any numbers to the Indian life style, adopting sandals, simplicity, and silence. I remember quite clearly walking along the Avenida Reforma in Mexico City in the late fifties and seeing other shabbily dressed beatniks—sandals, peyote bags, Indian paraphernalia on our belts. Seldom did we speak to one another, rather our communication was unspoken and symbolic, each of us on our own special odyssey of discovery, reflective and open to the nuances and spirituality of the Mexican Indian, but at the same time wary. We knew we had found something, and we also knew that what we had found had to be discovered by each individual; it couldn't be transmitted by guidebook or conversation. Each of us who discovered the riches of rural Mexico, the humbleness, simplicity, human dignity, and warmth, realized that our discovery had to be protected, even from one another, for in our hearts we knew that what we had discovered was bound eventually to be lost, simply because of our discovery.

The beats' sojourns to Mexico during the fifties heralded what would happen later. When they returned to North Beach and Greenwich Village and Venice West with their five- and ten-pound dope stashes—for personal use mostly—they opened the first chinks in the youthful wine-oriented culture that was just beginning to burgeon in emulation of the beats themselves. Already the Bohemian ghettos were swarming with the first disciples, kids who had left their home towns to come to North Beach to stand on the street corners waiting for something to happen.

What happened was that the few beats who made a buck or two off their stashes returned to Mexico for more. In a semi-Bohemian world where any functioning outside the establishment was an accomplishment, marijuana became the source of income for a lot of people. There was hardly an artist or writer who lived in North Beach during the fifties and early sixties who didn't get involved in dope in one way or another, either as an outright dealer and user, or as simply a funnel for information for those who did deal and use. The change came fast: During my first trips to Mexico in the late fifties, I didn't even think of marijuana; when I went to Mexico in 1962, marijuana was my reason for going. And the place I headed for was Mazatlan.

Mazatlan is one of the most popular resort towns in Mexico. It is also one of the centers for marijuana procurement in the state of Sinaloa. Many gringos make their first connection in and around Mazatlan. Unlike Culiacan, which has no constant stream of transient tourists entering, hanging around for a week or two, then leaving, Mazatlan is still used by dealers and entrepreneurs and smugglers despite the prevalence of heat. Deals are always going on and weed is always available—if you know from whom to cop it.

The town's advantages are obvious. If there is any delay in making a connection (there inevitably is), the hanging around is in comfortable surroundings, on the beaches, in nice hotels. There are also thousands of tourists constantly moving in and out of town, so a potential smuggler can remain relatively inconspicuous among the crowds. Naturally, the popularity of Mazatlan among smugglers and dealers is not unknown to the Federales, so the town is also a dangerous place to do business. Hundreds of informers work the streets, operators paid by or forced to work for the police to ferret out unsuspecting gringos who've come down to score. For this reason Jesse and I had to be particularly careful when we entered Mazatlan.

Our problem was avoiding other dealers, smugglers, entrepreneurs, and informers who might know us, or know about us. People who engage in illegal activities for any length of time fall into patterns that are difficult to break. They tend to drive the same kind of cars, frequent the same places, eat the same kind of food, and frequently look the same from one trip to the next. Jesse and I recognized this habit in ourselves in as simple a thing as the restaurants in which we chose to eat. Every waitress in a string of restaurants from Nogales to Mexico City could recognize our photographs if the Federales happened to flash them. Both of us had also been involved in many deals, pickups, and purchases where a number of Mexicans had been present; people were constantly falling in Mexico, and we could never be sure that someone present at one of our deals had not fallen and decided, or been forced, to work for the other side. It was not likely to happen, but it is always the farfetched impossibilities that cause smugglers to fall, and neither Jesse nor I could afford to take any chances.

We wanted in particular to avoid the long-haired newcomers in
Mazatlan. Most of them were innocent kids down for a few weeks'
surfing, but their weed-copping brothers looked just like them, and the
methods they chose to score with brought tears to a professional's
eyes. Most of the busts in Mazatlan involve street-level riffs where
youngsters arrive in town and attempt to score immediately from a
cab driver or a stranger they meet on the beach. Until they are hipped
to the realities of the situation, most of the kids act as if the mere
mention of the word "marijuana" will open magic doors for them.

On many levels this used to be true. Before the great invasion of
longhairs, before 1965, Mazatlan and all of Mexico were extremely
tolerant of the young gringo visitors. The beats, who had come earlier
had few problems with Mexican authorities. Although they smoked
weed, their primary reason for visiting Mexico was not marijuana but
movement, getting away from the U.S. They were on the road, repu-
diating America, its progress, its stultifying sameness, its frenetic
striving after money and success. Also the beats were generally older
than the hippie invaders and took more time to inform themselves
about Mexico before traveling there. Most beats arrived, despite their
rejection of American life, with a respect for the culture and social
mores of Mexicans.

In 1959 I visited Isla Mujeres, off the coast of Quintana Roo. I was
with a girl named Anna, and not long after arriving we took a stroll
through the village. Anna wore shorts and as we walked down the
main street toward the plaza, every eye was on us. At this time the
island was undiscovered, we were the only gringos there; as we walked
along we could hear the mutterings and curses of the old crones
observing us from their doorways. It was an instant lesson in Mexican
decorum. Anna immediately returned to her room and changed into
a dress, and we resumed our walk. Nothing was ever mentioned of the
incident, and for the next two weeks we strolled and visited every part
of the island, and became close friends with many of the people who
lived there.

The fact that Anna was able to understand—and care—that we
were offending the islanders allowed us to correct our behavior immediately. Nowadays, when confronted with a similar situation in

which a local custom is affronted (as many are), most of the longhairs are at a complete loss as to what is wrong simply because they cannot understand the language. They enter Mexico with no other preparation than the rumors they have heard about fabulous dope and cheap beer and beautiful beaches and no hangups or cops or hassles. Because of these tales, the sensibility that glued itself to a corner in the Haight-Ashbury bumming for spare change figures it can do the same in Mexico. After all, the country has just as many corners, and less need for spare change because things are cheaper. Things don't quite work out that way, for not only is the general populace of Mexico living on a much lower economic level than most Americans, especially those with spare change, but the underlying Catholic moral hangups of Mexico won't allow behavior that the young gringos take for granted.

In 1966, when the drug revolution erupted, most of the kids coming to Mexico were coming not to escape any stultifying madness inherent in their own country, but to score weed—if not to smuggle, at least to enjoy while they were in Mexico.

As long as the kids were cool, copping and blasting a little weed didn't disturb the Mexican authorities. When the trickle of heads became a flood, however, and every kid on the street was either blasting, trying to score, or on his way home after scoring, the Mexican authorities were forced to crack down. They started making sweeps up and down the beaches, in the rented cottages and rooms where the longhairs stayed, and they even began to roust the caravans of psychedelic buses that were edged into the parking lots like multicolored elephants nosing water.

It wasn't the actual possession of marijuana that prompted the crackdowns. A kid could score his dope and take it home with him, or even smoke it quietly in his room or on a deserted beach and not receive too much of a hassle from the Federales. However, many of the young longhairs came to Mexico with the misguided notion that they were entering a completely unrestricted society, with absolutely no requirements as regards customs, manners, and good sense.

Many gringos who travel in Mexico—or any foreign country, for that matter—fail to learn the few elemental rules of the road, indeed, disregard all rules. Many Americans regard a trip abroad as license to forget all upbringing, all manners, all tact. When in Rome, do as the Romans do—should be guide enough for anyone, straight types with cameras slung over their shoulders, hippies and beats with their seemingly conscious effort to offend. Most Mexicans are extremely uptight about marijuana. The Mexicans who do use weed—and as a group they are becoming considerable—do so discreetly. The myth among Americans is that if you're in Mexico, you can blast away as freely on the beach or in the plaza as you can in the security of your own room. This attitude, plus the many bad trips, especially with acid and STP, trips that usually culminate in some wild, erratic behavior, has been responsible for much of the heat on the less affluent and nonconforming tourist in Mexico. Once I was visiting a church in Puerto Vallarta, and while the service was in progress a group of stoned longhairs started mocking the priest. During the taking of the sacrament one of the kids staggered over to the side of the church and urinated against the wall. Because of this type of behavior, not uncommon in Mexico nowadays, raids and longhair roundups have become commonplace in most resort areas of Mexico. Also, many innocent people are turned back at the border simply because their appearance matches that of others who had proved to be outrageous guests.

Part of the mystique of younger people, especially those in or on the fringes of the drug society in America, is their desire not to condemn or judge—especially themselves. This is a noble ideal—a person is free and just doing his thing when he takes off his clothes in the middle of the plaza or copulates on the beach—perhaps in proper context not a bad thing. In Catholic Mexico it is not a good thing. A man's freedom also includes the right to sit in the plaza with his wife and children and not be outraged.

While criticizing the young longhairs here I must also say that their actions were not entirely unexpected given the circumstances of their environment and their time in history. Most of them are products of middle-class homes and laissez-faire discipline, so lack of discipline and carelessness has to be their style. Also, the stories about hassle-free Mexico that the older beats brought back had served to create

myths that the longhairs could not know they were shattering, not, that is, until they found themselves in the *cárcel* awaiting deportation —or worse. The reports the beats carried back to the United States about the freedom and worry-free environment of Mexico were not false, for fifteen years ago the country was loose and relaxed and free. But the beats' discovery meant the end of it.

The loss of the myth means the appearance of something else though, and the very gringos who are so ignorant of Mexican attitudes and customs and traditions—both good and bad—are unconsciously changing those traditions because of their presence.

Today no part of the world is immune from the influence of American youth. Mexico is one of the countries most affected by gringos, and today on Isla Mujeres, where Anna could not appear in shorts, bikini-clad girls, both American and Mexican, frolic on the beaches, as they do all over Mexico. Hair styles, clothing styles, attitudes, manners, customs are all changing in Mexico, primarily because of the influx of American youths, and because of the universality of advertising. The streets of Mazatlan as much as any in Mexico reflect these changes. Ten years ago the traditional courtship rituals inherent in Catholic cultures, rituals that involved elaborate introductions, visits with parents, first dates with half a dozen chaperones, gifts to the family, and slow, careful nurturing of the partnership predominated; now the wealthy young señoritas meet their boyfriends along the *malecón* in their cars, spend time at private clubs and drive-in movies, and are relatively free, mobile, and independent.

One of the big catalysts in this change in manners and morals has been the arrival of young gringa girls from up north. The chicks, who come to Mexico by the thousands, either singly or with guys or other girls, are revolutionizing the Mexicans' sexual attitudes, manners, and morals. Their actions and behavior outrage the sensibilities of many of the old-line Mexicans—and many who are not so old-line. Nowhere is this more apparent than in the changing attitudes of the young, Mexican males.

Traditionally the upper-class Mexican male has been involved with only two types of women—the virgin and the whore. He sleeps with

the whore and then marries the virgin. In fact, the only requirement for a successful courtship in upper-class Mexican society seems to be that the chick be a virgin and the dude be able to provide her with a servant when they're married. The system is pretty well structured in Mexico, as it seems to be in most Catholic countries, and up until the massive gringa invasion of recent years, few Mexicans overtly complained. Of course, there were many private complaints and frustrations. I once went to a grand ball in Culiacan and watched the young Mexican studs from the area's finest families squire their brides-to-be around the floor, formal, polite, and intense. The young men and women were at the age when the glands were most susceptible to rubbing thighs and lanquid eyes. Toward the end of the evening, when you could have cut the sexual musk hanging in the air with a knife, Carlos, the friend who had invited me to the dance, grabbed my arm and pulled me out the door. We jumped in his car and split for the *zona roja*, the whorehouse district, just like every other dude in the place. I know how the young Mexican men got rid of their sexual tensions that night; what the young Mexican women did, I have no idea.

Young gringas are changing this. It's a truism to repeat that cultural opposites attract, but everyone knows that any gringa visiting Mexico has absolutely no problem attracting a panting horde of Mexican males. The young chickybabies down from the States for a two-week fling and the hundreds of divorcées with children who have found the country both economically and physically attractive can see this for themselves. The status of American divorcées in Mexico is particularly interesting. If statistics were available, I am sure they would show that at least one-fourth of the foreign residents who have chosen Mexico as a more or less permanent place to settle are divorcées with one or more children. They have discovered the merits of living in a country where their divorce-deflated egos can not only be rebuilt, but enshrined on altars so high that they have to become more than a little suspicious of their worshipers' motives.

The whole male-female relationship in Mexico becomes somewhat maddening to many gringas just because of this female worship trip

so many Mexican males indulge in. If a romance is established, and especially if it becomes anything remotely serious, an American woman often finds herself locked into terrible Mexican male-ego problems, trapped, as it were, on an altar whose foundation is as wobbly as the Mexican male's sense of manliness. The trip he lays on the American woman begins with lavish attention, flowers, songs, gifts, whispered entreaties, and supercool amorousness, and quite often ends up with the woman a virtual prisoner; any relationship or attentions, even innocent ones, outside the orbit of that one particular male are subject to immediate and sometimes deadly contests. More than one gringa I know who has had an affair with a Mexican has ended up with her Mexican dream shattered. When a girl I knew decided that she could no longer be part of a relationship that involved so much hysterical-jealousy-ego-*macho* game-playing on the part of her lover, she found herself hounded not only by her ex-lover but by her ex-lover's friends, who couldn't live with the thought of her being free to choose her own relationships. To the ex-lover it was a simple situation, be involved with him or not be involved at all. The girl found herself unable to walk down the streets with another man without putting the second man's life in jeopardy. When she continued to exclude her ex-lover from her life, however, he solved his massive ego problem in a typical Mexican way: He reported her to the authorities as an immoral and undesirable person and she was deported from the country.

This is perhaps an extreme example of how some Mexican men react in their relationships, but it is by no means a rare occurrence, as many gringas have painfully discovered. The fact that all gringas in Mexico are known as easy lays contributes to the conflict, because their sexual liberalism brings out many of the pent-up furies and frustrations of the Mexican male. It has always been traditional in Mexico that a girl who sleeps with a man before she is married is not worth marrying. Any Mexican girl who does sleep around is marked for life, because no man of any standing will have her, even though the man may have been the one who marked her. The longhair invasion is changing this attitude. Although the longhairs didn't in-

vent sex, and gringas have been balling Mexican men ever since they discovered Mexico, the invasion of the longhairs and their super-liberal sexual attitudes are leaving their mark on the Mexican, both male and female. The fact that well-educated, well-heeled young American girls from good families can be casual and free with their personal wares and still not suffer from ostracism or abandonment has been revelatory to the Mexicans.

Seeing it work for someone else and having it work for yourself are not the same, however, and Mexican men are wrenched by the balls when such sexual conflicts arise. The Catholic cultural hangup that turns chicks into either virgins or whores is not entirely one-sided either, for it is the Mexican men who blackball any chick found sleeping around. And even though the Mexican stud latches onto the gringa chick because he knows she sleeps around, his personal ego problem and cultural upbringing will not allow her that freedom once she is with him. The young gringas are twisting the Mexican's head around, though. The industrial revolution of sex does not imply that the chicks are whores or cheap pussy, but simply girls from another culture who don't mind bedding willing boys; that fact is gradually getting past the Mexican stud's psychic foreskin, and seeping into his consciousness. As a result of this sexual industry, a corollary of the longhair invasion which is one of the results of the continuing search for marijuana, many of Mexico's customs, even those as old and entrenched as sexual mores, are changing. There is weakening of tradition, an easing of restrictions and taboos among young Mexicans, especially the more urbanized and sophisticated, and also a concomitant repression by Mexican authorities of the gringos who have helped bring this about.

American boy meets Mexican girl is another story. Except in the very sophisticated society of Mexico City, where the mores and manners of Europe have more or less been emulated by the upper-class, educated Mexicans, a gringo dude will find it tough going with Mexican chicks. As a friend of mine expressed it after a few months in the country, "Mexico is a sexual desert!"

As far as upper-class Mexican girls are concerned, I must agree

with him. The Catholic rituals prescribed for courtship and romance involve incredible precourtship proceedings. I remember the first time in Mazatlan during the carnival; I was sitting on the retaining wall above the *malecón* watching the promenade, a nightly ritual in Mexico in which the young girls walk around the square in one direction, and the young men walk around in the other. During the carnival the promenade had been transferred to the *malecón,* and I was delightedly witnessing herd after herd of beautiful Mexican maidens parade by. During the course of passing me for the fifteenth time, one young girl whose eyes had locked on mine sat down. Her name was Lupita and I asked her out. The following evening, when I met her as agreed at the entrance of the Hotel Belmar, I found her accompanied by her four brothers, her mother and father, and three sisters. Lupita was twenty-five years old and was not allowed out of the house without a chaperone. During the course of the evening I asked her brother Francisco what Lupita did. "She stays home all day and embroiders," he said.

Lupita, like so many young girls in Mexico, was a prisoner of her culture, unable to escape for even the briefest of trysts. As with so many of her aunts, she would probably become an old maid, sitting alone all day knitting and embroidering, growing bitter, thin-lipped, and old, all because of the incredible social and sexual and religious hangups prevalent in Mexico. When the Lupitas of Mexico see the young gringas, who operate under a completely different cultural and sexual code, their attitudes change. No longer are they willing to sit in the background, moldering into old age as the world changes around them. The changes needed are many and they are far from complete, however. The drug and sexual and moral revolution that turns on so many Mexican males must complete its work on them first, then they, with their new attitudes, and with some help from their more ambitious friends, must complete the work on the Mexican girls. And even more important, on the parents of the Mexican girls who are locked into a tradition almost as old as weed itself.

The sexual attitudes and manners of the lower classes of Mexico differ from those of the upper classes. Lower-class girls are much

freer, primarily because they are poor and must work. When a chick
gets out of the house to work, she meets men. Also, lower-class girls
and boys quite often simply start living together without benefit of
civil or church ceremony. Naturally this causes many hardships for
Mexican women, for when the dude gets tired of the arrangement he
may split. The wife of Luis Echeverria, the President of Mexico, has
recently instigated a series of "public marriages," wedding ceremo-
nies for thousands of couples at a time, which make the unions lawful.

While one social level of Mexico is locked into a set of rigid moral
precepts and unwritten laws that prevent common mingling and
meeting, other levels operate in just the opposite manner. This isn't
a sociological tract and I don't want to go into the differing social
attitudes of various segments of the Mexican population, suffice it to
say that the very attitudes that lock one level of Mexican society into
a rigid code of rules and manners, lock the lower levels of society out.

Ignorance isn't the only reason why young gringo longhairs flaunt
the cultural and sexual traditions of Mexico, however. The whole
mystique behind the use of weed on the part of many young gringos
demands an openness that, in their heads anyway, the weed itself
expresses. The general tenor is to not conceal one's use of the weed,
but to smoke it openly, freely, to confront society directly with the
realities of marijuana. In other words, marijuana acts as a cultural
detoxicant, opening one up to expressions of naturalness and honesty
that are normally repressed. If you are going to smoke weed and then
conceal the use of it, that act goes against the nature of the weed itself.
Also, many of the young people who are into smoking grass feel that
the harsh marijuana laws have to be changed. Many are willing to
spend a year or two in the joint if the sacrifice will help to bring about
changes in those laws. There is also the mystique of martyrdom, youth
against an uptight establishment that condones and promotes the use
of its own turn-ons—alcohol, pills, tobacco—but condemns the use of
marijuana. Many kids feel that a fall on the border or even a bust on
the street is a sign of identity, a merit badge to be worn with honor.
Most of those who fall are young enough to absorb the two or three
years in prison they are made to suffer, and so the end result is the

creation of a growing army of rebels *with* a cause, to the mystification of the establishment.

For the older users of marijuana—the beats and Bohemians, the musicians and ghetto roustabouts who have been using weed for years —this is not the case. The older users have a healthy respect for the harsh marijuana laws simply because so many of them have already fallen and are unwilling to play crusader again. To the kid who shouts out to the judge who is sentencing him, "You'll understand what you have done when your own son is standing here before you!" the older heads can only nod in sympathy, knowing that for some time ahead in America, and Mexico too for that matter, most judges will sentence their own sons right along with the rest of the crowd.

When we arrived in Mazatlan, Jesse turned left along the esplanade and drove to the south side of town and then back, a ritual we went through each time we arrived in town. The ritual had its function; in that short circumnavigation of Mazatlan we could get a feel of what was going on, spot all the gringo cars, notice the climate and pace, sense the street activity and the general aura of the place. This first intuitive impression helped more in avoiding hassles than any concrete information friends could give us. Both Jesse and I had our trouble wands tuned to be on the alert for strange vibrations, and after completing the circuit around town, we stopped at a small out-of-the-way hotel and took a room. Both of us needed to shower and rest. We wanted to visit Luis, our connection, that afternoon.

Luis is a large weed dealer who operates a string of taxicabs as a front for his smuggling operations. Luis is known by all of the heavies in Mazatlan and he covers his scene with money in the right places and a brother who works in the police department. Luis also runs a wrecking yard to supplement his taxicab operation, employing a group of greasemonkeys and carpenters to work on his cars. The carpenters work on smugglers' rigs when they are brought in, building stash compartments in the cars so the weed can be packed properly for the trip to the border. Before smuggling became such a crowded profession, Jesse and I felt secure driving our car right into town and

parking next to Luis's wrecking yard. We no longer did that. On one such run in early '66 we drove up in front of his place and one of Luis's men ran out in the street and jumped in our car. *"¡Vamos!"* he said. "Let's get out of here."

I put the car in low gear and beat it out of town. Tomas, Luis's man, directed us thirty kilometers out into the campos to a small rancho Luis owned. Luis was at the door when we drove up. *"¿Qué pasa, hombre?"* Jesse asked once we were inside the house.

"Oh, man," Luis said. "Some sumbitch gringos were popped at the border last week an' they geeve my name to los Federales. Maybe you know the guys, a tall *cabrón* with a mustache, and a short fat *pocho.* They said they were from Los Angeles."

"What kind of car did they drive?" Jesse asked.

"A Ranchero, a blue one."

"Did you load them?" I asked.

"Are you crazy, man!" Luis looked at me. "I never load no wan I don' know. I don' even talk to heem, they worked through Ramos, a friend of mine."

"Why do you think they mentioned your name?" Jesse asked.

Luis shrugged a resigned Mexican shrug. I had to laugh when I saw it. Seeing Luis's shrug was like seeing all the pain and poverty and hard work of Mexico wrapped up in one resigned lift of the shoulder; in Luis's shrug was the Mexican-American war, Santa Ana's sell-out of the country, the 1910 Revolution, Zapata rising up out of the fields, and Pancho Villa being shot to death in the back of an old Dodge phaeton in the streets of Hidalgo del Parral in 1923 all at the same time; Luis's shrug embodied all the bad luck and bad land and bad politicians and bad dope deals in Mexico, and it was done with a helpless lift of the shoulder, like a victim raising up one more load, one that was all the heavier because it was part of his heritage. "Foking greengo pinche cabróns!" he said. "They come down here to buy mota an whan they geet pop they geeve my nombre to keep the heat off they own man. I gonna keel those sonnovebeeches whan I see heem!"

"What do you want us to do?" Jesse asked.

Photo by Roberto Ayala

"You better spleet for awhile, two weeks maybe. I'm out of business until this heat dies down. I'll keep you car here an' whan you come back it'll be loaded."

What had happened was that the drug revolution had caught up with us. Mazatlan had become inundated with gringos, mostly amateurish longhairs who didn't have their scene worked out properly, but who were scoring or attempting to score, many of them falling in the process. In falling they brought the heat down on the rest of us.

Since that close call Jesse and I had established a more sophisticated system for scoring. We still used Luis, but now when we arrived at the border we called a mutual connection who had a phone and informed him of our approximate time of arrival. The contact informed Luis, who would have another man meet us outside of town when we arrived; there we would exchange cars and the man would drive our car back into town and stash it in one of Luis's garages. Jesse and I would continue on in the other car to another town further south and spend a few days on the beach, then return, again at night, and pick up our car and head for the border. In this manner neither we nor our car was ever spotted in town. Casual informants and undercover narcotic agents were beginning to work the known weed distribution centers in Mexico in increasing numbers. For the informant, who is paid a fee for finking, any gringo car is suspect. All he has to do is phone the border and give the license number to the officials, and that car will be subject to a thorough search, even though it belongs to innocent tourists.

Jesse and I were particularly conscious of the problem in Mazatlan not only because of our experience with Luis but also because of the experience of another Mexican friend named Valdez.

Valdez was a retired politician from Mexico City who had moved to Mazatlan and opened a restaurant to keep busy. He was a generous dude, extremely tolerant of the first waves of longhairs who began arriving in Mazatlan during the middle sixties. The young kids dug his Mar Vista restaurant because of the relaxed atmosphere and because Valdez was always ready with a meal on credit and a place to throw a sleeping bag if a kid needed it. Jesse and I had known Valdez

for a number of years and were in the habit of stopping by his place whenever we were in town. If we stayed for a few days Jesse inevitably ended up acting as interpreter, for not only were the young gringos woefully lacking in even the most rudimentary Spanish, but Valdez and his crew knew absolutely no English.

By 1966 the Mar Vista was so popular that Valdez began thinking of building a newer and bigger restaurant on the tip of the peninsula —really just a large rock—that jutted out into the Pacific behind his original restaurant. He had some architectural renderings made which he showed religiously to all the young gringos, asking their opinions, always seeking new ideas and improvements for what was going to be his masterpiece, as he said. According to the rendering, Valdez planned to build a bastardized Holiday Inn, with plastic paraphernalia performing weird design functions, acres of glass and colored lights, a few plastic palm trees, and tons of Neapolitan glitter. It was comical watching the various architectural experts advise Valdez. Each gringo remembered some particularly ugly feature from a restaurant back in Southern California that had to be included in the final plan. Valdez's inherent trust in the advice of the young kids was comical to them. Even Jesse's and my advice was sought, Valdez weighing our opinions heavily as he sat at our table.

By 1966–67 the Mar Vista's popularity with the new breed of doper-surfer-longhair, combined with Jesse's dislike of being called on as interpreter by every gringo who wanted a Coke, finally drove us out of the restaurant. What really forced our decision to avoid the restaurant, however, was the attitude and actions on the part of the young kids who had made the place their headquarters.

Unlike the beats, who came in ones and twos, the longhairs arrived in herds. They parked their giant buses, inevitable psychedelic insignia painted on the sides, in the Mar Vista's parking lot like so many raggletaggle Conestoga wagons around a communal campfire, almost as if they were fearful of Mexicans. The longhairs seemed to have a need to travel in groups, a need that can be partly explained by what I refer to as the Kesey syndrome; that is, buy a bus and pack it with people and take off. Not only does this type of travel allay the fears

of going into the unknown (and for many kids Mexico is the unknown), it also provides a veil of anonymity. In large groups timid kids can act brave; actions they would never consider if they were alone become *de rigueur* in a group. By 1968, one year before the instigation of Operation Intercept, the Mar Vista, despite Valdez's attempts to keep the place clean, had become headquarters for every freak driving down the west coast of Mexico, drop zone for dealers and amateur smugglers, shooting gallery for junkies, street corner for spare-changers and stranded drifters waiting for money from home. The hippie or drug problem (the two terms are synonymous in Mexico) had reached such proportions that the Mexican authorities felt obliged to do something about it. Not only were Mexican officials pressured by the U.S. government to stop the illicit marijuana traffic, they were also fearful of the growing influence young gringos were having on Mexican youth. Mexican authorities began a series of long-hair roundups. Any gringo on the streets of Mazatlan—and any other resort town in Mexico, for that matter—who didn't look like a well-heeled tourist was subject to arrest and deportation. Since neither Jesse nor I fit the Establishment image of a gringo tourist, things were apt to be difficult for us. Our attire reflected our longtime life styles, and neither of us could see changing our appearance simply because a bunch of assholes had made it anathema to Mexican officials. My own attire, Levis, boots, and sombrero, had been part of me so long that changing it would have been like changing my skin—I just wouldn't be comfortable. To avoid the problems the new Mexican policy created, Jesse and I avoided the areas where longhairs hung out. We also took other precautions; Jesse was an amateur photographer and always carried his camera with him. I was a writer and I carried press credentials from a San Francisco magazine. In case of an emergency we could pass ourselves off as a journalistic team on assignment, actually not too far from the truth.

Documents are important in Mexico, as anyone who has spent much time in the country can attest. Many countries in Latin America —and elsewhere—give undue importance to uniforms, and to documents. Anything with official-looking seals and signatures, especially

if the bearer's photograph is affixed, opens doors otherwise immovable. Credentials that affirm an individual's occupation as a journalist are better than money, and many officials of extremely negative disposition become positively friendly when confronted with them. As a gringo in Mexico representing an American magazine I had a certain amount of juice, even though I did dress in Levis and a sombrero.

Jesse and I felt that Valdez's fondness for the young longhairs was bound to cause him trouble. During our travels in Mexico we had developed a sixth sense about certain people and places, and our security wands warned us that his open-house policy was super dangerous. We foresaw the Mar Vista's downfall, although neither of us expected the blow to be as severe as it turned out to be. When the repression of the young longhairs began, Valdez defended them, bailing them out of jail and using his expertise to expose some of the more blatant acts of repression by the Mexican police. This angered the powers that be in Mazatlan, and the Mar Vista became a special target for repression. Within a few short months Valdez was set up by the police, who planted some marijuana in his restaurant. He was arrested as a supplier to the young gringos who hung around his place. A week later the Mar Vista was closed.

The heat the young longhairs brought down on Mazatlan was nothing compared to the volcano that erupted in 1969, however, a volcano that sent reverberations throughout Mexico and changed the nature of the weed industry.

The drug culture, after gestating for a decade or more, was born between 1962 and 1964. As it expanded, the weed industry, until then relatively piddling, expanded with it. Obviously there was little need for sophisticated operations before there was a market for the fruits of that industry. To understand how the drug culture itself emerged, though, we must go back even further, to the mid-fifties.

Until then, marijuana was not a popular high in the United States. Weed had gone through a period of favor during the thirties, especially among jazz musicians, and it had always been one of the major turn-ons in most urban ghettos, Bohemian and otherwise, but until the early fifties it had never been used by white middle-class kids.

Immediately following World War II, however, and partly as a result of the bracero program, marijuana began appearing in the white high schools and colleges on the West Coast. The braceros, imported to work the large farms, were bringing their stashes with them when they crossed the border. This still did not make for a drug culture, however, and if you were dealing in marijuana during the early fifties you would have had a difficult time offing it. A friend of mine who is very big in the industry today describes how in the early fifties he had a garage full of weed that he couldn't give away. If he had been in North Beach or Greenwich Village he would have had little trouble unloading his weed, but all of his connections were Chicanos and Blacks, in San José and Oakland and East Los Angeles, and they were interested in heroin, not marijuana.

When the beat culture erupted during the middle fifties, marijuana became one of their mainstays. Why this happened I have no idea, except that beats were jazz-oriented and most of the jazz musicians at this time were into weed as well as heroin. It was during this period that some of the pioneering beats began making their first trips to Mexico. It was no big thing to score a load of weed cold off the streets in 1957–58; there was little heat involved because no real marijuana traffic pattern had been established, so anyone with a small amount of cash and a car could make it across the border and return with twenty or thirty kilos almost at will. He could carry his stash to any number of Bohemian communities that had sprung up on the West and East Coasts and dump it within a week or two for a good profit. Inevitably a few of his customers watched the deals go down and decided that they could make the same trip—so they did. These ripples in the weed trade became waves in 1967.

Scoring for weed on the street in 1967 was not like scoring for weed on the streets in the late fifties and early sixties, however. During the beats' initial odysseys the borders were relatively open. There were no dogs. The roads were bare of *aduana* checkpoints. The towns from which weed could be easily acquired were not universally known as weed centers. During this time the state of Sinaloa was the center of weed smuggling and the largest grass-producing state in Mexico.

Most of the grass produced in Sinaloa was processed in Mazatlan and Culiacan, the two largest towns in the state, and then shipped to the border towns, especially Juarez and Tijuana, where it was delivered into the hands of Mexican-Americans for smuggling into the U.S.

When the beats started coming to Mexico to score, they headed directly for Culiacan and Mazatlan, sometimes with the name of a connection, often not. If a dude had no connection it was a simple thing to hang around town for a few days until he could hit upon someone, or until he was hit upon. This casual manner of scoring worked fine as long as the weed industry was small, as it was when Jesse and I started. Prior to 1965 we could move with relative impunity throughout Mexico. We felt no hostility from the Mexicans, had few hassles, never had to deal with informers, saw no heat, and had relatively sweet sailing on up to the border once we had our shit together. After Mexico was invaded by longhairs in psychedelic buses, however, the same towns we had operated in quite freely became hotbeds for young gringos. We had to consider informers, inquisitive police, even local Mexican youths who would accost us on the streets shouting, "Marijuana, do you want to buy marijuana?" aloud in our ears. The Mexicans did this not because we were known smugglers, but simply because we looked somewhat like hippies and it was assumed that every hippie wanted weed.

In a sense this was true. The longhairs who had made a couple of successful buys at the Mar Vista and got their load safely home and disposed of were now back, moving into the smuggling game in earnest. Their presence in the country and the industry not only caused smugglers like me and Jesse grief, it also created problems for established Mexican dealers like Luis. So many young gringos were floating around the country with pockets full of money that a whole bagful of fly-by-night Mexican dope dealers immediately appeared to service the neophyte smugglers. Most of the Mexican dealers were as new to the game as the gringos themselves, and together they not only upset the traditional price equilibrium established in the industry, they also disrupted the methodology of scoring and smuggling itself. Jesse and I had to change the areas in which we operated, and we had to change

From the collection of Roberto Ayala

our heads as far as methods and prices were concerned.

None of this was as critical as what was happening at the border, however. As the young gringos began moving increasingly big loads, many of them getting popped while doing so, the customs people tightened up the border. Every nonconforming tourist was getting a stiff shakedown, more guards were hired, and electronic checks were beginning to be used. Repeat visitors to Mexico would have their license plates checked, a telecommunications system was set up along the border, and finally a program was started to train weed-sniffing dogs. In 1964 a bust of fifty kilos on the border was considered a big-time operation; by 1968 a bust of fifty kilos was the mark of an amateur, someone who didn't have his shit together enough to use an airplane or boat.

In 1972 electronic sensors were placed along hundreds of miles of border between the U.S. and Mexico. Now a border guard can sit in his office and wait for a bell to ring or a light to flash announcing an unauthorized border crossing. Despite the occasional false alarms sounded by stray cows and burros, the sensors are effective. In September, 1973, three Mexican-American marijuana smugglers were shot to death by U.S. border patrol agents when they were caught sneaking a load of weed across the border near Jacumba, seventy miles east of San Diego. The sensors had sounded their warning and the border patrol had staked out the trail leading from Mexico into the U.S. When the border cops attempted to arrest the smugglers they opened fire to protect their load.

By early 1969 the weed traffic crossing the border from Mexico to the U.S. had reached such proportions that the U.S. government decided to take dramatic steps to halt it. In September, 1969, Operation Intercept was put into effect. Customs and immigration officials were to stop and search *all* traffic, both vehicular and foot, crossing the border from Mexico to the U.S. The operation was a blatant attempt on the part of the U.S. government to blackmail the Mexican government into cracking down on the drug traffic inside Mexico. Mexico has always considered drug traffic a problem of the United States, reasoning that if the gringos didn't want weed, there'd be no traffic at all.

Operation Intercept continued for one month, until October, 1969, and was discontinued for a number of reasons. In the first place, the hue and cry set up by American tourists and the Mexican government caught the U.S. government off guard. U.S. officials had expected some outcry from inconvenienced tourists, but the extent of the Mexican reaction was much greater than expected. Powerful interests who control much of the business along the border pressured the Mexican government to lodge formal complaints with the U.S. government. Relations between the two countries plunged to the lowest level they had been in years. Business had fallen way off along the border. The U.S. government yielded to complaints and ordered Operation Intercept halted.

The amount of illegal drugs confiscated during Operation Intercept's one month of formal functioning was the lowest in months. The operation was so well publicized that only an idiot would have attempted to cross the border carrying a load. After the operation was formally abandoned (it still functions informally, concentrating now on the young, long-haired, and weird-looking), officials from the United States and Mexico met in Mexico City and came up with an alternative—Operation Cooperation.

Under Operation Cooperation, the U.S. government would allow business to go on as usual along the border and concentrate instead on helping the Mexican government halt the illegal drug traffic inside Mexico itself. The U.S. would supply guns, equipment, men, money, and know-how to the Mexican government to take the battle into the mountains, burning crops, spraying fields, setting up roadblocks, and hiring more undercover agents.

Operation Intercept illustrates the naïveté with which the U.S. government approaches the Mexican pot industry. While the operation was in effect, hardly any drugs were confiscated. The big-time smuggling operations were actually glad to see Operation Intercept put into effect. It disrupted many of the amateur operations and lessened the pressure within Mexico. As soon as the initial shock of the operation wore off the big-time smugglers began using boats and airplanes, smuggling methods that Operation Intercept could hardly affect.

In essence the U.S. government was nabbing small fry and letting the big boys go. Aside from disrupting the economy of Mexico, straining relations between the U.S. and Mexico, and hassling thousands of tourists, the intensive border checking did nothing but stop a few college kids and hippie longhairs with a few ounces of weed and some pills.

Operation Cooperation was greeted just as derisively by the pot industry, because it also was based on a fallacy—two fallacies, in fact: the first one being that the weed industry is a problem in Mexico.

Mexico has reasoned all along that marijuana is a gringo problem because it's the gringos who are after the weed. What the Mexican politicians fail to say, however, is that many of them are involved, either directly or indirectly, in the weed industry. Which brings up the second fallacy behind Operation Cooperation—that any money funneled into Mexico to fight the weed industry is actually going to find its way to the weedfields.

The U.S. government policy feeds large amounts of money and equipment into the hands of Mexican officials, acting on the assumption that there is a large, organized weed industry to suppress. If such an industry does exist, it exists with at least the tacit approval of many of the officials who are receiving the money, and who don't see weed as a Mexican problem. When one considers the methods the U.S. government chooses to deal with the drug problem in Mexico, one can only conclude that the American officials who jet back and forth between Washington and Mexico City for international drug conferences are completely ignorant of the realities of Mexico. No amount of money and equipment delivered into the hands of Mexican politicians to fight the "drug menace" is going to be effective as long as the people who receive the money and equipment are involved in that industry. True, the helicopters will scout the mountains and a few already-picked-over fields will be burnt, and a few squads of soldiers will be bivouacked in some obvious weed-growing areas, but most of the money and equipment sent into Mexico will end up in the pockets of generals and politicians, governors and businessmen whose sole operating policy has always been *take care of me first.*

The only really effective club the U.S. government holds over the Mexican government to curb the flow of illegal drugs is the threat of curtailing the tourist industry. The U.S. government can say to Mexico, stop the drug traffic in Mexico or we'll put sanctions on U.S. citizens visiting your country. Even that threat is hollow, though, for the tourist industry is controlled almost entirely by Americans. The planes that fly gringos down are American, the hotels in which they stay are American, and most of the stuff they buy is directly or indirectly controlled by Americans. Mexicans know their economy enriches already rich gringos, and helps Mexico very little. In the long run the tourist industry that so many Mexican officials gloat over actually hurts Mexico's economy; it takes young men and women who might become teachers and turns them into waiters—because waiters make much more money than teachers. It also deprives campesinos of their land, and any reason for working that land because the big gringo outfits, in consort with a few rich Mexicans, buy up all the land for their hotels. So to curb the tourist industry is a move that will end up hurting gringo businessmen more than it will Mexico. When Operation Intercept was initiated the gringos along the border screamed the loudest. The unholy yell put up by the Mexican government was on account of all the rich Mexicans who are partners with gringos in the big hotels and businesses that line the border and inundate the resort areas of Mexico.

The initial derisiveness expressed toward Operation Cooperation didn't last. There were enough dedicated politicians and government officials to cause serious disruptions in the weed trade. Not that Operation Cooperation has stopped the traffic. No government operation will do that, but it did create new problems.

Because of Operation Cooperation Mexican entrepreneurs have had to change their *modus operandi.* Smugglers used to go directly to warehouses to choose their weed; now loads were suddenly being stalled in the mountains, sometimes for weeks, while the transporters waited for soldiers to leave the area. Also, not only were soldiers guarding the trails leading out of the mountains, they were also being dispatched into the mountains themselves, searching out fields and

burning them. Increasing numbers of shootouts involving marijuanos and soldiers were occurring, shootouts that brought tremendous heat down all over the areas in which they occurred. When marijuanos shot down helicopters, as they sometimes did, large platoons of soldiers were immediately dispatched into the area and bivouacked there, sometimes for months at a time. Farmers refused to move their weed out of the mountains unless paid in advance, and once they did agree to move a load all responsibility for the journey was placed on the purchasers. Many loads that were moved prematurely fell, victim of either the soldiers, or a new hazard of the industry, *bandidos,* who roamed the mountains in search of marijuana caravans.

On the Mexican roads smugglers ran into additional problems; unexpected roadblocks manned by new people, and troops who had not been paid off. Even the *mordida* was no longer a sure thing along the road. Luis Echeverria, who was elected President of the republic in 1970, instigated a new policy of punishing bribe takers, a policy that, while far from completely effective, did instill a certain sense of patriotism in many of the younger officials. No longer could a smuggler drive down the road with the assurance that even if he were stopped a simple payoff would get him through.

Many of the changes wrought by the cooperation between the Mexican and American governments made the marijuana industry stronger, however. Whereas before it had been an industry composed of many separate operators, including innumerable fly-by-night newcomers, now the amateurs were sifted out. For the professional smugglers, it was a simple matter of survival—organize and help one another, as the Mexican and American governments were doing, or perish. And the organization was not limited to smugglers alone; it also involved dealers and entrepreneurs and eventually the farmers themselves.

The structure and organization of the weed industry has evolved as the industry itself has, and can be broken down into definite links that form a chain leading from the mountains of Mexico to the streets of every city in the U.S. Starting with the farmer who grows the stuff, weed goes through the hands of the entrepreneur, the Mexican con-

nection, or dealer, the gringo smuggler, the buyer, or dealer, the middleman, and finally the user. Often one or two links in the chain will perform more than one function, as some entrepreneurs will act as dealers and some dealers will also be smugglers.

When Jesse and I started out, we were not only smugglers but also dealers and middlemen. Like all amateurs, our first few runs were accomplished on the street, utilizing the equivalent of the Mexican middleman. We didn't have to score cold like a lot of amateurs, but we did buy our first few loads from Mexicans who were in the same position on their side of the border as we as smugglers were on ours. After a few trips though, Jesse and I wanted more weed than our street connection could handle, so we moved up the chain and came into contact with a dealer. Mexican dealers can provide more than just a few kilos and therefore most gringo smugglers never progress past the dealer link in the chain. However, since our dealer was also an entrepreneur, that is, a dealer who bought direct from the farmers in the mountains, we were able to progress up two and eventually three links in the chain simply by being in contact with him. As the weed industry matured and more people got involved, it became dangerous to perform more than one function. The links then separated, putting as much space as possible between them. By the late sixties almost every professional gringo smuggling operation was manned by people who performed a specific function within the organization, one man copping the weed, a second man smuggling it, a third man dealing it out to middlemen who in turn peddled it to the actual users. In Mexico the industry structured itself around the entrepreneur, the individual most responsible for the organization of the weed trade on the Mexican side of the border.

"Entrepreneur" describes the top-echelon weed dealer in Mexico. He can also be called *jefe, contrador, fuerto,* or any other term that implies top man. Entrepreneur means a little more than just top man, however, it implies a certain expertise and organization that goes beyond just being a big dealer. Many big dealers prefer only to be middlemen. Some middlemen are actually bigger dealers than many entrepreneurs, but the one thing their organization doesn't have is control in the mountains, a necessity in order to be an entrepreneur. Entrepreneur means a big dealer who has farmers growing for him in the mountains. Many entrepreneurs supply their growers with money and supplies during the off season to keep them going; they also contract for most of the grass grown in one particular area or by one group of farmers.

The entrepreneur acts as intermediary between the farmers who grow the weed and the gringos who buy it. No industry can succeed without this connnection. In the early days it was often difficult for farmers to link up with buyers. Every connection was haphazard, consequently the farmers planted only as much weed as they thought they could get rid of that season. When the weed revolution occurred and the demand shot sky high, often there just wasn't enough weed around to satisfy the demand. During these early days dealers perspicacious enough to recognize what was happening went into the mountains and to the growers, often hiring farmers who had never grown grass before to cultivate it on an organized basis. Many of these first marijuana entrepreneurs ended up controlling the finest grass-producing areas of Mexico. Between the birth of the weed revolution and the implementation of Operation Cooperation, a period when a lot of big bread was made in the industry, these powerful entrepreneurs consolidated many of their holdings, creating channels of delivery and a series of connections that funneled hundreds of tons of marijuana into the United States. When the heat came down, this network was disturbed, and many entrepreneurs and smugglers were forced out by a series of busts and accidents. The remaining ones linked up in a cooperative effort that forms the basis for the industry today.

Since Operation Cooperation, marijuanos have found that they could no longer afford to operate independently, so they began to assist one another with information, equipment, men, dope even, especially if one dealer who was short needed some to make up a load. One practical way this cooperation began manifesting itself was in the changing attitudes on the part of entrepreneurs toward the gringo smugglers. Before Operation Cooperation, an entrepreneur would make his delivery, grab his money, and split, leaving the gringo to face the road alone. Because Operation Cooperation resulted in so many smugglers falling even before they reached the border, however, and the entrepreneurs began losing customers, they started taking a more active interest in the smuggling operation as a whole. No longer was a gringo abandoned on the highway with his load; the man who sold him his weed assisted him to the border, and in some cases even got his load across for him. Many entrepreneurs entered into partnerships with gringo smugglers, providing them with credit for large amounts of weed; in this way they are paid closer to retail prices for their kilos instead of the wholesale prices they charge when buyers pay cash.

The hierarchy of entrepreneurs which operates on a more or less regular basis in Mexico is fluid, with different echelons of dealers dealing with one another at some time or other. The whole industry, while élitist and controlled in the higher echelons, among the government officials, diplomats, and wealthy businessmen who deal in dope to make their real money, is still open and responsive to novice experimenters and even part-time dealers in its middle and lower echelons. Through necessity the industry has a self-governing network of information and communcation, developed so that entrepreneurs on all levels can keep abreast of who's buying what, how much, and where it is going. Because of the nature of the organization, and the fact that new blood is constantly entering and dropping out, the industry is almost impossible to control in any Mafia sense. It is made up of individuals and small organizations that operate together and separately, depending on the circumstances, which explains why the industry can absorb so many busts and still keep on functioning.

The high-level figures who take over a complete segment of dope traffic, controlling distribution and supply and prices, operate primarily in the heroin/cocaine field. They avoid marijuana because of its bulk, which makes it difficult to smuggle in any great quantity, and because of its profit level, which is relatively small compared to hard drugs. When a smuggler can turn ten kilos of heroin into the same street profit that 500 kilos of marijuana will bring, why bother with marijuana? Heroin and cocaine are more easily controlled be-

EUGENE ANTHONY

From the collection of Roberto Ayala

cause there is less of it around and supply is restricted. Marijuana grows everywhere, and anyone with a little cash and a connection can buy and peddle his share.

As for those involved in marijuana entrepreneurship in Mexico, they fall into every category, from powerful businessmen to politicians to campesinos who have made it big. For many years one of the biggest weed dealers in Mexico was governor of a state. As far as I know he is still active in the industry, along with his extensive family and connections. Most of those involved in the weed industry are not politicians, though. Many entrepreneurs are successful businessmen who started out in dope and have financed a legitimate business behind whose façade they operate. The financial character of free enterprise in Mexico is somewhat bizarre, by American standards. The country operates almost solely on foreign investments and investments on the part of the government. Mexicans who have money—and when a Mexican is rich, he is usually very rich—are reluctant to invest in their own country. Most of them invest it in foreign banks, although this habit has changed somewhat in the last decade. Middle- and lower-class Mexicans who have nothing to invest must be consummate hustlers to survive in a society that pays its minor officials a weekly wage about equivalent to that paid an American laborer for a day. In Guadalajara a traffic cop, paid only about twenty pesos per day, is expected to supplement his salary by stopping traffic violators and biting them on the spot. Certain corners in each city are awarded to various cops by their value, such and such a corner worth 500 pesos a day, etc. The cop is expected to bite enough traffic violators to produce the estimated sum, and part of it goes to the captain. Without this everyday practice the traffic cop would not be able to live. The consequences of this practice are that on every street corner you have deals, in marijuana, appliances, typewriters, cars, or whatever. I went to a dentist once who asked me after ten minutes in his chair if I was interested in buying some marijuana. When I said no, he told me he also dealt in appliances, guns, amphetamine, and hot cars. The hustler who is able to acquire a car and turn it into a taxicab is well on his way to becoming a minor entrepreneur with his own business. Lesser

officials with access to forms, licenses, stamps, and documents can extend their favors, the basics of success in Mexico. With these tools they can establish stakes and influence with which they can branch off into other enterprises. It is common knowledge that the lucrative posts along the border are changed regularly so that every official has his chance to make some money, and also to keep any one official from growing too rich and powerful. Inevitably in his rise to stature and position, the Mexican bureaucrat, be he policeman, agent, border guard, or whatever, gets involved in dope. This is because dope is so much a part of Mexico, there is so much money in it, and the biggest customer lies right across the border.

I was exhausted as I lay down on the bed. Outside my window I could hear the sounds of the city. Beyond the traffic noises the sea beat up against the *malecón*. Jesse and I were going to wait until after dark before venturing out. We knew that we would look suspicious to a lot of idle Mexicans the minute we set foot on the street. Neither of us dug the realities of the street situation in Mazatlan, but since we were in the weed trade we had to face them. As I listened to the sea, I thought of all the changes I had gone through since my first trip to Mexico, changes that manifested themselves in the way I approached the country, the streets, and the people. Mexico was no longer the carefree land it had once been for me; now every move I made was thought out in advance, and people on the streets were no longer just people, but potential finks and informers, police and dealers and coconspirators. Before getting involved in weed I roamed all over Mexico at will, completely oblivious to the possible ramifications of my presence. Nowadays Jesse and I avoided many areas of Mexico, and visited others only at night. We never entered strange towns before finding out something about them; if they were even remotely known for handling, storing, growing, or moving weed, we avoided them unless specific business took us there. We did not establish this habit out of any arbitrariness but on the recommendation of Mexican entrepreneurs who knew the danger to strange gringos who snooped around their territories.

Many gringo smugglers ignore this basic rule, which suggests that Jesse and I display an unrealistic paranoia, considering the setting in rural Mexico. One of the weaknesses of many gringos in Mexico, however, is an assumption that most Mexicans are rather dumb, and don't fully realize what's going on. This has often proved a fatal misconception.

There is no one more closed, taciturn, lonely, and sorrowful than the Mexican—and he is also friendly, charming, quick, and deadly. The Mexican never exposes himself; he keeps locked within all secrets of the self. He won't be ridiculed. It is unmanly to need, therefore stoicism is manly. The Mexican uses language as a weapon; words can wound him—the wrong words can kill. Attitudes and mores are important to the Mexican; they are foundations upon which he has established himself. When changes occur he is unsure of himself and therefore dangerous. The Mexican personality is complex, alert, and suspicious, and while a gringo may think he is moving about the country completely unnoticed, in actual fact a hundred eyes are on him, casually watching, noting his mannerisims, eyeing the stranger simply because he's a stranger. This is not to imply that Mexico is a country of spies, far from it. It is simply to say that out of a natural inquisitiveness and curiosity, little gets by unseen in rural Mexico.

For this reason, Jesse and I adopted another rule while on a smuggling expedition in Mexico. We never carried a stash or smoked any weed while we were getting a scene together. Many smugglers stay stoned whenever they're not out actually scoring, and many are stoned even while scoring. This is stupid, not because I think a person can't operate while stoned on weed, but because most of the fuckups that occur in any weed-smuggling operation are usually attributable to small things like ounces left on dressers where maids can see them, or the smell of marijuana smoke reported to the heat. Many runs have been aborted because the big-time dudes running them couldn't wait until they got their shit together before lighting up.

Whenever Jesse and I scored it was important for both of us to have clear, unstoned heads so that we could properly sample the marijuana being offered. Our method was to take one good toke off *one* joint; if

that didn't get us off fairly well the grass wasn't worth buying. Many times I've seen buyers come into warehouses so stoned they couldn't tell righteous shit from cow manure. The Mexican entrepreneur spreads his samples out and the gringo heavyweights light up and nod conspiratorially at one another and agree that they're really smoking loady stuff. When they get their shit back to the States nobody but squares in the avenues will buy it because it's Culiacan garbage, so bad that some dudes have even smuggled it back *into* Mexico so they wouldn't have to look at it.

One of the reasons Jesse and I were so anxious to get into the mountains was so we could find and record the cultivation of really righteous shit. We weren't interested in Culiacan garbage or any run-of-the-mill weed. We wanted to find the *primo* that grew on the slopes of the west-coast range in the state of Guerrero. We knew it was up there. As far as I knew, no other gringo had ever visited the mountains where the rancheros were located, especially on a mission such as ours. A few years previously, Luis had invited me to go into the Sierras with him, but that had been a spur-of-the-moment invitation and involved nothing more than accompanying him and his men on a negotiating run. I had declined because I was due back in the States in a few days, and I had regretted my decision ever since. When Jesse got out of the shower I expressed my enthusiasm at the prospect before us. "I can't wait to get up into the Sierras," I said.

"Well, we'll see what happens when I talk to Luis. I'm going to call him this evening."

"He seemed pretty confident in his letter. Do you think we'll have any problems?"

"I don't know. I didn't tell him about taking pictures. That might cause us some problems."

"How are you going to broach the subject?"

"I don't know. We'll just have to take things as they come. The important thing is to get up into the mountains, then worry about the cameras."

I lay on my bed thinking of the mountains. Unlike the United States, which has few areas left that aren't accessible by automobile,

Mexico is dominated by Sierras that in many places are completely inaccessible except by mule or helicopter. The people who live in the mountains seldom leave them. They are mountain people, alone, aloof, remote, cut off from the rest of Mexico by time and distance and the canyons and valleys where they were born. It is in such inaccessible valleys and canyons that marijuana is grown. The people who grow it are suspicious, silent, unused to visitors. They are also wary of any authority, especially as it manifests itself in Mexico in the dull-green uniform of the Federales.

Looking back, I realize that I imagined (rather naïvely, as it turned out) that our trip into the Sierras would be a gentleman's camping trip, a short jaunt on horse and muleback up into the mountains so Jesse and I could survey the scene and prepare it for Gene to come down later and take pictures. What eventually happened was far from my preconceived scenario. I was filled with boundless gringo enthusiasm, however, and the realities of Mexico do not announce themselves on public bulletin boards. What I was to learn is that Mexico speaks through her silences, and the silence of the mountains is a language one can understand only by going there.

That evening Jesse and I left our hotel room. While Jesse called Luis, I walked along the *malecón*. From one end to the other it was crowded with promenaders, girls and guys, arm in arm. There were a number of gringos strolling along the sea's edge. Mazatlan looked like a suburb of Newport Beach. After completing a circuit of the *malecón* I entered a restaurant to meet Jesse. "How'd it go?" I said.

Jesse shrugged. "We've got problems. Luis can't take us into the Sierras."

I was dumbfounded. "What happened?"

"Do you remember Nacho?"

I nodded. Nacho was one of Luis's men. I had met him three years before. He was a likable dude, immense, happy-go-lucky. He controlled Luis's operations in the mountains.

"He was ambushed last week in Rosa Leon. Federales are bivouacked in the area. No one can go near the place until the heat dies down."

"Jesus," I said. "How'd it happen?"

"No one knows. All they know is that Nacho and two other campesinos and four soldiers are dead. The heat's all over the place."

"Is Luis involved?"

"Only peripherally. It was his stuff being moved but he's not giving out any details. All he'll say is that we can't go near the place."

"What are we going to do?"

"Luis is going to introduce me to a dude who has some ranchos in Jalisco. We'll see him tomorrow."

Jesse seemed undisturbed. I was concerned how this bad news was going to affect our trip. Whenever a shooting occurred that involved soldiers, troops were immediately moved into the area to investigate and to quell any further disturbances. Often a number of areas within a state will be shut down, areas that are not necessarily the scene of the shooting but are shut down anyway just so the heat can die down. Luis's operation would probably come to a complete standstill for three or four months—or until Luis thought it okay to resume. The problem with a shooting is that the disturbance doesn't stop in the mountains. Troops would visit Nacho's home and the homes of his friends. Some of Nacho's friends would be as upset by his death as the soldiers were by the death of their friends. It wasn't uncommon for a disturbance to snowball, leaving many campesinos and soldiers dead before it ended. To prevent just such a thing, Luis would move all his men out of the state, or send them underground. When the soldiers showed up at the homes of the marijuanos, all they would find would be the women—and Mexican women are as silent as the mountains themselves.

Jesse wasn't particularly worried about our stroke of bad luck, nor was I for that matter. We both understood the nature of the weed business. The hangups and incidents and aborted beginnings are as much a part of the industry as the weed itself.

Consider: When Jesse and I entered Mexico, it was as reasonably knowledgeable operators. We knew all the names, could go in a minute to an entrepreneur and negotiate for a ton of grass to be delivered in Tucson, Arizona, for $30 a kilo, one ton minimum, $30,000 cash on the car hood. Or we could pick up our load in a

cornfield on the outskirts of Chilpancingo for $20,000 and worry about the border later. Jesse and I had negotiated many cornfield rendezvous and weigh-ins surrounded by M-16–carrying campesinos, our own .38-Supers lugging heavily in our belts, everyone smiling but cautious, sharing tequila from the bottle—as necessary to any negotiation as the money itself; then paying off, slowly counting the bills, the mad, dark eyes of the Indios reflecting a mountain sadness only Toltecs understand.

Jesse and I did not want a ton of marijuana delivered in Tucson or in a cornfield outside of Chilpancingo, however. We wanted to go into the mountains and see the grass in the fields, touch each leaf with our own hands, and then have Gene come up and take pictures for *Life*. Try to explain that to the Indios. Try even to explain it to a sophisticated entrepreneur like Luis, whose daily bread comes from plane flights to the fields carrying seeds and fertilizer to the farmers and back with sixty-kilo sacks of marijuana. Especially try to explain the camera, whose cyclopean eye looms more ominous to marijuanos than the muzzle of a Mauser.

Luis, our long-time associate, could not understand our mission. "You want mota?" he asked. "How much, *mano*? I'll deliver it for you. . . ."

"We want to go into the mountains, Luis, we want to see it growing, take pictures. . . ."

"*Ay, mano . . . los Indios . . . son locos!*"

We were crazy too, because for the next six weeks Jesse and I roamed all over Mexico searching for the connection who could and would take us into the mountains. Despite our close association with Luis, and others like him in the business, we found that a cactus curtain had been drawn across the mountains that was to prove almost impenetrable.

A Mexican will never refuse a stranger advice and directions. Stop a Mexican on the road and ask for instructions to find a particular place and you will be given them fulsomely—even though your informant has never heard of the place. To the Mexican it is discourteous not to know, so he tells even when he doesn't know. It is an infuriating experience to be guided down a dozen different false roads.

Such was the case with Luis. After he had expended all his possibilities, introduced us to all of his friends who might possibly help, all to no avail, still he led us on. He was determined until the last to lead us into the mountains. Jesse and I were helpless victims of Luis's courtesy. After seeking his aid it would have been discourteous to insult him by implying that he wasn't helping us. So for three weeks we blasted around a crazy Mexican wagon wheel, Mazatlan being the hub and the roads to a hundred small villages throughout Mexico the spokes that we thundered to and fro on.

No experience on this earth is quite like a Mexican auto ride. Like most entrepreneurs, Luis's life-long ambition had been to own *un Galaxie,* as they say in Mexico, that is, a Ford Galaxie especially equipped with heavy-duty springs and General Popo tires that are fit to do battle with the roads. Luis owned his Galaxie, and when he came by our motel to drive us out into the campos, both Jesse and I gaped in amazement. We were going fifty kilometers into the country where roads are a thing of the imagination, and his Galaxie was packed full of campesinos, crazy Mexicans waving tequila bottles and wearing sombreros as big as bullrings.

Luis threw open the door of his car and beckoned us in. "Get in, hombres! *¡Ándale!*" he cried. "There's no room, Luis, it's packed," I said. "*¡Ay, mano, mira!* Plenty of room!" He pushed a campesino and made room on the seat for a midget. Jesse and I shrugged. "Chuy! Ponce! Get out!" Luis shouted to two of his men. They fell out of the automobile. "Now, compañeros, there's plenty of room, get in!" Jesse and I got in. "*¡Ándale, cabrónes!*" Luis shouted to Chuy and Ponce. The two piled in on top of us and off we shot.

Three weeks after commencing our search with Luis, we still hadn't found the connection who could take us into the Sierras. We sat down in a café one morning to discuss the matter. "There is one further possibility," Luis said. "I know of one man, unfortunately he doesn't live here, who might be willing to take you into the mountains."

"Where does he live, Luis?" Jesse asked. Luis was silent. He sat for some time and ordered another beer before answering. "This man is an old friend of mine and he owes me a favor. If you like I will write him a letter."

"Where does he live?" Jesse asked again.

Luis waved his hand. "South. In the mountains. Guerrero."

Jesse and I looked at one another. Guerrero was where we both wanted to go, but dared not hope to get there. The state was the wildest in Mexico, dangerous, rife with bandits and Federales and marijuanos. "Write your friend a letter," I said. "If we have to go to Guerrero, we'll go."

Although we were tremendously excited about the possibility of going to Guerrero, Jesse and I still had to consider alternative places in case Luis's letter led us to another blank wall. At one point we considered returning north, to Tijuana, and looking up Roberto and Juan Hernandez, whom Jesse had known from his prison days.

Los Hermanos, or The Brothers, are big-time dope dealers in Mexico, especially along the border. Getting involved with them, however, had its drawbacks. The advantages were obvious: immediate access to almost any connection in the industry. Both Jesse and I knew, however, that that kind of carte blanche treatment tended to have its drawbacks. If we utilized Los Hermanos to get into the mountains, we knew we'd be marked in a peculiar way, cast as part of an organization that, despite its power, perhaps even because of it, would taint our mission, color it in such a way that we would find confining and eventually regret. I felt that if we utilized The Brothers, not only would the organization expect more from us than we were prepared to offer but also we would come on with credentials that in the long run we couldn't back up. I did not want to get involved with The Brothers. I felt that even if we had to blunder through Mexico for another three months looking for our own connection, it was better than being taken under the wing of a heavy syndicate dope operation whose influences and power might eventually cause us more grief than benefits. Plus both Jesse and I knew that The Man was as familiar with The Brothers' operations as we were, and the possibility of there being an undercover narc in the organization was more real than we wanted. Once before when Jesse and I had had difficulties on a run we had

linked up with an organization that came with heavy credentials and seemed to have all their shit together—big-time boats and lots of money and electronic communications equipment, plus a crew of dedicated and experienced dope smugglers—and when the whole number came down we found out that we had loaded a ton of weed on a boat crewed by an undercover narcotics agent. Fortunately for both me and Jesse, we were far enough removed from the actual action on the beach that we couldn't be incriminated, although we did lose a ton of weed and $35,000.

Despite the risks, however, we had to discuss the possibility of utilizing The Brothers, simply because we couldn't afford to ignore any possibility. "We could make it back to Tijuana in two days and probably save ourselves a lot of time in the long run," Jesse said.

"Man, I don't like Tijuana. I get the creeps every time I pass through that place."

Jesse shrugged. "We're not getting damn far with Luis. Maybe his letter will work, maybe it won't. We may have to go back."

"Who's to say we'll be able to find The Brothers? Shit, they may be in Mexico City for all we know. I don't think we should go back."

Jesse and I were agreed on one thing. Neither of us dug Tijuana. There's an aura of evil over TJ, a malignancy that seems to cover the place like poison gas. Crossing the border from the U.S. into Tijuana is like stepping into a foul-smelling sewer which both countries are contaminating, and every time I stand on the streets I feel like a maggot scurrying along with a hundred thousand other maggots, each of us after our own little piece of shit. And it's not that the town is bad, it's just that a certain lurking evil seems to prevail there because of its juxtaposition with the United States. Every time I approach Tijuana a chill goes through me; the place is hustle city, and everyone there is on one scam or another, they have to be in order to survive.

Making it across the border to work in the U.S. is the goal for many Mexicans, and a lot of U.S. Immigration officers are willing to help them—for a price. Mexican women are considered trash by most of the thin-lipped, hard-edged cowboy types who seem to predominate in the Immigration Service, and a little present to the boys on the border is often the price for a green card that enables a woman to work in the U.S. I've been told hundreds of tales of Mexican women being raped, manhandled, or molested in the course of crossing the border to work. Often the Mexican women who have legitimate green cards are obliged to suffer humiliating skin searches every time they cross. In fact, one of the reasons why so many gringo tourists are now suffering indignities and hardships at the hands of Mexican officials within Mexico is because of the treatment accorded so many Mexicans at the U.S. border.*

However, the hustles and scams along the border don't bother me as much as the genuine desperation of so many of the people in Tijuana and other border towns, campesinos and country people by the thousands who have hitchhiked and bummed their way up through Mexico from Central and South America, peons from Peru and Indians from Chiapas who've come to the border to grasp the chain-link fence that separates them from the United States, and to stare across the lush farmlands of *el otro lado,* the other side. The fact that the great majority of them make it no further than Tijuana, and then are left broke and homeless in a strange town, contributes to the sense of desperation prevalent in the place. It's not without reason that so many deals are constantly going down in TJ. Every scam on the board has a hustler playing it, including all the dope scams. In fact, the dope scams along the border are among the worst of the lot, and if I have one rule to impart to potential dopesters it's this: avoid Tijuana.

Because of our shared feeling about the border, Jesse and I preferred to deal in central and southern Mexico. Also, neither of us wanted to turn north from Mazatlan. Once on the road it's difficult reversing your forward rhythm.

That afternoon we went back to see Luis, and he wrote a letter of

---

*Recently the U.S. government has instigated an investigation of the Immigration Service and a number of officials have been arrested, not only for some of the offenses alleged above, but also for collusion in marijuana smuggling. The investigation touches only the tip of the iceberg, however, since it is patently obvious to anyone who has spent any time at all on the border that corruption and dishonesty are rampant, among even the highest officials.

introduction for us—and promised to write a letter to his friend in Guerrero that same day. Jesse and I had made up our minds. Even if the letters didn't work, we would go to Guerrero anyway. Neither of us knew what would happen, but the magic of the road and of Mexico lay before us.

The next day we checked out of our room and said goodbye to Luis and his family. As we drove out of Mazatlan, I peered across the mudflats to the shipping channel where three large freighters were tied up. It was on this same mudflat ten years before that I had had my Mexican vision, the one of the small girl and the tarpaper shack, the vultures and the bloated dog, and outside in the channel itself, the gleaming white yacht. There were fewer shacks on the mudflats now, uprooted perhaps, so the channel could be widened to make room for the big, oceangoing ships. A radio-station antenna rose out of the dike where before only gloom and detritus lay, and along the road leading out of town were bustling hovels and tin-roofed huts where Pepsi and beer, tortas and enchiladas were sold.

A few kilometers outside of town the road, which had been running east, turned right and headed south, straight into the heart of Mexico. As our car picked up momentum I looked up and saw a giant jet airliner gliding over the fields to the right of the road, drifting in for a landing at Mazatlan's new international airport. The old airport was right downtown alongside the *malecón,* and it had been abandoned because it was too small, and the new jets made too much noise and the big new hotels complained. The giant jets floated in over fields where beasts of burden trudged along with wooden plows piled high with stones to make them bite into the earth, and men walked along behind prodding the animals with sticks. I tried to imagine what the campesinos thought when they stood still to watch the large planes drift over them and roar to a stop beside their fields. To many of them flying must have been as strange and unknowable as it was to that tribe of aborigines in the mountains of New Guinea whose totems were monumental re-creations of the silver birds they saw winging through the air above them.

As we drove south down Highway 15 the heavy diesel rigs and automobiles thinned out and the late afternoon light began to soften. Huge cumulus clouds looking like the soft white underbellies of cows piled up on the horizon. Further away, toward the sea, the sky darkened and turned a deep majestic purple. In the far distance occasional lightning flashes lit up the sky. We passed cars and men on bicycles pedaling along the road, some of them holding flashlights against the dark. We were in the tropics, and even with the lightning flashing and the darkening sky it was still warm. Outside the car the air was heavy, though it began to cool as it got darker. When I could no longer see any details alongside the road my mind traveled back to all the times I had driven down this road, first in 1957 and every year since that time, sometimes four or five times a year. A lot of changes had occurred in Mexico, dramatic and overwhelming ones that I had not noticed, or had noticed and not paid attention to. Perhaps if my visits had been fewer I would have noticed the changes more, like one notices the differences in a friend after not seeing him for many years. As it was, I suddenly was struck by how different Mexico was now, beyond even the changes one would ordinarily expect. Where were the white-suited campesinos? old men with backs bent over carrying firewood, or leading burros loaded down? I knew they still existed somewhere off the road, in the small hovels and villages, back in the foothills, in the wide-open spaces. Along the highway America marched rapidly south with its jet planes and automobiles, its sharp-pointed shoes and plastic sports clothes, and somewhere out there the old men still carried their wood, bent over and alone, standing still among the mesquite and silence while the gringos and the rest of Mexico hurried by.

Later that evening we crossed the Rio San Pedro bridge. Jesse pulled the car to a stop in a rocky parking lot full of diesel buses, motors fuming and stinking. The bus passengers were streaming into a restaurant. Jesse and I pushed in after them.

The restaurant was a familiar one to us. Built alongside the river, it was a rest stop for all the trans-Mexico buses making the run up and down Highway 15. A road cut off Highway 15 on the south end of the bridge, heading for Tuxpan, and around the intersection was spread an informal market, vegetable and fruit stands, small shops, and laden tables where local people from the small villages in the hills sold their poultry and grain, watermelons, etc. When the buses stopped, small children hawking goods ran up to the windows, holding their wares high so that the passengers not wishing to alight could poke out their pesos for morsels which they ate in their seats.

In 1958 I stood at this intersection waiting for a ride. A beautiful young gringa in a new Jaguar roared around the bend and spotted me, reversed her car, and picked me up and took me all the way into Mazatlan. On the way we stopped at a river and swam, dove nude under the water while Mexican ladies beat clothes out on the rocks and watched us from the other side. It was one of the really fine rides of my life. When we reached Mazatlan we walked on the beach and I showed her some of my favorite places, a small seafood restaurant, and a spot on the hill from where you can see all of Mazatlan spread out below you. We spent the night in a hotel. The next day she drove away in her Jaguar and I never saw her again.

The crossroads restaurant was a large one, divided into two dining areas, in front an enclosed one jammed full of chrome dinette tables and tin chairs, and in back an open area overlooking the river furnished with metal cerveza tables. The kitchen, in the back and open to view, was occupied by half a dozen laughing mammas slapping tortillas, stirring great bowls of soup, squeezing fresh oranges into juice.

Unlike restaurants in the U.S., most eating establishments in Mexico are social places, especially the less expensive ones along the roads and in the small towns and villages; they reek of communication and activity and life shared at the tables. Sit down at a roadside restaurant

Photo overleaf by Roberto Ayala

in Mexico and you are immediately deluged by children, peddlers, bystanders from other tables, waitresses, dogs, parrots, even goats; it's like a big family gathering for dinner, people table-hopping and yelling, in one corner a musical trio playing, a drunk *vaquero* reeling from wall to wall in another part of the room, bus drivers and passengers slapping and joking, dogs barking and chickens and cats mingling. The typical gringo who sulks in a corner aloof from this activity is soon brought out of his lethargy by the warmth and friendliness emanating from every table.

For Jesse eating was a ritual and he enjoyed playing elaborate verbal games with the young señoritas waiting on the tables. He seemed to get a perverse delight out of kidding them, speaking in broken Spanish, pseudo-Tarascan, a broad Texas accent, or in just plain playing dumb.

"What would you like, *señores?*" a dark-skinned young lovely asked us when we sat down.

"What do you have?" Jesse asked.

"We have *mole, carne, frijoles, sopa, blanquillos,* whatever you'd like."

"*Blanquillos,* what are those?" Jesse asked.

The señorita did not want to say *"huevos,"* the Mexican word for eggs, because she knew she would be leaving herself open to laughter and jokes from the men in the room for whom *huevos* always means balls, specifically, the man's balls.

Huevos has such covert implications in Mexico, especially in rural parts of the country, that most women will not use the word at all. Instead they refer to eggs as *blanquillos,* or "little whities." If they mention the word *huevos* and there is a man present, more often than not he will make some sexual innuendo, as if it were his balls the women really wanted. Jesse knew this, and his little verbal trap was designed to get a few laughs.

After eating, Jesse and I serviced our car and continued south. It was past midnight and we were beginning the long climb into the mountains that lead to the Nayarit Plateau. Out of the soft night air the smell of bananas and corn came to me as we drove through the fields planted on the steep, rocky slopes on each side of the road. Still higher, in fields miles distant from these, marijuana grew. As our car twisted through the night I felt close to the farmers who lived in the small huts on the high mountain ridges. Each kilometer Jesse and I traveled took me closer to them, each curve and each whiff of growing corn reminded me that the journey whose preamble had taken so long was really about to begin.

For those who travel the roads and highways and dusty back trails of Mexico extensively, time becomes abstract, unreal. Each road leads to another road, each individual leads to another individual. Every experienced marijuano knows that the pace cannot be altered, nor can the destination be reached before the time is right. Each rendezvous is like a scene in a play; act impatient and the play falters, the characters miss their cues, everything falls apart. Above all else in Mexico, and especially when dealing with any aspect of marijuana, a man must have patience.

Jesse was well suited for this Mexican aspect of smuggling, while I, the hulking gringo, preferred the moment of truth at the border. Together we successfully combatted the forces that usually defeat the freelance smuggler. Gringos operating together cannot help acting as gringos, a fatal mistake while dealing in weed in Mexico. A gringo and a Mexican operating side by side balance one another, one pushing and prodding, the other holding back and deliberating. Thus we traveled south to meet Jesus, the entrepreneur Luis had told us of. In each town and village we stopped in, Jesse would talk with the people, sound them out. He liked to get the feel of the place, sense the land and the people. I was always eager to get on, intent on the next goal, the entrepreneur who would take us into the mountains.

For the next three days we drove through Mexico, across the Grand Barranca between Tepic and Guadalajara, past the ruins and volcanic graveyards, through canyons and over mountains on the way to Guerrero. When I drive the roads of Mexico I fall into a reverie, brought on by the movement of the car perhaps, but also by the realization of the startling dichotomy that exists between the Mexico of my imagination, an image engraved indelibly in my mind and reaffirmed on every crossroads corner, children and animals standing mutely still, watching as our car sails by, and the real image of sad, poignant, thunderous Mexico that exists behind the mountains, behind the silence, behind the stillness of the faces staring at me. There are many Mexicos, and the one you choose is the one you are bound to get. The one I chose was the one of silences and the sweet sad stares of children, of the campesinos, the people of the fields, of the countryside and the aloneness that makes so much of the Odyssey in Mexico a combination of bitterness and ecstasy. It has been said many times that Mexico is a country of contrasts. This is true of many countries, but nowhere is it more true than in Mexico. Born of conquest, the nation behind the mountains still struggles in the conflict, each drop of blood reeks of rebellion and deprivation, misfortune and contempt. On the surface much of this is hidden, but once inside the true character of Mexico, a startling hostility and violence emerges, violence left over as part of the afterbirth of the Revolution, but inherent, really, in the blood of the people since before Montezuma.

I ask myself when I'm in Mexico, why am I here? The almost physical lust I feel when I enter the country is soon curdled into something else, disgust perhaps, as if I were a disappointed trick who had paid for the services of a provocative whore. Yet something always brings me back. The same conflict that rends the country rends me. I am attracted and repelled, fearful and bold, energetic and slothful in turns. The road in Mexico brings all of this out in me, a strange wistfulness and excitement and dread, an insistent yearning for some undiscovered secret, and fear that the secret, when discovered, will be more than I can bear.

Photo overleaf by Roberto Ayala

Guerrero bears the scars of the history of Mexico in every village and crossroads campground. This wildest state in Mexico still remembers the independence and courage of those days in 1910 when the campesinos rose up out of their fields with hoes and sticks and machetes to protect their land. The state is the most violent in Mexico as far as shootings and knifings are concerned. Revenge shootings and vendettas are part of the everyday violence, undisturbed and uncontrolled by government edicts and troops and police. The state is rich in marijuana and the farmers who grow the stuff are these same people, at home in the mountains like they never are on cobblestones and city streets. Fierce defenders of their fields, they don't sit idly by when government troops invade their mountains. They fight openly

Three days after leaving Mazatlan, Jesse and I arrived in Huatama-quilpa. The town was small, spotlessly clean around its central plaza, and alive with a jumpy energy accentuated by the music from loud-speakers set in the trees. The plaza was full of people so we chose a side street to park the car. We entered a small restaurant on the square. If you dig watching people, Mexico is the place to be. I can sit for hours in Mexican plazas watching the parade, have my shoes shined over and over again, observe the patterns, note the habits and rituals every Mexican indulges in. Huatamaquilpa was an ordinary Mexican town, a little livelier than most, with the aura of Guerrero hovering over it. The aura of Guerrero is one you don't forget. The state is alert, independent, and aware of strangers.

and bravely for what is theirs. They nurture their fields and tend their crops, and few strangers disturb them. They also grow some of the best marijuana in the world!

Many parts of the mountains have become the private domain of the growers. No one not part of the scene dares go into them, especially without a good connection who is familiar with the people and the area. Federales seldom venture far into the mountains of Guerrero, for when they do inevitably a few of them remain "to help the plants grow," as the saying goes.

Jesse and I had no illusions about our trip. The fact that we wanted to photograph the fields added to our problems. If it was simply going into the mountains and observing, our task would be relatively easy, but we had to be able to get pictures. For that reason we decided to

ROBERTO AYALA

take it easy, just roll along with whatever breezes and personalities fate and our friends dealt us. Fortunately, Jesus solved the problem of getting into the mountains.

Jesus had a rancho fifteen kilometers outside Huatamaquilpa. When it was sufficiently dark we headed for his place. The road leading to the rancho was unpaved and our car bumped and swayed with the ruts. Twenty minutes along the road we saw the lights of another vehicle approaching. We turned off the road to allow it to pass. When the vehicle drove abreast of us the driver stopped and stuck his head out the window. "*¿Qué pasa?*" he yelled.

"*Ola, hombre,*" Jesse said. "I am looking for Jesus Jaramillo, he has a rancho around here."

Two men in the pickup talked rapidly with one another and then

the passenger opened the door and stepped out. He stood on the opposite side of the pickup, behind the hood. The underbrim of his large sombrero reflected the light from inside the truck. "Why do you want to see Jesus Jaramillo?" the driver asked.

"I am a friend of Luis Montoyas in Mazatlan," Jesse said. "Luis told me to come here."

The man standing beside the pickup spoke in rapid Spanish to the driver. Then he walked around and stood beside our window. "I am Jesus Jaramillo," he said. "Are you Señor Jesse?"

"*Sí*. And this is my *compañero*, Jerónimo. I have a note from Luis."

"No matter. I knew you were coming. Luis sent me a wire." Jesus gestured to the driver of the pickup. He got out and stood beside our

car. He handed an object to Jesus, who in turn thrust it through our window. It was a bottle of mescal.

Jesse and I both drank from the bottle and then Jesse handed it back. Jesus and his companion drank from it. Jesse and I got out of the car.

"It's good you arrived today," Jesus said. "I was just leaving for the frontier. This is Eduardo, my driver."

We shook hands all around and then stood beside the road for ten minutes drinking and talking. Suddenly Jesus and Eduardo jumped in their pickup and beckoned us to follow. They whipped their truck around on the narrow road and took off. Eduardo drove like all Mexicans, the pickup careening from one bump to another as it flew down the dirt road. Jesse followed as close as possible, both of us nearly blinded by the cloud of dust. Ten more minutes along the road and we turned off onto another, bumpier road that led to the rancho. Jesus jumped out of his pickup and opened the gate for both vehicles, then jumped back after we'd passed through. When we reached the rancho I saw that it was composed of a number of buildings, half a dozen or so structures built around a plaza. The main house fronted on the patio, where a number of vehicles were parked. There was a small grove of trees behind the main house. I couldn't see the rancho distinctly because of the darkness, but the next morning I had a chance to wander around the place and I discovered it to be extensive, with outbuildings and small sheds to house the dozen families who worked for Jesus.

We entered the main house when we arrived. Two women immediately rushed into the kitchen and started preparing food. The bottle of mescal was replenished with a second one and we sat down at a large table to talk.

I was curious about Jesus' house. More than anything else, a man's home denotes his "place" in Mexico. Jesus obviously had a lot of recently acquired money, for not only was his house being expanded (workmen were building two new additions to the main house), but the main living room was crammed full of new-looking furniture, most of which looked like it had been boosted from the foyer of the Hotel Plasticano. The large, angular, overstuffed couches and chairs were covered with the clear plastic Mexicans so dearly love, and a nine-foot-long color-television console dominated one corner of the room. It was perched on a dais two feet higher than the rest of the furniture. The set was on full volume and a number of women and children and two old men were gazing at it. Jesus paid it absolutely no attention, conducting his conversation below the rumble from the set. There were bright wool rugs on the floor and the red tile gleamed from constant mopping. From my corner at the table I could see into the kitchen; a bright-chrome dinette set dominated that room.

I have a wealthy Mexican friend named Salvador whose home is the standard by which I judge all other wealthy Mexican homes. As I sat at Jesus' table I thought of the differences between his home and that of my old friend Salvador. To me, Salvador's home epitomized a

Photo overleaf by Roberto Ayala

certain attitude and temperament that seems indigenous to many wealthy Mexicans. This attitude manifests itself not only in the house and the furnishings in the house, but also by the aura which dominates such places.

The first time I entered Salvador's house I was impressed by the sense of wealth, but it seemed to me that it was wealth spent unwisely, squandered with little of the taste and feeling real money is capable of serving. The television set sat on its altar in the corner, and in a semicircle around it were four incredibly large "American-style" couches and chairs, covered with the inevitable clear plastic. The room reeked of chill and impersonality. Salvador's house reminded me of a hotel with large public rooms used as buffer areas, greeting rooms where the formalized life styles of wealthy Mexicans can be displayed. Later, Salvador took me through the house to a back patio where coffee was served on a glass-topped chrome dinette set. The patio was beautiful, surrounded by caged parrots and other birds. The coffee was brought in a beautiful sterling silver serving set by a mestizo girl, and served in plastic cups. There were at least half a dozen mestizo servants bustling and cleaning around the house, mopping, ironing, serving the coffee, etc.

What struck me in Salvador's home was the fantastic conflict that exists in the wealthy Mexican—and all of Mexico for that matter. Plastic cups beside silver serving sets; exotic caged birds in beautiful patios next to rooms crammed full of plastic-covered furniture; dark-skinned mestizo girls from mud huts across town polishing chrome dinette sets. The two cultures that are rending modern Mexico were manifesting themselves before my eyes; the one Indian, dark and silent, imbued with a natural good taste, the other one ersatz gringo, plastic and tasteless, shiny and cheap. The modern Mexican denies the one and attempts to emulate the other. I remember thinking when I first walked into Salvador's house that there was no sense of the Indian tradition at all, no handwoven rugs, no Indian pottery, no decorations suggesting the Indian heritage in Salvador's blood. I saw Catholic icons and pictures of the Virgin Mary, but nothing Indian, nothing from the land. It was as if that part of Mexico were buried, forgotten. The only reminder of it was the whisk-whisk of the long rag mops the mestizo girls moved across the floor.

In Jesus' house things were different. Despite the chrome dinette set which I saw in the kitchen (chrome dinette sets are ubiquitous in upward-moving Mexican households; I believe that after the first major, conspicuous purchases, the automobile and the color television set, the Mexican family on the way up buys a chrome dinette set; it's the first large utilitarian purchase), an Indian aura pervaded the place. There were handwoven rugs on the floor and Indian pottery to drink out of, and in the kitchen the women were making tortillas over a brazier. The tortillas themselves were an indication of Jesus' Indian legacy, for they were not served in Salvador's home.

Many books have been written about the Mexican's denial of his roots, and none has adequately explained it. It is inevitable, I suppose, in a stratified society like Mexico's for the upper levels of society to forget their blood. The consequences are manifested, however, on every level of Mexican society. In Mexico City the women refuse to shave their legs, sure that hairless legs are a sign of Indian blood. All Mexicans are imbued with Indian blood—indeed, the Indian blood is what makes Mexico Mexico—a fact to which many Mexicans can't reconcile themselves. Indian roots are denied, foreign influences praised and emulated, and tradition and history abandoned. As Octavio Paz says in *The Labyrinth of Solitude,* "It is astonishing that a country with such a vivid past—a country so profoundly traditional, so close to its roots, so rich in ancient legends even if poor in modern history—should conceive of itself only as a negation of its origins."

Almost every Mexican of any social standing is sure to mention in his first conversation with you that his grandfather or father or some distant relative came from Spain. If you point out that he is denying his true birthright for the elusive snobbery of an ancestry in one of the most backward European societies, he doesn't listen. This shortcoming of the Mexican character is exposed on all levels of society, but is most apparent in the treatment accorded the lower classes, the campesinos and lower-class mestizos and Indians, the people who bear the weight of the country upon their backs.

The lower-class mestizos and Indians are the children of conquest, misfortune, denial, and contempt, completely ignored in the contemporary life of Mexico. On all sides the media scream for every Mexican to take part in the rapid industrialization and commercialization of the country, but the campesino is nonplussed because none of the media acts as though he exists—at least in his dark-skinned form. It's like the refusal of American advertising to recognize until recently that there are Blacks actually living and purchasing and consuming in our own country. When a campesino goes to a movie he doesn't see anything relating to himself or his own life—save in a few antiquated Zapatista movies where he's relegated to the back of the crowd; what he sees are people and lives and advertised products and a whole world relating to things he cannot imagine existing. The blond, blue-eyed creatures staring out at him from movies and advertisements and billboards might as well be from another planet. Things non-Indian are constantly advertised and purveyed in contexts that are incredible to the people of the fields. This does not leave the Indian unaffected. Who is he? Where does he live? What does he live with? These are all questions the advertisements and billboards and movies not only ignore; they don't even hear them.

The evidence that Mexicans deny their Indian heritage is available on every street corner. The mestizo, product of the mixture of Spanish and Indian blood, abandons his huaraches and struggles for months in order to purchase a miserable pair of cheap, badly designed imitation gringo shoes, pointy-toed contraptions that pinch and bite his feet and cost upwards of 150 pesos a pair. In the meantime, the beautifully designed and functional huaraches that can be had in his own market place for 25 pesos are ignored. The gringo-designed shoes are what's advertised though; they are "American" and therefore add to the wearer's status in the streets. That they are uncomfortable and impossible to work in and wear out in two months is beside the point, the fact that the wearer has graduated up from huaraches to foreign-style shoes is what's important. The pointy-toed shoe syndrome is now driving the Indians and campesinos to the supermarket instead of the market place.

This hostile, negative attitude on the part of Mexicans toward their Indian heritage receives a jolt when young gringos visit their country. Struggling mightily to lift himself by the huarache straps out of a violent and poverty-stricken past, the average Mexican is shocked to see the young gringos from the richest and most powerful nation in the world emulating Indian ways and denying the middle-class Mexican's. This is difficult for the Mexican to understand because he has been indoctrinated to believe that the Indian is culturally and spiritually inferior. This belief is not Mexican alone, but is held in all Latin America. In Latin America the attitude is that the aristocrat must always remain the aristocrat and the servant the servant. People are grouped and identified by birth in a way that creates a chasm between those with light skin and those with dark skin. The fact that so many of the longhair gringos, when they arrive in Mexico, emulate the bottom half of society, abandoning their $40 shoes for the $3 huaraches of the Indian, literally blows the Mexican's mind.

Once I visited the state of Chiapas with some wealthy Mexican medical students. The students were amazed that I would bother to take pictures of the Indians. They would thrust themselves in front of my lens, eager to have themselves photographed in their new clothes and gringo shoes. The one student with a camera spent all his time taking pictures of the group's new car. To them it was incomprehensible that I found the Indians worth bothering with.

To me Mexico's denial of its Indian half and the inevitable and inexorable Americanization of the country is a sad thing. The loss of the Indian personality, indeed, the complete denial of it by most of the middle and upper classes of Mexico, will eventually force on the country the same straitjacket of conformity and rootlessness so many Americans wear today. I don't think of Americans as being an especially happy people, in the sense that they have much of a feeling of fulfillment in their daily lives. Whatever personal identity individuals have is programmed out of them at a very early age. To me, Americans are the pioneers of the rootless 1984 society. Divorced from the land, divorced from tradition, divorced from one another, divorced from any concrete reality, they march to the beat of an increasingly alienated, mechanically monitored claptrap society. Sold a bill of goods, subsequent generations of Americans have sought to justify it, creating a fantastic plastic mechanized culture that takes for its fuel the lifeblood of the land and the people.

It is a lesson in alienation to walk down the average American street: eyes that see but do not meet; faces that look but do not speak; voices that sound but are not heard. It's not surprising that increasing numbers of American youth are abandoning the "American way of life." When their journey toward freedom and fulfillment takes them to Mexico, a hegira thousands of them are undertaking with almost religious fervor, their presence and deportment affect Mexico as much as the fact of their leaving affects the country they left behind.

Alienation partly explains the drug revolution taking place not only in the United States but all over the world. Young people recognize that their parents have made a mess of things, that they have denied reality for a plastic unreality, and that's one of the reasons why weed has become so important in their culture. Marijuana acts as a detoxicant, giving the youths a more relevant reality. Then again, perhaps weed just makes some kids more able to live in a completely fucked-up world without going completely insane.

The constant denial of the Indian heritage on the part of the Mexican creates a tremendous schism in his psyche, and the insecurity of so many Mexicans—and the country itself, for that matter—is partly a result of it. Indian blood surges through the veins of Mexico today, and it is noble and vital blood. That educated, aware Mexicans put down the 90 percent of their blood that is so rich and powerful in favor of the weak drippings of a dried-up European spring is a fact that can be understood only in the larger framework of history. It is the mixture of two bloods, Spanish and Indian, that has made Mexico what it is today. Perhaps it's simply fashion that dictates which face will peer out of the screen and sell Coca-Colas. In the years since the emergence of the mestizo as the power in Mexico, Indian features have come to dominate the country. More and more the two races have merged into one, and more and more it is unlike the blond, blue-eyed stereotype. Until the Mexicans realize and live with this—

the fact and glory of their Indianism—there will be strange, violent encounters, overtly brought on by some insult or affront, but in reality brought up out of a cauldron of mixed and mixed-up blood.

Happily, and partly, I believe, because of the influence of gringo youths and marijuana, this attitude toward their Indianism is undergoing a change among many Mexican youths. In 1968 I went to a party in Mexico City with a number of architectural students from the university. I was surprised to see more than half the students wearing ponchos and huaraches—and smoking grass. Of course, most of the students were part of the élite and were semi-Bohemian to begin with, but the very fact that they are beginning to recognize their Indian heritage is important.

The reason Jesus was still linked so closely to his Indian culture was because he had only recently acquired his wealth and had not yet had time to enter into what I call the gringo-emulation phase. Jesus had not been born to money like Salvador, but had made it through a legitimate business which he later turned into a marijuana entrepreneurship. Originally Jesus started out as a farmer, possessor of a few *hectarios* of land on which he planted maguey, the spiny cactuslike plant that's used for the manufacture of tequila and pulque. His maguey farm thrived, and when he got enough money together to acquire more land the drug revolution hit Mexico. Instead of purchasing more land for maguey, he went into the mountains and hired some farmers to grow marijuana for him. He still maintained his maguey farm, and even increased his acreage after his weed farming began to pay off. He was an excellent administrator and his business prospered. When Jesse and I met him he had over forty farmers growing for him in the Sierras of Guerrero and Michoacan—plus his regular workers who lived on his rancho and worked his maguey land.

Jesus, a wire-thin, taciturn man, had four wives in various small villages in Guerrero. Each wife had a house and a number of children, and Jesus rotated among them weekly. He had a wry sense of humor which Eduardo complemented by making great fun of his tired, hangdog look. "Each of his wives is pregnant right now," Eduardo whispered. "He has twenty-two children and he loves them all." When

Jesus smiled, his face opened up in a skeptical dark leer. When I looked into his eyes I could see ten thousand years of suffering. Despite his look of pained exhaustion, it was enjoyable to be around Jesus. He spoke in a slow monotone as he described his business, calmly sipping from the bottle of mescal each time it came past. While he was self-deprecating when he spoke, I sensed in him a great strength.

While we talked he held his smallest child on his knee and bounced her up and down. The child was a dark, fierce-looking girl of about eighteen months, when she glanced at me out of her well-deep black eyes, she looked like a Zapotec princess.

"What is it you want of me?" Jesus asked after we had eaten.

Jesse and I looked at one another. We both knew we had to be out front with Jesus and tell him exactly what we wanted. It was up to him to take it from there. Jesse spoke: "We have been smuggling marijuana for a long time, Jesus. My *compañero* here has been arrested for smuggling marijuana and right now he is in a very delicate position, in Mexico illegally and subject to arrest and imprisonment if the authorities find out. But he is here for one reason, and one reason alone. We have been offered an opportunity by a very large magazine in America to show what marijuana is all about. If we can show the people in America what marijuana is, who grows it and how it is grown, who smuggles it and how it is smuggled, then we believe that many of the misconceptions and lies told about marijuana will be forgotten. We have come to Mexico to tell the truth about marijuana. We want to go into the fields and talk to the farmers; we want to take pictures of the fields, the plants, of the people who work in them. That way we can show the people in America that what we are doing is not bad. We can show the truth about marijuana."

"The truth about marijuana is money," Jesus laughed. "It is the best crop we can grow in the mountains now, because of you gringos."

"Marijuana is more than money to a lot of people," I said. "Many gringos feel that it is a gift, one that can help many people."

Jesus shrugged. "Mota is many things to many people. For the people in the mountains, it is a livelihood, a source of income. For

others, it is more, a panacea for their many problems. For still others, it is an excuse to abuse people. For me it is an accident, a happy one I am glad to say."

"An accident?"

"Sí. I did not go out of my way to cultivate marijuana, it came to me accidentally. I was a simple farmer growing maguey. Maguey is a good crop. For each peso I invest, the next year I can make seven pesos. When I saw friends of mine going into the mountains, however, and paying los montaños to plant mota on their slopes and between their rows of corn, I asked a few questions. The people in the mountains cannot grow maguey, for that you need relatively flat land—and one peso to buy each maguey plant. The people in the mountains do not have pesos, but they do have land—and time. My friends told me that for the cost of a few seeds, mota can be planted almost anywhere. And if a man cares to get industrious he can make a good living growing mota. So by accident I got into mota. For each peso I invest, the next year I can make 500 pesos."

"Can you take us into the mountains to see the mota growing?" I asked.

"I can take you into the mountains," Jesus said. "Whether or not you can take pictures is up to the farmers."

"If we can get into the mountains, I am sure the farmers will be sympathetic," Jesse said.

"We'll see," Jesus said. "When I get back from Juarez we'll go up there, I have to deliver some supplies to the farmers anyway."

Jesus was leaving in the morning for the border. He was going to ride shotgun with a ton of marijuana he had sold to the Texas Syndicate. El Sindicato Texas is made up of a group of Mexican-Americans who operate one of the biggest weed-smuggling rings in Texas and the southwest. Most of those involved in the organization have family connections in Mexico. It was through the family connections that they had linked up with Jesus, who was known for his ability to deliver high-quality weed regularly. One of the interesting aspects of the syndicate weed-smuggling operation is that the people involved in it are interested not in the quality of the weed they smuggle but in the

act of smuggling. The Texas Syndicate people are into weed in such bulk quantities that quality is secondary; their primary concern is getting ton loads of weed into the States, and Jesus was helping them.

Jesus explained that before Operation Cooperation he did not usually accompany loads to the border. Now, however, there were so many soldiers on the roads that it had become difficult moving large shipments, so he rode shotgun with loads he had sold to ensure their delivery.

And the new *aduana* stops on the highways were not the only problem. Roving gangs of bandits operating in rural areas of Mexico were eager to knock off unprotected marijuana shipments and were becoming a menace. The *bandidos* piqued my sense of the comic in much that goes on in Mexico. For a bunch of outlaws to go through the whole illegal scam, raising the money, planning the run, making careful anti-cop considerations, and then having the whole trip clobbered by a gang of equally rascally *vatos locos* who were just as illegal and probably even more desperate seemed humorous to me—and even appropriate. My head has always been on the side of the outsider, and in a weed-smuggling operation it seemed to me that the *cabrones* trying to rip off loads moving out of the mountains were even farther outside than the marijuanos doing the moving. However, the *idea* of bandits knocking off a load of weed and the *reality* of it are two different things. Jesse and I had once lost 400 kilos of mota to a group of bandits in Zacatecas, and there had been absolutely no humor in the situation. In fact, there had been a death.

Because of a mechanical fuckup I was late in arriving at a certain spot with our truck to pick up our weed. The campesinos guarding the load got worried and attempted to move it back into the mountains. They were ambushed by bandits and a young farmer named Alphonso was killed. Although both Jesse and I felt partly responsible for Alphonso's death, there wasn't anything we could do about it except make token payments to his family. The rest of the growers involved in the shooting were philosophical about it and matter-of-factly went about running the bandits down and killing two of them. Later, Nostromo, one of the growers involved in the shoot-out,

showed me the hole in his side where a bandit's bullet had gone clean through. Needless to say, the experience colored my dealings in Mexico, giving them a sense of reality I hadn't felt before. My romantic idea of the comic nature of the conflict between marijuanos and *bandidos* wasn't so romantic after all.

Once Jesus had solved the bandit problem in the mountains, the border was nothing; the Texas Syndicate had the whole border wired and it was no hassle getting a load through Juarez into El Paso and beyond.

Jesus' organization is reasonably sophisticated. It is controlled entirely by himself and one partner, and is connected in a loosely organized series of link-ups with other entrepreneurs throughout Mexico. Jesus has his own area in the mountains where he supports the farmers and buys all their crops, and his connections with other entrepreneurs are used primarily to keep track of what's happening in the industry, how much weed is available, where it's moving to, who is moving it, etc. The connections also serve as a mutual-protection society. If a big order comes through that Jesus is unable to fill from his own sources, he can contact another entrepreneur in another area. The federated dealers also keep one another informed as to the movement of soldiers in the mountains, and new roadblocks and *aduana* checks that might have been set up. On the other side of the coin, the mutual-protection society also keeps itself informed of large busts, fingers, informers, and government figures who are notoriously prone to accepting bribes, and when they will accept them. One of the facts of life is that government officials change their minds and their alliances; officials who take bribes occasionally get honest, and other officials who never take bribes sometimes get into financial difficulties. The marijuana game requires keeping yourself informed. The man who knows the most is the safest.

Jesus' organization is more sophisticated than most because of his equipment and connections. He has two airplanes and a large fleet of trucks to move his stuff. His maguey rancho justifies so much equipment, and also makes it easy to move loads along the Mexican roads. As far as his weed fields are concerned, Jesus is blessed with some of the finest ones in Guerrero. He also has a brother-in-law who operates in the state of Michoacan. Together the two of them are able to utilize one another's resources. The fact that Jesus was connected with El Sindicato Texas was also important. This established Jesus as a big entrepreneur, who could be counted on to deliver big loads when and where they were wanted. Entrepreneurism in the weed industry requires expertise, capability, and dependability. An entrepreneur who can't deliver, or can't deliver in certain areas, is decidedly less valuable.

When Jesus accompanied a load of marijuana to the border, he occasionally stayed there for a few days of fun. Jesse and I had to find out how long Jesus intended to stay at the border this time. As the evening progressed, however, we got too drunk to discuss business. We spent the night at the rancho and got up the next morning for an early breakfast.

After breakfast Jesus informed us that he was going to be gone for a week. "You can stay here at the rancho, or you can drive over to Acapulco for a few days and enjoy yourselves," he said.

Jesse and I decided on Acapulco. I hadn't seen the place for seven years. That afternoon we saw Jesus and Eduardo off for the border, and we left for Acapulco. We were to return to the rancho in five days. From there, Jesus would fly us into the Sierras.

My first visit to Acapulco was in 1957. I hitchhiked down from Mexico City and spent two weeks on the beaches, saw the divers leap from the rocks, met a girl, got busted for sleeping on the beach, and discovered the real Mexico in the back part of town.

My trip was fortuitous from the start, beginning with a ride out of Taxco in a '48 Chevy packed with thirteen young Mexicans heading for a picnic on the river. They stopped for me, refused my protests, and crammed me in the car. Just like Luis crammed Jesse and me in his Galaxie when we were hunting connections in Mazatlan. Off we went, shooting down the canyons and barrancas out of Taxco, heading for the river. When we arrived at the riverbottom the Mexicans piled out, pulling me with them, and began spreading blankets on the ground, and started gathering firewood. The girls spread heaps of delicious food on the blankets while the men broke out bottles of beer and tequila. I helped gather firewood until the music and food started, then jumped in and started eating and drinking with the others. While guitars played and men sang, I fell into my first tequila drunk, stumbling and laughing along the river's edge, happy to be alive and in Mexico. Pepe, the leader of the gang, wanted me to return to Taxco with them, offering to put me up and show me the town. I said no, I had to get to Acapulco, and as the crew was packing I staggered across a field to a road where Pepe said a bus heading for Acapulco would stop for me. It was one of those magic days that happen occasionally, and the minute I stepped out on the empty road a dilapidated bus wheezed around the corner and rumbled to a stop. A sign on the window said Acapulco, so I aimed myself for the door and stumbled aboard.

Inside the bus were pigs and fowl and Indios and children and cages and birds. I lurched to the back of the bus and an old Indian who looked like Zapata's grandfather stood up and offered his seat to me. He was carrying an ancient shotgun, and his toothless smile bid me sit down. I was too drunk and too happy to argue. All night I talked and laughed and spoke pidgin Indian as the bus swayed and lurched on its way to Acapulco. The campesinos sat quietly and made room in the back for the gringo *borracho,* who alternately rambled, sang, smiled, shouted, and moaned. The honesty and grace and simple dignity of the rural people of Mexico, a profound strength, seem to be missing in the people born into higher levels of society.

Acapulco, like no other city in Mexico, points out with an explicitness the two faces of the country. The three faces really, for although Acapulco is in Mexico, and its Mexican poverty and wealth exist back to back, the city has an American face too. In 1940 Acapulco had less than 6,000 inhabitants. Today there are over 250,000. Of the more than one hundred large luxury hotels in Acapulco, only a few are owned by Mexicans. The United States so dominates Acapulco that it can be considered an American resort, save for the back part of town, where most of the original inhabitants live, crammed into dingy hovels and lean-tos, subsisting as they have always on the horse meat and tortillas and leftover fish that doesn't make it to the kitchens of the fancy hotels. The explosion in building has been so frenetic that developers have raced over *ejido* land, land that is the communal property of the campesinos, and built their American-financed and controlled hotels and highrises. Naturally this was done without the consent of the campesinos, and only recently has anyone suggested that it might be proper to pay the poor people for their loss.

During my first visit to Acapulco in 1957, there were no highrises extending south down the beaches on *ejido* land, and when the second-class bus labored up over the final hill I moved up from my rear seat to one in front (most of the passengers had long since left, gone into the hills to their huts and shacks, toiling slowly away down some dark path with a passel of chickens or a pig on a rope). I was not surprised to see spread out on the bay below me a jewellike resort, with a dozen or so large hotels along the shore of the bay, but mostly it was a small town with golden lights along the water, the crownlike heads of cliffs across the bay just beginning to catch the rays of the sun coming up behind me.

That first day I walked through the town getting my bearings. I visited the beaches and strolled along the *malecón*, probed the back parts of the town, visited the market, saw what the town was made of. Acapulco throbbed with a rustling, incipient energy that I could sense in the streets. Kids and campesinos swarmed over the rocks and beaches, bustled through the town, hawked their wares and stared at

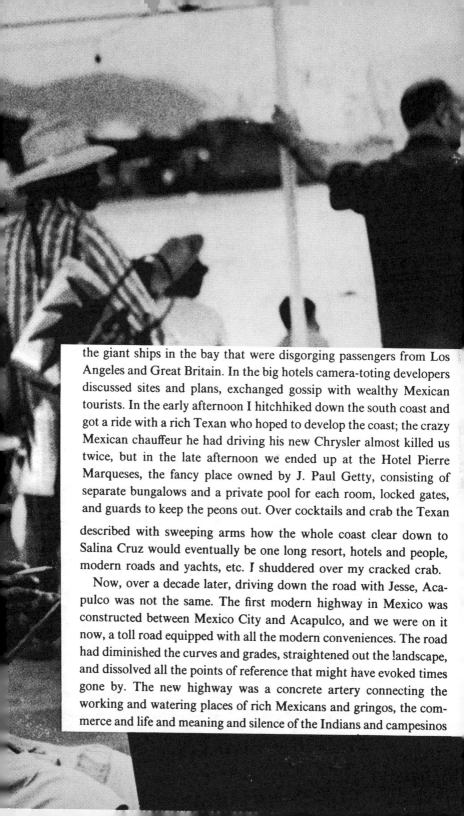

the giant ships in the bay that were disgorging passengers from Los Angeles and Great Britain. In the big hotels camera-toting developers discussed sites and plans, exchanged gossip with wealthy Mexican tourists. In the early afternoon I hitchhiked down the south coast and got a ride with a rich Texan who hoped to develop the coast; the crazy Mexican chauffeur he had driving his new Chrysler almost killed us twice, but in the late afternoon we ended up at the Hotel Pierre Marqueses, the fancy place owned by J. Paul Getty, consisting of separate bungalows and a private pool for each room, locked gates, and guards to keep the peons out. Over cocktails and crab the Texan described with sweeping arms how the whole coast clear down to Salina Cruz would eventually be one long resort, hotels and people, modern roads and yachts, etc. I shuddered over my cracked crab.

Now, over a decade later, driving down the road with Jesse, Acapulco was not the same. The first modern highway in Mexico was constructed between Mexico City and Acapulco, and we were on it now, a toll road equipped with all the modern conveniences. The road had diminished the curves and grades, straightened out the landscape, and dissolved all the points of reference that might have evoked times gone by. The new highway was a concrete artery connecting the working and watering places of rich Mexicans and gringos, the commerce and life and meaning and silence of the Indians and campesinos in the hills and valleys beyond the road meaning less than nothing to the roadbuilders and politicians and engineers. To me the new highway manifested Acapulco, and the city was not now one a person who truly loved Mexico could respect. Acapulco and the new highway were all straight lines and high buildings and displaced campesinos and Colonel Sanders fried-chicken shacks and hamburger heavens and a jangling dinero-oriented jukebox madness that had no inkling of the little stops at night along the old road where girls sat at tables with comic books under gas lamps, where the coffee was served in pottery cups on flyspecked tablecloths, a radio playing in the background tuned to a station in Chilpancingo, a fan whirring overhead one revolution per minute, and calendars on the walls picturing, for me, the true magic of Mexico, the arrival or departure of the *vaquero* at his wife's door. It was this memory, the memory of nights on second-class buses riding down the now-abandoned road, that made me, when I thought of the Acapulco I was heading toward, shudder slightly under my blanket.

My disappointment met expectations when Jesse and I reached Acapulco. The town had blossomed into urban sprawl that clung to the edges of the bay, spread over the hills, and climbed the mountains behind the town. Everything had a price on it, even a spot of beach on which to stand. The Americanization was almost complete in the ticky-tacky roadside stands that blurted out their neon messages twenty-four hours a day. Things were so bad that even the Mexicans were beginning to cringe; they had just passed a law that all new gringo enterprises must adopt Mexican-sounding names. They were also considering a law that would ban the Indian hawkers who peddled their wares around the town to make a few pennies a day. Bad for business, the people in charge said, having those ragged folk around our beautiful new hotels. New visitors to town must have wondered what all the famous stories were about, the ones of the beauty and peace, the silence and drama of old Acapulco, for all they found when they arrived were the same claptrap joints they'd left behind in Los Angeles and Miami Beach. The old Acapulco had died and no one but a few old-timers mourned its passing, for on every street people hurried and scurried on their hustles and scams, beggars

Photo overleaf by Roberto Ayala

and beautiful Indian babies selling jewelry from fists no bigger than peas, carting, hauling, bicycling, motorscooting, running, walking, yelling, screeching, all to the tune of car horns and bus roars, shrieks and blasts and moans as the city throbbed and grew almost visibly in front of your eyes. What could possibly bring people here any longer? Surely it wasn't the peace of the place nor the beauty, for the peace and beauty had been buried. It must have been the myth, the myth that now belonged to some other part of the coast. Jesse and I spent a day in town and then drove north toward Zihuatanejo, the town where Timothy Leary tried to start his LSD colony in 1963.

When Leary was thrown out of Harvard he decided the best place for him was Mexico, so he came to Zihuatanejo. Zihuatanejo lies about 250 kilometers north of Acapulco and is a sleepy little village between the sea and the jungle. Zihuatanejo is what Acapulco must have once been. The reason Leary chose to settle in Mexico was because at the time it was one of the few countries where one had access to the chemical LSD-25, which was manufactured in Switzerland under the Sandoz drug label. Sandoz LSD-25 was the first acid available in any amount in the United States. It was also some of the best that has ever been available, including Augustus Owsley III's famous acids. Leary hoped to start a drug-experiment colony in Zihuatanejo, and actually had one going for about six months. When the Mexican government found out what he was doing, however, they ran him out. Leary's hassles with the Mexican authorities were, in fact, the first rumbles signaling the birth of the hippie-longhair invasion that was to come later. When Leary was asked to leave Mexico, a contingent of his colony under the leadership of a thin, messianic dude named Thad moved to Ajijic, the small resort town on the shores of Lake Chapala in Jalisco. Ajijic and Chapala, the town from which the lake gets its name, are havens for middle-aged Americans who flock there to retire. The towns are controlled, in fact, by American Legion and mid-America types who have settled in the communities along the lake because of the low cost of living and the abundant and cheap booze. By the late fifties and early sixties quite a few beats had left their North Beach and Greenwich Village pads and also settled around the lake. It was this thriving community that the Zihuatanejo expatriates wished to join.

When Thad and his followers arrived in Ajijic, they set up shop in a place called The Mill, an abandoned granary that became a center for LSD experimentation for the next few years. This was during the hiatus between the death of the beat movement and the birth of the hippie-longhair movement. Neither the death nor the birth occurred spontaneously, however, and it is interesting to note that the small town on the lake near Guadalajara was one of the more important wombs of the worldwide drug culture.

Shortly after his arrival in Ajijic, Thad talked the University of Guadalajara Medical School into conducting experiments with LSD-25, using members of the beat colony and some Mexican students as guinea pigs. These experiments were shortlived, however, because the scene was beginning to get out of control back in Ajijic and Chapala. Thad, like Leary himself, had an insatiable desire to turn everybody onto LSD, and was gathering more and more kids around him at The Mill. Word had spread in the underground back in the U.S., and hundreds of kids were descending on the area. This, combined with the increasing demand for marijuana, created a lot of heat. The old crowd of retired boozers had never gotten along with the Bohemian crowd that lived along the lake, but at least they had tolerated one another. When the LSD freaks started traipsing into town, the scene changed from tolerance to intolerance. Many of the beats were into marijuana, and it wasn't unusual for their homes to be used as warehouses for shipments of the weed going up to the States. When kids wearing weird hair (the Beatles were just getting popular) began falling out in the streets while stoned on acid, the lush-head legionnaires began complaining to the Mexican authorities. After receiving numerous complaints the Mexican police started rousting *los existentialistas*, as the Beats were called, the word meaning in the Mexican sense, "those who, when night falls, make that their home." When the heat came down a lot of homes were busted and some weed was found. In 1963 I rented a house in San Nicolas de Ybarra, a small village on the lake south of Chapala. In 1964, a few months after I left, the house was busted for being the center of a drug cult. The Mexicans arrested over forty gringos, drug freaks and occult nuts, according to a report printed by *¡Alarma!,* the Mexican shock newspaper. By now Ajijic had become a hotbed for longhairs, and it was dangerous walking the streets of the town if you looked slightly beat or Bohemian. The roundups that were to become commonplace in every Mexican resort town started occurring weekly, primarily at the instigation of the older gringo legionnaires who ran the town.

Jesse and I avoided Ajijic and Lake Chapala now, and as we drove into Zihuatanejo I thought of the changes Leary's little expedition had spawned in Mexico. Not that the changes wouldn't have occurred without Leary, undoubtedly they would have, but the sensibility that demands such wholesale turning on without regard for conventions or manner or traditions always seems somewhat perverse. It seems to me that a lot of gurus attempt to exorcise their own devils with the minds and bodies of others. This book is not about LSD, but it strikes me as strange that the leaders of such experimental groups, be they Timothy Learys or Thads, always seem to desire a group of people under their thumb. I don't believe they start out like this. I believe that at first they want to let others know of the fabulous possibilities that hallucinogens offer, possibilities of seeing themselves and others as unique parts of the universe, all together, none separate, none unequal. Unfortunately, few kids who enter into these relationships are adequately prepared for the experience, nor are their teachers.

Zihuatanejo was still unspoiled, still beautiful, a few more shacks now, but not yet taken over by the tourist plague. Jesse and I camped out on the beaches for a few days and then packed up and headed back to Huatamaquilpa. It was time to go into the mountains.

3.

THE MOUNTAINS

Jesus was at the rancho when we got back from Acapulco, preparing for the flight into the mountains. That evening we drove into Huatamaquilpa in his pickup to meet Sanchez, the man who would be our guide. On the way into town, Jesus asked me where my sombrero was. "Back at the rancho," I said. He reached under the seat and pulled out a sombrero. "Put it on," he said. "All Mexicans wear sombreros around here."

I put on the sombrero.

"If someone sees you in my truck without a sombrero, they'll remember it. Three Mexicans with sombreros is nothing."

I was silent the rest of the way into town. I knew I had goofed. I could feel the tension between me and Jesse. I was pissed off. A forgotten sombrero isn't the end of the world. It was as if Jesse had been reading my mind.

"It's the little fuckups that do a scene in," he said. "You can plan for the big fuckups and avoid them. The little ones you have to know subconsciously so you can forget them."

A carnival was in progress in town. The square was full of towns-people and campesinos from the surrounding villages. Jesus skirted the square and drove to the opposite side of town. He parked in a deserted side street and went to find Sanchez. Jesse and I waited in the pickup.

I could hear the sounds of the carnival. Jesse was quiet. The street we were parked in was dark except for a small patch of light cast against an adobe building at the corner. This was a poor section of town and the electricity was turned off early. I couldn't get over how much time we spent on this trip waiting, waiting in cars, waiting in trucks, waiting in motel rooms—now sitting in a pickup at night in a deserted street in a strange town waiting for a man I barely knew to bring another man I didn't know who would guide us up into who knew what at what price. At times I felt insane to be there, masochistic in the trusts and times and alleys and darkness I put myself through.

Jesse lit a cigarette, and the glowing tip illuminated his face. He used to buy chicle from the kids on the streets and when he got nervous he popped four or five pieces in his mouth and chewed furiously. His mouth was full of chicle and I watched his jaws moving up and down. He had one foot propped on the dashboard and he tapped his toe in rhythm to his jaw. Jesus had been gone forty-five minutes.

"Maybe Sanchez isn't home," I said.

"If he wasn't home he'd be back by now," Jesse said.

Sometimes on the road together Jesse and I got edgy. Little things that ordinarily wouldn't bother us started to grate. Now I was infuriated by Jesse's jaws clacking up and down. "For Christ's sake," I said, "can't you get rid of that gum?"

Jesse continued chewing. I looked down the street at the spot of light. Too many days on the road, too many hours in the car. I felt like opening the door and bolting down the street.

"Goddammit, sit still," Jesse said. "Here comes Jesus."

Jesse removed his foot from the dashboard. Jesus was standing beside the pickup door before I realized it.

"Sanchez was at the carnival," Jesus said. "I had to find him. He's waiting for us."

Jesus and Jesse took off and I followed, stumbling over the cobblestones of backstreet Mexico and along dung-covered footpaths. The carnival noises and the sound of a church bell beckoned from across town, an out-of-tune call to Mass. Then it was quiet, just the sound of our walking, Jesus' form dark against the darkness. Sanchez' house was across a gully. "He's in the process of building it," Jesus said. "The fee you pay him will help." There was a light in the house. I could see the tile roof and white columns supporting it, like fingers holding up the top edge of a cliff. We stumbled across the gully and climbed the path to the house. Jesse and I stood back in the darkness and Jesus knocked. He didn't have to. Sanchez stepped out of the darkness and spoke. His voice was low, soft, complementing his appearance; quiet, deceptively soft, limp handshake, .38-Super stuck in his belt, huaraches on his feet. Sanchez and Jesus talked and Jesse joined in, low, subdued, the voices like the sound of nature, the brush of a dry leaf against the house, a mule rubbing against a fence post, a woman coughing somewhere behind a wall.

We moved off the porch to an alley beside the house. I sat on the hard, dusty ground with my back resting against a wall. A strip of light illuminated Sanchez' forehead. The three sombreros bobbed and moved in the darkness. The next day when I saw Sanchez clearly I saw his eyes, very clear but with a perpetually pained or sad or perhaps innocent look in them. Standing still, his belly pooched out. Later, when walking in the mountains, he would leave me far behind.

After talking for twenty minutes, the arrangements were complete: Sanchez would guide us for $250. He didn't know if we could take pictures; that was up to the farmers. Yes, there were good fields, but hard to reach. We would meet in the morning and Jesus would fly us up into the mountains. *"Gracias, señores, hasta mañana."*

We walked back down the hill to the truck in the darkness. On the way the church bell struck ten. We walked through narrow passageways between stone walls. When we reached the truck, Jesse and Jesus talked quietly. Three campesinos trudged by, laughing and drunk. One of them stumbled against the truck and then all three of them stopped and pissed against a stone wall at the end of the alley.

We drove out of town back to the rancho with our sombreros pulled down. Behind the dark mountain shapes lightning glittered.

The next morning we were up at dawn to make final arrangements.
Jesus left to check out his airplane while Jesse and I ran through our
supplies—clothes, sleeping bags, ponchos, Polaroid and Pentax cameras. We intended to get some preliminary photographs before Gene
Anthony came down, mainly to get the farmers used to the idea of
cameras.

At mid-morning Eduardo, who had taken Jesse's pickup into town,
returned with Sanchez. We threw our gear in the back of the pickup
and climbed in. There was a small airstrip on Jesus' rancho and we
were to rendezvous there. Jesus kept his planes at the small airport
in town when they weren't in use. He had gone there to get his Cessna.

While we waited for Jesus to arrive with his plane, Jesse and I
talked. "Our troubles aren't over yet," Jesse said. "Once we get to the
village in the mountains, we still have two or three days on muleback
before we get to the fields." Sanchez agreed.

"The most difficult part is ahead of us. We not only have to hire
mules, we have to convince the growers that we're good guys, so they
won't shoot our asses off while we're up there."

"The campesinos in the mountains have no reason for letting us up
there in the first place," Jesse said, puffing reflectively on a Fiesta. "It
can't possibly do them any good, and it sure as hell could do them
harm. In fact, Sanchez is a little worried that they might be down on
him for bringing us in."

"Then why is he doing it?" I asked.

"Because we're friends of Jesus, and Jesus is the biggest buyer in
the area. Without him we wouldn't be going anywhere."

I glanced at Sanchez. He was squatting back on his haunches. His
short body seemed soft and flabby at first glance. A second look
revealed the passive strength lurking beneath the surface. His dark,
knotted feet looked like roots inside his huaraches, like they could
send shoots down into the ground and grow if he stood in one place
long enough. When he shook hands it was with a limp, dishrag gesture
that was disconcerting. The whole aura of the man was one of slow,
casual indifference, a passive solidity set off by the .38-Super tucked
in his belt.

Photo overleaf by Roberto Ayala

Sanchez heard the plane first. He stood up, slapping the dust and wrinkles out of his clothes. I stood up too, although I didn't hear anything, and rubbed my knees. They had grown stiff from squatting. Only then did I hear the motor. In an instant a small blue and white Cessna hit the end of the dirt strip and bounced to a stop in front of us. Jesus held the door open while Sanchez grabbed a number of sacks of fertilizer and our gear and threw them inside. As I entered the plane, I noticed that Jesus had a pistol tucked in his belt—the badge of the Mexican! Jesse and Sanchez jumped in and Sanchez pulled the door closed. Within seconds Jesus was gunning the aircraft down the strip.

I held my breath as we lifted off, sighing with relief when I felt the plane leave the ground and climb into the clear Mexican air. A lone hut drifted under us as Jesus banked the aircraft and started to climb over the first ridges leading into the mountains. In the distance I could see white smoke from fires which farmers had set to burn off their fields. It mingled with the mountains and disappeared as it drifted upward. Jesus leveled the plane out at 11,000 feet, and we continued

northwest. Villages, rivers (muddy from the recent rains), and canyons rolled into view and fell away. The whole country seemed like a vast, prehistoric garden, rich and tumbling beneath us, a verdant, organic palette on which gods mixed their rainbows.

I looked over at Sanchez, whose seat next to Jesus faced the rear of the plane. He was holding onto the safety strap above the door, and peering over his shoulder into the mountains ahead. I felt as though I were flying into some irrational, half-primitive, half-mechanized dream world—Sanchez with his cracked, ground-beaten feet, and the hawkish shadow of the plane flitting silently across the valleys and mountaintops below. As the ragged landscape unfolded, I thought of the ancient myth of the Indians, of the white man who was to come from the east one day, either from the sea or from the sky, and I wondered if marijuana had anything to do with that vision. I looked at Jesse, the Tarascan blood etched in his cheekbones, my friend for more than ten years, and recalled the prophecy recounted many times in the huts and tents and hogans: Some day the Indian would regain

his gods, and the white man, who had destroyed them, would be taken in hand by the children of those Indians and led back to the ancient deities. Perhaps the young gringo kids turning on to pot, actually an Indian hallucinogen, and traipsing about the country in their restless searches for some honest answers were acting out that myth. Hundreds of kids had gone to New Mexico, Nevada, and Arizona to join the Indians and live in hogans and tipis. As the plane drifted over the mountains I felt my own self drawn irresistibly toward them. We were all Indians, on a journey in search of gods.

The mountains we were flying over were like a vast nether world, fantasmagoric and beautiful, yet ominous and strange. Because we were up so high the peaks below appeared flat; I could see only the color, deep and rich in the canyons and bright gold on the mountaintops. A dark chasm cut through the landscape directly below us, disappearing under the airplane and reappearing on the other side. I strained to see what lay in the gorge. Jesse had said the village was scattered somewhere along its edge, clinging to the sides of a river like detritus lodged there after a great flood. I saw no village, but as we flew across the gorge I could see a slow fluttering of white objects and recognized them as birds lifting off the peaks at the sound of our craft. Below the birds I could see their infinitesimally small shadows gliding over the ground, and by following the shadows could see the ground dip and weave and drop away into thousand-foot gorges. I gasped. The landscape below me was like a vast blanket quilted by a mad woman who had sat huddled over her work for a thousand years, a million years, who still sat over her work, embroidering, stitching, restitching, making new and anew her wonderful earth blanket.

I snapped out of my reverie as the plane swooped down from the clouds and circled a small village perched on the banks of a swift river. Down below, a white statue raised its arms amid the blues and greens of the mountainside, and as the crosslike shadow of the plane flitted overhead, a bevy of white birds took flight like flowers thrown into the air. The landing strip we were approaching was smaller even than the one we had left an hour and a half before. It was hacked out of the cliff, and the high bluffs rising on either side of it made landing

Photo overleaf by Eugene Anthony

dangerous. A dozen people stood at the end of the strip as we swept over it and then turned for our approach. I held my breath as we dropped toward the ground. Jesus landed and brought the plane to a jolting stop, and whipped it around for the takeoff. Before the plane stopped, Sanchez was out the door. Jesse and I threw our bags out and followed him. Then two Indians who had been standing beside the plane jumped in and threw out the sacks of fertilizer. When the plane was empty, Jesus gunned it down the strip and took off. I watched the plane go with a certain wistfulness. Jesus was supposed to pick us up in two weeks, but I wondered if I would ever see him again.

ROBERTO AYALA

Jesse and I waited in the shadow of an adobe hut while Sanchez went to see about renting mules. Curious children stared at us, their wide faces smiling and friendly. It was about ten A.M. and the morning sun stretched high above us. We were in a small valley settlement about 6,000 feet up in the mountains—a few huts clustered around the end of the landing strip, two or three more substantial houses, and dozens of burros, pigs, chickens, and children.

A few of the men were shooting at one of the chickens, taking turns with a slingshot. One man finally killed it with a well-aimed rock to its head. The other men laughed, and they all chipped in a few pesos to quiet the woman who owned it. Each of the men carried a pistol in his belt, and even without holsters, they seemed anxious to display their weapons properly. From time to time one of them would take his gun out, aim it at some imaginary target, and then wipe the barrel across his pantsleg before stuffing it back in his belt. Here in the mountains a gun is both an ornament and a necessary tool. Each man has his piece and knows how to use it. One of the men stood fifty yards from a tree and squeezed off three rounds, plunking berries with his weather-beaten pistol.

EUGENE ANTHONY

In Mexico the gun serves as instant judge, jury, and executioner in many personal confrontations. Almost every Mexican carries a gun, including city Mexicans, and every day one newspaper or another carries a story of individuals resorting to the gun to settle differences —or simply to demonstrate their *machismo*.

In Michoacan a small-town mayor bragged of his prowess with a gun to a group of his drunken friends. "I'm the best shot in the state," he cried. "Bah!" his friends scoffed. "You couldn't hit a *piñata* with a shovel!" The mayor pulled out his pistol and aimed it at an Indian sitting across the plaza. "Go ahead, shoot!" his friends goaded him. The mayor pulled the trigger and shot off the back of the Indian's head.

The Mexican is so concerned with his manhood that he wears his balls on his shoulder, so to speak, to show that he has a pair. An incident, a friend's taunt, an unexcused bumping on the sidewalk, a minor traffic accident, can lead to a confrontation. This attitude is manifested in the *macho,* the super-male. The *machista* is fearless, has *huevos,* and takes no shit off anyone, neither his woman nor his enemies.

From the collection of Roberto Ayala

Originally *macho* meant the male mule, a strong, stubborn animal. *Mula*, or female mule, which is by implication the opposite of strong, is a Mexican slang term for prostitute. A *machista* therefore is a strong, heavy dude who doesn't leave himself open, who doesn't expose himself to anyone or anything, while a dude who lacks *machismo* is like a prostitute, open, exposed, vulnerable, weak. To be *macho* is to be strong, physically, sexually, politically. A bull which acquits itself well in the ring is *macho*, as is the man who dominates others in business or bed. The *macho* is closed, cold, unconcerned with the feelings of others; at the same time the *macho* dominates and is dominated by appearances; thus a gesture or glance or a slip of the tongue can take on major significance under certain circumstances.

In Mexico City a gringo saw a pretty señorita walking along on the sidewalk and gave her the familiar American greeting; shave-and-a-haircut-six-bits, with his car horn. Within minutes half a dozen Mexicans had abandoned their cars, many of them in the middle of the *glorieta*, and were tearing at the gringo's automobile. Only a policeman was able to pull the *machistas* off the ignorant gringo. What he had inadvertently done was insult the mothers of every Mexican within the sound of his horn. Shave-and-a-haircut-six-bits means "Go fuck your mother, *cabrón*," in Mexico, and every Mexican who heard the horn was sure that it was he personally being insulted.

Mexico is a country dominated by the male. From a very early age boys are treated better then girls. If a Mexican's first child is not a son he is humiliated, angry, and mocked by his friends. There are hints that his *huevos* are not entirely adequate. Naturally one is careful not to insult a man who carries a gun in his belt, for although his *huevos* may not be adequate enough to make a boy, his pistol is capable of making you dead.

The homosexual connotations behind the Mexican's use and abuse of the gun cannot be ignored. A shaky manhood is steadied by a .38-Super tucked under the belt. Even the *idea* of a .38-Super is enough for some people. In Mazatlan I saw a group of young studs prancing along the *malecón* on Saturday night. One of the dudes carried a cigarette lighter made in the shape of a .38-Super. At first glance the lighter looked like a real gun—and was worn so by the kid.

The shiny cold steel of the lighter-gun against his abdomen reassured him, represented an element of manliness, and made him feel less vulnerable. At first I thought it was ridiculous because the lighter-gun could do nothing but light cigarettes; then I realized that its secondary function—as symbol—was really its primary function. As a symbol it said, "Play around with me, fuck with me, insult me, and you have big trouble."

The constant testing of one's manliness in Mexico sometimes reaches ridiculous proportions. I was sitting in the Plaza de Mariaches in Guadalajara when a man came around with a magneto. For a peso you could hold a metal rod in each hand as he twirled the crank to test your ability to withstand a shock. At the table next to mine sat six Mexicans and their wives or girlfriends. At first they ignored the magneto man, but when one of the men was finally persuaded to grab the metal rods, both the magneto man and I knew that each man at the table would pay his peso to test his strength. Sure enough, the metal rods journeyed around the complete circle, each man holding on grimly as the electric shock surged through him. After each man in turn had received a jolt, the first *macho* told the magneto man to turn the current up before he tried it again. Again the rods circled the table. Fortunately the magneto's power was limited, or the rods would have circled the table until one of the men had proved that he had real *huevos*, the implication being that the rest of the men were pussies.

Under different circumstances this attitude can lead to a fatal confrontation between Mexicans. If the magneto had been a gun, the men would have been playing Russian roulette. Each man would have had to spin the chamber and pull the trigger. The game has to go on until one man is the winner or one man the loser. If one man had refused to play, then he would be the loser, and the butt of jokes for the rest of the night. He would also, I imagine, take the pressure off his companions. The term *macho* implies the existence of its opposite, and it's someone's lack of *huevos* which enhances the *huevos* of the rest of the crowd. Quite often in Mexico the tongue replaces the gun in contests of superiority, and Mexicans have raised to a high level the art of cutting, or repartee. Similar to the verbal game called the dozens, played by Blacks in the U.S., the Mexican's verbal jibes and puns are usually imbued with heavy sexual overtones and innuendos. The *macho* uses words to wound and defeat and defend; naturally there is always the possibility that the dude who runs out of verbal ammunition will resort to his final weapon—the bullet. Under certain circumstances though, the *macho* loses his balls if he resorts to violence. I was in a whorehouse where a *maricón* was teasing a *charro*. The *charro* had come in from a day's fiesta and was dressed in his finery, tight leggings, wide-brimmed sombrero, inlaid boots, and a very large pistol strapped to his side. The *maricón* was getting laughs from the crowd by mimicking the *charro*, prancing behind him, making obscene humping gestures as he walked. Under the circumstances the *charro* was helpless except for his tongue. With words he could do battle with the homosexual; if he resorted to his gun or fists, he would be putting himself in the same position as the queer, ball-less, without *huevos*, an object of ridicule and scorn.

Machismo has come under severe criticism recently, not only in the United States, where feminist forces have seized on the term and its attitude, but also in Mexico itself. Recently José G. Cruz, a millionaire publisher and illustrator of comic books in Mexico City, published a thirty-six-page booklet entitled *El Nefasto machismo* (Tragic Machismo) in an attempt to counteract the violent, exaggerated sense of male superiority and manliness that requires the Mexican man to prove constantly that he is tough and forceful.

Usually Cruz's comic books deal with popular romance and adventure stories or an occasional historical and political biography, but aware that most Mexicans read only comic books, if they read anything, he has recently published comic books dealing with contemporary phenomena. After the student riots of October, 1968, in the Plaza of Tlatelolco in Mexico City, where more than three hundred students were massacred while protesting their country's spending millions of pesos on the Olympic Games while the Mexican people were starving, Cruz published a comic book entitled *Treason to the Fatherland*, wherein he raked the subversive students over the Mexican coals for not loving their country more, and not supporting it in all its manifestations.

When the longhair invasion from the United States began to influence Mexican youths, Cruz published a comic book entitled *La*

Basura hippie (Hippie Garbage). In it he warned his countrymen of the dangers to young Mexicans who imitate the behavior of the perverted American youths from up north. Cruz describes the Hippie Garbage as "irresponsible, loose-living," and "a dark malignant cancer." The cover depicts a massive pig, behind which sit a dude and a chick with long hair and beads, marijuana smoke curling around their faces. He ends the booklet with a patriotic plea to Mexican mothers to raise their children with a sense of cleanliness, beauty, and personal decorum.

Despite efforts such as José Cruz's to counteract some of the manifestations of machismo, however, the attitude is ingrained in the Mexican psyche, and will be for a long time. Not all connotations of machismo are negative. *Macho,* in certain circumstances, implies good qualities that have nothing to do with an exaggerated sense of manliness, or the need to be forceful and tough. A Mexican who is *macho* can be a dude who is straight, who will back you up in an emergency, who will not let you down.

The term *macho* is difficult to understand because, like many words which are used to describe attitudes, it has as many meanings as there are inflections in the human voice. The way the word is spoken can denote a certain thing; whether the term is cut off short or drawn out, and what the eyes are doing while the tongue is speaking, all lend import to the particular meaning intended at the moment. Understanding the various meanings does not come from studying, but from the incidents themselves.

I leaned against the adobe hut and watched the Mexicans playing with their pistols. For a fleeting moment I imagined myself making some blunder, a gesture or word that insulted one of them. The thought was not entirely without justification. Once in a bar in Patzcuaro I innocently declined a drink offered by a drunk campesino—and quickly regretted it. The campesino was insulted that I refused to drink with him and pulled out his pistol. Needless to say, I hastily apologized. "A thousand pardons, señor, I misunderstood you," I said, gulping the drink down. One does not refuse a drink when it is offered in a bar in rural Mexico. You understand this or you don't enter rural bars. Naturally custom dictates that once you have accepted a man's hospitality, you then offer your own, so I bought a drink for the campesino. Many drinks later we both staggered out of the cantina and into the street. While the campesino weaved and groped for his pistol so he could demonstrate his marksmanship on the street lights, I fled down the street to my home, drunker and wiser.

Rural Mexico is ritualistic, and the mountain dwellers of Mexico are the most ritualistic of all. While watching the men play with their guns I thought of Jesse's and my position. We were essentially alone in the mountains, at Sanchez' mercy, with almost $5,000 in our pockets. Neither Jesse nor I carried a gun. I knew that if a Mexican was insulted, or even thought he had been insulted, likely as not he would draw his gun and shoot. If he killed someone, it would be a run in the

EUGENE ANTHONY

Sierras for him, as the saying goes. Death is not the same in Mexico as it is in the United States. Perhaps because the Mexican lives so close to the earth, he is more prepared to send one or be sent into it. The very aggressiveness toward life of so many Mexicans is a far cry from the aloofness to life that most *norteamericanos* display. For the Mexican death is close. In the United States, death tends to be invisible, and therefore life itself takes on a deathlike quality.

When Sanchez returned, he had only one mule. "The rest of them are in the mountains," he said. "I've sent word up to have the men bring them down. They'll be here in a few hours." We loaded our gear on the one available mule and walked into the village. Mules are at

From the collection of Roberto Ayala

a premium in the mountains. A good one costs about $200. Compared to total income, that's about as much as an American pays for his car. We paid fifty pesos ($4) a day to rent each mule. Because they are so valuable, we hired a boy to come along with us and care for them.

The trail to the village sloped down a bit, then rose to skirt the cliff above the river. The water boiled against the rocky walls of the canyon; trees and bits of timber tumbled in the current. Above the blue slate walls of the canyon, rich, verdant brush took hold and spread up toward the timber line. We walked in single file along the trail, passing through half a dozen tunnels hacked through solid rock. As we emerged from the last tunnel, I saw the village clinging to the cliffs above the river. With its cobblestoned streets, its ancient stone buildings, and the old church thrusting up its lonely spire, it looked like a scene from the Middle Ages.

As we entered the town, I saw the remains of a large sign painted on one of the buildings: *Plata.* We were entering an old silver mining town. I could see the mouths of old tunnels in the cliff face, and a number of abandoned ore cars lying bottom up along the trail. The village was larger than it had seemed from the air. As we entered it I saw the red roof tiles stretching up and around a bend in the river. We passed the church and walked down the narrow streets to the village square. The square was like all other village squares in Mexico, except that this one was in miniature. It measured no more than 40 by 100 feet. The rococo bandstand, with its floral curlicues, colonnades, and grills, looked like an illustration for a children's book.

Sanchez left to check on the mules and Jesse and I sat in the plaza and talked to the crowd of children who gathered around us. Suddenly, as we talked, a door of a house fronting the plaza flew open and Sanchez emerged with a grizzled old campesino in tow. The campesino strode rapidly to where we were sitting and threw his arms around Jesse. After the *abrazo* he thrust a bottle at me. "*¡Aquí señor, toma!*" I looked quizzically at Jesse and Sanchez. "You're being welcomed into town," Jesse said. I reached for the bottle but before I could grab it the old man turned away and strode rapidly back across the plaza toward the open door. I followed Jesse and Sanchez after him.

From the collection of Roberto Ayala

Inside the door was a cantina, really just a bare room with a large plank lying across two barrels. On the wall behind the plank bar were wooden shelves holding three or four bottles of clear liquid. The adobe walls of the room were blackened by smoke from oil lamps, giving one the impression of being inside a cave. Stooping under the plank, the old man, Refugio, pulled the string that lit a dim light bulb and grabbed three glasses from under the bar, wiping them thoroughly on the front of his shirt. Filling them carefully to the very brim, he thrust one at me. Somewhat selfconsciously, while the rest of the men watched, I drained my glass in the traditional campesino style, in one gulp. Yak! The stuff hit me immediately. My mouth felt like I had just stuffed a handful of hot coals into it and they were rapidly burning their way down through my guts. With tears streaming from my eyes I held onto the bar, gasping for breath. Neither Sanchez nor Jesse had touched their drinks. Refugio filled my glass again but I shook my head no, I wasn't going to touch that stuff again. As I fought for my breath he calmly poured a little of the liquid out onto the bar and struck a match to it. It burnt with a blue flame as it ran along the bar. Everybody broke into laughter at my expression; it could just as well have been my guts burning there on the bartop. Refugio then took his glass and drained it down without expression. "It's homemade mountain mescal," Jesse said. I nodded my head. I had been initiated.

The village had no restaurant, but we were invited into the home of one of the women who fed campesinos when they came down out of the mountains to go to church on Sunday. Señora Sala's house was a typical adobe mountain home. The kitchen was open to the air and a *pila* containing fresh water stood in the yard. There was a rough wooden table with four chairs beside the *pila*. While her nieces made tortillas, Señora Sala prepared chicken *mole,* a dish cooked in a hot sauce.

Everything was done in the old way: the adobe oven, the charcoal stove, the rough-hewn table, the utensils—all had centuries of use behind them. Even the sounds were old, the slap-slap of the girls' hands as they worked the tortilla dough, the clack of the mules' hoofs on the cobblestones outside. The scene in Señora Sala's house was to

From the collection of Roberto Aya

repeat itself again and again in the mountains, each time we stopped to eat or rest. The ancient, patient manner of the women, who knew exactly what their tasks were, who knew that when the men came in to eat, no matter what the time, they were to be fed. Wherever we went in the following weeks, when we arrived at a small hut stuck away in a mountain canyon, the man was always there to invite us in and the woman always ready with food on the table.

While we were eating, the mules Sanchez had arranged to rent were brought down from the fields by their owners and tied up outside the house. "Why don't the campesinos use horses?" I asked Sanchez. "They are no good in the mountains," he replied. "They don't have the balance or the stamina of good mules."

When I looked sceptical, Sanchez explained further. "The trails here in the mountains are very steep. Sometimes there are no trails at all. At night a horse will get frightened and slip and maybe fall. Mules can see in the dark, also they can carry a much heavier burden much farther than a horse. No one uses horses in the mountains, they are impractical."

Later on I saw a horse in the village square. It seemed out of place. Sanchez saw me looking at it. "It's not used to go up into the Sierras," he said. "The man who owns him only rides on Sunday."

After eating, we packed our gear on the mules and said our good-byes. Raul, the young man Sanchez had hired to care for the animals, came over to me and double-checked my load. He untied my trucker's knot, which I was extremely proud of, and bound my load down with rawhide thongs, then led us through the village toward the trail. I looked in the open windows of the houses as we walked through the village and saw dark eyes staring out at me. Occasionally a young girl's face would appear and then abruptly disappear. I was worried about mounting my mule because I had never ridden before and I didn't want to look ridiculous. When the village ended and the trail began, Raul motioned me up on my animal and we were off.

The mules set a brisk pace and I felt myself bouncing up and down like an idiot. At a wide spot in the trail I let Jesse and Raul go by me

From the collection of Roberto Ayala

and then brought up the rear. I wanted to learn how to ride with no eyes on me. When we came to the first switchback in the trail I turned around and looked back at the village. It had lost all appearance of a village; the red-tile rooftops were linked together in a ragged jigsaw puzzle, a geometric pattern reminding me of a cubist painting. The houses and church looked like huge tumbled rocks and boulders which had lodged along the banks of the river. Above me the mountains beckoned, stretching higher and higher, peaks folding into other peaks like gigantic steps leading into the clouds. Far above, the brilliant blue sky stretched over everything, a majestic sea rolling over the whole world.

There was no noise except that of my own animal. The silence was incredible, a quietness beyond the creaking leather stretched over wooden saddles, the iron hoofbeats on rocks. As I looked down into the valley the silence seemed to beat up out of the canyons, permeating everything. The world seemed to have come to a halt along the river. As I watched, a lone hawk dropped below me, circling from one saddlehorn of rock to another, far, far below.

We rode for two days, climbing higher and higher into the steep canyons. The trail was steep at times, and at other times it simply meandered along the ridges. Space and silence were everywhere, mile after mile of rolling ridges sweeping westward toward the sea. Fantastic cumulus clouds paraded over our heads like vast ships struggling over mountainous waves. When we crossed arroyos, leaves swept up out of them, borne upward by the stiff breezes blowing out of the canyons. At times we rode through fields of yellow flowers, so tall and profuse we lost sight of one another. Other times we picked our way past cornfields, the furrows planted on hillsides so steep it seemed impossible anyone could stand there, let alone till and work.

Occasionally we met other riders on the trail, *montañes, los que viven en las montañas*—those that live in the mountains. Inevitably they appeared out of nowhere, silent, many of them carrying weapons on their backs. Whenever we met them, we would stop. Sanchez would converse with the men, slowly, courteously, the conversations

Photo overleaf by Eugene Anthony

From the collection of Roberto Ayala

echoing with a strange formality. If there were young boys in the group, inevitably they would reach out and take Sanchez' hand and kiss it. The gesture surprised me. I saw Raul do it when we first hired him to care for the mules, but I thought it was a gesture of thankfulness. The gesture was repeated often though, always with young men reaching out and kissing Sanchez' hand. I realized it was part of the mountain code, the way the young men showed their respect for an older, dignified visitor. Sanchez was no stranger to these mountains. I saw that he was considered an important person, someone to be honored and respected. The mannerism seemed rooted in the past. I spoke to Jesse about it later, and he said the gesture was the result of a cultural accident. During the 1860s, when Juarez was climaxing his drive to rid Mexico of Maximilian and the French, a number of French soldiers deserted and fled into the mountains. The ones who survived assimilated with the Indians, marrying and having children. The offspring of these children still lived in the mountains, light-skinned, blue-eyed campesinos. Many of the campesinos back at the airstrip where Jesse and I first arrived in the mountains had strikingly blue eyes and fair skin. Jesse said they were a legacy of the French soldiers who had fled into the mountains, and the custom of kissing the hand was a legacy of those same Frenchmen.

Entering the Sierras of Mexico is like entering a world bypassed by time. The mountains themselves take on a prehistoric quality, and I found myself drifting off into vague reveries about "first man." Occasionally I got separated from the rest of the party by a half-hour or so, and when that happened a strange feeling crept over me. I wasn't frightened; in fact, the feeling was quite nice. But I had never felt more alone. The ridges above me and the valleys below me took on an abstract quality, a tentativeness that brought my whole existence into question. I began to wonder who I was. I could feel myself becoming amorphous, drifting out over the ridges and mountain tops. When that happened I spurred my mule to catch up with the rest of the group.

At times the trail was so steep we had to dismount and walk beside our animals. Sanchez had incredible stamina, tramping up the trail with a steady pace that left the rest of us far behind. My ass felt like raw hamburger from the hard wooden saddle, and I welcomed each moment of walking. I had long since removed my jacket and shirt to pad my saddle. Each moment on the mule's back was agony, and I gazed upward longingly, hoping our destination was in sight.

I am proud to report that before I left the mountains I was riding as well as any man, the campesinos themselves complimenting me. Now though, each rest period was like a reprieve from hell, and when Sanchez motioned for us to stop, I fell off my mule and lay panting on the ground. During rest periods I gazed down the trail we had climbed and saw it disappear in shadows far below.

In the late afternoon of the third day, we passed the first dwellings I had seen since leaving the village—a nest of adobe huts perched on the edge of a field. The field was fenced off with a stone wall. People watched as we passed, saluting Sanchez, who waved back from his mule. Across an arroyo I saw a large two-story adobe house. One end of the house was buried under a magnificent bougainvillaea. I pointed it out to Jesse. "That's where we're going to spend the night," he said.

The house looked magnificent in the late afternoon sun. The rough adobe walls and dull-red tiles contrasted beautifully with the brilliant blue and purple flowers of the bougainvillaea. The house belonged to Sanchez' family. At the moment, Rafael, Sanchez' brother, ran the place.

As we dismounted, three men and two women came out to greet us. We shook hands all around and the men took our mules away to be fed and watered. The women invited me and Jesse into the house. The house was immense, with a large back room containing two old-fashioned beds and a loft which was reached by a crude wooden ladder. The front of the house had a patio-like room whose walls were a series of arches open to the outside. One wall of the patio-room was waist high, beyond which was the kitchen, ancient, dark, exuding exciting smells.

It was harvest time and the floor of the patio was covered with piles of beans and pea pods. Sacks of beans stood in the corners, and two young girls were busy shelling peas, their hands moving swiftly over the piles. On the walls hung the working paraphernalia of the mountains: mule trappings and leather lariats, blankets and halters, and a romantic 1940 calendar depicting a bandit and his beautiful señorita in their mountain hideaway, the bandit either just returning or just leaving, the girl in tears at the door. In the corners of the room hung strings of chilis and corn and onions.

The two women who ran the household were Sanchez' mother and Rafael's wife. They bustled into the kitchen after we arrived and soon the smell of boiling coffee filled the house.

The two women worked in the kitchen in perfect harmony, each knowing exactly what to do, one stirring pots and cutting pieces of chicken, the other slapping cornmeal into tortillas and preparing the coffee. I mentioned the harmony to Jesse. "No one seems to be the boss," I said.

"There's no need for anyone to be boss," Jesse said. "There's just work to be done. Mexican women have no jealousies or animosities when their men come in from the fields, they know exactly what to do."

I thought of the States, where every kitchen is a sanctuary which other women enter at their peril. In rural Mexico, tasks have not yet been broken down into ill-defined areas. In the mountains every job is explicit, the woman's in the house among house things, the man's in the field among the animals and outside things. The intermingling of tasks that has appeared with the lessening of roles in the United States was not apparent here in the mountains.

"Women's liberation is a luxury of bored women," Jesse said. "Here in the mountains a woman does not have time to be bored. It would be ridiculous for a Mexican man to go into the kitchen, he would never do it. If he did the woman would laugh him out of the house."

I was interested in what Jesse said. During my years in Mexico I had often observed the rigid separation of duties in the typical Mexican household. Although the separation was tending to break down a little among urban Mexicans—despite the cult of machismo—here in the mountains there was absolutely no sign of a breakdown. At the same time I couldn't get over the feeling that women—or at least the idea of woman—tended to dominate Mexican society. There was always the image of the woman, the earth mother, the hovering female presence that seemed to loom over everything like a vast, brooding bird with soft, warm wings. Despite the super-masculinity of the typical Mexican's attitudes, I felt Mexico to be a feminine country.

When the food was ready, Jesse, Sanchez and I were seated. I was given the first helping, hot chicken *mole* and tortillas, rich black beans, and a large mug of steaming black coffee loaded with sugar. I tore into my food. I especially dug the chicken *mole,* piping hot with a rich, chocolatey taste. Chicken is evidently the only meat eaten in the mountains except on special occasions, for in every house we entered we were fed chicken *mole* or some variation thereof.

After Jesse and I were through eating, the other men sat down beside Sanchez and ate, the women serving second and third helpings of whatever was desired. I noticed that after all the men had eaten, the women themselves sat down to eat. They had cheated a little though: while they were cooking, both of them continually stuck morsels into their mouths.

After eating I walked outside and stood under the bougainvillaea, gazing into the valley below. I saw the shadows of clouds moving across the valley floor, soft, ominous shapes almost invisible except for the muted changes they made in the colors of the trees and rocks and canyon walls. The vast panorama below me appeared like a vague Technicolor dream, the shapes and shadows shimmering in a delicate light. Across the canyon I saw the peaks of other mountains, one after another, marching westward to the sea.

After everyone had eaten, we saddled up again and began the final leg of our journey up to the fields. Jesse and I wanted to inspect the fields, and Sanchez wanted us to hurry so we could return to the house before dark.

We climbed steadily for two hours, passing through grasslands, cornfields, and barren, rocky stretches of land. Finally we entered a grove of oddly formed trees whose limbs were twisted as though tortured by the hardships of their lives, or a fanatical gardener had

From the collection of Roberto Ayala

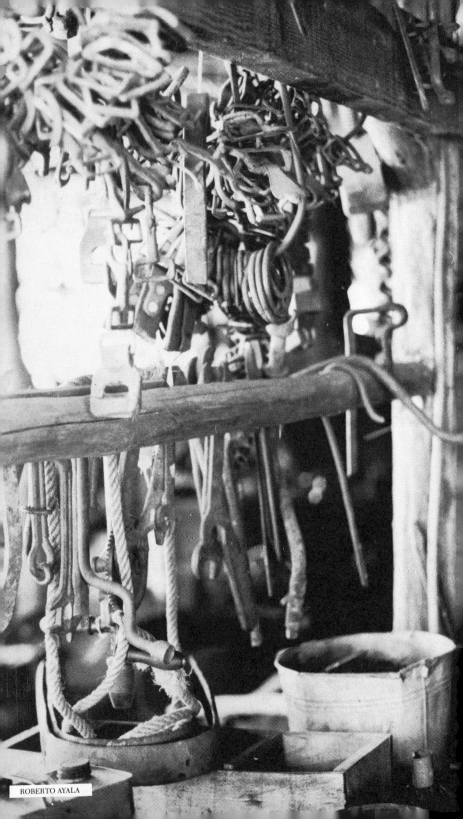

ROBERTO AYALA

spent years misshaping them into weird mountain topiary. Beyond the ill-formed trees we entered the final rise of the mountain, heading up a chasm formed between two high ridges. At the head of the chasm Sanchez raised his gun and fired, signaling the man guarding the field that we were coming. We all dismounted. From here on we would walk.

We tied our mules to some bushes and followed Sanchez up a steep, narrow trail. The undergrowth was so dense we had to fight our way through it in many places. About 200 yards up the trail, Sanchez signaled us to be quiet, then he cupped his hands to his mouth and yodeled into the distance.

The sound of my breathing seemed much too loud as I waited with the others for the answering call. When it came, Sanchez started down the trail, crossed a small stream, and climbed another slope toward the marijuana field. Jesse and I hurried after him.

When we reached the field, I saw the farmer scurry into the underbrush, his gun on his back. The marijuana plants stirred softly in the breeze and the sun glinted off the bright golden leaves. Jesse and I looked at one another; we had made it! Row after row of cannabis plants stretched quietly up the hillside. A lower half of the field was in the process of being planted. The rows had been tilled, and an irrigation hose fed water to each terrace. The upper half of the field was redolent with hemp, the foxtails glistening in the late afternoon sunlight.

Leaving us standing beside the field, Sanchez climbed the path skirting the field and disappeared into the brush. Jesse and I carried our gear up to the middle terrace and I sat down to rest under a small tree. A cool breeze played over the field, and it felt good to lie back in the shade and think of the long journey that had brought us here. More than six weeks of work and sweat and hardships. If nothing else happened, if we went no further than this, to me it was still worth it.

Jesse, perhaps, thought differently. It was getting late and he didn't waste time musing. He worked his way down the rows of plants, inspecting each one by squeezing the *colas*. If the grass is good, a sticky residue of cannabin will stick to your hand when you grasp the foxtail. After squeezing half a dozen plants, Jesse held up his hand and smiled. His palm was covered with resin. By the time Sanchez returned, Jesse had inspected half the field. We walked back down the trail to our mules and set out for the rancho. In the morning we would return and talk to the man who owned the field.

That evening Jesse and I gorged ourselves on the dinner Señora Sanchez prepared. After dinner we sat back and looked at the stars while Sanchez broke out a bottle of mescal. Everything was beautiful, the incredible starlight, the mountains, the shrill sound of the cicadas. We talked for an hour or so, then I left the group to relax under the bougainvillaea with a joint. The moon disappeared behind a cloud and

Photo overleaf by Roberto Ayala

ROBERTO AYALA

ROBERTO AYALA

the stars came down to join me, seeming to share in my contentment. Seeing the stars so bright reminded me of a night in Big Sur when I had dropped some acid and walked out on my porch to gaze at the stars; every constellation seemed hand-drawn, golden lines connecting stars into instantly recognizable pictures, Andromeda, the Pleiades, all the constellations one read about but never saw. In my acid hallucination I recognized every constellation and knew where the Mayans got their images. They came from the stars! The geometric configurations which I had seen on the temples of Chichen Itza and Bonampac stared down at me from the heavens. I remembered standing on my porch in Big Sur transfixed; I was wearing a Huichole Indian costume that I had bought from an Indian in Tepic, and the sense of drama was so great that it seemed like I was being drawn up into the heavens, sucked into a vortex, attracted and frightened at the same time. My fixation on the stars that night in Big Sur was so profound that for a moment I was afraid for my sense of reality. With the least prodding I would have stepped off my porch (there was a thirty-five-foot drop to the ground) to join them. At that moment I decided that such distances were beyond me, so I stepped back inside.

Tonight was different. I hadn't taken any acid, just smoked some good dope, and as the moon moved in and out of the clouds, the stars dimmed and the landscape took on a soft, unearthly glow. The whirring of the cicadas gradually ceased, and in the distance I could hear a mule cough, then the yapping of some dogs. I spread my poncho on the ground underneath the bougainvillaea. As I was stretching out, Señora Sanchez, Rafael's wife, came out of the house and grabbed my shoulder. *"Venga, venga,"* she said. I got up and followed her. She led me inside to her bedroom and pointed at her bed. *"Es suyo,"* she said (It's yours). I stared at her in stupefaction. Jesse looked up from the circle of men sitting in the patio. "The guest always gets the master bed," he said. "They're doing you an honor." "I don't want the master bed, I want to sleep out under the stars." Jesse grinned. "Too bad, if you refuse they'll be insulted."

Dumbly, I walked outside and dragged in my sleeping bag. I knew

I couldn't offend Rafael's hospitality. I threw my bag on the bed and began undressing. I felt miserable. To add to my embarrassment, everyone watched as I took off my clothes. They stared in surprise when they saw I wore no undershorts. The señora blushed and quickly turned her back. I blushed too, feeling more stupid by the minute. I had undressed in front of everyone because everyone was standing in the room and I thought that that was part of the custom too. The men grinned at my discomfort. I was suddenly too tired to care.

As I crawled into my bag, Señora Sanchez returned and began yanking blankets out of the corner. I asked her what she was doing. "I am going outside, señor, to make a bed so I can sleep." I leaped out of bed. "Wait!" I cried. I grabbed my clothes and struggled into them, stumbling outside. The men looked up from their discussion. "Where're you going?" Jesse asked. "I'm not going to take her bed, she has to sleep on the ground if I do." "Don't worry about it." "Bullshit!" I said. "I'm not going to sleep in that bed, courtesy or no courtesy!"

The men laughed as I stumbled over them, dragging my sleeping bag behind me. Stammering, I turned to Rafael. "Señor, I appreciate your courtesy but it is such a wonderful night and I really desire to sleep out under the stars tonight." "¿Cómo no?" Rafael answered. He stood up and grabbed several large burlap sacks, the kind marijuana is stored in, and spread them out on the ground. I rolled my bag out on the sacks and crawled inside. My high, which I had completely lost in the bed hassle, returned and once again I gazed up at the stars. They moved with unearthly stillness across the heavens, seeming to be close at hand and infinitely far at the same time.

The next day we returned to the field. José, the farmer who had disappeared with Sanchez when we arrived the day before, was waiting for us. He was a small, thin man with a pockmarked face. He stood beside his mule, which was tethered under a tree.

Both Jesse and I were carrying our cameras. José looked at them suspiciously. Sanchez explained to José that we wanted to photograph the field, and get some pictures of him as he worked. José looked at us uncomprehendingly, his eyes darting from our faces to the cameras. He looked at us as if we were holding guns on him. The idea that

someone would come all the way into the mountains to take pictures of his field was crazy. He shook his head from side to side.

"José," Sanchez said, "these men are good friends of Jesus. He brought them up here; they come with his recommendation."

"*Claro, hombre,*" José said, "but this is my field. Jesus does not pay me to grow mota. If the señores want to buy mota I will sell it, but I cannot make any money with pictures. . . ."

Jesse and I looked at one another. This is what we had expected but had hoped it wouldn't happen. The Mexican campesino is naturally distrustful, not only of gringos with cameras, but of anything outside his mountains. José had no reason to let us approach his fields, let alone film him working in them. He was in a peculiar position because of our friendship with Jesus, however, and I could see he was uncomfortable. All the same, he was adamant. He wasn't going to let us photograph anything.

Sanchez said nothing, just stood beside his mule looking unconcerned. For him the trip meant being paid to guide us. It did not matter whether our trip was successful or not. I could sense that he too was uneasy around our cameras. Both of the men were probably thinking that Jesus was a fool for letting Jesse and me come into the mountains in the first place. My feelings were ambivalent. On the one hand I respected José, and on the other I was pissed off that he was making our job difficult. Jesse was more practical, however. He put his camera away and told me to do likewise. "*Bueno, hombre,*" he nodded to Jose. "Forget the cameras. We'll help you work in the field."

ROBERTO AYALA

With our cameras out of the way, José loosened up. We followed him along the rows of plants as he displayed his crop. He was proud of his work. Many of the farmers in the mountains are relatively unsophisticated when it comes to growing weed, throwing seeds into the ground and forgetting them, except for minimal clearing and care, until they are ready to harvest. José obviously was different. He took care of his plants, and the field showed it. Each plant had a small dike built up around it for irrigation. All the rocks had been cleaned out of the field and tossed into the arroyo below. The field itself was terraced down the hillside in two-foot-wide steps, and each row of plants was slightly higher than the one below it. As we moved along the rows, José stopped at each plant and plucked off a few bottom leaves—the garbage leaves, he called them. He was trimming the leafy growth that produced little cannabin but at the same time used up a lot of the nutrients that should be going into the rest of the plant.

José had fifty-pound sacks of commercial chemical fertilizer that had been supplied by Jesus. In the old days, he explained, when marijuana had been cultivated by Indians, each plant was fertilized with a small fish buried alongside it. I queried José about the practice, wondering how the Indians got the fish up into the mountains. He was vague. Later Jesse confirmed his story. In the old days, however, there had been no danger in cultivating marijuana since there was no law against it, and it was grown freely in the lowlands. "Grass was very popular with the Indians of ancient Mexico," Jesse said. "They used it as a medicine." I knew that many Indians in Mexico did use grass medicinally. When I visited Quintana Roo in the late fifties, marijuana grew wild everywhere. Once I stopped at a Mayan settlement along the coast and one of the delicacies I was offered was grass—not as a high but simply as an Indian remedy for fatigue.

As we followed him down the rows, José caressed each plant, holding out the long branches to show off the colas. The average height of the plants was approximately seven feet, and each cola was about ten to twelve inches long, thick with resin and seeds. José explained that high noon was the best time to harvest the plants because the resin oozed out of the plant in the hot sun and glistened on the leaves. In late afternoon the resin was sucked back into the plant, and the leaves were relatively unsticky. He grabbed a cola and squeezed it. When he held up his hand, his palm glistened with resin.

Every so often I noticed a dried, frazzled-looking plant which looked dead. I asked José about them. He said that they were the *hombre,* or male, plants, and most of them were pulled out of the ground before the female plants matured. His explanation was that if they were left growing they would fecundate the female plants and thereby decrease the resin content of the flowers. I asked him how come all the male plants were not removed from the fields. He shrugged his shoulders. "It's not necessary," he said, and let it go at that.

One of the myths among cannabis aficionados is that the male plant must be removed from the fields before it fertilizes the female plant. José's confirmation interested me, but what interested me even more was that he felt he could safely leave a few male plants in the field. He seemed to think that a little pollen wouldn't hurt his crop, perhaps reasoning that it would be cruel to deny the female plants all male companionship. I knew that the female plants were pollinated by the action of the wind, not by insects, and I reasoned that such a minute number of male plants could hardly fertilize more than a few dozen female plants. Nevertheless, as we walked down the rows I saw that all the male plants were dry, shriveled husks, obviously beat after supplying so many females with their pollen.

The process of marijuana cultivation has changed considerably in the last few years. Before weed got popular the whole process of growing, packing, selling, and shipping was extremely casual, with few standards. This casualness was epitomized in the mountains, where, for the most part, the farmers simply threw seeds in the ground before the rainy season began and then harvested the grass when the plants looked mature. Any other agricultural considerations were unheard of. The quality of the grass that resulted could be anything from substandard to dynamite, depending on a number of circumstances. If the soil was especially fertile, the sun reasonably hot, water abundant, and the plants allowed to mature properly, then more than likely the weed would be potent. On the other hand, if the soil was poor, water scarce, and the growing season short, garbage grass would be the result. The casual cultivation by the farmers was due partly to the nature of the cannabis plant itself, which grows wild wherever seeds are dropped. In the years since the marijuana business has become serious, the cultivation techniques employed by the farmers have improved.

In the first place, many entrepreneurs began to provide growers, along with tools and equipment, potent seed, probably the single most important factor in producing powerful weed. They also impressed upon their growers that care was needed to produce higher-quality weed, and that better weed would bring more money. Now farmers like Rafael prepare their fields carefully. When the seedlings emerge from the ground, they are meticulously cared for. In Mexico the first crop is planted in May or June, right before the rainy season begins. In a few weeks the seedlings emerge from the ground and must be protected from rabbits and deer and other predators. In a month or so the plants are from a foot to three feet tall, and the farmer must spend every day in his field. Quite often he lives beside his field in a small hut.

It's hard work for a farmer to grow a marijuana crop because he must also take care of his corn or bean crop, which is often hours away from his weed patch. Successful weed farmers sometimes hire other men to care for their corn and bean fields, and sometimes a few farmers will band together in a weed patch, sharing the work. This has become especially common in the last few years as the demand for weed has increased. The cooperatives work together not only for security, but also because of the sheer amount of labor involved. After the plants have shown their sex, the male plants are removed from the field. Then comes the job of trimming the garbage leaves, or fingers, as they are called, from the female plants. It is a pruning process that goes on as long as the plants are growing. The farmer must make sure his plants receive enough water, but not too much, for too much water will cause the roots to rot. The best soil for growing marijuana is light and sandy, the kind that water drains through quickly. Usually water is no problem for the first crop since plenty of rain falls in the high mountains during the season. It is the second crop, the one planted in October, that needs watching. The second crop must be irrigated, and many farmers string plastic pipe from a nearby stream down to their field. Obtaining the plastic pipe is next to impossible for the unaffiliated farmer. It is the farmers who are linked with entrepreneurs like Jesus who are able to string irrigation pipe to their fields.

Before weed got popular, few farmers bothered growing two crops, most of them being content with the one crop that grew during the rainy season. Like everything else though, success breeds industry, and now many farmers grow two crops. Some even attempt to grow three crops in one year but few areas in Mexico are suited to support three growing seasons. Most of the weed grown in these four-month periods is harvested while immature, and therefore is not of very high quality.

The average growing period for marijuana is six months. In that time the plants have a chance to mature properly and to flower. The harvesting time is crucial for good marijuana. If the plant is left in the ground too long after blossoming, it will lose a lot of its potency. Most farmers harvest their weed a week or so after the flowers bloom, cutting them down during the hottest part of the day when the resin is thick on the leaves.

Jesse and I worked all day with José, helping him trim the garbage leaves off each plant and repairing the dikes that had fallen down. Each dike was carefully cleaned of weed and debris and then rebuilt, leaving a small aperture for water on the upper edge. At the end of the rainy season water gets scarce in the higher canyons so José had constructed an elaborate irrigation system to water his plants. The system involved a small dam which he had built across a nearby stream and a long ditch from the dam to the field. In the ditch he buried 400 feet of plastic irrigation line, covering it with leaves and dirt so it couldn't be spotted from the air. When he watered the plants he moved the end of the irrigation line up and down his field, feeding each terrace individually. The water would run down the terrace and fill each dam through the little gaps we had left. Each plant was watered twice a week. The soil in José's field was light and sandy and perfectly suited for his crop. Although the plants didn't grow tall (José explained that he kept them trimmed down to avoid detection), they did spread out quite fully. Each day José devoted half his time to his field, trimming the garbage leaves, checking for rodents and pests, and repairing his dams. In two or three weeks his field would be ready for harvesting.

In the days before marijuana was as popular as it is now, at harvest time the whole plant was cut down. After the weed had cured for awhile, and sometimes even before it had properly cured, all of the leaves and stems and flowers were bricked together, with no attempt at segregating the good parts from the mediocre. Now the farmers are more particular, primarily because of the fuss made by smugglers and entrepreneurs, and the plant is carefully separated into different parts before it is packaged. First the colas are cut off the growing plant and dried separately. The colas are the most potent part of the marijuana plant. They are the flowering tips and most of the cannabin resin is concentrated in them. After the colas are cut off, the plant is often allowed to grow another two weeks or so before the rest of the plant is harvested. When the plant is finally cut, the bottom half is segregated from the top half. The top part of the plant is considered quality grass, and the bottom provides commercial grass, not the quality of the top half or the colas, but still good enough to get you stoned.

One interesting development in the last few years is the growth of super grass, or dynamite, as it's called in the trade. Before 1966, any marijuana that made its way up to the United States was eagerly gobbled up by incipient heads, quality not being much of a consideration. The only criterion was availability. With the popularization of marijuana and the growing sophistication on the part of so many smokers, however, a demand for better quality began—especially among the young professionals and rock musicians who had money. They would get a taste of some especially succulent variety and realize what grass could be, so they started demanding quality. Many of them started subsidiary careers in smuggling to provide the kind of grass they and their friends wanted.

During the early days of weed smuggling it was never easy to score quality grass, however, simply because there just wasn't much available. In the middle sixties, when Jesse and I were providing a fair amount of grass to the San Francisco Bay area, it was relatively easy to sell anything, and a deal never fell through because of quality. One time, though, when we were making our rounds a customer handed us a small can with some grass in it. "That's the kind of grass I want," he said. Inside the can there was an ounce of weed, golden and sweet smelling. When lit it burnt sweetly and caused harsh coughing for a moment until the high took hold. It was the remnants of a mature cola, and the dude had tasted enough grass to know that with some imagination and bread he could probably find a source for it. Jesse and I took the can of grass with us when we returned to Mexico and showed it to a number of entrepreneurs. Naturally every entrepreneur we showed it to said that he could provide the same type of weed. When it got down to the actual cop, though, we found that few of them could, at least in any quantity. This was the first time, to my knowledge, that smugglers had taken a sample down to Mexico to duplicate. The night we showed the sample to our main supplier, he took us into a small town in central Mexico to see a ton of grass that had been set aside for us. To inspect the ton, we pulled out each sack and opened it, searching for the colas. As usual they were mixed up haphazardly with the rest of the grass, and it was a tedious job separating them. The Mexicans stood around dumbfounded as we slowly threw the colas into one stack and the bulk of the plants into another. After working all night we ended up with about 300 pounds of colas, the basis of what was to become known as Michoacan, the super-grass imported from that mountainous state.

Jesse and I became known as the gringos who wanted only *colas de zorras,* the foxtails, and we would pay extra for them. For a long time it was difficult convincing our own entrepreneur that the plants should be segregated as we had done. Eventually we had to drop him and work directly with another man in the mountains. After my arrest in San Luis in 1966, and while I was on probation, Jesse spent many months in the mountains of Guerrero and Michoacan showing the farmers how to segregate the various parts of the plants, instructing them in elemental precautions like not harvesting too soon, waiting for the resin to appear before cutting, then curing the weed properly, which meant slowly. While we were doing this, other smugglers were doing the same thing in other parts of Mexico. One smuggler in particular spent all his time roaming through the small villages of Mexico searching out the particular varieties of grass that were super-stony. Oftentimes there are only a few pounds of heavy dynamite in a whole crop, but if that grass can be found and segregated, then it forms the basis for a business back in the States without equal. Jesse and I never concentrated on this super-special type of weed that could only be found in small amounts; what we were after were relatively large shipments of Gold, the kind of weed that no sophisticated head will refuse.

Quality is still the exception rather than the rule in the Mexican grass industry. There are hundreds of gringo smugglers who are so eager to cop any type of grass that they will pay high prices for garbage and consequently spoil the industry for those who are constantly seeking to improve quality. Many times Jesse and I have gone to bid on a crop and found ourselves dealt out by our own high standards—simply because there was some *gringo rico* who was eager to buy the whole crop and quality be damned! The Mexican entrepreneur is eager to sell to this type of buyer because he knows he is dealing with an amateur. He also knows that he will receive few complaints from the gringos later. Most entrepreneurs are quite ethical in their dealings, however, despite the ease with which they can sell anything, including garbage weed, to many smugglers. Jesse and I found that reputable entrepreneurs always back up their quality and weight once you have dealt with them for a while. For this reason we usually dealt with the same people, unless they had nothing available. If we or our customers were ever dissatisfied, it was no problem making up on shortages on the next run.

There just isn't enough dynamite grass available. It always amuses me to hear stories, common in the industry, of ton cops of Gold or thousand-kilo scores of Zacatecas Purple. I know from my own experience in copping some of the best grass in Mexico that it is rare to score 500 kilos of really top-quality marijuana. Often you will find that 75 percent of such a score is high quality and the rest is average, or just the reverse. Smugglers who have established connections and routes in the mountains are the ones who usually score the best grass. In the last few years some high-powered Mexican entrepreneurs have started warehousing the colas from their crops and selling them in pound lots for very high prices. There are some warehouses in Mexico where, during the height of the season when lots of grass is available, knowledgeable smugglers can walk down row after row of kilos and pick the type they want—by the variety and price, Gold going for so much a pound, and Michoacan for so much less, etc. Dynamite weed, however, doesn't stay around any warehouse long.

The mythology of the weed business is manifested in the names for the different varieties of marijuana peddled in the last few years. The mystique of the name is quite often more important to the dealer and user than is the weed itself. Heads love to sit around and rap about the fine Gold or Panama Red or Colombian they enjoyed last week, and dealers pride themselves on being the bearer of the latest, loadiest variety.

There is a type of marijuana that turns the color of light gold when it is cured. The marijuana is favored by a good climate, rich soil, and a high altitude. Because it grows in the mountains surrounding the resort city of Acapulco, gringos call it Acapulco Gold.

Ask a Mexican for Acapulco Gold and he will laugh at you. To

him, there's only good weed and bad weed. If the weed is good it will get you high, if it's bad it will give you a headache. Acapulco Gold, however, has become the name for a type of weed which is the standard by which most other varieties of marijuana grown in Mexico are judged, and smugglers vie with one another to cop weed of Gold quality. Since high-quality weed is not confined to the mountains of Guerrero, however, many smugglers score other varieties of weed from different states and label them as Acapulco Gold. In fact, the use of the name Acapulco Gold has become almost a generic name for quality grass, no matter where the weed came from.

Other varieties of marijuana are just as potent as Acapulco Gold, some even more so. Jesse and I were responsible for some of the first loads of Michoacan, named for the state where it's grown, to be brought into the Bay area. The weed has a dark-green color, and a joint of it is comparable to a joint of Gold.

Sinsemilla is another extremely potent grass. The name means "without seeds" in Spanish. For a long time weed mythology had it that Sinsemilla was grown only by women in the high mountainous regions of Oaxaca, in southern Mexico. The truth of the matter is that Sinsemilla is simply a variety of weed that produces fewer seeds than other varieties, although it does produce some, and it is grown in many areas of Mexico, although the best crops are grown south of the Tropic of Cancer. Often the farmers who grow Sinsemilla (men grow the crops) shake the cured plants to remove the few seeds that do actually grow on the colas.

In the late fifties some weed made its way to Chicago wrapped in sugar bags. Smoking the weed left a distinctive, sweet taste in the mouth. That flavor let you know you were smoking Chicago Sugar Bag. Actually the weed was probably a very good-quality grass that had been sugared when it was bricked. Chicago Sugar Bag was a nice name, though, and it stuck.

Zacatecas Purple is a variety of marijuana that grows in a particular high mountain valley in the state of Zacatecas. When cured, the seeds from the colas have a distinctive purple hue, and the weed is extremely potent, especially if it is allowed to cure properly. In the late sixties

Photo overleaf by Eugene Anthony

a beatnik dealer planted a crop using some Zacatecas Purple seeds in the mountains of Big Sur. The resultant weed came to be known as Big Sur Holy Weed, and holy it was, too.

Other varieties of marijuana also exist: Guadalajara Green, Yucatan Red, Colombian Red, Nayarit Yellow, and one of my favorites, Popo Oro, which grew on the slopes of Popocatepetl.

Popo Oro was a special shipment of weed that a smuggler got into San Francisco and sold only to his friends. After the shipment was exhausted the smuggler returned to Mexico to get another load but the grower who had been responsible for the harvest had been wiped out by Federales and the field was gone.

There are also many names that denote bad weed: Culiacan Garbage, Tijuana Regular, Johnson Grass, etc. The need for mythology in the weed business arises out of its illegality, and because the realities of smuggling are unknown to most people. Marijuana smuggling may be no stranger than any other enterprise, but when you have an illegal product, and outlaws bringing that product to you, mythology prevails. The names that are invented to give substance to the myths are real, and will live on long after the weed trip is over.

Quality marijuana is not created by mythology, however, it is created by hard work in the field. Like any crop, the hemp plant improves under the proper circumstances, and rapidly degenerates under adverse circumstances. The simple matter of too much or too little water will drastically alter the resin content of the plant. The plants may be cultivated to throw all their energy into creating fine stalks, producing the good fibers that used to be popular with rope and basket makers. Under different circumstances, with less water and more sandy soil, for instance, the fleshy stalk remains thin and dry and the energy goes into the leaves and flowers—thereby producing more resin, essential for good smoking grass. Hemp plants were once cultivated in the United States for their fiber content, and the descendants of this strain, which grows wild in the Midwest, are still primarily fiber-producing plants, not resin-producing ones. This accounts for the poor high the plants produce. Kids who smoke the leaves produced by Midwestern hemp plants are doomed to bum highs, headaches, and little else. On the other hand, seeds taken from good Mexican hemp plants and cultivated properly will produce grass as good as any available in the world, including the highly touted ganga from Bangkok and the Near East. I have smoked some marijuana grown in various parts of California that was produced from Mexican seeds, and can say that the high experienced was capable of scaring the shit out of anyone, no matter how sophisticated a weed head he pretends to be. My own particular name for this type of grass is "snakes in the trees." When I get loaded on it, every limb on every tree turns into live, writhing snakes.

Few things are more relative than the quality of marijuana. Any knowledgeable dealer realizes that his super-weed may be your bum trip, grass that makes me paranoid may send you into paroxysms of laughter. Serious smugglers know that the super-grass grown in one area may produce a high entirely different from the super-grass grown in another area. I have found, for instance, that grass produced in the mountains of Michoacan, which is of excellent quality and much sought after, gives an entirely different type of high than, say, the grass produced in the state of Jalisco, in central Mexico. Cultivation factors undoubtedly have much to do with the differences, things like soil, water availability, minerals, strain of plant, etc. However, it is difficult convincing buyers that the super-grass they bought last week which produced such a loady high may be no better than the super-grass currently for sale which is just as potent, but produces a completely different type of high.

One of the problems of the industry is that there are no standards and the only way a person can tell what he has is by smoking it. One time I contracted to supply a half-ton of weed to a dealer in Berkeley, a client whose only requirement was that the grass I import be super. Super what, I could have asked him—super downer? super sleeper? super worker? After being in the industry for awhile, knowledgeable smugglers can almost pick their high, the only real problem being to satisfy the particular customer's demands. For many heads the standard for really super-weed is that it knock them on their asses for half a dozen hours. Granted, marijuana that does that is potent, but for me it's a bum high.

I've often been chastised for scoring weed that is mellow, giggly, and kind, rather than the very stony type of grass that renders you comatose for half a day. For some inexplicable reason, known only to those heads who prefer that type of grass, knockout weed is always referred to as the heaviest, the loadiest, when in reality the high may be a bad one. For the next guy, the grass that gives him the giggles for twelve hours is super-grass, a glorious, freewheeling, mirthful high where everything is ridiculous, funny, insane. My own particular delight is the kind of grass that gives me a feeling of mellow contentment, a benevolent, calm, sensual high, turning me onto activity rather than off it, and rendering me completely open to every sense and sensation.

To say that each type of grass is different is also to say that they are the same, however, for the truth of the matter is, all types of grass and every high involve many of the same characteristics. One of the first effects of any strong weed is a slight feeling of paranoia, a paranoia that either goes away after a short time or grows stronger, depending on the circumstances. The user of marijuana will be greatly influenced by the state of his own head, by who he is with, and by where he is at the time he gets stoned. But for those who want a mellow high, for those who like working grass, and for those whose kick is cannabinol knockout drops, all kinds are available, ready for the picking.

One of the unique things about Mexico, aside from the many varieties of marijuana that grow in the country, is that it is the only country in the world that is blessed—or cursed, depending on where your head's at—with over 200 natural hallucinogens. Most of the hallucinogens were known and used by the ancient peoples of Mexico as sacraments in their religious services, and also for medicinal purposes. Many years ago in Mexico I heard a rumor about the existence of a fantastic illustrated manuscript that contains not only sketches and descriptions of the 200 plants, including cacti and mushrooms, many of which are no longer known, but also detailed observations on the various states of mind each hallucinogen puts the user in. The manuscript was supposedly compiled painstakingly over the years by one of the first monks to come to Mexico after the conquest, and has been in the hands of the Vatican for over 300 years.

Of all the hallucinogens illustrated in the manuscript, none is as well known as marijuana. Two others which are only slightly less well known are still used by Indians in Mexico, peyote by the Huichole in the western state of Nayarit, and the magic mushroom by the Zapotec in the southern state of Oaxaca.

Mexicans as a whole frown on the use of hallucinogens, considering them slightly barbaric. During the last few years this attitude has hardened because of the influence gringo youths have on Mexican youths. To the average middle-class Mexican, if such a creature exists, marijuana is *malo,* bad! If anything, his attitude is even more rigid than that of his counterpart in the United States, where the general feeling toward marijuana has been loosening up. For years though, the general conception of marijuana in the United States was that it's a drug used only by black and brown ghetto dwellers and, even worse, artists and Bohemians. In Mexico, according to the Mexican middle class, only Indios and low-class country people smoke marijuana.

It's hard to say who actually does smoke marijuana in Mexico. I have heard countless stories of wiry old campesinos who still work sixteen hours a day in the fields and at night come home to their Corona-size joints; also, who knows how many tokes guys like Rafael and Sanchez take on Sundays before hiking down the mountains to church? When I was in the mountains I seldom saw the farmers smoke any weed, unless I rolled a joint and offered them some. Even then, their acceptance of the joint seemed more a matter of politeness than of desire. When Jesse and I visited growers' huts and sampled various qualities of marijuana, the campesinos always sat back and watched. They seldom smoked themselves. Once I asked Sanchez, "Who smokes mota in Mexico?" He replied, *"La policía y la aduana"* —the police and the customs.

In a sense what Sanchez said was true, even though he meant it partly as a joke. Only Indios and low-class campesinos smoke marijuana, according to the Mexican middle class; only the police and the customs people, according to the Mexican campesino. When the middle-class Mexican scorns weed, though, he is actually scorning the

Indian, the campesino, the people of the fields. When the campesino says that only the police and the customs people smoke marijuana, he is calling them hypocrites because they spend their time arresting farmers who grow and transport marijuana, yet turn around and deal the weed themselves once the farmers are out of the way.

One segment of the Mexican population where the use of marijuana has more or less always been accepted is in the army, where a bag of mota is part of the standard issue, at least in popular Mexican mythology. Whether soldiers are actually issued marijuana, or whether it's just easily available, I haven't been able to ascertain. No one denies, though, that the Mexican soldier has always enjoyed his weed. In most cases marijuana is cheaper than alcohol in Mexico and much easier to obtain. The use of marijuana among soldiers is due also to the fact that most of the troops are campesino conscripts, from the land where weed has always been used.

Jesse and I worked all day in the fields with José, returning to Rafael's house late in the afternoon. Already I was falling into the mountain rhythm, and looked forward to the meal the women were preparing. After unsaddling our mules and washing, I sat among the circle of campesinos who gathered in the patio. I was introduced to Lupe, a tall, thin man who had just arrived. I shook his outstretched hand firmly, then relaxed my grip as a slightly pained, rather bemused look appeared on his face. In my usual gringo enthusiasm, I had forgotten that Mexicans don't shake hands like gringos, and Lupe's dishrag hand was no exception. When I first shook hands with the campesinos I was put off by the limp, listless handshake, having been brought up on the gringo concept that unless a man's handshake is firm and strong, the man himself is somehow weak. For Mexicans the handshake is a formality the strength or weakness of which means nothing. In essence all they do is touch palms. The real greeting among friends in Mexico is the *abrazo,* the arms around the shoulders and the free hand slapping the back. The *abrazo* is done only between friends, however, never new acquaintances like Lupe and me. Later, after we got to know one another and actually became friends, we too would use the *abrazo.*

Lupe was a farmer who had a field elsewhere in the mountains. He had come to Rafael's house when he heard Jesse and I were there. I felt an immediate regard for the man. His thin, narrow face was the color of walnut, and his finely chiseled lips looked like a small girl's. When he talked his eyes flashed, and the quick way he handled the mescal bottle, gesturing with it before and after drinking, revealed an appealing litheness. Lupe smiled when he talked, his lips parting to reveal flashing teeth. "I have very good plants," he said, "and it would be an honor for me to show them to you." Word had gotten out in the mountains that Jesse and I were interested in looking at fields.

While Jesse talked with the men, I cleaned my Polaroid camera. A number of children stood around the circle, their big eyes clamped on me. I aimed the camera at one small boy and clicked it. The children jumped like goats, shrieking with laughter. In a minute I had the print out and the children gathered around. It showed the small boy, a look of mock horror on his face. All the children crowded in to have their pictures taken. I lined them up against the side of the house under the bougainvillaea and aimed the camera. They scowled seriously as the shutter snapped.

Soon every man, woman, and child was crowding around to see the magic prints. I arranged everyone in poses to take best advantage of my limited film supply. Lupe stood in the line, severe and noble, with his hair wetted down and his rifle held across his breast. After all the women and children had prints, the men who had not stood up to be photographed looked at me nervously, not knowing whether to risk it or not. The picture I took of Lupe was magnificent, showing him standing regal and still against the edge of the house. His eyes burnt out of the picture, and I could tell that the rest of the men needed little prodding to stand in front of my camera. Jesse had removed his 35-millimeter camera from its case while I had been shooting the kids, and started photographing. He moved among the people, snapping away. They were disappointed that no magic pictures came instantaneously out of his camera but soon were back dancing in front of my Polaroid. By the time it was dark I had shot up a dozen boxes of film, and everyone held an image of himself in his hand. Even José, who had shied away from our cameras up in his field, stood quiet and

reserved in front of my magic box. He smiled widely when I gave his print to him, blowing on it delicately to dry the sticky coating as he had seen me do.

The next day Jesse and I accompanied Lupe and another campesino named Jorge up to his field. We carried our cameras slung over our shoulders. Lupe's field was on the opposite side of the mountain from José's and it took us half a day to reach it. On the way we passed Lupe's house, a hut made of stones topped with small poles. The poles that formed the upper half of the structure were bound together in a loose weave that allowed the air to pass through. As we approached the hut, Lupe's wife ran inside. It took much coaxing on Lupe's part to get her to come out. Finally she did, three children tagging after her. Lupe wanted me to capture them all with my magic box. When he explained to his wife what he wanted, she rushed the children inside and scrubbed them down and dressed them in their Sunday clothes. The children hung behind their mother's skirt, shyly peeking out as I focused on them. Lupe dressed in his Sunday finery also, and I took another picture of him, then the whole family together. The simplicity and grace with which they posed touched me. For them it was indeed a magic instrument, never before seen in the mountains. When Jesse moved around the group with his camera they paid no attention, assuming he was pretending, since nothing came out of his box.

After the picture-taking, Lupe's wife fed us. She moved about her open hearth gracefully, slapping the tortillas into shape. The fare was simple, beans and tortillas and coffee, but we ate with relish. After lunch we continued on to Lupe's field, which was hidden away in a remote arroyo.

One of the things that surprised me when I first set eyes on the marijuana fields was their size. I had expected big fields, plantations really, but what I found were small plots, most of them encompassing less than half an acre, cultivated in arroyos and along rivers. Obviously they were kept small so they wouldn't be detected. Lupe's field was typical, a long, thin patch of weed growing in a steep arroyo. The slopes above the arroyo were covered with corn, and tall corn plants

even grew among the marijuana. From the distance of a few meters the field couldn't be detected. Most of the farmers in this particular mountainous region kept the location of their fields secret—even from their neighbors. Still, there was a loose pattern of familiarity among the growers, the unspoken commandment being that no one visited another grower's field unless specifically invited to do so. Most of the fields were one-man, or more correctly, one-family operations, being cultivated jointly with a crop of corn or beans or melons. The farmer would work his food crop during the morning and then spend the afternoon caring for his marijuana plants. When the two fields were together, as in Lupe's case, the crops were worked at the same time.

Once in the mountains, the hazards of cultivating marijuana seemed remote to me, it all seemed so natural, so distant from the paranoia and tension of the city. Still, I could not get over Lupe's precautions as we approached his field. Half a mile from his field he had us tether our mules. Jesse and I stayed behind as Lupe and Jorge left the trail to approach the field. After Lupe examined his field, he returned and beckoned to us. As we walked I asked Jesse what that was all about. "It's simple security," he said. "Even up here the growers aren't one hundred percent sure that their fields haven't been discovered. Every time they visit their fields they take a different route; they want to make sure there're no strangers present. That's why no farmer ever visits another farmer's field without being invited. In the first place, it's none of his business, and in the second place, he might get shot."

"It seems to me they wouldn't have much to worry about up here. Hell, we're days from any heat hassles."

"It's not only the heat that worries the farmers," Jesse said. "There are a whole lot of complex things going on in the mountains all the time, things you don't even know about unless you're part of the area."

"What d'you mean?"

"You don't see it because you're a gringo and a lot of the subtleties of the language are lost on you, but back in the village when Sanchez was hiring our mules, there was a conflict. Some of the campesinos

Photo overleaf by Eugene Anthony

were pissed that their mules weren't hired. We're bringing a lot of bread into the area and the campesinos know it. Everyone wants some of it and it's up to Sanchez to see who gets it. It's a problem for him too."

"Shit, we can't hire everyone," I said. "What do they expect Sanchez to do?"

Jesse shrugged. "What he's doing, I suppose. He'll pick his friends and not his enemies. I don't know what kind of feuds the mountain people have going among themselves, but I do know that it's not as easy as it looks."

"What about the grass then? How come José didn't want us to take pictures of his fields so he could make some bread?"

"I don't know. Maybe Sanchez wanted too big a commission. It's all very tangled when you get into the hills, everyone has to have his little piece. You notice how he talked to José for a couple of hours when we first got to his field—and then the next day Lupe showed up. Lupe wouldn't have come unless he had been invited. Sanchez is working his angles just like we're working ours."

"Well, you can't blame him for that," I said.

"No, you can't," Jesse said. "It's difficult making people who aren't familiar with Mexico or the mountains understand the dangers involved. Most gringos have a romantic idea about the whole marijuana game and that's why they're in it. There's nothing romantic about it in the mountains, however, it's deadly serious to the people up here. You notice that the fields are built at least a couple of hours away from the growers' homes. . . ."

"Why's that?" I asked.

"So if any troops do come into the area, ownership of the field can be denied. Obviously if you plant a field in your back yard, you can't very well deny ownership if the heat comes."

"I don't even see how the heat could get up here," I said.

"Yeah, and the farmers couldn't either until a few years ago. Now the heat comes in helicopters. Last year a helicopter was snooping around some fields south of here and the farmers shot it down. Shooting down a helicopter is bad business, though, because the next thing

they know, a company of troops is in their midst, shooting, pillaging, raping. Most gringos think I'm bullshitting when I say this, but when Mexican soldiers come into the mountains no one's safe, no home, dog, mule, garden, or daughter. To protest is useless because campesinos are not allowed to protest. The only thing they can do is what they have always done, stand up and fight. If that fails, then it's a run further into the Sierras."

Jesse's view was sobering. I knew that what he said was true, however. I had newspaper clippings to prove it. In 1971, government troops entered the rural village of Realito in search of marijuana. In the process of turning the town inside out, twelve people were killed, including one soldier and a twelve-year-old boy.

"I don't know what gets into the soldiers when they come into the mountains," Jesse said. "They seem to go insane. Maybe it's because they have to tramp all over the hills looking for marijuanos they can't find. Maybe it's because they know they'll get shot if they don't shoot first. It's all part of the Mexican trip though, no compassion and no restraint."

"God, it's amazing to me that anyone grows marijuana," I said.

"What do you expect them to do?" Jesse said. "These people are rooted in poverty. There's no money in the mountains except in weed. For the growers it's a way of life, their daily bread on the table. What amazes them is the hassles involved in growing marijuana. There's nothing wrong with the weed to them. They've been using it for centuries. Hell, their fathers and grandfathers used it. The mystery for them is that a bunch of crazy gringos will go out of their way to pay a lot of money for weed, and an equally crazy bunch of soldiers will go out of their way to keep the gringos from getting it."

"And they're caught in the middle," I said.

"They're not only caught in the middle between soldiers and gringos, but they're also caught in between official policies that change from one moment to the next. Hell, a couple of years ago there was no danger in growing weed, all they had to do was give the local general his bite, pay off the troops down on the roads, and deliver their loads. Now that the heat's on in Mexico City, the generals have to

Photo overleaf by Eugene Anthony

clean up their act, so they bring the heat down on the villages. Military patrols that used to accept bribes and let weed go through now stop shipments and rip them off. If the farmers protest, they get shot. If anyone squawks, the helicopters provided by the United States government come in. It's a crazy business."

When we reached Lupe's field he conducted us through it with obvious pride. He was a careful farmer. Each of his plants was well trimmed, and the earth cleared away around each stalk. The plants were seven to eight feet high, and very leafy. Without testing I could see the resin gleaming on the foxtails. Lupe's dog, Noche, rubbed against the stalks and nibbled at the lower leaves. "He likes it," Lupe said. "It makes him *muy contento.*"

While Jesse accompanied Lupe and Jorge through the field, I climbed a small bluff and looked back over the trail. It wound in and out of the canyons and finally disappeared behind a ridge. The corn stalks surrounding me rattled in the breeze. It was the only sound I could hear. To the west the mountains receded in ridge after ridge toward the sea. Below me a hawk circled slowly, his shadow rising to meet him as he swept toward the ground to strike at a gopher or rabbit. The mountains had a prehistoric quality about them, silent, austere, beautiful.

We spent two hours in Lupe's field and then returned to his home. Jesse and I were excited by the field. We wanted to use it for our story. Jesse asked Lupe about it. He smiled and shrugged. "A man makes no money from pictures," he said. "If you want to buy my mota, I will sell it to you."

Jesse explained to Lupe what we wanted to do. We would pay him for the use of his field, then he could sell the grass to other buyers. He could make money both ways.

"Other buyers are not here now. If you want my field you can buy it. Then you can take pictures."

Jesse and I looked at each other. It had not occurred to us to buy a marijuana field. I asked Lupe how much he wanted for the whole field. Lupe spoke rapidly with Jorge. After some calculation he looked up. "I will sell my field to you for twenty-five pesos per plant. And Jorge and I will harvest it for you."

Jesse and I figured there were approximately 2,000 plants in Lupe's field. At 25 pesos per plant, the whole field would cost us $4,000. If we could get the price down to 15 pesos per plant we could afford to buy it. Either that, or we could buy half the field.

"Lupe," Jesse said, "we have $2,500. If you will sell your plants to us for 15 pesos each, we will buy the whole field."

Lupe and Jorge figured again. There was much talk of burros and men to move the marijuana. Jorge wanted to make it clear that moving the grass was not included in the purchase price. If we bought the field, they would harvest it but we would have to pay extra to move it out of the mountains.

"How much will it cost to move the marijuana out of the mountains?" Jesse asked.

"Each man must be paid sixty pesos per day," Lupe said. "And each burro costs fifty pesos per day. Besides that, two or three *pistoleros* must be hired as guards. They cost seventy-five pesos per day. If there are any delays or losses along the trail they must be borne by you, that is the way it is done."

"How long does it take to move a load down?"

"If we move the whole load at once we must plan to take at least one week, perhaps more. Loads can only be moved at night, it is very tedious and there are many risks. Things are very difficult in the mountains now, there are many soldiers camped in the villages along the coast."

"How many burros and men will be required?"

"We will need ten burros and five *muleteros,* plus the *pistoleros.*"

Jesse and I figured that the men and burros would cost 1,000 pesos per day, about $80. Ten days on the trail would cost $800. A cheap price for what we were getting. I turned to Lupe.

"Lupe, we would like to buy your field. There are a few problems involved, however. We have another friend, a photographer, who has to come down from up north. It will take him a week or so to get here. Will it be possible to harvest the field and move it down from the mountains at that time?"

"My field will be ready for the first cutting in ten days," Lupe said. "After that it depends on you. As far as hiring the men to move the

load, I will take care of that. If you want your friend to take pictures though, he must be here within two weeks."

Jesse clinched the deal that night. He gave Lupe 10,000 pesos as a down payment on the field, the rest to be paid when the field was cut. I was giddy. Jesse sat calmly in the corner talking with Lupe. It seemed incredible to me that we had solved our major problem as easily as we had.

The only hassle would be what to do with the weed we had purchased. Neither Jesse nor I had made any preparations for smuggling a ton of weed. The logistics involved in such an operation are considerable. We could, of course, give the weed back to Lupe once we had our photographs. That would ease our burden, but it would also be giving up a considerable amount of bread. The trip was going to cost a lot more than we had figured originally, therefore it behooved us to consider contacting some people in the States who could help us. The professional thing to do would be to move the weed out of the mountains, store it someplace until we could contact friends, then smuggle it into the United States. That would take time and money though. We could also move the weed out of the mountains and sell it to some of the young smugglers who were operating in and around Acapulco. However, neither Jesse nor I wanted to get involved with anyone we didn't know. In the end we decided to solve the problem one step at a time. First we would contact Gene and get him down. After he got his photos, then we'd decide what to do next. The important thing was that we had a field; everything else was gravy.

That night, we slept at Lupe's and then returned to Rafael's big house the following day. Jesus wasn't going to return for another week, so for a week Jesse and I stayed with Rafael helping around the house and visiting other marijuana fields nearby. Two days before Jesus was to return, Jesse and I thanked Rafael for his hospitality, gave him 500 pesos for his services, and started down the mountains. Sanchez led on his mule and Jesse and I followed. Raul brought up the rear. The trip down was uneventful. When we reached the village we went to Señora Sala's place to eat. It amazed me how the rhythms

Photo overleaf by Eugene Anthony

seemed to work out in the mountains, for just as we rode up in front of Señora Sala's place, the doors opened and she welcomed us in. On the table were bowls of hot *mole* and tortillas, black coffee, and ripe oranges. Jesse said there was nothing surprising about the food being ready, the people of the village had seen us coming for hours. We ate a beautiful meal and then at what seemed an appropriate time I searched out a place to throw down my sleeping bag. I was dead tired. As I was preparing to unroll my bag, an old man came in and gestured to me. "*¡Venga! ¡Venga!*" (Come! Come!) he said. I looked at Jesse questioningly. "*Yo tengo mota buena*" (I have some good marijuana), he said.

Word had spread through the village that Jesse and I were looking for marijuana. The old man had a patch he had grown and he wanted us to come with him to sample it. We followed him through the square and up a narrow alley to a dimly lit hut. When we entered the hut, two women stepped outside. There were five men inside sitting in a circle on their haunches. Spread out before them was a large sack of marijuana, all colas, thick as small wrists. Jesse sniffed the weed, then bit off a piece and chewed it. "It looks good," he said. "Why don't you try some?"

I rolled a joint and lit it, taking one long toke. I offered the joint to the other men and they all refused, their eyes intent on me. For a minute I felt nothing, so I took another toke. I felt slightly embarrassed in front of all the people, the hulking gringo sitting on his haunches smoking weed. I had the sudden feeling that if I didn't like the grass, they would shoot me. Waves of paranoia swept over me and I actually felt frightened. Each of the men wore guns, and two of them actually held their weapons between their legs as they looked at me. The chatter of the women outside the hut sounded like rebukes. I was able to understand Spanish perfectly clearly when I was stoned, a fact that always seemed remarkable to me, and I knew the women were just gossiping, but I felt threatened by their voices anyway.

As the power of the weed rolled over me, I felt a sense of vertigo and almost tumbled to the ground. I put out a hand to stop myself from falling and it seemed to take an eternity for my hand to reach the ground. I realized I was bombed. I felt a great desire to get out of the hut. I wanted to smell the fresh air and see the stars. Jesse was talking with the old man though, discussing the availability and price of the weed. Suddenly he stopped talking to the old man and addressed me. It took me some time to realize that his voice was directed to me. "How is it?" he repeated a number of times. For a minute or so I didn't know what he was talking about. Then I remembered the weed. "O, está bueno," I said, rather glibly I thought. My paranoia was such that I was beginning to question the sound of my own voice. I was suddenly worried that I hadn't okayed the weed forcefully enough. I wanted another chance to elaborate on what I had said. "It's great!" I blurted out.

Everyone looked at me. Jesse had often rebuked me for speaking English in the mountains, and when I spoke his head shot up. I sensed anger in his face so I stood up and walked outside. In a minute Jesse joined me. We walked back down toward the square. The old man followed us. I said nothing as we walked. My feelings of paranoia were being replaced by giddiness. I was concentrating on walking, noting where I placed each foot on the cobblestones, dodging the manure and chuckholes, daintily tripping out in an awkward dance.

When we reached the square, Sanchez was waiting for us. Our gear was tied on a giant mule and he motioned for me to get on. "Where are the other mules?" I asked Jesse. "They've been returned to their owners," he said. Sanchez motioned me up again so I cocked my leg over the animal and settled into the saddle.

The mule was a magnificent animal, as big as a horse and beautifully caparisoned, the usual wooden saddle replaced with a tooled leather one. The owner of the animal obviously took pride in it. When I mounted I towered over Sanchez and Jesse. I flashed that I was going to be riding down a narrow trail at night while I was stoned out of my mind. The thought was both appealing and frightening. I was frightened because my experience with mules was minimal and the path was narrow and dangerous. The idea was appealing though, because I knew that whenever I got stoned and tried something, it inevitably worked out fine.

The minute I mounted the mule a sense of excitement rushed over me. I was no longer in a small village in the mountains of Mexico, and I was no longer on a mule. I was transplanted back into the eighteenth century and I was mounted on a gigantic horse. It is difficult to explain the sensations I felt while stoned, but I was no longer imagining my feelings, I was living them! The horse hoofs rang out on the cobblestones. The narrow street twisted and turned. The towers of the small church loomed over me as magnificently as any towers of Chartres or Notre Dame. I felt in complete control of the animal, prodding him forward, reining him to stop. He was impressive in his strength and balance. We danced, horse and rider one, down the narrow streets toward the river. The path was only five feet wide and it was a forty-foot drop to the river below. Boulders as big as houses lay in the river bottom, but I felt supreme confidence in my animal. When we reached the narrow bridge that I was especially worried about, I goaded my animal across at breakneck speed just to test him—and me. In seconds we were on the other side, reining up to wait for Sanchez and Jesse. I was impatient, wanting to dash ahead.

It was pitch black and all I could see were the glows of two flashlights behind me as Jesse and Sanchez walked down the trail. One of the lights hurried toward me. It was Raul, the boy we had hired to care for the mules. There were tunnels along the trail where one had to duck to pass through, and he was running forward to shine the light for me. I knew this instinctively although I had never thought of it before. I remembered the tunnels from the time we had entered the canyon on our way up into the mountains. Raul ran ahead of me into the first tunnel, shining the light on the heading. I had no need for the light, however. When my animal reached the mouth of the tunnel, he paused and snorted. I ducked and he entered. Ahead of me Raul's light flashed on the roof.

As I emerged he ran forward to the next tunnel, three or four hundred feet down the trail. Outside the tunnel my eyes adjusted to the darkness. I could see everything clearly. The stars were bright; the moon was not yet up. I had the strangest sensation while riding alone. I felt as if I were floating along in a universe and a time so perfect that

I wanted it to continue forever. I consciously thrust out my hand and grasped at the bushes growing along the trail. I grabbed handfuls of leaves and rubbed them on my face. The animal and I were united. I was amazed that I had never before imagined the sensation of being part horse, of floating over the ground, of the sheer speed and power my new form assumed. Occasionally the brim of my sombrero brushed overhead branches, causing me to duck. The rocking sensation of my body as I rode along was comforting. I could feel every bone and muscle working in place, as if I were an infinitely complex machine whose every part was functioning perfectly.

The ride down the trail took an hour. I emerged from the last tunnel and rode on to the group of huts surrounding the dirt landing strip. Beyond the strip on the edge of the bluff was a large adobe house. I had seen it when we first landed ten days before. We were to spend the night there.

I waited at the edge of the strip for Jesse and Sanchez. When they arrived, Sanchez untied our gear from the mule and released the animal to Raul. We continued on to the house, carrying our gear. On the way we passed a small hillock, with a structure on top. I asked Sanchez what it was. "A cistern," he replied. "It used to hold water for the big house." I dropped my bag and ran up the hillock to the cistern. It was round, with a flat top. Standing on it, I could see all around, the landing strip, the big house, the mountains rising on all sides. I ran back down and continued on to the big house with Jesse and Sanchez. As we approached, a half-dozen dogs came out to greet us, barking furiously. The barks flashed in my head like explosions, destroying my feeling of tranquility. The caretaker of the big house came out and quieted the dogs, and said we were welcome to sleep on his veranda. "I'd like to sleep on the cistern," I said. "*¿Como no?*" the old man replied.

While Jesse and Sanchez talked with the old man, I trudged back up the hill to the cistern and spread out my sleeping bag. My footsteps echoed in the well, a hollow booming sound that reverberated in my head. I could hear water dripping inside. When I lay down I noticed a small structure a few yards away, like a small hut. I got my flashlight

ROBERTO AYALA

out of my pack and climbed down to look. It was a grave. I flashed my light on the headstone: "Otilla Clark, *esposa de* Floyd Clark, *año* 1926. Dead at the age of thirty-seven years."

The house whose cistern I was preparing to sleep on used to be the main house for the silver-mining operations in the area. Otilla Clark was the wife of one of the American engineers. Her first name was Spanish so I assumed she must have been a Mexican girl. As I stretched out in my bag I thought of Otilla, dead over thirty years before. I wondered if she loved these mountains. I wondered if she had chosen this place to be buried. Maybe she and Floyd used to climb up here to watch the sunsets. It was a nice place and I felt comforted having Otilla near me.

Inside the cistern the water dripped and echoed. Inside the grave, the bones of Otilla Clark metamorphosed into the mountains she loved. On top of the cistern I snuggled deeper inside my bag. Above the mountains I saw the Big Dipper, so bright and clear that I imagined nectar dripping from it. For the first time in my life I lay still enough under the stars to see them wheel across the heavens. Just before I went to sleep, Jesse and Sanchez came up and spread out their bags. The old man from the big house was with them. Then Jesse did an insane thing. He pulled out his battery-operated slide viewer and started showing slides to the old man, Kodachrome transparencies of Puerto Vallarta and Guadalajara and other odd places. The old man looked intently into the projector as the stars slid over his head.

Jesus returned the next day and we flew down from the mountains. I called Gene from Acapulco and told him that everything was ready. He said he'd meet us in Acapulco in a week. I then took a plane back to San Francisco to make arrangements for the ton of weed we had bought. I also wanted to straighten out my probation officer. Jesse and I had decided to go for broke, we wanted Gene to get photographs of every aspect of a smuggling trip, from the field on down. I had some friends in Berkeley who were into smuggling and I wanted to see them to arrange for a boat. As luck would have it, when I did contact them they said their boat was already in Mexico. It had never carried weed

before but the owner of the boat was broke and willing to make a run for some money.

Don, the fellow I talked to, was a big-time acid dealer in San Francisco who had recently turned to dealing marijuana. He had actually hired the boat before I spoke to him and sent it south to Mexico hoping for the possibility of a score. The fact that I came just at this time with Jesse's and my scam was sweet news to him, so he called his skipper in Mazatlan and we made the final arrangements, agreed to terms, and shook on the deal.

After completing those arrangements, I saw a friend in San Francisco who owned an airplane. I didn't want to use an airplane, but I wanted one available in case I had to. Dr. Billyboy, the dude I talked to, owned a Cessna 240. He said he was ready to move at a moment's notice, all I had to do was call him from Mexico and tell him where to land. I didn't trust Dr. Billyboy completely, mainly because he had a Texas Ranger complex and liked to walk around with .358 Magnums tucked in his belt. His credentials were good though. He had made a dozen runs that I knew of personally and he always did them well.

At the end of a hectic week I had all the preliminaries ready, a boat in Mexico, a plane that could come down at the first phone call, and another contingent of dudes who agreed to bring down a truck to move the load on the ground. Neither Jesse nor I were ready to move the weed along the Mexican roads without assistance. We wanted some good equipment to rely on. We needed a couple of radios, a house to store the weed if necessary, and we also needed more money. The bread *Life* magazine had given us was almost gone. We owed Lupe $2,000 for the rest of the field and another $800 to $1,000 for the actual moving. We had the two grand for the field but we didn't have any more, so it was up to me to get it. Before I left on the return flight to Mexico I contacted some old friends who were in the music business and arranged for them to finance the trip. They put up $5,000 for a double return on their money, plus the right to sell a third of the load at wholesale prices. I agreed to the deal, and left for Mexico three days before Lupe was to harvest our field.

Gene and I flew to Acapulco the same day. Jesse met us at the airport and drove us to Jesus' rancho. Early the next morning Jesus picked up Sanchez and flew us back into the mountains. He carried a load of fertilizer and irrigation pipe for some of his growers, so we were packed into the plane on top of the supplies. Gene shot pictures all the way, the takeoff, the flight, the landscape below us, and the landing. When we landed, Raul was waiting for us with six mules. The trip up into the mountains the second time was a repeat of the first trip, although I considered myself a veteran now, pointing out things to Gene along the way. Gene's camera was in his hands all the time. The campesinos didn't seem to mind, as my Polaroid had broken the ice.

We stopped at Señora Sala's for breakfast and Gene shot her portrait. Then we took off for Rafael's house. It was comical watching Gene adjust to the mule's saddle as we started up the trail. I sympathized with him, remembering my own battle a few weeks before. When we reached Rafael's house he welcomed us. Lupe was there, with his wife and children. Our arrival was somewhat ceremonial, and I was glad I had remembered to bring some mescal. That night we all got gloriously drunk and Jesse and I put Gene through the master's bed routine. Finally I told Gene to grab his bag and sleep outside with me, which he gladly did. As we lay on the ground looking at the stars, fireflies burst out of the bougainvillaea like miniature searchlights, lighting up the area. Gene was full of the same mystery and admiration I had experienced on my first trip, and I listened quietly as he talked. The need to communicate one's feelings about the mountains is overwhelming. As he was re-creating his experiences, I fell asleep.

The next morning we breakfasted early and mounted our mules before it was light. Gene wanted to get some pictures of the sunrise and Jesse and I wanted to be in Lupe's field as soon as possible. Lupe and his family had returned home the night before, after Gene and I had gone to sleep. I was amazed that they had taken off in the dark but Sanchez said it was no problem; they were used to the mountains.

We rode the same trail as before, going faster this time because our mules were fresh. When we reached Lupe's house, half a dozen campesinos were there, sitting around a fire. We were introduced all around. Lupe explained that he had hired the men to help with the harvest. They had brought along seven burros to carry the marijuana.

Lupe's wife had a meal prepared so we had a quick bite. Gene shot pictures and none of the campesinos seemed to mind although they averted their faces when the camera was pointed their way. Then we remounted and rode to the field. When we arrived the campesinos tied up the animals and moved in among the plants. Wielding machetes, they began lopping off the foxtails and upper branches. The foxtails were set aside in separate piles as they worked. While the campesinos cut the plants, Jesse and I carried the bundles over to the edge of the field. Sanchez had brought along several large burlap sacks for the marijuana, but we didn't stuff the marijuana in the sacks, instead we wrapped the sacks around the bundles of grass and tied them with twine. The marijuana wouldn't be sacked until after it was dry.

It amazed me how few plants it took to make a large, twenty-kilo bundle. In a few hours Jesse and I had thirty bundles tied at the side of the field. Gene photographed the whole process, moving among the tall plants as the campesinos worked. I was fascinated by the quickness and dexterity of the campesinos. They moved with grace and agility. One old man named Diego, who seemed to be *jefe* of the group, was especially agile, jumping around the plants like a young kid as he mowed them down. Diego had a high-pitched twangy laugh that echoed through the field. His running commentary on everything kept the rest of the campesinos laughing. During the day I grew fond of him, and he reciprocated by tossing especially beautiful colas at me every chance he got. *"Aquí, Jerónimo,"* he'd yell. *"¡Fume ésta! ¡Te pone muy loco!"*

By two o'clock the field was harvested. One of the campesinos brought the burros down and we tied the bundles on their backs, four bundles on each burro. The loads completely covered the small beasts. After securing each load, Diego led the group in single file down the trail, heading for Lupe's drying shed. The shed was located in a distant part of the arroyo, some five miles beyond the field. The fact that Lupe had a drying shed pleased me and Jesse. Any farmer who lives in the high mountains and goes to the trouble of constructing a drying shed is obviously serious about his business. To the gringo, whose access to tools is enormous, this may not seem like much, but to the campesino in the high Sierras, an effort such as Lupe's is impressive.

It was especially significant when you consider that most of the marijuana grown in Mexico suffers from inadequate growing time and little or no curing. It is cut before it is mature and bricked before it is dry. There are a lot of reasons for this, not the least of which is the hard-up entrepreneur who, in his impatience to fill an order, makes the grower harvest his crop before it's mature. Not all entrepreneurs are guilty of this, but enough are greedy so that a lot of mediocre marijuana is smuggled into the United States. Another reason why so many farmers harvest their crops early is the Federales. In many states in Mexico, especially the west coast states of Michoacan, Nayarit, and Sinaloa, it's a matter of harvesting a crop early or not harvesting it at all. Much of the grass produced in Sinaloa is mediocre— although Sinaloa does produce some of the finest mota in Mexico— because most of the farmers in the state grow extremely paranoid toward the end of a six-month growing season, when they see the small aircraft used by the Federales buzzing around their mountains. The Federales know when marijuana matures as well as the farmers, and one of their favorite games is to seek out the fields just as they are being harvested. That way they hope to corral as many growers and helpers as they can. When the soldiers discover a field being harvested, they move in with their flame throwers and machine guns. To reduce this possibility, farmers in Sinaloa and Nayarit plant and harvest early, hoping against hope that they will be able to harvest a mature crop.

A third reason why so much marijuana is harvested early is simply because of ignorance on the part of the growers. Many farmers harvest their plants as soon as they are head-high, and then brick the grass before it is dry. These farmers aren't particularly concerned about quality; after all, they still get their 50 or 60 pesos per kilo whether the weed is mediocre or not.

When we arrived at the drying shed the burros were stripped of

EUGENE ANTHONY

From the collection of Roberto Ayala

their loads and allowed to roam free. The campesinos spread the marijuana out on the ground around the shed. The foxtails were taken inside and spread out on special racks. The drying shed measured about 15 feet square, and was made of thatched material so it could breathe. The four walls were lined with racks. As Jesse and I watched and Gene photographed, the campesinos filled the racks with colas. Lupe explained that the colas would be allowed to dry out of the direct rays of the sun, while the rest of the weed would lie in the sun. At night the grass lying outside on the ground would be strung up with twine. In the morning it would be spread out on the ground again.

After the campesinos spread out the marijuana, Lupe paid the men and thanked them. He arranged for them to return in a week to help move the load out of the mountains. As they were preparing to leave, Diego came over and shook my hand. "You have the box that makes pictures," he said. "Show it to me." I pulled my Polaroid out of my bag and handed it to him. "Where do the pictures come out?" he said. "You put the film in this end," I said, holding the camera for Diego to see, "and when you push this button a picture is made." "Make me a picture," Diego said.

While the other campesinos watched, Diego jumped up on his mule. He sat stiff and formal in the saddle, his ancient shotgun balanced on his thigh. I snapped the shutter, waited sixty seconds, then pulled the picture out. I handed it to Diego. He held it delicately in his remarkably fine hands, gazing at it. After five minutes, a big smile broke on Diego's face. *"Increíble,"* he said, shaking his head. *"Increíble."* The other campesinos crowded around to see Diego's picture. Then they too wanted pictures. I photographed each one sitting sternly in his saddle, gun balanced carefully on lap or shoulder. After they all had their pictures taken, Diego shook hands with me again. *"Una semana,"* he said, smiling. The men rode out of sight.

For the next week Gene, Jesse and I hung around Lupe's house. Every morning we rode up to the drying shed and rotated the plants, shifting the colas from rack to rack, and turning over the branches on the ground. Sanchez and Raul went down to the village below to arrange for more burros. They were due to return at the end of the week.

From the collection of Roberto Ayala

I easily slipped into the mountain life. Each morning I awoke and wandered down to the stream and bathed, plunging my arms deep into the cold water. Sometimes Lupe's children accompanied me, little Tomas, six years old, scowling like a chimpanzee, while Ester, nine years old, stared at me in wonder.

Ester was a strikingly beautiful young girl, so slim and perfect when she removed her clothes to bathe, my heart stopped. Her hair hung down in cascades, like a black spring erupting off her head, and her skin was of such a luscious, golden brown it was hard for me to take my eyes off her. I was struck by the enigmatic womanliness of the child, she was both child and angel, goddess and devil, earth mother and temptress, holy madonna and mudfaced urchin all in one. Ester was not only a woman, she was all women, and her stern-faced canyon-deep eyes gleamed at me with a million dark fires, like ten thousand tons of coal were burning behind her brows, sending billows of lightning out of them.

Antonio, the two-year-old, toddled and stumbled after us when we walked down to the stream, his little half-erect penis leading him along like a divining rod. Each morning after bathing, I was guided back to Lupe's hut by the slip-slap of Nadia's hands making tortillas. When I reached the hut the smell of coffee was so strong my stomach jumped. I had never had such an appetite, and the thought of eating what Nadia was preparing was delicious torment. I spent long hours each day either anticipating Nadia's food, eating it, or remembering it.

Lupe's family rarely ate meat, and for two days I watched silently as a baby goat wandered about the house. One morning Lupe slaughtered the goat. Watching the metamorphosis of that animal from a small living creature to skinned carcass to succulent chops on my plate that evening was both appalling and satisfying. To expunge some of the guilt I felt, I got up after dinner and went outside and offered a little prayer for forgiveness to the baby goat's spirit.

Four days later, Sanchez and Raul returned with six burros. The marijuana was dry, so we stripped off the small branches and stuffed them into burlap sacks. The colas were sacked separately, then bound firmly with strong twine. Under ordinary circumstances the mari-

From the collection of Roberto Ayala

juana would have been bricked at this time. Jesse and I were adamant about keeping our grass in bulk form, however. Bricking not only destroys the quality of the marijuana, but sophisticated buyers in the States are reluctant to buy bricked kilos. Not bricking our weed meant that it took twice as many burros to move it out of the mountains.

Many growers still brick their weed—bulk marijuana is still the exception rather than the rule in Mexico. To brick weed, it is spread out on a large tarpaulin and dampened with water. Much of the commercial grass in Mexico is actually soaked in a sugar solution, presumably so that the sticky sugar will help bind the kilos in brick form. Actually the sugar is put in to add weight to the kilos, for plain water will bind the bricks. Each kilo of sugar weighs one kilo, however, and when you're selling weed for $30 a kilo, why not add twenty or thirty kilos of sugar—especially when it costs only a few cents? A lot of the rip-off dealers who work the border employ special sugar men, dudes who are hired to brick the marijuana once the load's brought out of the mountains. The marijuana is taken to a special warehouse where it's spread out on tarpaulin and sprayed with the sugar solution out of a 55-gallon drum. A 100-kilo load often ends up weighing over 120 kilos after it has been sugared. When a gringo buys his sugared kilo, it weighs 2.2 pounds, but when he gets it back to the States and unwraps it, he finds that it has shrunk down to a pound and a half.

Most growers use crude presses made from old automobile parts to brick their grass. The presses are made in all sizes, but the favorite ones make cigarbox-size kilos, a convenient size. The presses are simple boxlike affairs into which the marijuana is stuffed by hand, then an iron plate is fitted over the weed, and a hydraulic jack used to press it down. Making bricks in this manner is a slow, laborious process. In the early stages of our careers, Jesse and I once worked for three days helping a group of Mexicans brick 600 kilos.

While we were stripping and sacking the weed, Diego and his men rode up with four more burros. We now had ten burros, enough to

haul the load out of the mountains. One of the burros would carry food and utensils for the campesinos. It was important that the caravan not be seen along the trail or in any mountain settlements, therefore the men would cook for themselves while hauling the load down. Three of the men with Diego were *pistoleros,* hired to guard the load from *bandidos.*

The emergence of *bandidos,* campesinos who roam the mountains and ambush unguarded loads moving down the trail, is a new phenomenon in the weed industry. Most of the *bandidos* are marijuanos or ex-marijuanos who prefer to rip off loads rather than to grow a crop themselves. There is an intense rivalry between various small communities in the mountains, and campesinos from one area won't hesitate to move in on another area—especially when large amounts of weed and money are involved. Often a group of campesinos will rip off a load to fill an order of their own, but most successful ambushes are the result of carelessness on the part of the transporters or the smugglers themselves.

Now, no load moves out of the mountains without *pistoleros* along to guard it. Timing is critical in transporting weed, and a delay on either end of the trail causes hardship not only for the campesinos moving the weed, but also for those picking it up. Sanchez' plan for moving our load was simple but effective. One man was to ride two hours ahead making sure the trail was clear, the *pistoleros* were to ride as flankers alongside the burros carrying the weed, and the *muleteros* would handle the animals. The rest of us would bring up the rear. Sanchez explained that we would be able to move during the daylight hours for the first two days only, or until we approached the outskirts of the small village below. After that, all movement must be at night. He also said that it was best that Gene and I not accompany the load any further than the small village, for the trail became very difficult after that and the men did not want to have to stop for any reason. Jesse, on the other hand, would accompany the load on down to make sure our interests were cared for.

I was somewhat peeved by the idea of not accompanying the load all the way down but realized Sanchez was right. Gene was certainly

in no shape to make the week's journey down the mountains, and even though I was, I knew the smart thing to do was to go along with Sanchez' suggestion. Four or five nights on muleback in the Mexican Sierras with a ton of weed and potential bandits and Federales and natural disasters is not my idea of a garden party. Besides, the logistics of the trip demanded that I get out of the mountains as quickly as possible so I could check up on the boat. I had to call Berkeley and find out if the boat had moved down the coast to where it was supposed to be; I also had to make sure that the two dudes I'd hired to bring a truck down had actually done so. Sanchez sensed my disappointment at not being able to accompany the load out of the mountains, and suggested that I meet it in a small village in the foothills. "Maybe you can bring your truck in to the village and meet us there," he said. "It would save us a day's journey."

"I'd be glad to pick up the load in the village, Sanchez, I'm sure I can do it."

"It is very difficult reaching the village I am speaking of," Sanchez said. "I will make arrangements with Jesus that you have someone to guide you. It takes six hours in a truck, over a very bad road."

"No matter," I said. "My friends are bringing down a good truck. I'll be there."

So it was set. Jesse would accompany the load out of the mountains, and Gene and I would drop out of the caravan and fly out with Jesus. I could then take care of the final arrangements with the boat and meet the load in the small village with the truck.

That afternoon the load was secured on the burros and we started down the trail. The advance man rode ahead, the *pistoleros* rode out as flankers, a couple of men accompanied the burros, and the rest of us followed. The last few hours of daylight saw the burros spread out along the trail, the *muleteros* casually riding among them. When it got dark the *muleteros* moved in and bunched the burros up so they wouldn't stray off the trail. The rest of us closed the gaps between our animals. At night it gets pitch black in the mountains and no lights were to be used. The mules themselves would find the way. The first few hours of darkness were exceedingly uncomfortable for me; not

ROBERTO AYALA

only was the steep trail causing me to ride up on my saddle, but I couldn't get over the instinct to keep my hand up to ward off branches. The *muleteros* moved fast, not the slow pace I had grown accustomed to when traveling with Sanchez. Behind me I could hear Gene puffing and wheezing as he attempted to maintain his grip on his mule, but I had no sympathy to spare. I was having the same trouble. Finally, after two hours of struggling, I sat back in my saddle and let my animal have his way. I found it much more comfortable to ride this way, hunched over the horn with my head down and eyes half closed. My mule kept his nose to the ground as he followed the trail.

That first night there was only one rest stop, at a small hut where an Indian family gave us water. We rested twenty minutes and then the *muleteros* drove the animals down the trail, switching their legs with leather crops. On one section of the trail we passed through heavy undergrowth and thousands of fireflies erupted out of the darkness, lighting up our caravan. The fireflies bounced off the men's shoulders and sombreros like sparks off stone.

To pass the time and keep my mind off my discomforts, I thought of our efforts in getting up into the mountains. It was satisfying to think that our labor was responsible for the load now moving down the trail. Forever after when I lit up a joint in San Francisco, I would appreciate the logistics involved in moving every little bit of mota from Mexico to the United States. All the lines and loops and links that eventually connect in one joint were slowly braiding together. I was pleased to see the whole structure, to be part of it and know its full value.

At dawn we stopped at a hut where breakfast was prepared. The woman of the house accepted coffee and beans from our pack animal and in less than forty-five minutes had fed everyone. Gene had a package of cookies in his pack and shared them with the men. I felt like I was breaking a long fast as I ate, and each bite tasted exquisite.

We rode all that day and into the night, stopping briefly to eat and rest. We were approaching the village, and the *muleteros* intended to detour off the main trail. Gene, Raul, and I were to go on through the village to the airstrip. Jesus was due to fly in the next day to pick

us up and take us out of the mountains. When we came to the fork in the trail, the men and burros went on and Jesse and Sanchez stopped to say goodbye. "Raul will take you on down to the landing strip," Sanchez said. "When Jesus arrives with the airplane, tell him we will be in Hostopan in four days' time and you are to meet us there with your truck. He will arrange to have a friend accompany you. *Bien viaje, hombre.*"

"*Bien viaje, hombre,*" I said.

Jesse held out his hand. "Have a good trip down, man, and make sure you get the truck to Hostopan. These guys can't wait around in that place more than two or three days."

"I'll be there," I said, "as long as Zeke and Hoff made it down to Acapulco."

That afternoon Gene and I waited beside the dirt airstrip for six hours. Both of us were beginning to think that we'd got our signals crossed, when finally Jesus' airplane flitted over the valley. The sound of his airplane was sweet to my ears. When he landed, he explained that he had to make an extra stop for other farmers in a distant part of the mountains. He also had a lot of material for the local farmers, including fertilizer and irrigation pipe. He demonstrated by hauling out a dozen large sacks of fertilizer and throwing them on the ground. Two noncommittal campesinos who had been waiting beside the field for hours quickly moved forward and took the supplies, lashing them on to their mules. Jesus spoke briefly with them and they rode off. He then grabbed our equipment and tossed it into the plane, motioning us in. Gene and I both jumped in and we were off.

After gaining some altitude, Jesus swung back around the canyon where Lupe and Sanchez were leading the string of burros down the trail. "If we can spot them," he said, "so can the Federales." I peered into the canyons as we passed over them. I could see nothing. "Everything stops when the sound of an aircraft approaches," Jesus explained. "From now on they will be moving only at night. It is exceedingly dangerous from here on in." I looked over the mile after mile of rolling mountain canyons and tried to imagine soldiers and farmers doing battle down there. Except for an occasional hut perched

up on a mountain top, there were no signs of life. "I don't see how anyone can see anything," I said. "To me it's like a patchwork quilt."

"You must have the eyes of an eagle," Jesus laughed. "And the silence of a snake!"

4.

THE COAST

From the collection of Roberto Ayala

The abrupt transition from mule to motel room was startling, but three hours after leaving the mountains Gene and I were taking showers in a motel in Huatamaquilpa. I had picked up the station wagon at Jesus' rancho and Gene and I were preparing to drive to Acapulco the following day. I wanted to make sure that Zeke and Hoff, the two dudes who had promised to bring down the pickup, were actually waiting for us.

Zeke was an old-time beatnik smuggler who had gotten in the game a year or so after me and Jesse. Jesse and I hadn't worked with Zeke except in a peripheral way, sometimes providing him with weed when his own connection was out of town or otherwise unavailable. We also loaded planes for him occasionally, since his specialty was barreling loads across the border in souped-up Cessnas. His running partner, Hoff, was a tall, thin dude who was the dealer of the outfit, his specialty being offing the weed once it reached the States. Zeke's half of the partnership, aside from insuring that loads got up to the States, involved raising money and copping the load. He was also the pile-driver behind the outfit, goading it on when it bogged down. He never flew planes across the border himself, preferring to hire Vietnam vets and out-of-work airline pilots instead. His one problem was that he lived in sort of a fantasy land and he tended to bullshit a lot, which put a lot of people off his case. In fact, the reason I had been able to hire him to drive a truck to Mexico was because his own scene had collapsed. Investors shied away from him, especially since his last two loads had gone down.

The functions of smuggler and dealer in the marijuana industry demonstrate, perhaps better than anything else, the actual structuring of the entire dope culture. Zeke is a smuggler, like me and Jesse, while Hoff is a dealer.

Smugglers are involved in moving marijuana from the interior of Mexico into the United States, whether by airplane, ground vehicle, or boat. The smuggler delivers the load to a dealer, who transports, distributes, and sells marijuana *inside* the United States. Sometimes dealers are also smugglers and sometimes smugglers are dealers, but this is getting rare. Dealing and smuggling are two different enterprises, connected by the product, but separated by Grand Canyon differences.

The people who smuggle weed come in all sizes, shapes, sexes, and colors. State senators' sons have been arrested for smuggling marijuana and so have janitor's sons. Hippies, beats, squares, straights, they've all been popped at the border with weed in their possession. There is no particular type that dominates the industry, although there are certain classifications into which most smugglers fall.

First, there is the old-time Mexican-American smuggler. The Mexican-American smuggler has been in the game for a long time, and is the primary supplier of most of the southwest and of the large urban ghettos. The Mexican-American smuggler is the most successful since he's been at it for years, with family and racial connections in Mexico that are well established and usually secure. Mexican-Americans form the Texas Syndicate, the largest organized smuggling ring in existence. The Texas Syndicate has good connections on both the Mexican and United States sides of the border. They don't have to worry about being popped, since everyone is paid off. They are never popped in Mexico, and if a fall occurs in the States, they know the officials who can be bought. The Mexican-American smuggler has little to do with the hip community. He sticks pretty much to his own areas and deals with his own people. Many of the Mexican-American smugglers have established legitimate businesses with the money they've made from weed. They put their profits in liquor stores, small construction firms, appliance outlets, laundromats, ranches. Except for the fact that they smuggle a hell of a lot of weed, most of them have little to do with the current drug revolution. The rash of arrest statistics at the border and the large amounts of dope confiscated do not reflect their activity, simply because they hardly ever get arrested. A final thing that differentiates most Mexican-American smugglers from their gringo counterparts is that they also move a lot of heroin across the border, something most gringo smugglers shy away from.

Second is the Bohemian-beat smuggler. These are individuals who have been part of the Bohemian scene for many years, who smoked weed in the fifties before it was popular, and who got into acid and speed before the invention of the Haight-Ashbury. Most of the Bohemian-beat smugglers work out of some type of creative bag, and fall into weed smuggling because it is a profitable and exciting way to finance their work. Most of them started out small, tripping across the border with a few keys for their personal use, not really intending to become professional smugglers. Because it was so easy when they got started (most Bohemian-beat smugglers got started in the trade during the early sixties), they continued on and became very good at it. Many of them graduated into big-time smugglers, in the sense that they consistently move two or three hundred kilos across the border each month. Jesse and I considered ourselves in this classification.

Third is the hippie-longhair smuggler. These are the young kids who entered the business during the last few years, primarily because of the fantastic demand for marijuana among their peers. Again, many of them started out very small but some are now very heavy smugglers, utilizing aircraft, boats, cars, trucks. Many of the hippie-longhair smugglers work out of some sort of music bag, and many of the operations are financed by rock bands. The reason for this is pure economics. If a band is blasting $500 worth of weed a week, why not finance a trip so they can score their own? From that beginning it's a simple step into peddling the smuggled weed to other bands and

people. Some of the biggest shipments of weed brought into the United States are financed by successful young rock and roll stars. Unlike the Bohemian smuggler, who tends to operate individually, the young hippie-longhair smugglers usually have quite an organization behind them, lots of bread, lawyers, good equipment. They enter the business like they play their music, totally and with great enthusiasm. The hippie-longhair smuggler is also the one who created the drug revolution. It is his peers who are demanding the weed, and it is his contemporaries who are creating the climate of oppression in Mexico that is changing the whole industry. On the other side of the coin, it is his example and all-pervasive attitude that will eventually create the changes in the laws governing the use of marijuana.

Fourth is the weekend smuggler. This is the tourist, college student, young longhair, or surfer who goes to Mexico for a short vacation and ends up scoring a kilo or two. Sometimes trips are made specifically to score, but the cop is seldom over five kilos. I personally think that before Operation Intercept, the largest number of kilos smuggled were moved by the weekenders, simply because of their number. Often the trips are one-shot adventures, but occasionally a successful weekender graduates into becoming a real smuggler. If he does, he automatically falls into one of the other groups.

Another category of smuggler that is quite new on the set, appearing since Operation Cooperation, in fact, is the granddaddy smuggler, usually a crusty old individual or couple who has been influenced by a younger family member, probably a young hippie rebel grandson, into driving loads across for fun and profit. I personally know of three of these operations, where white-haired old folks merrily trip their way across the border in their Winnebagos with two or three hundred kilos stashed inside the panels. This type of operation is especially popular among old-time dudes who were on the set when booze was outlawed, many of them remembering smuggling liquor in their youth. Prohibition and the current laws against weed are similar. This category also includes some old renegades who have lived all their lives outside of society, boat captains and adventurers who find smuggling weed satisfying and profitable. The last time I was in Mexico I met two men, both in their sixties, who were either scoring or waiting to score. They were vibrant old dudes who had already made half a dozen trips.

Aside from the common denominator of weed, most of the above-mentioned classes of smugglers have little or nothing to do with one another. They approach their craft differently, utilize different tools, and often expect different results from their endeavors. The primary difference between the Texas Syndicate-type smuggling operation and the modern Bohemian-beat-longhair smuggler, what I like to refer to as the California smuggler, is that the one utilizes border connections and violence if necessary, and the other doesn't. The California-type smuggler relies on a smaller ungreedy operation that prefers to move smaller loads with ingenuity and cool, relying mostly on the fact that less than five percent of the border traffic can be physically checked. During our own trips neither Jesse nor I ever carried guns, always figuring that if we did fall we would either split at that moment, or else take the fall and work it out later in the courts.

The Texas Syndicate-type organizations, on the other hand, have a predilection for using force if necessary. If a member of the organization is accidentally popped and none of the covering efforts (*mordida,* etc.) prevail in smoothing things over, the smugglers are not adverse to removing the obstacles by more direct methods. This is what happened in 1966, when the Bono brothers, two Mexican-Americans from Los Angeles, were accidentally popped by two green immigration officials near Mexicali. The brothers had a ton of weed in the back of an old army four-by, and the officials, thinking they might be illegal aliens, stopped them. They discovered the load and refused to make a deal, so the brothers overpowered them, tied them up in an abandoned shack, and set fire to it, killing them.

This is not an altogether uncommon experience for border guards when dealing with the Texas Syndicate—or Mexican-American smugglers in general. Their particular code of ethics, rooted as it is in the Mexican personality, does not normally consider surrender or acquiescence in any way. They are ready to work things out, share their load as it were, if the border people are reasonable; if they aren't, the guns are under the seats.

No smuggler, Mexican-American or gringo, likes this type of trip to go down. It brings the heat all along the border, and the individuals responsible are usually caught. The reason it doesn't happen oftener is because of the grease that is spread out along the border; everyone slides along nice and easy and no one gets hurt. When someone does get killed, it's usually because either green guards or inexperienced dope smugglers have been involved.

Not all of the young gringos who get involved in weed are immune to violence, however. In recent years, because of the fantastic amount of publicity surrounding weed and weed smuggling, an ominous pattern has developed along the border. Hundreds of young gringos with little experience in Mexico or in weed get a stake together and hightail it to the border looking for a fast score. These kids are a perfect setup for the ripoff artists—both gringo and Mexican—who work the border. The kids get to the border with a third-hand connection or no connection at all, and attempt to score, hoping for the quick trip back home with a stash. There is no way of knowing how many of the young dudes have been taken for a ride in the desert "to see the stash" in the last few years, but every month or so a couple of bodies are discovered. The finds warrant an inch or so in the local newspaper, that's all.

The ripoff trips are not confined to towns along the border. Both Phoenix and Tucson have become known as real bummers, towns where a dude has to be pretty slick to hold on to his stake.

The ruthlessness that has invaded what I call the border dope trade, a trade that has little to do with the smuggling industry going on in the interior of Mexico, incidentally, has occurred because of a number of factors. For one thing, many of the one-shot dudes who come down to the border to score approach the industry with such naïveté that they ask to be ripped off. The profit potential available in the weed industry has also attracted hundreds of petty criminal types, hoodlums and gangsters who find the relatively innocent weed-heads easy prey. The important thing to remember about the burgeoning weed industry is that it was initiated by noncriminal types, youths who, if they had any previous criminal experience at all, were probably involved in nothing more serious than joy-riding or shoplifting. Many

of the more serious criminal types who are getting into smuggling in a big way are prone to violence, which is occurring with increasing regularity along many parts of the border. There's an old Mexican saying that goes, "A man who uses his hands on a woman doesn't know what his tongue is for"; the same is true of dope smugglers who use violence. It's a bum trip all the way down the line, and, like the Bono brothers, who after murdering the border guards were captured and are now in prison, doomed to defeat. Violence goes against the nature of weed itself, and the people who approach the game like junior high school gangbusters usually don't last long.

In recent years, the sophistication of the antiweed forces both within Mexico and along the border has necessitated a specialization on the part of those involved in smuggling and dealing. The structuring of the weed business, with each participant doing a specific job, did not occur accidentally, nor did it happen overnight. It was the natural culmination of many trips and many falls, and the eventual recognition of the facts of life.

When Jesse and I first started smuggling weed, we copped the loads together. I drove them across the border and Jesse sold them in the States. We soon found out that this wasn't where it was at, however. Any man who risks his ass at the border, whether in a plane, a car, or a boat, is a fool to risk his ass on the street. After a couple of close calls where Jesse almost got popped, we changed our operation and linked up with some dealers. In fact, we formed a partnership with the dealers. They provided us with the money to cop, we did the copping and delivered the load, and they sold it. Jesse and I realized that offing weed wasn't our scene. We didn't have the time. We didn't have the social grace. We didn't have the temperament. I myself never did like getting stoned with a bunch of weed-smoking squares while they sampled our product.

The people we linked up with were good dealers, able to run the social set down and bullshit with customers and blast weed all day. Our partnership was a success because we kept the ends of the industry separate. The dealers did the selling and Jesse and I did what we did best, moved weed across the border.

The efficacy of this pattern is not always easy to impress upon dealers, however, especially when they are putting up the bread. Whenever money moves south across the border, I don't care whose hands it is in, it enters into a sort of never-never land, tending to disappear mysteriously, wafted into the mountains, as it were. For this reason almost every big dealer I know of has tried at one time or another to smuggle his own weed. This way he can not only control his bread, if he is smart he can cop his weed cheaper—since he will be buying direct from the source. Also, hired mules are cheaper than smugglers who are partners, so he can save money that way. There is still another reason why dealers often attempt to do their own smuggling, however. There is a mystique running with the dealer who has the reputation for being able to cover every aspect of the set, from fields to street, as it were. It impresses customers, who assume that if a dealer is getting his weed direct from the source, it must be pretty good weed. It also makes them feel good to be able to buy from a dealer who is able to furnish them with weed when other dealers can't. In many cases, dealers who go to Mexico to take care of the smuggling end become permanent smugglers because they find that their talents lie in that direction. Also, some smugglers switch their roles and become dealers for the same reason.

Any reasonably sophisticated smuggling operation that is successful today is structured somewhat along the lines of Jesse's and my trip. We have entered the baroque period of marijuana smuggling, and those knowledgeable in the trade consider that if a dude is copping the weed, running it across the border, and selling it, then he is doing it wrong. Most small operators have been squeezed out of the marijuana industry in the last few years, and the sophisticated operations have taken over. I do not mean sophisticated in the sense that the operations are Mafia-controlled or bankrolled by big-time gangsters, but sophisticated in that all the loose ends are together. Marijuana has really become an industry; weed cooperatives have taken over to fight the antiweed cooperatives set up by the Mexican and American governments.

Specialization has occurred in the weed industry not just because of the antiweed forces, however. The different natures of the two ends of the weed business are also responsible. The difference is reflected in the attitudes not only of smugglers and dealers, but in the attitudes of the public toward smuggling and dealing.

Smugglers and dealers have different heads. That is, they think differently, have different motivations, and they approach their problems from opposite sides of the border. Leaving marijuana out of it for a minute, and at the risk of oversimplifying, I would say that smugglers are in the game for the *rush* and dealers are in it for the *money*. The smuggler gets his kicks outwitting the border and the dealer gets his kicks driving a Mercedes 280 SL in front of his friends. Smugglers live in a sort of Old West fantasy where it's them alone up against the baddies (United States Customs); dealers live in a sort of 1920s Great Gatsby flapper dream, waiting for the chauffeur to open the door of the Duesenberg.

In the public's mind the differences between the two are reflected in the attitude that smugglers and smuggling are romantic (especially among the young), and dealers and dealing are dirty and evil (especially among the old). Both of the images are true and both are untrue, but the relevant fact here is that smuggling things across borders (anything and any border) does have romantic connotations not normally associated with dealing and peddling. The romanticism is not confined to squares on the street either, the smuggler himself is a victim of it. He is neither immune from imagining himself romantic, nor can he ignore the fact that others think him so.

When you talk to a smuggler you usually find an individual who considers himself a rebel, a loner, a sort of daredevil. Most smugglers are smart, have been involved in many scenes, have had some experiences in Mexico before marijuana became the reason for going there, and have an interest in the country beyond weed itself. In fact, many smugglers engage in the business because it is the only trade that allows them to remain in Mexico. Most smugglers live outside the mainstream of society and are discontent with reasonable, secure pursuits. Most of them are victims of a vision that places them on the edge of life itself. I believe that many smugglers enter the game because it's something like war, a pastime where life is lived on the edge, where the games played are real games, where nothing is hidden, and where every move has to be conscious. A lot of smugglers enjoy the rush, the intense energy that explodes through the body when a border is approached. At the border the rush is on the surface, a real prick-retractor, as a smuggling companion of mine says. And then, some smugglers are enamored of weed itself, considering it a tool that if introduced to and used properly by mankind, will save society, alleviating some of the hassles that plague the world today. These smugglers feel compelled to deliver as much weed as possible into the hands of kids. For them smuggling is a mission.

Finally, a lot of smugglers get into the game because they enjoy the direct conflict with the establishment. This is especially true now when so much energy and equipment of both the Mexican and the United States governments are being brought to bear against the border. There are hundreds of new guards, weed-sniffing dogs, electronic teletypes that relay messages and monitor traffic, radar, informers, drone aircraft flying the borders, and all the other man-made and natural snags that smuggling is heir to. To overcome these obstacles and make money and not be dependent on an eight-to-five job and be able to do what you want when you want is why a lot of people get into smuggling.

My own reason for getting into smuggling—to lend specifics to generalities—was to obtain freedom to write. When supporting a family while trying to write became impossible, I fell into smuggling. I didn't plan it that way; it just happened. I have never been interested in smuggling *per se,* nor have I been particularly interested in weed as a salvation for youth. For me smuggling was a means to an end. True, the rush was important when I approached the border, because it is somewhat like the rush experienced when creating something. It never overwhelmed me, however. My desire to write got me in the smuggling game and my writing about marijuana got me my first exposure in print, a fact I look upon with a Zen Buddhist's appreciation. The rhythm works in wondrous ways. The money was never important beyond its ability to provide the freedom I needed to write.

Surprising as it may seem to cynics, money is not the motivating force that leads all people into smuggling. In truth, very few dope smugglers make a great deal of money in smuggling. The difficulties and hassles and hardships and falls and lawyers' fees take up so much of the bread that the smuggler who ends up with a hacienda in Mexico, every smuggler's dream, I imagine, is a rare bird.

Dealers, on the other hand, are essentially businessmen who happen to be dealing in weed rather than automobiles or whatever. Most dealers use other people's bread and make their money doing other people's shit. They don't like the rush and can't take the border. Many of them don't like Mexico. Dealers are sociable; smugglers tend to be solitary. To be social is necessary for a dealer, however, since dealers are salesmen. Dealers also, especially if they are successful, attract large crowds of people around them, other dealers and middlemen and hangers-on who enjoy the peripheral benefits all successful dopesters provide. Smugglers usually like to run alone, although sometimes they run as partners, like me and Jesse, and sometimes as couples, man and wife teams who use that guise to aid their smuggling. Dealers are more money-oriented, they get their rush in status and material things, property, cars, legitimate businesses. They also crave the accolades of people in their set.

Other interpreters of the drug scene may disagree, especially some dealers who pride themselves on their anonymity, but I believe many dealers have a definite need to be recognized, especially by their peers. This need exists despite the fact that if a pop occurs, it's usually because of someone in the set, not someone out of it. A maxim of the weed industry says there's no such thing as a well-known, successful dope dealer; the attributes are contradictory. Many dealers refuse to follow the maxim though, and end up falling behind the sidewalk rush, the need to be known, to expose themselves, to sit in coffee houses, to announce their success by driving big cars and buying big houses or acting big-timey in front of the squares on the avenue. For a lot of people dealing is like being a rock star, however—you have to be noticed to be appreciated.

Dealing, as opposed to smuggling, must be considered the yardstick for the whole hippie-longhair-Bohemian drug culture of the last few years. During the early days of dealing, a small group of people took a hell of a lot of risks and made a lot of money. They also set the stage for most of the changes that eventually occurred in the drug culture. In 1965, there were no bankrollers around who would put up ten or twenty thousand dollars to finance a run for weed. Consequently, all the bread had to be raised on the street a dollar at a time. Participation in the financing of a run required a sense of morality that seemed to pervade most dealing; this was before the era of universal ripoffs and burn artists.

Perhaps I can explain dealing better if I speak in terms of acid and other drugs rather than marijuana. The short history of acid dealing demonstrates the change in dealing and handling all underground drugs better than marijuana, because it was acid, not marijuana, that made dealing popular among white, middle-class kids.

During the first few years of acid dealing, from 1963 to 1965, when the drug was entering the American consciousness, the only acid available came from the Sandoz Laboratories in Switzerland. It was very expensive and difficult to get, so only a few people could deal it. During these first few years of drug discovery, all the hallucinogens were approached with a sense of spirituality by users and dealers; the whole process of copping, dealing, and using was almost reverent. I was living in Patzcuaro, Mexico, in 1964 when a friend stopped by my house. He had just driven in from Yucatan, where his wife had given birth to a baby while under the influence of peyote; the whole delivery had been conducted under the influence of peyote, the husband and midwife also eating the buttons. "This is a holy plant," he said, handing me a button. "You must be very careful how you use it. It can do you as much harm as good."

The hallucinogens were considered powerful medicine at this time, and the individuals who had been initiated into their use considered themselves fortunate, dwellers in a Garden of Eden, privileged to be partaking of a sacrament. Bad drugs, adulterated drugs, ripoffs, and burns were unheard of. Dealers were considered priests of the new religion, a religion predicated on new chemicals and stimulants provided by—who? They came from nature, everybody said.

LSD became popular, and backyard chemists like Augustus Owsley the Third started manufacturing and selling it in gram lots. People saw the money dealers were making and the good life they were leading and decided they wanted to get into the Garden of Eden also. Pretty soon every community had its dealer, just like it had its local rock group. And like the rock stars, many of the early dealers, guys like Goldfinger, Charlie Running Dog, and The Ghost and even Owsley himself, became folk heroes in the underground, adding not only status to the dealer image, but mythology as well. As more acid became available, more dealers dealt it.

Because it was so expensive—acid sold for $4,000 a gram wholesale in 1966—a lot of second-rate bathtub chemists without Owsley's talent or concern for quality started mixing their own batches. Other dealers hired commercial chemists who were hungry, and as a consequence, quality became secondary. A lot of bad acid hit the streets, acid that was laced with methadrine and strychnine, and whose primary purpose was not to produce magic, but to provide peddlers with money. Bum trips were common, and the great ripoff was on. The element of sacredness, of spirituality, disappeared—if it had ever been there. Acid became just another high, and the more you could take the better. Kids on the street opened their conversations with accounts of how many "mikes" they dropped the night before, and how this was their thousandth trip, and did anybody have any more acid so they could get on with their second thousand?

The changes acid use went through affected marijuana. As the backyard chemists flooded the market with acid, the price went down. At the same time, marijuana, which had been available fairly cheaply from Mexico, started going up in price. In 1968 you could score tabs of acid on the street in Berkeley for a dollar, yet the kilos of marijuana that had sold for $100 now cost three times that. Acid was suffering not only from being adulterated, but also from a bad press, and marijuana went up in popularity. Many acid dealers stopped dealing acid and moved into marijuana. A hell of a lot of money had been made in acid, and those bankrolls were turned loose in the weed fields.

At the same time, the big bread being made by a lot of the rock groups was being used to finance marijuana runs.

A new methodology evolved in the weed scene. Semi-hip business-men, many of them very straight and very successful in their busi-nesses, heard about the profits being made in marijuana and decided they wanted in. Those who were hip enough to have connections in the underground contacted dealers who needed financing and were willing to accept partners. One friend of mine who operates a very successful legitimate business in San Francisco while also dealing a hell of a lot of dynamite weed tells of being approached by dozens of straight business types, real estate agents and used-car dealers, law-yers, and other entrepreneurs who wanted a piece of his scam. They had the money, all they needed was someone who knew his way around. Almost any dealer will accept an investor as partner because it lessens his own financial risk. The investors have little or nothing to do with the actual smuggling or dealing; in fact, that's usually one of the conditions of the partnership. All they do is put up the capital for the run and then sit back and wait for their bread.

The emergence of bankrollers changed the nature of smuggling and dealing, but was a natural result of the separation of duties caused by Operation Cooperation. Many smugglers became hired hands, work-ing for dealers who in turn were working for bankrollers. Some smug-glers who weren't into working for others, but still understood the necessity for leaving the dealing to someone else, started selling runs; that is, they'd cover the scene in Mexico themselves, arrange for a load of weed on credit or with a small down payment, then return to the States and find a bankroller to finance it. Thus they reversed the process so they could keep better control of their own end. One of the hassles working with dealers and bankrollers is that inevitably a boss emerges—one has to, as far as I'm concerned. Jesse and I always kept our operation south of the border from any takeover on the part of financiers or dealers, entering into agreements only after it had been established that we would take care of things down in Mexico, and they would handle the United States end.

Part of the mythology of dealing lies in the fact that, like the smuggler, the real dealer never hits the street. Most of the action that occurs on the street involves middlemen and brokers, dudes who are setting up sales, finding weed for one source and selling it from another. It's in the street where all the head trips and bad scenes go down, the street has always been that way. The dealer who has his shit together can remain mythological because he can remain invisible, known only to a few select middlemen. The fact that so many dealers fail to remain anonymous is due partly to that ostentatiousness that infects so much of the rock underground. Dealers don't put out hit records though (except for a few dealers who are successful rock stars), so their reputations must be promoted by a sleight of hand, now you see him now you don't, does he or doesn't he?

Sometimes dudes enjoy the reputation without becoming dealers, instead they become the victims of dealers. Such a dude is Frank Werber, once a successful folk-music entrepreneur, and now involved in an extremely successful restaurant catering to dope dealers, rock stars, and narcotics agents. Werber's myth blossomed behind a dope bust where he was supposedly set up by two mules who were popped at the border and said they were working for him. When he was acquitted of the charge and the two finks themselves were punished, Werber was on top of the heap. He had a big-time music rep, a big-time dope rep, and he was a partner in the favorite hangout of everyone in the trade.

The glamour is so great, in fact, that some lawyers defending clients like Werber get involved in the dope trade themselves, financing trips and becoming silent partners by doing so. I know of two lawyers in the Bay area who make as much money financing weed runs as they do defending clients who've been busted for dope.

Dealing was simple in the old days, now it's an integral part of underground economics. Half the new-car dealers and real estate agents in San Francisco would go out of business if dealers stopped buying. There are more Mercedes sedans in San Francisco than there are in Berlin, and they're mostly owned by rock stars and dope dealers. In 1971 a young longhair was stopped by the police while hitchhiking across the Golden Gate Bridge. He was carrying a briefcase containing over $75,000 in cash. Since the money wasn't stolen and the kid had no record, he was released. A few months later, another young kid walked into a showroom on Van Ness Avenue in San Francisco and paid cash for a new Rolls Royce. Many of the kids with big bread are beneficiaries of a new movement in the drug culture, a movement brought on in some respects by the U.S. government itself. After acid and grass, dealers discovered hard drugs, and the one drug that has served as the link between marijuana and hard stuff is cocaine.

When Operation Intercept was implemented along the border, a curious thing happened within the drug culture. The government operation didn't stop the old-line weed smugglers, the Mexican-Americans and others who had family connections in Mexico, but it was relatively successful in stopping many of the young longhairs, the ex-acid dealers and rock stars who were into supplying their people, plus the white middle-class, university-oriented crowd. In 1969, when the weed supply dried up on the street, kids who had been into marijuana started substituting other drugs. And obviously, if a thousand newly trained guards and dogs were stopping the weed traffic, the only drugs that would be getting through would be the easily concealed stuff—heroin, morphine, barbiturates, pills, etc. Dr. Roger C. Smith of the Drug Free Clinic in Marin City told a Senate subcommittee that, "It is interesting to note that the use of dangerous drugs by adolescents increased dramatically following the implementation of Operation Intercept and the subsequent shortage of marijuana at their level."

Kids who had been smoking a little bush started dropping pills, shooting speed, taking barbiturates, anything to keep a head on. It was during this period that heroin started filtering into the white, middle-class underground. Kids who had never touched smack began chipping it, and riding in on the coattails of heroin came the rich man's high—cocaine.

With the increased hassles in Mexico created by Operation Cooperation, many of the hippie-longhair smugglers moved into cocaine and, on the other side of the world, hashish. Both drugs are easier to transport than bulky marijuana, and both bring higher profits on the street. Dedicated weed smugglers stuck to marijuana despite the difficulties, however, because they didn't believe in moving hard drugs. Cocaine is not only the rich man's high, it is also the drug that made hard drugs respectable in white, middle-class communities.

The single-mindedness of many weed smugglers and dealers is not difficult to understand given the nature of marijuana itself. Heroin is almost exclusively smuggled and dealt by heroin addicts, individuals who have gotten into the trade to support their habits. Cocaine, on the other hand, while recruiting many ex-weed dealers, is still a hard drug. Each drug has its own mystique, and users are drawn to them for specific reasons, reasons that are manifested in the drugs themselves.

William Burroughs describes cocaine as the most exhilarating drug he has ever used. The drug effects are very short-lived. When the user is high on cocaine, he experiences fantastic amounts of energy and power—but he must continue snorting or shooting it to stay high. Coca leaves, the source of cocaine, are chewed by the Indians in Peru to enable them to carry heavy loads for long distances in extremely high altitudes. A street name for cocaine is "incentive," and the drug does give one that, even though the incentive is temporary. Prolonged use of the drug causes sleeplessness, destroys the mucous membranes of the nose and throat, and eventually the brain itself, and makes some users hostile and aggressive when high. Cocaine acts as a powerful aphrodisiac for some people, its devotees maintaining that until you've balled on cocaine, you haven't balled. "It's all in the orgasm," is the way a friend of mine put it.

Cocaine has always been popular among the wealthy intelligentsia and politicians of Mexico, and among entertainment people in Hollywood. It seems to be the drug you fall into after having gone through all the others. When weed dealers discovered the popularity of coke, many of them started moving increasing amounts of it into the United States from Mexico, Panama, and Peru. Uncut cocaine costs $4,000 a kilo in Panama. Any coke worth its name can be stepped on (cut) four times, so a dealer who buys a kilo of uncut coke will end up with about eight pounds of incentive to dump in the streets. Since an ounce of good coke goes for from $700 to $1,000, depending on how heavily it's been cut, the final street value of one kilo is close to $125,000.

Marijuana, unlike heroin and cocaine, is nonaddictive. Marijuana is a sensitizer like cocaine, and heroin is a desensitizer. In fact, heroin is the super downer, it deadens every aspect of a person's sensibility. When a person shoots smack, he is on an escape trip, a trip back to the womb. Nothing bothers a person high on smack, not even the fact that he might be dying. In fact, the ultimate smack trip is to OD; every addict secretly longs for that journey over the rooftops. Heroin also, for reasons I have never been able to understand, always seems to involve a lack of trust. Perhaps it's the nature of the drug itself; anything that creates such a need in the body, a need that has to be satisfied at all costs, is inherently dangerous. Anytime you deal with an addict, you are dealing with a person you can't trust. An addict's primary concern is always his own need; if that need is fulfilled regularly, then things can go along very normally; if the need isn't being fulfilled, every aspect of every deal is trepidatious. The addict will lie, cheat, fink, steal, even kill to satisfy his need. For this reason alone most weed smugglers stay away from smack. The karma behind it is just too heavy.

Marijuana is another thing entirely. In the first place, you can't get addicted to weed and therefore you're not going to be dealing with people who need something desperately. This is not to say you don't meet people you can't trust in the weed industry, far from it. The problems that arise out of weed trafficking almost always involve peripheral aspects of the industry, however, money, personality hangups, general time and organizational fuckups, misunderstandings, etc. They seldom have anything to do with the nature of marijuana itself.

After spending the night in Huatamaquilpa, Gene and I drove to Acapulco. We were to meet Zeke and Hoff at a motel outside of town. I was apprehensive as we approached the motel because one of the hangups in the smuggling game is organizing people to be on time.

Half the fuckups in the industry are caused by people who don't keep appointments, who misconstrue instructions, who dally along the road while a load is waiting to be picked up. Timing is all-important in the smuggling game, the judge that sentences every operation to success or failure. The difficult thing for most gringos to understand is that Mexicans move on one time plane while gringos usually move on another. There is also a third time plane involved when weed is being moved.

If I had to use one word to describe the nature of the marijuana business, that word would be *waiting*. Waiting to score, waiting to meet the man, waiting for the man who will take you to meet the man, waiting to pick up, waiting to deliver, waiting to wait. In Mexico, smuggling marijuana is a life lived in motel rooms, on the street, in towns that become scary from too much time hanging around. Mexican time is not time in the ordinary, *norteamericano* sense, but spatial, time moving on a different plane. Successful dealers operate on the assumption that time in Mexico does not exist, or if it does, it exists somewhere in the back of the imagination, lingering over you like old age or death. In Mexico, four P.M. at the cafe means midnight, *mañana* means next week, and next week means we don't even bother thinking about it. A load of weed promised by Tuesday next means that you make a phone call next Tuesday from Acapulco to see if your marijuana is out of the mountains yet. "Oh, no, *mano*, but *mañana*, I'm promising you. . . ."

My own experience with Sanchez told me that when he said he would meet me in four days, he would be there. If I was late with the truck, a dozen men would have to hang around a town they were not a part of—an unpardonable sin in smuggling. I also knew, however, that there was a chance Sanchez and the load could be delayed a few days somewhere along the trail. That meant that I would have to hang around an unfamiliar town. The logistics involved in moving weed get more critical the nearer you get to the road. Once on the road, or next to it, there is no room for fuckups. Things have to be timed perfectly —trucks, people, boats have to be in place, nothing can be where it isn't supposed to be. The difficulty of all this is that everything also

has to be prepared to be someplace else—immediately. No plan can be final; every plan has to leave room for contingencies. The real danger occurs when the people involved aren't ready for contingencies, when someone can't move immediately—after days and weeks of hanging around doing nothing.

Like many things in Mexico, marijuana smuggling is sort of a patiently evolving chaos. Successful gringo smugglers in Mexico are recognized as supreme masochists. When I started my smuggling career as a mule, or runner, driving loads across the border was a pleasure compared to the endless hours spent waiting in motel rooms, the days and weeks spent passing time in towns grown stale from too many visits, and the countless conspiratorial assignations to fix dates and times for further assignations.

When Gene and I drove up to the motel where we were to meet Zeke and Hoff, I was relieved to see a nice new four-wheel-drive pickup with California plates in the parking lot. As we parked our car and headed for the office, a door opened and Zeke stepped out. "Whaa whaa whaa," he laughed. "You guys ready to go hunting?" He grabbed me in an *abrazo* and pounded my back.

"Goddamn, you made it," I said. "I sure am pleased to see you. How is the setup here?"

"Purty as a pitchur. We booked a room for four, tol' 'em our two buddies would be arrivin' soon, an' t'morrow we got a guide t'take us huntin'."

Zeke laughed as he helped us carry our gear into the room. I always dug being around him, his whole demeanor was one of hulking good will. He kept everyone in stitches with a vast repertory of tall tales. In fact, the one hangup with Zeke was that his tall tales grew on you and you began to believe them. He told his stories with such sincerity that half of California and all of Mexico was snowed. Whenever he operated in Mexico, Zeke put on what he referred to as his "outfit": a fifty-dollar stetson, hundred-dollar Tony Lama boots, and a four-hundred-dollar custom-tailored western jacket. "You gotta play the game when you come down here, goddammit," he'd yell. "The Mex's expect it and this is the real me anyhow, haw haw haw!"

ROBERTO AYALA

Inside the room Hoff was lying on the bed reading. He jumped up and shook hands. "How about a shot?" He held up a jug of tequila and filled four glasses. "To celebrate a successful hunting trip," he said.

"If Stretch's brought down his boat to where he's supposed to be, it'll be a success," I said. "How long have you guys been here?"

"We got here yesterday. We already checked out the road up north. It's good all the way, no patrols, no nothing. Tomorrow when we go hunting we're going to take the rig off the road. The manager here knows the country and he's got a brother-in-law who'll guide us. We're going after jaguars."

"Fantastic. I'll drive up the coast tonight and see if Stretch has moved his boat down. You guys can hunt for the next two days and then meet me in Aquila. Then Zeke and I will go meet the load."

"Solid, baby." Zeke slapped my hand.

I was beginning to feel the rush, the excitement that builds up when the threads start coming together. It always makes me feel good. Part of the success of any operation is keeping a rhythm going. It pleased me that Zeke and Hoff had organized the hunting expedition. The knowledge that coworkers are doing their part is important. The hangups possible in any smuggling operation are so numerous that any sloughing of responsibility always puts a burden on someone else. It also creates tension and causes mistakes. I was especially pleased that Zeke had arranged to hire a guide for the next day. Every tourist in Mexico has to have a reason for being there. If you're not hanging around the big hotels and beaches, you'd better have some scam ready to cover your presence. Hunting is popular all along the west coast of Mexico, and Zeke and Hoff were natural hunters. As far as Gene was concerned, he could hunt with his camera. It was a good cover for our real hunting expedition.

That evening we went into town and got slightly *borracho*. When we returned to the motel I packed a small bag and got ready to take off for Laguna de los Leones. Stretch should have moved his boat down from the Sea of Cortez by now. If he had, everything was set. If he hadn't, I'd have to call Dr. Billyboy in San Francisco. He could fly down in twelve hours. If the boat was where it was supposed to be, I intended to forget about Dr. Billyboy's airplane. For one thing, Stretch's boat could carry all the weed Jesse and I had, and for another, I personally didn't like to move weed with airplanes.

During the mid and late sixties, 95 percent of the weed smuggled across the border was moved in ground vehicles. All types of vehicles were utilized, cars, campers, vans, pickups, trailers, even giant diesel-powered semi-trucks. Most of the large shipments of weed smuggled across the border by the Texas Syndicate moved in large semi-trucks carrying legal shipments of frozen fish, scrap metal, and vegetables. A ton of weed can easily be concealed under such a load. One outfit working through Juarez smuggled their weed concealed under tons of animal entrails, oozing across the border for months until customs agents got wise to them. When Operation Intercept was implemented in 1969, smuggling methodology, which was being revolutionized anyway, abruptly changed. Most big smugglers started using aircraft and boats, ignoring surface vehicles completely.

Few things cause more controversy among smugglers than how to move weed. Each method—land, sea, and air—has its devotees, and each devotee has his own particular style of operating with his chosen method. After cars and trucks became impractical, Jesse and I started using boats. I dig boats. For one thing, smuggling by sea has a long tradition behind it, and both Jesse and I had experience with the sea. Jesse had been a commercial fisherman and I had once been a merchant seaman. We also had access to a boat, which is the most important factor of all. The Mexican coasts are ideally suited for boat traffic. There are literally hundreds of small inlets, lagoons, bays, and deserted beaches where a smuggler can anchor, load, lie in if necessary, and, not least of all, hide. Another factor that increases my enthusiasm for boats is that most of the weed grown in Mexico is grown within fifty miles of the coast. A load can, theoretically, move from the field down to the coast and be put aboard a boat without once having moved on a road.

The disadvantages of boats are that they are slow, they require an experienced crew, and they cost a lot of money to outfit. There is also a hell of a lot of organization involved in making a successful run. The slowness doesn't bother me because I believe in doing things slow and easy—especially when dealing with weed. The one factor that is a pain in the ass is the crew. One never knows until that critical moment just how the hired hands will react in an emergency.

One time, on a smuggling operation somewhat similar to the one we were now on, the skipper of the boat we had hired decided at the last minute not to take the load. Jesse and I had moved three-quarters of a ton of weed out of the mountains, sat for three days on it in a small town in Morelos, then went to the coast to meet the boat. The skipper of the boat thought he knew Mexico as well as he did his boat, and when we arrived with the load in the middle of the night in a dense fog he had made up his mind that the vibes weren't right, that he should hang out for another day or two and clear his papers properly with the Port Captain before taking on the load and splitting. "Jesus Christ," I said, "what d'you want to be, a legal smuggler?"

"I just don't feel right about it," he said. "The timing's not right!"

"Fuck the timing! That's our job. We've been sitting on this weed for a week and you say the timing's not right. Man, you're gonna take on this load."

I'll never forget what happened next. Leo, the skipper, was a bull-headed German with no smuggling experience but with a master's knowledge of the sea. I looked straight into his eyes. "You were hired to pick up a load and deliver it to northern California. That's all you have to do. You don't have to fuck with the Mexicans, worry about papers, or hassle with the man. All you gotta do is load this shit on your boat and get out of here, do you understand?"

I was so mad I was shaking. For the first time in my life I felt that if I'd had a gun I would have shot somebody. Leo looked at me, clenching and unclenching his fists. "Man, I'll take it on, but if anything happens, I'm holding you responsible."

"That's right, I am responsible. And once the shit's on your boat, you're responsible. Now let's both of us do our jobs."

Any type of smuggling run that involves a number of people is inevitably tension prone. Leo was worried because he had never smuggled weed in his boat before, and still wasn't attuned to the fact that when you do something illegal, every aspect of that trip is illegal. If he had waited around to clear his boat with the Port Captain, perhaps the trip would have still gone down all right. There's also the chance the Port Captain might have gotten suspicious of Leo, maybe wanted to bite him or otherwise get some coin. Leo's problem was that he didn't trust me. The one thing about a smuggling operation, however, is that each person in on it has to trust the others implicitly. The fact that Leo got scared when it came time to load his boat illustrates one of the inevitable hassles with working with a boat—time. A lot of dudes can stand ten or twelve hours' pressure, the time required on a plane trip, not many can take the three or four weeks of pressure, which any boat trip requires, however.

I have never liked to use airplanes on smuggling runs because I know so little about them. Jesse and I had loaded a number of aircraft on bandit runs, but the trips were always put together by others. Our job was simply to cop high-quality weed and deliver it to the plane. Many smugglers who used to be very heavy into ground vehicles now use airplanes exclusively and swear by them, refusing to have anything to do with any other type of rig. A few smugglers have even taken flying lessons so they can pilot their own planes. My theory about moving weed precludes using an airplane, because I don't like to get involved in any trip that, come an emergency, I can't personally handle every aspect of myself. Obviously, if I can't fly an airplane, I can't handle every aspect of a plane trip.

Another thing about smuggling with planes that bugs me is, unless you own your own plane there is a good chance you can fall behind somebody else's bummer. I've heard reports of smugglers renting aircraft that had just returned from another smuggling caper run by someone else. The number of airplanes for rent is limited, and the heat knows what's going on at most airports after a few dope runs. A new gimmick The Man is installing on rented aircraft nowadays is a transponder, an electronic sensor that feeds information back to a master control center as to the plane's whereabouts at all times. More than one run has fallen because the dude piloting the plane was followed all the way down and back by a little electronic beep. The main thing that disturbs me about airplanes, though, is that once they go up they have to come down. If you're packing 500 kilos of primo in your back seat, sometimes you just don't want to come down.

Boats are something else. If you have an experienced crew working your boat, any emergency can be tempered by time and distance. The sea is very big. It is also, theoretically at least, international territory once you've passed the twelve-mile limit. In practice the twelve-mile limit doesn't mean much, especially when the Coast Guard is bearing down on you at thirty knots, but a reasonable person has a fighting chance in a boat. If he has things set up right, he's prepared to dump his load on a moment's notice, or even the whole boat if that becomes necessary.

Smuggling methods change with the times though, and the smugglers who are flying planes and sailing boats today will be driving trucks or maybe even be mailing their weed home by parcel post tomorrow. Many successful smugglers have, in fact, started using cars and trucks again for the simple reason that the feds are getting too good at nailing planes and boats. Smugglers who return to ground vehicles rely on percentages, figuring that there's so much traffic moving between Mexico and the United States that a goodly number of loads are bound to get through no matter how much surveillance there is. All kinds of ground vehicles are still being used, but the successful rigs work in cycles, with the customs people usually six months behind the smugglers. Mules will drive loads across concealed in especially rigged motor homes, the retired-folks rig, as they are called. When the heat pops a few of them, all those type rigs are suspect and the smuggler switches to something else. The secret of success with ground vehicles is always to be a couple of steps ahead of The Man. As long as you set the pace, always being inventive and ingenious, then it's the dudes who copy you who will fall. Some of the most successful rigs working the border right now are nondescript family cars that have been taken apart and completely rebuilt at great expense. The smugglers who use these rigs specialize in moving small loads of extremely high-quality weed across the border, often making two or three trips a week. There is one dude in San Francisco who is considered a genius at building this type of rig. He has already built a total of seven cars, the first of which has been running regularly since 1967, and none of his cars have ever been popped.

Rocky, the genius who builds the pop-proof smuggling rigs, and Space, his running partner, are a legendary dope-smuggling duo in the industry, at least among longhairs. Rocky is a tall, gangling dude who looks like Little Abner and runs around San Francisco in bare feet and a blue work shirt with the tail hanging out. He's an authority on wines and mathematics and metallurgy and he's absolutely brilliant when it comes to blueprints and welding rods. His specialty is creating smuggling rigs with hermetically sealed compartments and special doors that require handmade tools to open. The compartments are so ingenious that one of the tests he gives his cars is a ten-hour shakedown conducted by expert smugglers. Space, his partner, s-s-s-s-speaks l-l-l-l-like t-t-t-this, absolutely unable to open his mouth without stammering so bad he's impossible to understand. In one of my last dope runs I agreed to load their latest rig for its first run. I copped fifty pounds of the best primo weed in Mexico (that's all the car would carry), and loaded the car. To give the car the super test, Space and Rocky drove it across the border themselves, Space with his machine-gun stammer and Rocky with his bare feet, long hair, and balls hanging out. As soon as they drove up to the customs shed, The Man thought he had a live one. They were moved into the secondary inspection area and everything came out of the car, clothes, seats, seat belts, floormats, even the ashtray. When The Man couldn't find anything inside the car, he went underneath it with mirrors and probes and lights, and thumped the sides. Finally a big German shepherd weed dog was brought out and he went over the car. Nothing. Not a sniff. After three and a half hours at the inspection station, Space and Rocky drove home with their fifty pounds of primo.

Because of the increased sophistication on the part of the weed industry during the last few years, many people are involved in peripheral aspects of the trade and must be considered smugglers, when actually they are only hired hands who have little or nothing to do with the behind-the-scenes realities of the industry. Drivers, or mules, as they are called, are people hired by smugglers to drive specific loads across the border. They have nothing to do with copping, nothing to do with selling, and often they never see the weed. They are hired, given the keys to a car in Mexico, and told where to deliver the load. They are usually paid a flat fee, half in advance and the other half upon delivery. In some cases mules are a regular part of the organization, partners getting equal shares. In other cases they have nothing to do with the organization, do not want to be part of it, and drive only for a straight fee. Many sophisticated organizations like to hire unaffiliated mules because it lessens the involvement—and the danger. The unaffiliated mule meets only the contact man in the organization, which insures anonymity for the rest of the group if the load goes down. If the mule breaks down, he can incriminate no more than the one dude he dealt with.

A number of criteria are used to pick mules—appearance, experience with the border, sex, personality, etc. The best mules tend to be anonymous, both physically and personally. Many couples work as mules, sometimes driving loads across with their children. A successfully organized operation utilizing a hired mule will often have some background details worked out in case of a fall. Sometimes an ad will be placed in a local newspaper in a town removed from traditional weed areas. The ad will request the services of a driver to transport a car back from Mexico for a retired couple who don't want to drive their own car back. The ad is legitimate, the individual who answers it is hired and drives the car back into the United States ignorant of the fact that it's loaded with weed.

A variation on the theme is for a smuggler to pick up a couple who are hitchhiking through Mexico and let them borrow the car. The smuggler lays a story down about a family member being sick, it's necessary for him to fly home immediately, etc. If the couple agrees to take the car and they get it across the border safely, a not unreasonable possibility since they won't be burdened by any of the paranoia vibes that usually plague hired mules, then it's simply a matter of the smuggler retrieving his car once it's across the border. Naturally the smuggler doesn't let his car out of his sight when it crosses the border, for when trips like this are set up, it's important to pin the action at the crossing. If the car is popped and the customs people believe the couple's story about driving the car home for a stranger, they will more than likely have the couple deliver the car to where it's supposed to go. If the smuggler's dumb enough to be there waiting for it, then he's popped.

A third variation is for a smuggler to work in consort with a garage in Mexico. When a gringo brings his car in to be repaired, a mechanic-accomplice loads it with weed. The smuggler finds out where the gringo lives, and once the car is home safe, goes there and rips it off and recovers his weed.

When mules are hired who are aware of what they are doing, certain criteria must be met. In the first place, common sense tells one that a mule should have no previous record. If a person is even remotely associated with weed via previous arrests, he shouldn't be hired as a mule. The mule should also be made absolutely aware of all the potential dangers he faces if he is arrested at the border. The customs people have a way of instilling fear in young arrestees at the border, and fear is usually what makes a mule crack. A mule must have a plausible story prepared and he must stick to it. And no matter what happens, the mule must be absolutely sure that he is not going to be abandoned by his confederates. If the customs people are able to make him believe he is going to be sacrificed by his crime partners, then it's all over for the smuggling operation. For this reason it is also important that a mule be paid commensurate with his task. Many smuggling operations go down behind simple things like not enough money at the right time, fear of being abandoned, no plausible story, etc. The smuggling ring that hires a cheap mule and then fails to back him up usually ends up with the whole load on their backs.

Since Operation Cooperation a new breed of mule has entered the smuggling picture; these are the professional pilots, more sophisticated, better trained, and more expensive to hire. Like their earthbound brothers, however, the flying mule's job is to get loads of weed across the border. Many of the flying mules are members of the hell-for-leather Vietnam war-baby breed who dig making runs low through the arroyos with their Cherokee 6's. There are hundreds of small airstrips like the one Jesus took me and Jesse to hacked out of the mountains in Mexico, and a pilot with a good eye and lots of nerve can make it in and out of a strip like that in fifteen minutes, provided his crew has the weed and spare fuel ready. The problem with smuggling weed by airplane is that the whole operation becomes extremely complicated, involving more men, equipment, and money. Smuggling runs have become much more complicated in the last year or so because flight plans are now required of all aircraft flying in Mexico, and no matter how remote the spot a pilot decides to land in, there always seems to be someone there. All runs that do make it into the mountains must provide for their own fuel, and in many areas this is an incredible task. Timing is all-important with aircraft also, five minutes one way or another can be fatal. Most fuckups that occur with airplanes involve timing, a man not where he is supposed to be, the weed late in arriving, unexpected headwinds, too heavy loads. Although smuggling by airplane is the speediest method when it works, it is also the one method that has all the sophisticated electronic paraphernalia of America working against it. Despite this, I would estimate that after the ground operations of organizations like the Texas Syndicate, most weed is smuggled out of Mexico in small aircraft.

That night I drove to Laguna de los Leones to reconnoiter with Stretch. There are two roads into the lagoon, a main road that's paved up to within five miles of the lagoon, and a back road that's unpaved, rocky, and hard. Jesse and I picked the lagoon not only because it was conveniently located, but because of the two access roads. We learned early never to take a load of weed into any place that has only one way in and out. Ideally, when we moved our weed down from Hostapan we'd be able to send lead cars down both roads to scout the way for us. One of the things I intended to do while rendezvousing with Stretch was to check out both routes. I wanted to see if there was any unusual activity along the roads, construction sites that might hinder us, idle soldiers or patrols lounging along the roads, or heavy traffic that could be considered dangerous. If one or both roads were unsatisfactory, then Stretch and I would have to choose an alternative loading place. Since it took time to move a boat up and down the coast, it was important that Stretch be at the lagoon.

I drove the main road into the Laguna de los Leones and arrived just after dawn. It's curious the rhythm an operation takes when things are going right. Zeke and Hoff had told me that before leaving the States they had the tarot cards read concerning the trip and the answer had come out, *A Dance.* They thought that was a good omen. When they crossed the border at Nogales they had their omen reaffirmed. They had brought along a small motorcycle which had no papers, and when they went through the vehicle-registration point just south of Nogales, a mariache band was playing and the officials waved them through after giving them permits not only for the truck, but also for the cycle. All along the route it had been a dance, according to Zeke. Our meeting at the motel in Acapulco was part of that same good rhythm. I knew the rhythm was important, just as the lack of it is important. Bum trips can be sensed in the timing. Lack of timing, missed appointments, misunderstood directions, are all signs set up by nature to warn the careless smuggler that he'd better be careful. Perspicacious smugglers always read the little signs and signals that are posted along the route.

When I turned off the paved road and started down toward the lagoon, I almost ran over Stretch and Phil. I braked to a Mexican stop (a rush of speed and a quick brodie that showers dust over pedestrians) and leaped out. We greeted one another with great backslappings and dances in the dirt. Phil, Stretch's first mate, stood quietly by as Stretch and I danced around one another.

"Man, we've been trying to hitchhike into town for two hours," Stretch cried. "We want breakfast and there hasn't been a car in sight."

"It's the rhythm, boys," I yelled. "It's all a dance." I told them about Zeke and Hoff and they laughed. We jumped into the wagon and headed for San Martin.

"Goddamn, I can't believe it. When you told me to move my boat down here I was pissed. I wanted you to haul the weed up to Alma. I'm glad you had us come down though. Phil and me had the greatest trip in the world. Phil caught a forty-pound albacore day before yesterday."

Phil was a short, dark-haired dude whom I had met only briefly in San Francisco. He was an expert meteorologist and navigator, and I had taken an immediate liking to him. I was to have my first feelings about him confirmed in many ways later when things got sticky. Stretch had built many boats and was an expert sailor. The two of them got along well, which was important. Next to having a reliable boat, it was critical that the people on board get along also.

After taking them into town to eat, we spent the day cruising the lagoon looking for the best place to load. All indications were that the south end of the lagoon was most favorable. We could drive the truck right onto the beach, and the waves there appeared minimal. The north end of the lagoon was open to the sea and was buffeted by heavy surf. Since we would be loading our weed into rubber rafts and motoring them out to the big boat, it was important that we not encounter any surf. If we dumped our load in the water, there would be hell to pay.

Late that afternoon I drove the secondary road back to Acapulco, a long slow drive over ruts and stones. There was no traffic and no unexpected detours. The road bisected a few hamlets, wattle and daub huts where campesinos stood alongside the road. Much of the road was built up on a levee. In an emergency, such as an army patrol approaching, a four-wheel-drive vehicle could plunge into the jungle, but the height of the levee made this almost impossible, so I checked the road out carefully with the odometer and marked each spot where a vehicle could drive off safely. By nightfall I was exhausted. I parked the wagon in a small clearing and slept.

The next day I checked out the rest of the road and returned to Acapulco. The motel room was deserted when I arrived, so I showered and took a nap. About ten P.M. Zeke and the rest of the boys came in. They were just returning from their hunting trip into the river basin north of Acapulco. They were full of tales of wild pigs and jaguars and the excitement of the day. No one had killed anything but everyone had had a ball. I told them what I had learned and we made plans for the next day. Gene and Hoff were to take the station wagon to Aquila and check into a motel room and wait for us there. Zeke and I would drive to Hostapan to meet Jesse and Sanchez. If everything went according to schedule, in two days' time our weed would be on Stretch's boat.

I called Jesus early the next morning and arranged to pick up our guide at the cutoff road leading into Hostapan. Zeke and I drove over to the spot. When we arrived, Hector was waiting for us. Hector was a short, dark campesino with one eye that was perpetually lidded over. One of his arms was also withered, about six inches shorter than the other. He explained that he had been involved in an "accident" in the mountains; soldiers had ambushed a load of weed he was transporting a few years before. Zeke and I said nothing as Hector guided us down the cutoff road toward Hostapan. After driving a few miles down the dirt road he had me pull the truck off the road under a large tree. *"Espérate aquí,"* he said. We waited while the sun went down.

While we were waiting I took the opportunity to unhook the interior and running lights on the truck. I also disengaged the light over the license plate. When it was dusk we took off for Hostapan. Although the town was only twenty miles off the road, those twenty miles were unlike any I had ever driven. There was no road, only occasional gashes cut out of the earth that showed where previous vehicles had gone. We followed cowpaths and arroyos, taking the path of least resistance. Many times I was forced to back up and start again when Hector lost his way. "I have never been on this 'road' in a pickup truck before," he said glumly.

Zeke and Hector braced themselves and hung on tight as the empty truck bounced and jolted over the ruts and ditches. I had the steering wheel to hang onto, but even that was uncomfortable. At the end of an hour I was exhausted. By the time we had gone five miles it was pitch black, which made driving all the more difficult. Occasionally

Hector had to get out of the truck and lead the way on foot, guiding us with his flashlight. I had been a little naïve when I had glibly informed Sanchez that I could make it into Hostapan with the truck. If I had known the condition of the road, I would have considered it for a long time before agreeing. It was too late to worry about it now, though. The weed was waiting.

Three hours after leaving the big tree we came to a small gate. Hector got out and opened it. *"Cinco más kilómetros,"* he said, after closing the gate and getting back in the truck. Five more kilometers. I knew as well as anyone that Hector's five more kilometers could just as easily be twenty-five more kilometers. Might as well ask a campesino how far it is to the moon as ask him how far it is to the next village. One time I drove from Ajijic to Puerto Vallarta by going over the mountains, a distance I had traced on the map as close to 150 miles. I found after driving fifty miles, however, that the road disappeared into a cowpath. I stopped a dozen campesinos along the way and asked them how long it took to drive to Puerto Vallarta. "Oh, two hours, señor," one would say. The next would convince me that it was a five-hour drive. Still a third knew it was a seven-hour drive because his patron had driven it last week. It was twenty-four hours and three ruptured tires later when I arrived in Puerto Vallarta.

I was sure it was the same with Hector's distance. Hoff looked at me and slowly shook his head. The new Ford pickup was disintegrating under us. The camper shell moaned ominously each time I twisted the truck down another arroyo. If we arrived in one piece we would be lucky; getting out would be something else. One thing that would help though, would be a load in the back. At least the truck wouldn't bounce over the ruts like a Mexican jumping bean. My arms felt like leaden appendages and my ass felt like it had been shoved halfway up to my shoulders. All of a sudden I saw a light. "Hostapan," Hector whispered. "Turn off the lights." I turned off the lights and Hector got out of the truck. He unbuttoned his pants and pissed on the headlights, then took handfuls of dirt and tossed them on the lenses. "Turn them on," he whispered. I turned them on and he threw more dirt on, making them dimmer. When they were almost completely covered he was satisfied. "Now we can go on," he said. "It's important that no one see us."

Twenty minutes later we stopped beside a rock wall. Hector got out. "Wait here," he said. Zeke and I waited in the truck for ten minutes. It was pitch black outside. The silence was ominous. From afar I could hear what sounded like music. It was a cantina in town, a jukebox. Suddenly a faint Mexican grito lifted up over the sound of the music and faded away. Campesinos letting loose after a hard day's work. I envied them. It was chilly, so I huddled under my sweater. Zeke coughed deep in his throat, and suddenly Hector reappeared at the door. Sanchez was with him. "*Bueno,*" Sanchez said, climbing into the truck. "I'm glad you made it. Go that way." He pointed toward my right.

We skirted Hostapan, which was bigger than I expected, and ended up on the far side of town. "Turn around and back down toward the cemetery," Sanchez said.

With the aid of Hector's flashlight, I turned the pickup around and backed down toward the cemetery. As I did so a dozen figures emerged from the darkness. Each one carried a large sack on his shoulder. Jesse was among them. "You made it," he said. "I'm damn glad. We've had this stuff buried in the cemetery since last night. Let's get it loaded."

Zeke opened the back of the camper and jumped inside. The men carried the sacks out of the graveyard and dropped them behind the truck. I handed them in to Zeke. There were sixteen sacks, each one containing fifty kilos of marijuana. It took us fifteen minutes to load them, stuffing each sack carefully inside the camper shell. When the last sack was loaded, Zeke covered the weed with a blanket and locked the door. We were ready to go.

I shook hands with Sanchez and Lupe. "*Gracias, hombres,*" I said. They gave me their limp hands and smiled in the darkness. The other campesinos came forward. I shook hands with each one, thanking them in turn. Zeke got behind the wheel. Hector jumped in beside him. He was going to guide us back to the main road. "*Bien viaje,*" Sanchez whispered, as Jesse and I jumped in the truck.

The trip out was smoother than the trip in. Even though the cab was crowded with four men, it was more comfortable because the laden truck took the bumps easier. It didn't feel like riding inside an empty tin can. Once we were out of sight of town, Hector cleaned off the headlights and we speeded up. It was important that we get out of the area before sunup. At three A.M. we passed through the gate.

Jesse filled me in on the trip out of the mountains. It had been uneventful except for one burro falling over a cliff. The burro was badly injured and had to be shot. Because the other animals were so heavily loaded, the weed had been buried back in the canyon. Lupe intended to retrieve it on the way back. I told Jesse how my end fared. "Everybody is where they're supposed to be. Stretch and Phil moved the boat down to the lagoon, and Hoff and Gene are waiting for us in Aquila. We should be able to make the run down to the boat late tonight."

Just before dawn we reached the big tree. Hector got out of the truck and shook hands through the window. "You know the way now," he said. "Go with God." "You too, friend," Jesse said. "*Muchas gracias.*" Hector disappeared in the dark.

Half an hour later we reached the main road. Jesse took over the wheel and aimed the truck toward Aquila. At the first Pemex station we came to, he stopped for gas. I got out of the truck and walked around the camper. I could smell the weed. "God, we've got to do something about the smell," I said. Jesse nodded. Fortunately the kid pumping the gas didn't know the smell of weed or didn't care. He was half asleep anyway. After gassing up, Zeke drove the rig a hundred yards down the road and parked it. We all three trudged back to the small restaurant beside the station to eat.

"We've got to cover that smell," I said. "It's just too damn strong. Every time we gas up it's going to cause us trouble."

"Maybe we can tape all the cracks" Zeke said. "That might stop the smell."

"We need some ground coffee," Jesse said. "It'll stop the smell for awhile. We can stop in Santa Rosa and get some."

Photo overleaf by Roberto Ayala

Santa Rosa was an hour's drive down the road. When we arrived there, Jesse parked the rig on a side street and I went searching for a market. After half a dozen attempts I found a small *supermercado* that was open. I bought fifteen pounds of coffee. The proprietor looked at me in wonder. I paid him in pesos and walked out.

Jesse picked us up and we drove out of town looking for a spot to open the camper. On the way Zeke cut open the coffee cans with his knife. Twenty minutes outside of town, Jesse turned off the road and parked behind a clump of trees. I jumped out of the truck and ran around and opened the back. The smell of cooking marijuana almost knocked me over. The inside of the camper was like a furnace. Sweat dripped from the blanket and windows. One of the big problems with transporting weed is disguising the smell it gives off. Even dry marijuana cooks when it's in an enclosed area. Smugglers try everything to hide the smell of weed and nothing seems to work. Even weed enclosed in air-tight packages is susceptible to the weed-sniffing dogs employed on the border. I have heard of dogs being able to sniff out dope stashed inside fake crankcases and transmission housings.

Our problem wasn't dogs though, it was the people who would be able to smell our truck from fifteen feet away if we didn't do something. Coffee helped because its own odor combined with the smell of weed to make a third odor. Coffee also soaked up the sweat from the weed. We quickly threw the loose coffee in on top of the weed. Fifteen pounds wasn't much but it would have to do. Jesse closed the back of the camper and locked it. I smelled around all the seams. An alert nose could discover something, but the smell was so weird that it would take a super sleuth to figure out what it was.

Back on the road we made our plans for that night. Once in Aquila, Zeke would take Hoff with him and drive the lead car to the lagoon. They would cover the main road first and then drive back around the secondary road to meet us. By going around the long way and returning up the secondary route, they'd be able to reaffirm my own conclusions about the two routes and find out if anything new had developed. We both were equipped with walkie-talkies. Once we made contact, Zeke and Hoff could take the lead and we would head for the boat.

Our walkie-talkies were effective for only ten miles so we had to stick fairly close together at all times. The map I had made on the previous run had every exit marked on it, so if anything unusual developed and Zeke radioed back, we would have time to race to one of the exits and disappear. It wasn't a foolproof plan by any means, but at least it gave us some protection.

One of the hangups that plague the smuggler who buys his weed directly from the grower is that he has to take care of all the logistics once the weed is moved out of the mountains. If we had been getting our weed directly from a big entrepreneur, it would have been no problem having him deliver it directly to our boat. Of course, we'd have to pay more for it. As it was, Jesse and I had taken over the entrepreneur's role without his facilities. This didn't present too much of a problem as long as all the threads came together; if they came unraveled somewhere along the line, then it would be a different story. In normal circumstances, the entrepreneur would have moved the weed out of the mountains and stored it in a rancho for a few days. We had no warehouse or rancho so we had to get our weed directly to the boat fast.

Ordinarily Jesse and I wouldn't have attempted an operation such as this. Moving a ton of weed through Mexico is always dangerous, and it's doubly dangerous when you're working off the cuff, as it were. The fact that we weren't set up properly lingered in the back of my mind, as I knew it did in Jesse's. Under ideal conditions we would have rented a rancho near Hostapan and then sat on the weed until all the tactical problems were worked out. In a sense we were ignoring the first rule of smuggling, which is, don't jam things through. The nature of the business is such, however, that despite rules, the rhythm also determines how things go. Even the best planned and coordinated smuggling operations sometimes fall, and the opposite is also true, some incredibly inept and hastily conceived ones succeed. The one dangerous aspect of our present trip was that we were leaving so little room for miscues; if there was a hangup in loading the boat, a mechanical breakdown in the truck, if any number of things happened, there'd be hell to pay. Now though my concern was with the smell,

Photo overleaf by Roberto Ayala

and meeting Zeke at the right time. We'd have to take everything else as it came.

We intended to meet Zeke about twenty miles from the lagoon on the secondary road at eleven P.M. The drive to the lagoon would take forty-five minutes and the loading should take another thirty minutes. Stretch and Phil were to meet us on the south end of the lagoon at midnight. If things went okay, they would be out on the high seas by two A.M. and in international waters by dawn.

The trip into Aquila was uneventful except for the super-paranoia we felt each time we stopped for gas. We stopped in Amotlan and bought another fifteen pounds of coffee to throw in on the weed, but even so, by the time we pulled into Aquila in late afternoon, the truck reeked. The smell emanating from the camper was a cross between mota and mocha, guaranteed to get you high—or at least stun you. We decided it was foolish to park the truck in town, so after dropping me and Zeke off at the motel, Jesse drove outside of town to sit on the weed. After I cleaned up I would have Zeke drive me out to relieve Jesse.

The emotion you go through on a smuggling run is like a spring that gets tighter and tighter. All the pressure mounts up in the final hours, tempers flare, arguments occur, plans are questioned, doubts and self-doubts plague you. While I sat in the truck waiting for dark, I tried to figure out if we had all the loose ends together, was there anything we had forgotten? As far as I could see, except for unexpected mechanical fuckups, we had covered every aspect of the operation. Stretch had his boat in the lagoon, Zeke and Hoff were ready to drive the lead car, Jesse and I would follow with Gene and the weed. The fact that Gene wanted to take pictures of everything complicated things a little, but he'd have to take his chances. If he could handle his part of the job while we handled ours, then it was okay with me. At this time, however, we couldn't afford to take time out for him— no hanging around waiting for the proper light.

At dusk I drove back into town and picked up Gene and Jesse. Zeke and Hoff had already taken off. Their drive around the lagoon and back up the secondary road would take them two extra hours. At

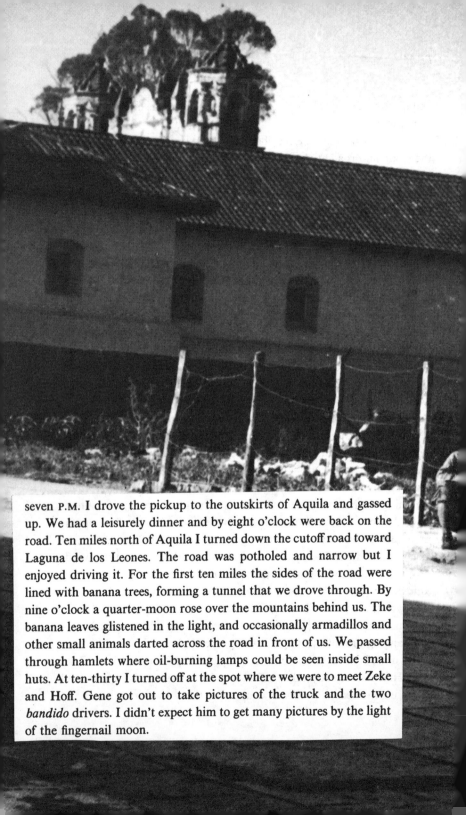

seven P.M. I drove the pickup to the outskirts of Aquila and gassed up. We had a leisurely dinner and by eight o'clock were back on the road. Ten miles north of Aquila I turned down the cutoff road toward Laguna de los Leones. The road was potholed and narrow but I enjoyed driving it. For the first ten miles the sides of the road were lined with banana trees, forming a tunnel that we drove through. By nine o'clock a quarter-moon rose over the mountains behind us. The banana leaves glistened in the light, and occasionally armadillos and other small animals darted across the road in front of us. We passed through hamlets where oil-burning lamps could be seen inside small huts. At ten-thirty I turned off at the spot where we were to meet Zeke and Hoff. Gene got out to take pictures of the truck and the two *bandido* drivers. I didn't expect him to get many pictures by the light of the fingernail moon.

While Jesse fiddled with the walkie-talkie, I wandered around the area. We were parked in a clearing surrounded by trees about thirty feet off the side of the road. Above the trees I saw the stars; they were incredibly brilliant. It was absolutely black among the trees, despite the sliver of moon. I felt a chill creep over me. I remembered stories smugglers told of their various adventures, but all I could remember were the fuckups, a few of which I had made myself. I remembered one time when I was driving out of Puerto Vallarta with a half ton of weed in the same kind of truck we were driving tonight, and I came face to face with a six-by full of Mexican soldiers. Some of the soldiers were strung out along the road with M-16s on their backs as I blew around the bend, and without thinking, without having time to think, I gunned the rig and swerved through them. They stared at me in amazement as my truck flashed past, not having time to jump in their truck and take off after me. They had no reason to take off after me since they didn't know what I had in back of my truck. Had they known, or had I been going slower and been stopped, for no reason as sometimes happens. . . . I didn't want to think about it. Another time some friends were driving a load of weed up north and they stopped in a service station to gas up. They smelled something burning and when they looked under the pickup bed they saw what it was. The false bottom of their rig was built too close to the muffler and had caught fire. Without waiting for gas they jumped in their rig and roared out of town. By the time they reached the outskirts the whole pickup was in flames, so they left it and ran into the desert. Twenty thousand dollars' worth of weed burnt up and them in the desert with no water. They hid out for two nights and then circled back into Guaymas and took a bus home, flat broke. When the bus passed by the spot where their rig had burnt, all they could see was a pile of junk. So it goes.

Of course, there were the good times too. All I had to do was think back long enough. One time a couple of young dudes with a beat-up truck and 200 kilos of weed rambled into Nogales, and their truck died right in front of the customs shed. "Get that pile of junk out of here," the customs man said. The boys shrugged their shoulders helplessly, so three guards and an immigration flack walked over and pushed the rig off the ramp. It was a busy day and people were hurried. Once through the gate the boys fiddled with their carburetor and got the truck going again. They drove home $20,000 richer.

There are a thousand apocryphal tales of border crossings, good and bad, and I think I have heard most of them. Trips in cars, trips in boats, trips on surfboards, trips in airplanes, trips in trucks, trips on burros, trips on foot. One time a group called the Bunkhouse Gang contacted Jesse for advice in moving 1,700 bricks across the border near Sonoita. They didn't want him to go along because they'd have to cut him in, they just wanted free information. They had a Dodge four-wheel-drive camper that could carry all the kilos, a couple of motorcycles to reconnoiter the desert, and cars to take the weed out of the area once it reached the road. "Who's driving the rig?" Jesse asked. "I am," a guy named Jonesy popped up. "That's my job." "Well, good, because it looks like you guys have everything pretty well covered. Just make sure you don't let the Mexicans drive your rig."

The following week the gang moved its forces down across the desert to pick up the weed. The Mexican connection had a ranch fronting the border, so the camper was driven across the border to the ranch and loaded. After the kilos were inside the truck, one of the Mexicans got behind the wheel. Jonesy, the driver, shrugged his shoulders and climbed in beside him. Just as they were crossing the border the big Dodge got stuck in an arroyo. The Mexican backed up and made a run for the opposite slope. No use. Back up again and make a stronger run. On the third run he broke the driveshaft. When Jonesy told us about it later, Jesse laughed. "Giving a Mexican a truck to load is insane. He'll load it too full and then drive it too fast. I told you not to let a Mexican drive the rig."

Photo overleaf by Roberto Ayala

At ten-thirty Jesse picked up Zeke on the walkie-talkie. They were a few miles away and everything was clear. I drove out of the clearing and headed down the road. In a few minutes we met. They turned around and headed back toward the lagoon. We gave them a fifteen-minute lead and then followed. No one said anything as we drove down the dirt road. All eyes were intent on the road. At eleven-thirty Zeke called back on the radio to say that they were at the lagoon. Jesse radioed back for them to continue on around to the north end of the lagoon while we arrived at the south end. After making sure there was no one at the north end, they were to return to help us load.

Everything was going smoothly. I traded places with Jesse, and he drove slowly toward the south end of the lagoon. The road ambled through coconut plantations, cutting back and forth at right angles as it skirted the fields. At one point three cows crossed the road in front of us, waving their tails imperiously as they let us by. Gene snapped pictures of the cows. The road was full of water-filled ruts. I held on as Jesse eased the truck through them. When we reached the south end of the lagoon, Jesse turned off the road. I got out and locked the hubs into four-wheel drive. We continued down the beach into a group of trees and parked the truck. We got out and walked down the beach. The bay was clear, too clear. I could see Stretch's boat sitting about 300 yards off the beach. The silver strip of moon was directly overhead, casting a slight glow on everything. It was eerie how far you could see. I saw some lights on the other side of the lagoon, a distance of fifteen miles. While we stood there I noticed the

surf. It seemed awfully high. In fact, the waves were crashing in on the beach. I knew when the moon started going down the waves would get higher. We had to move.

While we stood there I heard muffled sounds of activity on the boat. Stretch and Phil were bringing the skiffs into shore. Stretch had a fiberglass skiff and two rubber life rafts which we intended to use to haul the weed out to his boat. As soon as I heard the sound I raced back to the clump of trees to get the truck. Jesse and Gene stayed on the beach. My heart was beating fiercely when I reached the truck. I climbed in and started it, and without turning on the lights, eased it out of the trees and started down the beach. The truck seemed to make a terrific roar, especially in compound low. I was sure it could be heard all the way into San Martin. When I reached Gene and Jesse, Phil and Stretch were just coming in. They were about twenty yards out, on the other side of the surf. The waves seemed gigantic to me, bigger than I had expected. And this was supposed to be the lee side of the lagoon.

While Stretch started the ten-horse outboard to hold the skiff out beyond the waves, Phil eased the two rubber life rafts over the surf. He came scooting in on a wave and crashed on the beach. "Damn!" he cried. "This surf is big."

"Don't worry about it, let's get this shit out of the truck," Jesse cried.

I had the back of the camper open and had already thrown the blanket out. I yanked the large sacks of weed out of the truck and threw them down on the sand. Phil and Jesse picked them up and loaded them in the rubber rafts. Each raft held four sacks. While we were loading them the outboard motor on Stretch's skiff died. He tumbled in on a wave. He was soaking wet. "Jesus Christ," he cried. "Let's go. I can't hold this thing out there all night."

Both rubber rafts were full and the rest of the sacks were lying on the sand. Jesse picked up one and threw it in Stretch's skiff. "C'mon," he said. "Take this load out and come back for the rest. It'll take two trips."

Stretch leaped in the skiff and Phil and Jesse pushed him off the

sand. He yanked the motor on and headed into the surf. The towline between the skiff and the first rubber boat went taut, so Phil and I yanked the rubber boat into the water. As Phil jumped in I dragged on the second rubber boat. Just then a terrific wave roared over me. Stretch and the skiff hurtled by upside down. A sack of weed floated serenely out in the water. I splashed after it and dragged it ashore. "Too big," Phil yelled. "The waves are too big. We can't load here."

At that precise moment I spotted a pair of headlights moving down the beach toward us. I stood stock still watching them. Oh, Jesus, I thought, here they come. For a panic-stricken second I had visions of weed spread all over the beach while the Federales drove up with their machine guns out. "Get the shit back in the truck," I shouted hoarsely. "Somebody's coming."

We worked like demons. While Jesse and Phil threw the sacks in the truck, I stacked them. It was important to fit them in well or we wouldn't get them all back in the truck. It seemed to take hours. I was so exhausted from yanking the large sacks around that I could hardly stand up. I looked for Gene. I hadn't even thought of him. The crazy bastard was standing to one side shooting pictures. This is insane, I thought. Just then, the headlights turned off the beach and disappeared. "Thank God," I whispered to no one in particular.

"Listen," Stretch said. "We can't load the boat here. These are freak waves caused by the moon. We'll have to do something else."

"What about the other side?" I said.

"It should be calm," Stretch said. "It was flat this afternoon."

"Let's go there then," Jesse said. "What about the outboard?"

"It's finished, water-soaked. We'll have to use oars. Let's leave one raft here and take the skiff and the other raft back to the boat. We'll get over to the other side as fast as we can."

"Can you guys make it? You'll have to swim those rafts out to the boat."

"We can make it, man. Get going!" Stretch grabbed the skiff and pushed it into the water. Phil dragged the rubber life raft in after him. The two swam the boats through the surf.

I dragged the abandoned rubber boat up on the beach and left it beside the blanket. Jesse and I jumped in the truck where Gene was calmly loading his camera. "These aren't going to come out," he said. "Too dark." I shook my head. "Fuckups, goddamit, fuckups. Why the fuck does this surf have to be so big?"

While Jesse drove around the lagoon, I fiddled with the walkie-talkie. After a few minutes I contacted Zeke. "Stay where you are," I said. "We can't load down here. We've got to load on your end. Make sure it's clear."

I was shaking with exhaustion. My fingers were raw from yanking the burlap sacks. Jesse's hands were gripping the wheel tightly. I could see he was pissed. "Damn," he said. "Why didn't Stretch tell us the surf was too big? That was his job."

I said nothing. We both knew it was our job to okay or not okay the loading. We were jamming, that's what. We were damn lucky not to have had our whole load jammed right back down in our faces. If we got the stuff aboard Stretch's boat tonight we would be lucky. We both knew that. We only had a couple of hours before the fishermen started out, and if we were loading weed when they got up, that would be the end of it.

On the north end of the lagoon were some abandoned structures and a group of fishermen's huts. We drove through the huts slowly as dogs barked. On the far side of the settlement we parked the rig and waited. I slumped over the wheel. My mind was completely boggled by the fuckup. I couldn't think. I wanted someone else to make the decisions. Jesse said nothing. Finally he broke the silence. "We could cancel out here and move on up the coast. In two days we could load off Cape Blanco. Just stop everything cold, stop jamming. It might be the best thing to do."

"God, I'd like to get this thing over with tonight," I said. "I don't know. . . ."

Jesse lit a cigarette and looked out the window. From the fishermen's settlement a rooster crowed. I looked at the sky. It already seemed lighter. We had to do something fast.

"I'm going to walk over to the beach," Jesse said. "If I see the boat I'll give you two flashes with my light. Bring the truck out then."

"I want to go with you," Gene said.

"C'mon, let's go." The two of them disappeared.

After they left I sat quietly in the truck. I saw headlights approaching, and Zeke and Hoff drove up. They parked and shut off their motor. "What's happenin'?" Zeke whispered.

I explained the fuckup. Zeke and Hoff spoke briefly. "If the boat makes it back over to this side, you can drive out to the beach on a levee over there," Zeke said. He pointed with his chin toward the sea.

"It's the only way to get out 'cause the rest of the area is flooded. Once you go out I can park my rig on the levee and no one else is gonna make it. Y'might think of that."

"How wide is the levee?" I asked.

"Wide as one car," Zeke said. "If I park my car in the middle of it, ain't nothin' gonna get by. The only way the Federales can get to you is if they have water wings or else drive five miles down the beach and cross over. I think you can do it."

Zeke's information got me going again. I was pissed off at myself for even thinking of quitting. Just then I saw a flash from the beach. I wasn't sure. "Did you see anything?" I asked Zeke. "It looked like a light to me," Zeke said.

I looked again and I saw the unmistakable arc of a flashlight. I started the truck. "You follow me out and block the levee," I called to Zeke. He nodded and started his engine.

As I drove out on the levee I could hear roosters crowing behind me. The fishermen would be getting up soon. Halfway out on the levee I picked up Jesse and Gene. "Stretch and Phil are over there," he said. "They've got the skiff and the rubber boat already on the beach."

Suddenly I felt better. I pushed down on the throttle and raced toward the beach. The levee was indeed narrow, one wrong move and I would have hurtled over the embankment. Three-quarters of a mile out Jesse pointed to a ramp and I turned left. We were on the beach now, hard-packed sand where we could move. I shifted the truck into second gear and raced over the sand. "There they are," Jesse cried, pointing ahead.

I saw the two boats. Phil and Stretch were huddled beside them. I braked to a stop and jumped out of the truck. The surf was absolutely flat, like a swimming pool. Stretch and Phil ran toward the

truck as Jesse and I yanked sacks out of the back. "Get 'em in," I cried. "Get 'em in. It's going to be light soon."

Working like madmen, the four of us hustled sacks out of the truck and loaded the two boats. In a few minutes the life raft and the skiff were full. Stretch and Phil pushed them into the water and swam toward the boat, pulling the load behind them. "We're going to make it," Jesse whispered. "We're going to make it."

I looked toward the mountains and shrugged. "We'd better make it, because if we don't now, we never will."

Jesse and I unloaded the rest of the sacks while the skiffs were making the first trip. In ten minutes they returned and we threw the remaining sacks in. "As long as we've made it this far, we might as well include everything," I said. I reached inside the truck and hauled out a case of beer. The day before we had stopped and bought the beer for the long voyage home. In the last-minute panic of our fuckup, I had forgotten it. When I threw it in the skiff, Phil smiled.

It took us twenty minutes to load the weed and bid Stretch and Phil goodbye. As they pushed the two skiffs out into the water with the last load, Jesse and I jumped in the pickup and raced back over the beach. Zeke saw us coming and backed the station wagon off the levee. "It's loaded," I called, as I came abreast of him. "Let's get out of here!" I shifted into low gear and rounded the corner leading to the fishermen's huts. The fishermen were just getting up. They looked at us as we drove past, and one of them waved. I waved back. On the south end of the lagoon I stopped to retrieve the blanket and abandoned raft from our first attempt at loading. As we sped over the road leading around the lagoon, I looked back to see if I could spot Stretch's boat. Just as the sky began to lighten I saw the boat heading out to sea.

Smuggling by sea is probably one of the oldest forms of smuggling known to man; it is also, despite its aura of romanticism, one of the most dangerous. Not only did Stretch and Phil have the Mexican coastal patrols to worry about, they also had to worry about the sea itself, probably, after the first day, their most dangerous enemy. The journey from the central west coast of Mexico up to northern California would take approximately three weeks under normal condi-

tions, and that's what we were planning on. There are no normal conditions on the high seas though, especially in a small boat. I trusted Stretch's ability to handle his boat, because I had seen him do it; and I had really come to trust Phil in the last few days. He was an expert seaman, meteorologist, and navigator; at least they wouldn't lack those skills.

The plan was for them to head out to sea for fifty miles and then turn upwind, beating their way north. The difficulty with the plan was that they would have to sail 1,900 miles against prevailing winds and currents. They could have chosen to continue out to sea for a thousand miles and catch the trade winds which would blow them up north, but that would have entailed a longer voyage—although an easier one. Stretch opted for the first choice for two reasons: first, although the trip was harder, it was at least one week quicker; second, if something did happen to the boat or one of the crew, they could always head in and hide out for a few weeks along the coast—until they could contact me, or Don in Berkeley. Either way there were risks involved, and it didn't matter much which risks you tried to avoid, there were always others lifting their heads.

What bothered me most about the whole venture was not the sea, because I knew Stretch and Phil could handle that, it was the head trip they might go through while babysitting a ton of weed for three weeks. The anxiety and stress that accompanies a smuggling run tends to take its toll after weeks at sea. I had known skippers who grew so anxious as they approached their landfall that they threw the weed overboard rather than risk taking it in. I had also known skippers who lost all sense of judgment, about the sea, about marijuana, about everything, once their boat was loaded down with weed.

The real dangers Stretch and Phil faced were readily apparent: The Mexican government had just purchased ten new minesweepers from the U.S. Navy, and they were using them to patrol Mexican coastal waters. Theoretically, of course, once Stretch's boat was beyond the twelve-mile limit he was in international waters and could not be touched by anyone, but theoretics don't mean much off the coast of Mexico—or off of any coast, for that matter. Any small boat is fair game on the high seas, especially small pleasure craft. If a boat is

suspected of carrying illicit drugs, the Mexican Navy could blast it out of the water with complete equanimity, and no one would be the wiser. The chance of one of the minesweepers being off the coast where we loaded was remote, however, and to keep Stretch and Phil from getting too paranoid, I had not told them about the boats. According to the information Zeke had received in Mazatlan, the minesweepers were engaged in patrols off the main harbors, and seldom ventured down along the coast and into the small coves and inlets smugglers traditionally inhabited. This is not to say that they couldn't show up at any moment, but that was a reality I didn't want to think about. Besides, it's the head trips that smugglers go through that usually cause a seagoing run to fall, not the government boats, which have an awful lot of ocean to cover. To bust a sea run, the Mexicans would have to be on top of it from the very beginning, and pop it either while the boat was being loaded or soon thereafter. If they missed the boat on the beach, in all likelihood the smugglers would face no more problems (except the sea itself) until they were ready to off-load in U.S. territory.

After watching Stretch's boat go out to sea, I drove back to Acapulco and gave Zeke the truck. To celebrate the successful loading of the boat we had a dinner with all the trimmings at a fancy hotel, rubbing elbows with the Mexican politicians and rich gringos down from L.A. with their plastic-haired mistresses. Later that night Jesse and I took Gene out to the *zona roja*, the red-light district, in the backstreets of Acapulco. The next day Gene and I left for San Francisco; Jesse made plans to stay in Mexico until he heard from me.

Two weeks after returning to San Francisco, I got a phone call from Don. "The boat's in Bodega," He said. "Phil called."

"You're kidding!" I said.

"Nope. And they're waiting for us. They don't want to hang around."

I was astounded because the boat wasn't due in for another five days. In fact, Don and I were supposed to have set up a watch on the beach, and I had been worried because the weather off the coast had been so bad. I was sure Stretch and Phil had been blown all the way to Hawaii. It was amazing that they had made it up the coast five days

early. I jumped into a rented van and barreled over to Don's place.

Don was ecstatic. "Man, Phil said the wind blew them all the way up. They're sitting up there with a ton of weed."

"Almost a ton," I said.

"Ton, half a ton, what difference does it make? Let's get our asses up there," Don cried.

I was excited too. The energy in Don's pad was electric. Half a dozen middlemen were in the pad, already counting profits. I cautioned them. "The most dangerous part of the whole show is right now. Most pops occur when you're loading or unloading. We've got to be super careful. What did Phil say, exactly?"

"He said they'd made it and they were in good shape and Stretch was going to hang off the coast until after dark. He let Phil off this afternoon and he's waiting for us in a seafood joint."

"Let's get going," I said. "Howard and I will go in my van. You take your station wagon."

It was dark by the time we had our shit together to make it up the coast. Howard hunkered over the passenger seat staring through the windshield. It was pouring down rain. "God, I don't envy those guys out in this shit," he said.

I was worried too. The weather was bad. I was sure we'd have difficulty off-loading. Our plan was to bring the weed in through the surf below Bodega. It seemed like a crazy plan in this weather.

"Maybe we should cancel out tonight and wait until tomorrow," Howard said. "Maybe it'll be better then."

I said nothing. If the size of the surf on the way up was any indication, we'd never get the skiffs through it. The waves were breaking over the rocks. I was having a hell of a time holding my van on the road because of the wind.

"We'll see when we get up there," I said. That's all I could say.

Two hours later we pulled into Bodega. The wind had died down a little but the rain was still fierce. I drove down to the seafood restaurant where we were to pick up Phil. The restaurant was closed. "Damn, where is he?" Howard said.

I drove back through the parking lot and looked inside the darkened windows. Nothing. Just then Don's station wagon drove up. We conferred.

"He's not here," I said. "Where do you think he could be?"

"Hell, I don't know," Don said. "Are there any other places open?"

"Yeah, there's a bar north of town."

As we were pulling out of the parking lot a figure emerged from a telephone booth. It was Phil. He ran toward Don's station wagon and jumped in. I pulled up alongside them. "How's it going, man?" I said.

Phil looked exhausted. He held up his thumb and smiled. "Let's go down to that bar and have an Irish coffee," I said. "We can talk there."

In the bar we relaxed around a table. We were all jumpy with excitement. The bar was crowded so we had to talk low. Phil told us what happened. "We had hassles the minute we left Laguna de los Leones," he said. "A boat followed us out and we thought it was the Mexican patrol boat they use down there. Stretch almost panicked. He wanted to dump the weed right then and hightail it. I told him to cool it because the boat didn't look like a patrol boat to me. It wasn't either. It was a fishing boat making it out early. Damn, we were scared though."

"That would have been a stupid move, throwing the weed out," I said. "The stuff would have floated right back to shore."

"I know. That's why I didn't want to dump it. Not only that, but why dump it when you don't know what's happening?"

"Did Stretch calm down after that?" Don asked.

"Yeah. Once we got outside the twelve-mile limit we both settled down. Man, you've never seen a boat fly up the coast like ours did. We had twenty- and thirty-knot winds all the way up. They blew us up here."

The journey up the coast was amazing. Usually boats have to beat their way north, but Stretch's boat caught some unbelievably lucky weather. "It's all a dance," I said.

Everybody laughed. I ordered another round of drinks. "Where's Stretch now?" Don said.

"He's tied up in the middle of the harbor. I told him I'd row out in the dinghy after I contacted you guys. I've been waiting in that phone booth for two hours."

We drank up and headed for the harbor. I parked my van a block from the jetty, and Howard and I walked toward the docks. Don and Phil followed us. It was after ten P.M. and the harbor looked deserted. There was one bar open with a few cars parked around it. At the south end of the harbor there was a breakwater. Just inside the breakwater we could see the mast light on Stretch's boat. He was anchored fifty yards offshore.

"Go out and get him and let's talk," I said. "We obviously can't off-load through the surf. We'll have to decide what to do."

Phil got in the dinghy and rowed out to the boat. We braced ourselves in the rain and watched him. The responsibility for off-loading was on my shoulders. I had told Don when I first contacted him about using Stretch's boat that I would take care of the loading and unloading. It was up to me to find a place and time to do it. I was extremely skeptical about the weather. If we tried to take the load in through the surf I knew we'd end up on the rocks. Any other place though, and there was a chance someone would spot us.

The dinghy returned with Stretch and Phil. When Stretch got out we all shook his hand. "Phil says you had a great trip," I said.

"Magic," Stretch said. "All we had to do was set the sails and hang on."

"Listen," I said. "We've got to get a place where we can talk. Let's rent a couple of motel rooms."

We drove back to the north end of town and rented two adjoining motel rooms. Phil cracked open a bottle of tequila which he'd brought from the boat. We drank, and my stomach started loosening up. I turned to Stretch. "Listen. What kind of activity did you see when you brought the boat in? Did you see any Coast Guard patrols? What's the status of this harbor?"

"Nothing, man. I saw nothing. The status of the harbor is there's nothing here. All the fishing boats tie up on the north end of the harbor and the pleasure boats tie up down where we are. The only Coast Guard boat I saw was tied up at its own dock alongside the fishing boats."

"Do you have to report to the harbor master if you stick around?"

"Yeah. Tomorrow I'm gonna have to check in and request a guest berth. Of course, I could just stay anchored out in the middle. They'd think that was funny though."

"What about up north where we were going to off-load? Did you check that out when you came in?"

"In this weather? Man, we made it straight into the harbor. I didn't want to go anywhere near those rocks."

"I don't think we should go anywhere near them now either. We may have to hole up and wait for a day or two before we off-load. I don't want to jam this part of it. This is where all the fuckups occur."

"You guys decide what you want to do," Stretch said. "I'm gonna flake out for a few hours. I'm dead."

"I guess all of you guys might as well sack out. We're here for the night anyway. I'm going to take a walk around town and check things out."

"Let me come with you," Howard said.

Outside, the rain had turned to a drizzle. Howard and I walked down to the waterfront. The whole town was dead. Just then a police patrol car drove up behind us. "Hey, you!" a voice shouted.

I was absolutely calm when I turned to the police. The cop sat in his patrol car and motioned us toward him with his flashlight. "You the guys driving that van I saw awhile ago?" he said. I nodded.

"Where's your van?"

"We got a room for the night. It's parked at the motel," I said.

"Whattya doin' out here?"

"We're abalone divers," I said. "We were supposed to meet a boat here tonight. We're looking for it."

"All the abb boats are tied up at the north end of the harbor. Down that way," he pointed with his flashlight. "The fishermen hang out at Gino's bar."

"Thanks," I said. The cop wound up his window and drove off.

"Jesus," Howard said. "That's all we need."

"At least we know what to look for now. I wonder how many cops they got working this place at night."

"He's probably the only one," Howard said. "It ain't that big a burg."

Howard and I walked up to Gino's bar and had a drink. Half an

hour later we walked back toward the south end of the harbor. Half-way there we saw the cop turn the corner and head for us. We stepped into a doorway and watched him drive past. "He's making his rounds," Howard said.

"Let's stay here and see how long it takes him to make it around again."

We waited in the doorway for thirty minutes. Once again the patrol car drove around the corner. He passed us and headed toward the north end of the town. "He doesn't even go down to the south end of the harbor," Howard said. "I guess 'cause there's no stores down there."

I noticed the same thing. The jetty on the south end of the harbor was a quarter of a mile beyond the road where the cop turned down. If the circular pattern was his regular route, then he didn't bother driving out on the jetty. There was really no reason for him to drive out on it since there was nothing to see. The boats were anchored out in the middle of the harbor. Maybe we could off-load on the jetty.

"Let's watch him one more time," I said. "If he makes the same round I think we have it."

The cop returned in exactly twenty minutes. His route took him along the waterfront to Gino's bar, then up into town, then back around to the road leading down to the waterfront. He didn't drive down the jetty at the south end of the harbor. We could drive the van down there while he was making his rounds on the other side of town. Howard and I hustled back to the motel and woke the boys. They got up immediately.

"Don, I want you to drive right into the middle of the main inter-section of town and lift the hood of your car. Pretend your car's stalled. If the cop comes by, he'll help you. Howard, you go down to the access road to the jetty and stand at the entrance. If the cop tries to go out on the jetty you stop him any way you can, wave your arms, yell, piss on his car if you have to, anything to get his attention. You can pretend you're drunk. Me and Phil and Stretch will drive out on the jetty and unload the weed. We should be able to do it in twenty minutes."

We hustled into our cars. Howard ran down to the waterfront road and watched the cop drive by toward the north end of the harbor. Then we drove down to the south end of the harbor and out on the jetty. Phil and Stretch jumped out of the van and rowed the dinghy out to the boat. I sat in the van and waited.

I peered out the van window. It seemed that Phil and Stretch had been gone a long time. I listened to the rain rattling on the van roof. Then I heard a louder rap. I almost jumped out of my seat. Phil was beside the door, motioning to me. I jumped out of the van to help unload the dinghy.

Stretch was holding the rubber boat against the rocks. Phil jumped down beside him and started tossing packages of weed onto the rocks. During the trip up the coast, Phil and Stretch had transferred the weed from the large burlap sacks to small, easy-to-handle packages. The packages were covered with arabol, so water couldn't get in. I grabbed the packages off the rocks and tossed them up onto the jetty. The dinghy was unloaded in a few minutes and then Phil and Stretch jumped back in and paddled out for a second load. While they were out, I loaded the packages in the van. After four trips we had all the kilos loaded. I jumped in the van and started the motor. When I put it in gear and let the clutch out, the wheels spun in the mud. I reversed and tried to back out. Nothing. Suddenly Stretch and Phil appeared in front of me. They pushed against the front of the van while I stepped lightly on the throttle. The van backed out of the mud. Phil and Stretch jumped out of the way as I turned around and sped down the jetty.

At the mouth of the jetty I stopped and Howard jumped in. "The cop hasn't been by," he said. "How'd it go out there?"

I pointed in the back. The packages of marijuana were stacked up roofhigh.

"Fantastic! We better cover it up with something."

"There's a blanket behind the spare tire," I said. "Use that."

Howard covered the weed while I drove through the silent town. There wasn't a sign of life. I skirted the main intersection and headed toward Highway One. Beyond the city limits I put my foot down on the accelerator and took off.

By dawn we had the marijuana unloaded and stacked in a warehouse in San Francisco. At ten A.M. Don arrived with two middlemen who were going to help him peddle the weed. I called my musician friends to come over so they could get their share. When everyone arrived we weighed the weed, one package at a time. There were 1,700 pounds. We valued our weed at $140 a pound, wholesale. Middlemen would sell the weed for anywhere from $165 to $200 a pound, depending on their customers. Users, those who bought pounds for their private stashes, would pay $200 to $300 per pound.

The musicians who had loaned me $5,000 agreed to take their double payback in weed, so we separated 72 pounds from the main pile and gave it to them. We also agreed that everyone involved in the trip would keep one kilo for his own personal stash. There were ten people involved, so we took 20 pounds out. The rest of the weed was divided into thirds; one-third for me and Jesse; one-third for Don and his people; and the final third for the musician backers, who would be required to pay wholesale prices for it. By letting them buy a third of the load at wholesale, we weren't losing anything, but they were gaining a lot. They could make $50 to $100 on each pound.

I doubt if any aspect of marijuana smuggling and dealing interests as many people—the heat, the public, the dealer himself—as the money; how much is involved, who gets it, what the weed costs and how much it sells for. Figures are difficult to come by, since no dealer is going to reveal his financial tote sheets, but through my experience and that of a few friends, plus statistics at the border, some reasonable estimates can be made. The price of weed is a good barometer of the industry, and nothing is as revealing as the cost of kilos themselves, and the changes it has gone through in the last few years.

In 1963–64, the year Jesse and I started smuggling, we could buy kilos for $8 each in the Mexican interior. On the border identical kilos cost $25 to $30 each. A dealer who didn't want to risk running the border could buy the same kilos in Los Angeles for $100 each. Once the weed reached San Francisco, the wholesale price rose to $175 per kilo.

During the years 1963 and 1964, little marijuana was being smuggled into the United States. This was the very beginning of the drug revolution, and big-time weed smuggling was still five years away. In 1964–65, less than 700 kilos of marijuana were being brought into the Bay area (Marin County to Monterey) each month. By late 1965, as the corners of the Haight-Ashbury began to fill up, hundreds of young longhairs were drifting south to score. It's difficult estimating how much weed actually moved through the Bay area at the time, but observers generally agree that during the banner years of 1967, 1968, and 1969, thirty to forty tons of pot were moving through the area each month of the season. The season is generally considered to last from November until late February, although in actual fact it begins in October and lasts through the middle of May. By the end of May, weed is getting scarce in Mexico. The summer drought takes over until the middle of September, when the next harvest occurs.

By 1966, the same quality kilos that Jesse and I bought for $8 in the interior of Mexico in 1964 were selling for $20. At the same time, the wholesale price in San Francisco dropped from $175 per kilo to $100. What happened was that the demand for weed by the new breed of longhair smugglers had created a seller's market in Mexico, raising the prices, and the success the smugglers were having in getting their loads across the border had created a buyer's market in San Francisco, lowering prices there. The problem increased in 1967, when the price for kilos in the interior of Mexico rose to $25 to $30, and the selling price in San Francisco dropped to $75 per kilo. Granted, many of the kilos sold at this time were underweight, but the price per unit was still low enough to create hassles for many smugglers and dealers. The market was so depressed that many dealers dropped out of business, or went back to selling LSD. Then in 1968–69 two things happened: dealers, tired of explaining to customers why their bricks were underweight, began selling pound units—and the United States government implemented Operation Intercept.

In 1967, 90,000 pounds of marijuana was confiscated at the border. In 1970, over 500,000 pounds was confiscated. Figuring that the customs people are intercepting five percent of the traffic at the most, we can figure that some 10,000,000 pounds, or almost 5,000,000 kilos, was getting through. Assuming that the average price paid to the farmer in the mountains in 1970 for bulk marijuana was $5 per kilo, an estimate which I think is reasonable, we can figure that between twenty and twenty-five million dollars was being paid for grass at its source. This wasn't the price the gringo smugglers were paying, however. It was the price being paid by the Mexican entrepreneur. By the time the gringo got his hands on the weed, he was paying almost $30 per kilo, which brings the amount paid by gringos for marijuana in Mexico up to almost $150,000,000. By the time the weed reaches the border the price goes up even further, so we can multiply from there.

The first smuggling trip Jesse and I made, in 1963–64, involved 80 kilos and $2,000. Our second trip involved 125 kilos and $2,500. On our third trip we worked in partnership with our connection in Mexico and brought back 524 kilos on credit. Our debt to the connection after we sold the grass was $7,000. These prices obtained in 1966 and earlier. After I was arrested and no longer involved in the operation, Jesse made a trip where he spent $15,000 for 1,000 kilos. This type of operation could be multiplied a number of times in 1966–67, and you would not even scratch the surface of the industry.

The large amounts of weed moving through the Bay area during this time (a lot of the weed did not stay in the Bay area, it was transferred and sold elsewhere) were partly responsible for the implementation of Operations Intercept and Cooperation. One such load is still talked about by observers of the industry. A freighter from British Honduras loaded with twelve tons of Panama Red came into port during Christmas week 1968, and while the regular stevedores were at lunch, the cargo was unloaded by a pickup crew hired by the shipping clerk, who was in on the scam. Not one joint of the Red was distributed in San Francisco. In a matter of hours the load was inside a semi-truck heading for the East Coast. Most of it was sold in Philadelphia and New York. The weed was so good that one of the dealers involved in the transaction sent $500 to Philly to get one of the kilos back for his own use.

This kind of operation reflected a growing sophistication and organization on the part of smugglers and dealers—and on users also. By 1967–68, enough people had smoked enough marijuana to be able to tell good weed from bad, or even average weed, so they started demanding only quality. As with any commodity, the good tends to drive out the bad, so in a very short time every customer in the Bay area was demanding good weed. The demand was reflected back in Mexico by the gringo buyers and smugglers who, like me and Jesse, refused to purchase anything but quality. In our case it meant educating our entrepreneur; other smugglers did the same.

The demand for quality weed, the change from kilos to pounds as the units of sale in the United States, and Operation Intercept all occurred within a very short time—and they all contributed to an increase in the price of weed in Mexico. By 1970 many buyers were purchasing only unbricked colas, refusing to have anything to do with bricked marijuana at all. A number of Mexican entrepreneurs began to cater to this type of buyer. The prices for unbricked colas were astronomical compared to bricked weed, reaching up to $75 and $100 per kilo in the interior of Mexico. At the same time, due to the scarcity of good weed in San Francisco, pounds of unbricked colas were going for $200 to $300. In August of 1972, unbricked colas of dynamite grass were selling for anywhere from $300 to $500 a pound, with many willing hands ready to snap them up when they became available.

A rundown on the price of kilos in Mexico and the U.S. follows:

COST OF KILOS IN MEXICO AND THE UNITED STATES FROM 1955 TO 1972

YEAR	THE MEXICAN INTERIOR	THE BORDER	LOS ANGELES	SAN FRANCISCO
1955	$ 2 to 4	$15 to 20	$ 50 to 65	$ 90 to 100
1960	5 to 8	20 to 25	50 to 75	90 to 110
1963	8 to 15	25 to 30	75 to 100	125 to 175
1965	10 to 20	25 to 35	100 to 125	150 to 175
1966*	12 to 25	35 to 40	60 to 100	60 to 100
1967	15 to 25	35 to 40	100 to 150	160 to 190
1969	25 to 35k	35 to 50k	80 to 175(lb)†	100 to 200lb†
1970	35 to 50k	50 to 75k	100 to 200lb	125 to 225 lb
1972	35 to 80k	60 to 100k	125 to 400lb	125 to 500 lb
1974	35 to 100k	100 to 150k	150 to 500lb	200 to 500 lb

*In 1966 a depression occurred in the price of kilos on the West Coast. This happened because incredible amounts of weed were coming into the U.S.; every longhair and his brother was in Mexico scoring marijuana, and more than that, were successfully returning to the U.S. with it!
A curious corollary to this is the fact that Mexico is now on the way to pricing itself out of the business. I believe that within the next five years the prices for kilos will be so great, and the surveillance so heavy within Mexico, that most gringo smugglers will discontinue smuggling. Already domestic weed is getting increasingly popular in the U.S. During the next few years I expect domestic marijuana to completely take over the industry.
†In the late sixties the unit of sale changed in the U.S. from kilos to pounds.

Since 1974, when Weed was first published, many changes have occured in the marijuana industry, including tremendous changes in prices. Ounces now sell for $200.00 where kilos did before. Domestic weed is more popular than foreign, although the industry is beginning to move back into Mexico.

In 1968, the year our smuggling organization brought out the load of 1,700 pounds, Don and I figured the wholesale value of the weed at $140 a pound. After subtracting the 72 pounds for the musician backers, and the 20 pounds for the participants in the venture, we had 1,608 pounds left to sell. We figured the 1,608 pounds was worth $225,500 wholesale. The financial breakdown of the run worked out approximately as follows:

Money invested in trip:

$	5,000	from *Life* magazine
	5,000	from musician backers
$	10,000	total invested

Expenses of trip:

$	250	to Luis, our original entrepreneur
	250	to Sanchez, our guide
	250	for the use of Jesus' airplane
	500	for Gene's expenses
	250	for round-trip air fare for Jerry, Acapulco to San Francisco
	1,500	for road expenses for Jesse and Jerry, motels, food, gas
	1,000	to Zeke and Hoff for expenses
	1,200	for boat expenses
	300	for personal expenses, mules, food, etc.
	3,000	payment for marijuana
	1,000	for transportation of goods—burros, men, pistoleros, etc.
$	9,500	total expenses

Income from trip:

$	238,000	received for 1,700 pounds of marijuana @ $140 per pound
	−9,500	expenses for trip
	−10,000	double return to backers (72 pounds)
	−2,800	to participants (one kilo each)
	−20,000	payment to Stretch, skipper and owner of boat
	−12,000	payment to Phil, crew member
$	184,700	net profit

The U.S. Government's plan to ruin the Mexican marijuana industry has helped ruin the Mexican economy too — by taking millions of U.S. dollars out of Mexico and sending them to Columbia instead. Things have again turned around, however, and because of the increasingly risky proposition of growing weed domestically, many growers are returning to Mexico to grow sensemilla.

The run Jesse and I put together was unusual because the weed itself cost us so little—and the other expenses were minimal. If Stretch's boat had not already been in Mexico, it could have easily cost us another $10,000 for a boat. The fact that Zeke and Hoff were willing to transport and help load the boat for $8,000 each also cut down on our expenses. They could have easily asked for and gotten a percentage—because when you're down in Mexico and need help, you don't quibble about money. Under ordinary circumstances the weed Jesse and I bought would have cost us a minimum of $25,000. Once you subtract the cost of the weed, then take out another $20,000 for the boat or plane, and another $10,000 or so for miscellaneous expenses, you don't end up with a very large sum of money.

The weed industry handles a hell of a lot of bread, but very little of it stays in one hand. Smugglers and dealers I personally know have collectively moved tons and tons of weed but the money always seems to drift away, not only in losing trips which tend to suck vast bankrolls dry, but in other ways too, by drinking it up, coking it up, or spending it on expectations.

There are unsubstantiated stories of dope millionaires in San Francisco. I know of a dozen or so individuals who have two or three hundred thousand dollars stashed away, but in general there seems to be a dreariness about dope money that keeps most dealers and smugglers scratching along, even though they are moving a lot of weed. Most dealers and smugglers who make big coin in weed invest their money in real estate. One of the folktales around San Francisco during the economic recession of the last few years was that the only people buying the big expensive homes coming on the market were dope dealers and rock stars. A lot of dealers who were smart enough to establish legitimate businesses with their bread did buy big homes, but others who attempted it were corraled by the Internal Revenue Service. A few dealers and smugglers have money in Swiss bank accounts, although the tales outnumber the accounts. Mostly the bread made on a good run goes to pay for previous bad runs, or is used up in subsequent bad runs.

Dope smugglers are like oil wildcatters. The big run can always be made, but that big run oftentimes demands bigger and bigger attempts, and every run, once completed, seems to have a way of turning into a practice run for the one that'll be really big, the one that will buy the hacienda in Mexico, or the new Mercedes 450SL and a house in Marin County. I have seen thousands and thousands of dollars disappear in just paying to keep pilots on retainer, looking for airfields, buying equipment and losing it before one kilo was ever smuggled. Also an awful lot of the money made in dope ends up in the hands of lawyers, who have probably made the most out of the weed revolution.

Another reason why there are so few really big moneymakers in the marijuana business is because dealers and smugglers are continually entering and leaving the trade, especially after they've had a successful run or two—and even more so if the runs have been unsuccessful! One of the tenets of the smuggling game is, "Don't get greedy!" It's the greedy ones who fall. After making what they consider a reasonable stake, many smugglers and dealers retire to pursue their original interests. Often the money made from dope is spent fairly quickly and some of the players reenter the game, but they usually have to reorganize from scratch. Nothing changes as fast as the weed industry. Old connections in Mexico are no longer in business, old customers have found new dealers, etc. Most of the new breed of smugglers and dealers aren't interested in becoming marijuana millionaires, and the few who do get into the game with the sole idea of making money usually end up getting popped anyway.

Most smugglers have a working life that lasts no more than four years, by which time they have either been successful enough to have a little bread stashed away, or they've reached the point where they realize that dope money is easy come, easy go, with a lot of risks along the way, so they drop out. Smugglers and dealers who stay in business longer than four years are either desperate or greedy. In either case they usually end up falling.

My own fall at San Luis, Arizona, on August 30, 1966, had a bizarre twist, and while it did not prevent me from returning to

Mexico to do the run I've just described, it did turn my head around. As I said at the beginning of this book, when Speedy Blue told me I was going to be sitting in Yuma County one helluva long time if I didn't talk, I spun a tale off the top of my head that I'm still proud of.

I don't know what it was that made me invent the story I laid on Speedy Blue, maybe the Percodan. All I know is that when he gave me that sly Okie smile of his, the whole story popped into my head in a flash, with all the details, ready for any little tricks Speedy or Gomez might try. I was a writer, I had gone to Mexico to work on my novel and to sell my car. A *pocho* dude from L.A. bought my car in Guaymas and I was delivering it back to L.A. for him. The weed in the car wasn't mine, it belonged to somebody else.

My mind was speeding up behind the Percodan, which was supposed to slow it down. Speedy and Gomez loomed over me like two border bulldogs about to swallow a cockroach. I could see the bulge of the .45 next to Speedy's gut. He had a slight reddish tinge to his face and nose that spelled too much booze and too much sun. Gomez's face was impassive, a Chicano working for the gringos, the traitorous bastard! I leaned against the cell wall as they fired questions at me. I fired right back.

"What's the story, who's in this with you?"

"Nobody's in anything with me. I went to Mexico to write a novel and sell my car."

"It's against the law to sell cars in Mexico."

"Hell, I know that, but people do it all the time. You can make a good living selling old cars."

"Or stolen ones."

"Mine wasn't stolen."

"What happened?"

"I met a guy in Guaymas who bought my car. He said he'd give me $500 for it if I drove it back to L.A. for him."

"You don't expect me to believe that crap do you?" Speedy said.

"You can believe it if you want," I said. "It's the truth."

Both Speedy and I knew that smugglers sometimes conned innocent gringos into driving loads of weed across the border. I reasoned that if I could make Speedy Blue believe my story, he'd have to follow up on it. If he did, then I'd have a chance to wiggle my way out—maybe. The thing about customs agents, or any police, for that matter, is that they want to believe your story as much as you want them to believe it. They don't want to rest on a simple pop at the border, they want to get the big boys, the syndicate operation they always imagine you're part of. My story was plausible because I had just enough circumstantial evidence in my car to back it up. I had an incomplete novel in my luggage, a broken-down transmission, and no record. And, when it gets down to the nitty-gritty, I can act honest as hell.

"Who is this guy you met in Guaymas?" Speedy asked. "Is he a Mexican?"

"He's a pocho. He calls himself Gordo."

"Gordo!" Speedy almost spit the word out. "You're lying, you sonofabitch."

I shrugged. The only thing I could do was stick to my story. Once you started changing it, you were lost. I repeated my assertion.

"Man, I'm telling you just what happened. I was talking to a guy in a bar in Guaymas. He said he knew someone who'd buy my car. When I met Gordo, he asked if he could drive the car. He kept it for three hours. When he brought it back he made me the offer."

"And you didn't know there was marijuana in the car?"

"I suspected there might be a little weed in it. Hell, I didn't know the bastard loaded two hundred kilos in it."

"Plus a little coke and some other stuff," Speedy said.

"I don't know nothing about that," I said.

The reason I copped to knowing there was some weed in my car was that I wanted Speedy Blue to feel a sense of honesty about me. I knew I couldn't play the completely gullible gringo, but if I could make him believe that I was naïve—and a little bit guilty—then he might believe me.

"Where were you going to deliver the weed?" Speedy said.

"I wasn't going to deliver any weed," I said. "I was delivering my car. I was supposed to take it to Los Angeles."

"You said you knew there was some weed in your car, then you were delivering weed."

"I *suspected* there might be a couple of kilos in it. Hell, if I had known there was all that shit in my car, do you think I would have driven across the border? I may be simple but I'm not stupid."

A great line. Not even Speedy could refute that logic.

Speedy Blue turned to Gomez, his running mate. "What do you think?" Gomez shrugged.

"Where in Los Angeles were you going to take your car?" Gomez asked.

"It isn't exactly in Los Angeles," I said. "It's in a place called Pacific Palisades."

My mind was whirring fast. The Percodan head I had on was still buzzing. When Gomez asked me the question I immediately flashed back to a newspaper article I had read two years before. The article outlined a bust that occurred in a parking lot in Pacific Palisades, on the Coast Highway opposite Sunset Boulevard. "I'm supposed to deliver the car to a parking lot on the Coast Highway," I said. "Opposite Sunset Boulevard."

Gomez looked at Speedy Blue. "I know that place. It's been used as a drop zone before. Maybe we have something."

"What were you supposed to do after you dropped the car?"

"I'm supposed to leave the keys under the floormat and make it on home."

"That's all?"

"That's all."

"What about your five hundred dollars?"

"Gordo already gave me half. He said he'd send the other half to Big Sur where I live."

"You expect me to believe that shit?" Speedy snapped. "You're lying."

"I'm not lying!" I yelled back. "Lissen. The whole car's only worth two hundred bucks. I already got two-fifty. I figured if he sent me the other two-fifty it'd be a bonus. Shit, the thing'll hardly move with that bad transmission."

Speedy Blue and Gomez stepped to the other end of the holding cell and conferred. Occasionally they looked at me. After ten minutes they returned.

"Lissen, jiveass. We're going to follow up on your bullshit. If you're lying, you ain't never gonna see the outside again."

That morning I was handcuffed in the back of Speedy Blue's air-conditioned Impala, which had been impounded from a popped smuggler, and whisked across the desert to Yuma to be booked officially. Gomez and Speedy drank beer and tossed cans out the windows into the desert. "You're littering," I said, from my handcuffed position in the back seat.

"Fuck you, freak," Speedy said.

I was taken to the Yuma police station and booked, then taken before the county commissioner and immediately released on bail—in the custody of Speedy Blue. Officially I was now working for The Man, trying to set up Gordo, the dude who had bought my car and loaded it with weed. Unfortunately Gordo was a figment of my imagination, and my imagination was going to have to get imaginitiver and imaginitiver to make Gordo real.

Speedy Blue's plan was to have Gomez drive my car to Los Angeles; I was to be flown to L.A. and the car would be put back in my hands to deliver to the parking lot. Once I delivered the car I would be put on a bus for home. Then I was to wait for a letter of indictment from Phoenix and return there to stand trial for smuggling. If everything worked out as I had said, and Gordo actually picked up the car full of weed, I would be released with nothing more than a slap on the wrist—my reward for finking!

That night, in my new roll of dumb mule now cooperating with United States Customs, I was taken out for a steak dinner (Order anything you want, Speedy said), and then put up in a motel to await the next day's flight to Los Angeles. Gomez took my sick station wagon to the police garage, where they discovered the transmission needed a few adjustments to make the journey into Los Angeles, then he took off, across the desert at night, 200 kilos of marijuana reeking in the back. The next day I was taken to the airport and put on a plane.

When I arrived in Los Angeles, fifteen United States Customs agents were at the gate to meet me, one in particular, a six-foot-seven behemoth dressed in dungarees and sweatshirt. "Kamstra," he said. "My name's Hugh. Glad to have you on our team. I talked to Speedy Blue on the phone this morning and he says you've been real cooperative. Lots of smugglers bilk guys like you into being mules. Don't worry about it. We'll get the bastard."

I nodded weakly.

"We're gonna make a dry run in an unmarked car first, to give you the lay of the land. After that, you'll take your station wagon down to the parking lot and drop it. Any questions?"

I shook my head.

It was a strange feeling sitting in a car with the heat, other cars following us, on a mission to drop a load of weed in a phony drop zone so a nonexistent dealer could pick it up. I was beginning to sweat. I wondered if I couldn't call the whole thing off, just confess that it was my weed and couldn't I go to jail and forget about it. I was in too deep though. As we drove from Sunset Boulevard, I looked for places to jump out of the car. Three unmarked cars followed us, each one containing four customs agents.

When we reached the Coast Highway, Hugh turned left. "That's the parking lot, isn't it?" he said, *sotto voce*, pointing across the highway with his chin.

"Yeah," I whispered back. "That's the one."

"We're gonna drive down the road a little and turn around and come back. When you bring your station wagon down here, take it over to that corner stall, understand?"

I nodded.

Hugh swung the car around in a U-turn and headed back toward the parking lot. When we drew abreast of it I couldn't believe my eyes. Three large telephone service trucks were parked in the lot, and a man was up on a pole working the lines. Across the street were two plain Chevy sedans. Inside each sedan were two men, reading newspapers.

"You guys can't be serious, can you?" I said. "This looks like a training film on how to blow a bust. Nobody's going to pick up a load with all the heat you guys have around. You can smell cops for a mile."

"Let us worry about that," Hugh said. "We're not taking any chances. We've been after Gordo a long time."

"Oh, Jesus."

We drove back to the drive-in where my station wagon was parked. Gomez got out and I got in. The weed had been taken out of the panels and stacked in the back. My sleeping bag was thrown carelessly over it. I sighed. "Jesus, you guys. All Gordo has to do is get within fifty feet of this car and he's gonna know something's up. Look at the stuff."

"Don't worry about it," Hugh said. "You let us take care of the details." He turned to the twenty agents milling around. "You guys ready to go?" They nodded.

I drove the station wagon toward the Coast Highway. Ten un-marked police cars followed me. I felt like the lead car in my own funeral. I had wild thoughts of putting my car in low gear and taking off, a wild pursuit up the Coast Highway, half the L.A. police force behind me. Yak! There was nothing I could do. The traffic bleated around me like hogs stuck in a slaughter pen. I looked in the car next to me. There were three chicks wearing halters. Heading for the beach. It was a sunny day and the surf was up and I was heading for a parking lot to deliver 200 kilos of weed to Gordo, a big-time Chicano dealer who didn't exist. It was insane! How did I get myself in these predicaments? All I wanted to do was write. Shit!

I eased off the road into the parking lot. The stall Hugh told me to park in was occupied so I parked in the next one. I got out and left the keys under the floormat. I couldn't lock the door without the keys so I opened the door and grabbed the keys and locked the door. Then I realized I couldn't leave the keys under the floormat if I locked the door. I unlocked the door and threw the keys under the floormat and walked rapidly away, leaving the door unlocked. Fuck it! It was insane anyway.

After parking the car I was supposed to walk up Sunset Boulevard for half a mile, then Gomez would pick me up and drive me down to the bus station. I walked a mile. Two miles. After three miles I began to worry. I turned around and headed back toward the Coast Highway. Gomez met me on the way. "I can't take you down to the bus station," he said. "You'll have to make it on your own."

"Jesus Christ, Gomez! What the fuck's happening? I don't have a dime to my name. How am I supposed to get home?"

"Here, take this." Gomez reached in his wallet and gave me a twenty. "Now get the fuck out of here. We don't want to blow this, we got thirty-five agents on the stakeout." He jumped back in his car and sped away.

I stood on the edge of Sunset Boulevard watching him go. I had two choices: up Sunset Boulevard or down Sunset Boulevard. If I went up Sunset Boulevard, I ended up in the Los Angeles nether land; if I went down, at least I ended up next to the sea. I needed the sea at this moment to comfort me. I walked back down to the Coast Highway. From the intersection I could see my station wagon. The telephone trucks were still there and it looked like half the U.S. Customs Bureau was parked across the street. Nobody paid any attention to me. I walked half a block down the Coast Highway and stuck out my thumb. Inside of twenty seconds a '61 Plymouth Valiant whipped out of traffic and blasted to a stop beside me. "Hiya, jump in!" a smiling Southern California mouth said.

Fags, I thought. I jumped in and settled back into the rear seat. Both queers were dressed in Bermuda shorts and T-shirts. They had rubber sandals on their feet. Very hairy and very blond with surfboard muscles and plastic teeth. A half-mile down the road the driver whipped the car off the highway and stopped in a cloud of dust. "Okay, buster, out!" he said.

"What the fuck's going on?" I said. I closed my mouth. The dude on the right was holding out a badge. It had L.A. Police on it. I sighed. Both cops hustled me out and spread-eagled me against the car. Jesus, I thought, is this really happening to me?

"Okay, hippie, where's your stash?" one of the cops said.

"What are you talking about? I don't have any stash."

"C'mon. We stop fifty guys a day along this stretch of highway and three-quarters of them are carrying stashes. Where's yours?" The big cop who'd been driving pushed me against the car.

"Well, if you want to know," I said, "I just left my stash a half-mile back. It's in my car."

"Huh?" the cop said.

"I'm serious. I just left my car back there in a parking lot. It has two hundred kilos in it."

The two cops looked at each other then threw me back in the car. They sped around in a brodie and took off back the way we had come. I relaxed in the rear seat. On the way I calmly explained that I had been popped at the border, that the customs agents had flown me to L.A., and that I had delivered the car to the parking lot just an hour or so before. The cop driving the car looked straight ahead and nodded as I talked.

When we reached the intersection of the Coast Highway and Sunset Boulevard, he pulled off the road and parked. One cop stayed with me and the other one got out and walked toward my station wagon. It's really happening, I thought. Across the Coast Highway I saw thirty-five customs agents' heads following the cop. When he reached the station wagon he paused a moment, then walked around to the driver's side and opened the door. At that instant two dozen agents burst out of the telephone repair trucks and automobiles and rushed him, guns drawn. I sat back in the seat of the Plymouth, as calm as could be.

After the L.A. cop and U.S. Customs fiasco, I was released to make my way up the Coast Highway to Big Sur. I heard nothing about my border bust from the federal government until I was rearrested six months later. I hired a lawyer and pleaded guilty to the nonpayment of taxes on illegally imported marijuana, and was sentenced to two years in the federal penitentiary, sentence suspended, and placed on five years' probation.

GLOSSARY

This glossary is meant to be a collection not only of definitions of words, but also of explanations. For example, everyone knows that Acapulco is a resort city in Mexico. In addition, however, Acapulco is a symbol. To a wealthy Mexican with a home there, it is a sign that he has made it. To the politically conscious Mexican, it is a sign of corruption, of the on-going sellout of Mexico to the *norteamericanos* that was begun by Santa Ana in 1836 and continues to this day. To the sensitive individual, Acapulco is the symbol of vulgarity, of the complete desecration of the land and of the country by commercial developers. To a dope smuggler or a head, Acapulco is the birthplace of the mythology surrounding the high-quality marijuana grown in the mountains encircling the area. Places and words and meanings are multidimensional. The meaning for dope smugglers or counterculture people in general, say, is not always the primary meaning for most people. That's one reason why I love words—they are so precise, and at the same time so imprecise. The words that follow, then, are words used in this book that I believe need some additional explanation.

abrazo In Mexico the abrazo is the traditional form of greeting between males. Instead of shaking hands, males clasp one another around the shoulders in an embrace, pounding one another on the back with the free hand. There is a famous photograph of Castro embracing Khrushchev in an abrazo when the two men met at the UN in 1960. It was insinuated in the press that there must be something funny about these two guys who would hug each other in public. Actually Castro was only indulging in a typical Latin American greeting.

Acapulco   See the introduction to this glossary.

Acapulco Gold   A type of high-quality marijuana grown in the mountains of Guerrero.

aduana   Mexican customs.

amateur   The smuggler who enters the game without any criminal orientation or intent. Professional in the sense that he makes money by smuggling, the amateur is not professional in that he would not kill to get a load through. The professional, on the other hand, will do anything required to get a load across. Amateur and professional have absolutely nothing to do with amounts of weed smuggled; quite often the amateur smuggler moves far bigger loads than the professional.

bad   Bad is good. When someone says "This is really bad shit!" he is saying "This is really very good marijuana!" Good, on the other hand, means mediocre. Good grass is commercial grass. You can sell it but you're not going to have people beating down your doors to buy it. Good grass isn't as potent as bad grass, and doesn't come anywhere near the quality of dynamite (which see). *Comprende?*

banker   When the dope trade became organized during the late sixties it structured itself around various organizational levels, and the banker emerged as one of the levels. In the early days of the game a smuggler would round up his own financing, go to Mexico, score, and bring the load back across the border himself; later the business needed the smuggler, the dealer on the U.S. side, the middleman, etc. The banker came in to provide money for runs. He took none of the risks and naturally made most of the scratch when the run was over. Many dope lawyers and rock-and-roll musicians became bankers. Nowadays some real bankers are dope-run bankers.

beat   I use the terms beat and beatnik throughout this book because I came of age and lost my innocence as a beatnik in North Beach,

San Francisco. My definition of beat does not define the term, it defines the era, that period falling roughly between 1955 and 1964. Although much of the beat phenomenon Jack Kerouac described in his books took place before 1955, it did not reach public consciousness and cause any cultural upheaval until after that date. By 1964 the beat period was over, the beatniks having been run out of North Beach by overzealous cops and greedy topless entrepreneurs. Many of the beats moved to the Haight-Ashbury section of San Francisco. From 1964 until 1965 there was sort of a cultural hiatus in America, a time for free-speech movements and political awakening, but nothing like the beat energy that preceded those dates, nor the hippie explosion that followed them. For me beat has always been an ambiguous term, and since I understand all phenomena only as they relate to my own life and the lives of my friends, I have always thought of the word and the era as one of awakening, desperation, nihilism, social upheaval, and eventually catharsis. I became a beatnik because I wanted to be a writer and wanted nothing to do with the traditional American college-educated, nine-to-five, slowly-up-the-ladder-to-prosperity-and-debts-and-split-level-retirement-at-age-fifty-and-death-by-heart-attack-a-year-later routine. The thing that held the beats together during the fifties and early sixties was a sense of alienation, rebellion, purpose, excitement, and magic. In 1957 a beard was unusual. If you wore one you were a beatnik. The beard was a badge of identity, a spiritual and intellectual signpost. In a sense, having a beard in the old days and wearing Salvation Army throwaways was a physical sign that you had already dropped out—long before Leary came on the scene. You knew whoever wore the clothes was of the same frame of mind—with various individual differences—as you. It was like smoking weed in the early days, you *knew* everyone who smoked had a certain sensibility. We were outlaws, and a camaraderie existed among us. Now everyone smokes weed and that camaraderie is no longer possible. What I am saying is that you can no longer trust the people who wear the funny clothes or who smoke weed because everyone does it—and who can trust everyone?

beatnik   A person who is beat. Phil Maguire, a beatnik carpenter friend of mine in Big Sur, defined beatnik this way: "When Jack Kerouac coined the term beat he meant it to mean beatific, blissful, beautiful. When Herb Caen of the San Francisco *Chronicle* coined the word beatnik, he was wordplaying on the then current phenomenon of sputnik, the first Soviet satellite. Sputnik in Russian means 'friendly traveler,' therefore *beat,* meaning blissful, or beautiful, and *nik,* meaning traveler, when combined must mean *beautiful traveler.*" I have never heard a better definition of beatnik than Phil's.

bite   A bribe. Also called *mordida* (which see).

blanco   Heroin.

blanquillos   Literally, little whities, which, in turn, means eggs. Mexican women do not ask for eggs when they want eggs because the Mexican word for eggs is *huevos,* a popular vulgarism for balls. Asking for some *blanquillos* is a nice way to get your eggs without getting a lot of hoots and a pair of hombre's nuts thrown in.

boo   A popular term for marijuana among jazz musicians, especially during the forties.

boogie   A post-beatnik era term for a dope run. Boogie came into use when the college crowd moved into dope smuggling. To do a little boogie means to do a number, which in turn means to do a dope run—or any kind of run.

bracero   Literally, one who works with his arms. The term *bracero* has come to designate the migrant farm workers who come from Mexico to this country to work on the large farms. In 1943 the United States and Mexico signed a migrant worker pact so Mexican laborers could fill the American manpower shortage caused by World War II. The pact was revised in 1953 to allow only agricultural workers entry into the U.S. In 1964, after much pressure on the part of American labor interests, the agreement was terminated. Even though the bracero program has been terminated, U.S. authorities estimate that more than one million Mexican laborers continue to work on U.S. farms. Most of these workers are illegal aliens, and as such are often underpaid, mistreated, and abused by their American employers. Each year more than 300,000 "wet-backs" are deported from the U.S. to Mexico. The Mexican government has sought to negotiate a new agreement with the U.S. which would permit up to 300,000 migrant workers legal entry into the U.S. annually—and to provide them with the same safeguards provided American workers.

The whole bracero program has been the subject of much controversy, the growers complaining that the Mexican workers are needed because domestic workers aren't available to do much of the stoop labor required on large farms. American migrant workers maintain, however, that this just isn't so, that the large farms want to employ Mexican braceros because they are easily controlled, low paid, and can be gotten rid of once a crop is in.

brick   A kilogram of marijuana in brick form. See *kilo.*

broker   A dude who acts as a go-between. If you know someone who has some weed to sell, and also know another dude who wants to buy some, and are responsible for getting the two together and also get a piece of the action, then you are a broker. If you consummate the deal yourself without introducing the two, then you are a middleman.

brujo   Witch, magician, spirit.

bummer   A bummer is a bummer. Nothing goes right and everybody feels bad.

burn   In the weed trade a burn refers to (1) the peddling of phony grass or bad grass after good grass has been promised; (2) collecting for weed out front and then not delivering; (3) an outright theft of money or weed.

bush   Marijuana.

bust   An arrest.

campesino   A person from the fields; one who lives on and makes his living from the soil.

campos   The country, the land outside, away from town.

card-carrying Mexican   Mexican who has a work permit that allows him daily entry into the U.S. Usually he cannot stay for more than 72 hours at a time.

Chicago Sugar Bag Some weed came into Chicago supposedly wrapped in sugar bags. When smoked it left a sweet taste in the mouth and it came to be known as Chicago Sugar Bag. In reality the weed was probably some high-quality marijuana that had been sugared. It was a nice-sounding name though, and it stuck. The Chicago old-time heads still refer fondly to Chicago Sugar Bag.

Chicano Originally I understood Chicano to mean a person of Mexican descent who had been born in the U.S. Not all Mexican-Americans are Chicanos, however, according to some Chicano friends I've talked to. Chicano has come to mean a politically conscious Mexican-American, usually a member of the younger generation, although the term does not necessarily have any age restrictions. Like the term beatnik, Chicano suffers from its ambiguity, and many Tio Tacos, the Chicano equivalent of the Blacks' Uncle Tom, have covered themselves with the Chicano banner, especially since the banner has gotten so prominent.

coke Cocaine.

colas The top part of the marijuana plant, the flowers.

cola de zorra. Literally, tail of the fox. The foxtails are the most prized part of the marijuana plant. Most of the resin in the cannabis plant concentrates itself in the colas. The colas are usually separated from the rest of the plant when it is harvested.

cold Without heart. Most cops are cold, lots of dope dealers are cold, many Mexicans are cold, and some campesinos are cold. A cold person will rob his own mother and then beat her for complaining about it. I had a friend named Armando who once contacted a Mexican connection of his to buy 500 pounds of marijuana. The deal was made. When Armando went to pick up the weed the connection wasn't able to deliver, but he wanted Armando's money anyway, so he killed him. That's cold.

cold bust A bust that occurs without any prior setup on the part of U.S. customs officials at the border. In a sense a cold bust is accidental, if any bust can be said to be accidental. A cold bust occurs not because the smuggler has been set up, but because he goofed, either through stupidity, bad judgment, or just plain bad luck. See *hot bust.*

colitas Small colas. See *colas.*

Colombian A type of marijuana grown in the South American country of Colombia. Because of its very high quality, it is much sought after by smugglers and smokers. Good Colombian sells for approximately $400 a pound in San Francisco as of early 1974.

connection The man from whom you buy dope. He might also be the man who leads you to the man you buy dope from. The connection gets things together.

contrabandista A smuggler.

cop To score, to buy, to acquire, to get, to admit to.

cop out To cop out is to fink, squeal, not follow through, not take care of business properly.

cover To have things under control. When you cover something you take care of business. If you've covered your scene properly, everything will work out all right.

Culiacan A city in the state of Sinaloa in Mexico. Culiacan used to be the main marijuana distribution center for most of Mexico. The town is now much too hot for dealing so most of the action has gone elsewhere, but the town is still important in the industry, many of the *jefes* living there, etc.

Culiacan Garbage, Green, etc. Types of marijuana, usually of low quality. Years ago the weed grown in Sinaloa was as good or better than any grown anywhere in Mexico. Lately, however, the farmers have been rushed into planting and harvesting too early, mainly because of the Federale patrols, and subsequently the weed grown in Sinaloa is usually of pretty low quality.

Customs Customs are the people who cause you all the hassles at the border. Customs agents also operate within Mexico, clandestinely, usually in concert with Mexican narcotics agents. The U.S. Customs Service has more authority than any other U.S. law enforcement agency. They are the only law enforcement agency that can pump a suspect's stomach against his will. See *Immigration.*

dealer One who deals, or sells dope. A dealer is not a smuggler. The smuggler is responsible for getting the dope from Mexico to the States. The dealer is responsible for the dope once it is in the States.

domestic Home-grown marijuana, not smuggled.

doobie A joint, a number, a marijuana cigarette.

dope Marijuana, heroin, cocaine, pills, booze, or anything else you can stuff in your mouth, arms, nostrils, anus, or under your eyelids. Dope in this book usually means marijuana, however.

dope run A trip to score marijuana, usually for smuggling purposes. A dope run can also mean simply a trip across town to score a lid.

dynamite Weed that blows the top of your head off.

ejido Lands owned communally by campesinos. They are usually farmed collectively and everything is shared.

entrepreneur A Mexican connection who controls every aspect of the marijuana chain, from the fields to the warehouse, transportation, etc.

fall To be arrested, busted, etc.

finger To incriminate someone. You can finger someone without incriminating yourself, by dropping a dime on him, or whatever. Your neighbor can finger you if he sees your marijuana plant sticking out the window. In Mexico a maid can finger you if she smells marijuana smoke coming out of your room.

fink To fink is slightly different than to finger. Finking implies incriminating someone after you've already been incriminated. The heat likes to get arrestees to fink on their compatriots, usually promising them all kinds of good deals if they do. What usually happens is that the finks end up getting just as much or more time than those they finked on.

flowers, flowering tops Colas de zorras, or foxtails. The flowering tops are the most potent part of the marijuana plant. This is where most of the cannabinol resin resides.

free fall The free fall is an institution among many Mexican nationals. If a Mexican national is living and working in the U.S. and commits a crime for which he is about to be arrested, he can, if he is able, make it back across the border into Mexico and avoid prosecution. The Mexican government will allow him to remain in Mexico without extraditing him. Of course, this policy doesn't always work. If the crime is heavy enough, and the U.S. government wants the culprit bad enough, nothing is going to keep them from getting him—if he can be found! Thus, when the Bono brothers, two Mexican-Americans who fled into Mexico to seek refuge with relatives after murdering two immigration officers, reached the border, they found not only the American authorities after their asses, but also the Mexicans. Everything works some of the time, nothing works all of the time—including the free fall!

gabacho   A gringo (which see).

garbage   A catchall term referring to all types of low-quality marijuana.

Gold   A catchall term referring to all types of high-quality marijuana.

grass   Grass is weed, marijuana, dope, boo, bush, mota, etc. It ain't hay.

green card   A work permit issued to some Mexicans. The card allows them to cross over the border every day to report to their jobs. Most green cards are good for a 72-hour period, but some are also good for longer periods.

grifa   Mexican term for marijuana.

gringo   Gringo usually refers to Americans, but can refer also to any non-Mexicans. Originally the term was a pejorative, and although it is still used pejoratively by some Mexicans, it is not usually meant to be so.

grito   A cry, a call to arms, a shout.

grower   A marijuana farmer. Growers usually have nothing to do with the rest of the marijuana industry, either dealing, transporting (except out of the mountains), or whatever. All they do is grow the stuff, usually under contract to an entrepreneur.

Guadalajara   The second largest city in Mexico. Guadalajara is one of the main distribution centers for most of the marijuana smuggled out of Mexico.

Guadalajara Green   A type of marijuana grown in the state of Jalisco, usually of a reasonably good quality.

head   Head implies one who not only smokes marijuana, but also is attuned to the marijuana sensibility. A head is an insider, has usually been a victim of antiweed law enforcement, and is, therefore, sympathetic to and involved in a fringe-type of existence. Not all marijuana smokers are heads. A head is not a weed-smoking square (which see).

heavy Important. A heavy dude is someone to be reckoned with. A heavy bust is one involving lots of dope. A heavy jail sentence is one involving lots of time. Heavy is the opposite of light. See *lightweight*.

hippie In the dope trade, hippie refers to the crowd of young dudes —and chicks—who entered the game in the middle or late sixties. Many beatniks are called hippies, mainly because both groups affected the same appearance, but there is a definite difference. The hippie in my book is younger, more rash, at the same time more bound by weird conventions than the beatnik. Beatniks opened the dope trade, hippies overran it. Beatniks discovered Mexico, hippies destroyed it. Naturally the opposite of these generalizations is also true, but in general this definition bears out.

homegrown Domestic grass. Grown in the U.S., not smuggled.

hot bust A bust which has been set up by U.S. Customs, usually as the result of a tip from a fingerer or fink. Most big busts are not hot busts. See *cold bust*.

Immigration The government service that stops and searches all cars and individuals crossing the border between Mexico and the U.S. The Immigration Service is not the Customs Service. If a hot bust is about to come down, the Customs Service is called in, it is not handled by the Immigration Service. Customs is also called in if the Immigration Service accidentally makes a cold bust. The Immigration Service always takes care of people problems, the Customs Service always takes care of illegal dope traffic. See *Customs*.

incentive Cocaine.

Indian Black Gungeon A type of marijuana that came originally from Africa. Especially potent, exceedingly rare. It was popular during the late forties and early fifties.

J. A joint, a marijuana cigarette.

jefe Chief, boss, top man.

Johnson Grass A pejorative term used by smugglers which refers to low-quality weed they wouldn't be caught dead with. It belongs in Texas.

joint   A J, a marijuana cigarette.

juice   Connections, power, weight, money.

key   A kilo.

kilo   2.2 pounds of marijuana, cocaine, heroin, or just plain horse manure.

labores   Fields. When referring to the fields where so many of them spend their time, campesinos often call them labores—hardworking places.

lid   One ounce of marijuana. The word came from the time when marijuana used to be sold in Prince Albert cans—one can was one ounce of weed.

lightweight   Not very important, without authority, essentially meaningless. There are lots of lightweight dudes who think they are heavy. See *heavy*.

load   Stash. Also, a passel of dope after it has been stashed.

lumber   Sticks and stems mixed in a load of marijuana. Lumber is useless weight.

machismo   The cult of super-manliness prevalent throughout Mexico. See text for complete discussion.

macho   One who practices machismo.

maguey   The spiny cactus from which tequila and mescal are fermented.

mano   Literally, hand. It is also an affectionate term meaning "brother," from the Spanish word *hermano*.

mestizo   A mestizo is a cross between a Spaniard and an Indian. Most Mexicans are mestizos.

Michoacan   A state in Mexico. Also a type of marijuana grown in that state.

middleman   The connection between the dealer and the ultimate buyer. Without middlemen, few deals could be made. The structure of the weed trade is dictated in many ways by the illegality of the product, and middlemen are the liaison between various segments of people who do not want to know, meet, or see one another.

mordida A bite, a bribe, a piece, whether of the action, the money, or the marijuana.

mota Mexican slang term for marijuana.

move To transport, sell, or otherwise get rid of marijuana.

mula Mexican slang for prostitute.

mule A hired hand who drives loads across the border. Sometimes a mule is part of a smuggling operation, more often than not he is an outsider brought in for one specific run. Sometimes mules are unsuspecting dupes, and their cars are used without their knowledge.

norteamericano An American, a person born in the north, beyond the borders of Mexico.

number A marijuana cigarette, a dope run, an experience. To do a number implies doing something, the exact thing depending upon the conversation you are having. For some people going to the bathroom can be "doing a number."

off To get rid of, whether it's dope or a person. Usually off means to do someone in physically, that is, to kill him. If a person offs a load of weed, he sells it, or gets rid of it.

offed Gotten rid of, sold, done in, or killed.

Operation Cooperation A cooperative venture between the Mexican and U.S. governments designed to stop the illegal narcotics traffic between the two countries. Operation Cooperation was instigated by the U.S. after the miserable failure of Operation Intercept. Under Operation Cooperation, the U.S. government agreed to provide the Mexican government with men, material, airplanes, and money. In turn the Mexican government agreed to use this assistance to bear down on the dope traffic within their own country. Up until the implementation of Operation Cooperation, Mexico had always treated the marijuana problem as an American one. With the U.S. government willing to give them so much money, however, they were quite willing to start harassing Mexican entrepreneurs. See *Operation Intercept*.

Operation Intercept A U.S. government operation designed to intercept all illegal narcotics traffic between the U.S. and Mexico.

Under Operation Intercept every vehicle and individual crossing the border was stopped and searched. On the first weekend the plan was put into effect, traffic was backed up for six hours at San Isidro, between San Diego and Tijuana. The operation netted hardly any drugs and was dropped after one month. See *Operation Cooperation*.

ounce An ounce of heroin, cocaine, or marijuana.

out front Open, honest, not holding anything back. *Out front* also means to give somebody some weed or dope without demanding immediate payment.

outlaw Outside the law. *Outlaw* does not imply gangster or murderer; the way I mean the term is a person who openly goes up against the establishment's guns by doing something that is illegal, not bad illegal like killing people, but nice illegal, like smuggling dope.

Panama Red A type of marijuana grown in Panama. Panama Red is often referred to as "Red." It is very high-quality weed.

Pocho A Mexican-American born or raised in Los Angeles. Pocho is primarily a Southern California term, used mostly by Chicanos. It is not necessarily pejorative, but sometimes is.

pop Arrest.

popped Arrested.

primo First, best, top quality.

Purple Zacatecas Purple. A high-quality marijuana that grows in the mountainous state of Zacatecas in central Mexico. Zacatecas Purple is distinguished by seeds that turn purple, or a rich, reddish purple color when the weed is dry. Extremely good weed, much sought after by heads.

Red Panama Red (which see).

riff Originally a jazz term for a particular little solo, a player showing his stuff. In the dope world, riff means essentially the same thing, someone doing his particular number, either copping a load, offing some stuff, or whatever.

rip off To steal. You can rip off people psychologically, physically, emotionally, financially. Usually ripoff implies some kind of value trip, however, taking something without proper payment.

ripped   Stoned, loaded, very high. Good weed rips you.

run   A trip, usually meaning a dope run.

runner   Someone on a run.

rush   Excitement. The rush is one of the incalculable factors involved in dope smuggling. Many smugglers are in the game for the rush as much as for the money. In fact, if there was no rush involved many of them would choose other forms of activity. See *outlaw*.

shit   Dope, marijuana, heroin.

Sindicato Texas   The Texas Syndicate (which see).

Sinsemilla   Without seeds. Sinsemilla is often spelled Sensamaya, and is a hybrid species of marijuana that grows in certain areas of Mexico, usually south of the Tropic of Cancer. The myth is that Sinsemilla is cultivated by only women in the mountains of Oaxaca. The weed is actually cultivated like any other marijuana, and even Sinsemilla does have a few seeds. When the plant is dry the seeds that do remain are knocked off.

smoke   Marijuana.

smuggler   A smuggler is not a dealer, middleman, or banker. The smuggler is the one who scores the load in Mexico and is responsible for getting it to the States. Usually he is not involved in any of the stateside activity. He prefers to remain as close to Mexico as possible.

sniff   Cocaine. Cocaine is also called snort, snow, incentive.

status trip   An emotional jackoff trip that a lot of smugglers, dealers, dopers, and people in general often fall into. Dealers are especially vulnerable to the status trip because of the curious unreality of any big-timey dope endeavor. Successful runs can mean big bread, but that bread has to be manifested in things that can be seen—Mercedes Benz cars, big houses, the street strut. The need for this material manifestation sends a lot of people into the status trip, and usually culminates in their downfall.

stepped on   Cut. If cocaine has been stepped on twice, that means it has been cut two times.

sticks   Useless twigs in a load of marijuana. See *lumber*.

sugared grass   Marijuana that has been adulterated with a sugar solution. Those involved in sugaring grass say that it's done to bind the weed into bricks. Actually it's done simply to add weight to the kilos.

taste Sample. You taste the weed before you buy it.

tejano Texan. Texans are not too popular in Mexico. Often the term tejano implies an asshole.

Texas Syndicate A loosely organized group of Mexican-Americans and Mexicans who smuggle tons of weed across the border—usually in the southwest. The Texas Syndicate is the closest thing in the weed industry to any organized smuggling concern.

toke A drag on a joint, a puff.

vatos locos Crazy guys.

vibes Feelings, intuition, the sense of things happening.

weed Marijuana.

weed-smoking square Someone who smokes weed but is not attuned to the head's sensibility. There are lots of weed-smoking squares around.

weight Large amounts of marijuana. Can he supply weight? means can he furnish a lot of marijuana?

Zacatecas Purple A type of weed grown in Zacatecas, a mountainous state in central Mexico.

zona roja Red zone, the whorehouse district.